Samuel Silas Curry

Imagination and Dramatic Instinct

Samuel Silas Curry

Imagination and Dramatic Instinct

ISBN/EAN: 9783337334659

Printed in Europe, USA, Canada, Australia, Japan

Cover: Foto ©Andreas Hilbeck / pixelio.de

More available books at **www.hansebooks.com**

IMAGINATION

AND

DRAMATIC INSTINCT.

SOME PRACTICAL STEPS FOR THEIR DEVELOPMENT.

BY S. S. CURRY, PH.D.

*Author of " The Province of Expression ;" " Lessons in Vocal Expression ;"
Dean of the School of Expression ; Instructor of Oratory in Yale Divinity
School and Newton Theological Institution, and formerly in
Boston University and Harvard University.*

BOSTON:

THE EXPRESSION COMPANY,

PIERCE BUILDING, COPLEY SQUARE.

PREFACE.

THIS book is a study of vocal expression, as the direct revelation of the processes of the mind in thinking and feeling; and as the manifestation of the elliptic relations of thought which words cannot symbolize, such as the convictions, the beliefs, the interest, and the purpose of the speaker. According to this view, vocal expression is a significant, not a symbolic language, and is more subjective, complex, and nearer to Nature than words, and hence cannot be developed in the same way as a symbolic or representative language, nor be made subject to the same mechanical rules.

The work is meant to furnish simple and practical suggestions. In nearly every case a poem or selection is placed before the mind of the student, and the remarks made are intended to aid in the study of the extract, and especially in its interpretation by the living voice. " To know a thing, we must do it " is a fundamental principle of education. The mind must be brought directly into contact with nature. Experiment is the true method of scientific study, but the principle applies even more to literary or artistic work. The student must be set to doing, — explanation must be subordinate, and only for guidance in the discovery or study of the principles for himself in practice. This book is an endeavor to furnish a practical means of studying and training the Imagination and Dramatic Instinct. It aims to bring the mind of the student into direct contact with the noble works of Literature, not merely to analyze or to understand the thought in such works, but to stimulate and awaken the faculties in the reader which are awake in the writer, to study the processes of the mind in creating and assimilating ideas for the true artistic interpretation of literature by the living voice. It furnishes a practical means of educating some important actions of the mind by the oldest of all artistic agents, the voice.

In certain cases problems are definitely stated, but more frequently there are suggestions which can be formulated by the teacher, or by the student himself. All great artists sketch and make studies of the objects of nature. This is the true method of art study; there is no substitute for it. Hence, the same method must be used by the student of literature, or of vocal expression. There must be long-continued study in the rendering of single lines or phrases. Such studies must be arranged for students according to their needs, and the student himself must direct his efforts to those points in which he is weakest.

In using the book in class, my custom is to assign certain selections a week beforehand and have students study and read them alone; then afterward with the teacher for suggestions and criticisms. The studies are to be read over to aid the student in comprehending criticisms and difficulties in the rendering of a poem, or to stimulate deeper studies or broader investigations. The student's understanding and assimilation of the principles involved are chiefly to be judged by his rendering of a passage, or by his method of speaking. Occasionally, questions should be asked to test the student's conception of the deeper meanings of a passage of literature or the apprehension of its vocal interpretation or by his understanding of the steps which are being taken. My own aim is usually to keep many things before the student's mind, such as the essential nature of all expression, of all artistic endeavor, the steps he is taking in vocal expression, the spirit of the literary work he is studying, or the speech he is trying to make, and also his own special needs or tendencies ; first one and then another of these is emphasized to stimulate his harmonious growth.

This work is intended to follow " Lessons in Vocal Expression." That volume takes up the simpler processes of thinking, the more elemental or logical relations of ideas, while this takes up the imaginative and sympathetic elements, the ideal and dramatic relations of ideas to feeling and experience.

Practice in vocal expression should always be connected with vocal training. At every stage of his progress the teacher should give the student definite steps for the training of his voice, using the same or different extracts. The student must realize the character of his tone, and the effect of his mind upon it. Do the qualities of his voice change with his ideas and feelings ? Does he feel his ideas, his imaginative conceptions of relations and background, his deeper feelings in the tones and modulations of his voice ?

The book has grown from practical struggles in teaching for twenty years, from a realization of the importance of awakening the Imagination and Dramatic Instinct of college, theological, or law students, and in fact of every man and woman of whatever aim in life. The volume is larger than it would otherwise have been on account of the neglect or misconceptions of many aspects of the subject at the present time. Many of the lessons may be easily extended or related to wider courses, the History of Humor, Forms of Poetry, History of Lyric Poetry, and many other subjects. In fact, the volume is intended as a companion to the student in the study of literature to throw light upon practical vocal interpretation as one of the chief means to get at the spirit of literary work.

No one realizes its inadequacy, its imperfections, more than the writer. It has been prepared in the midst of the continual and engrossing duties of practical teaching. It is hoped that, while it has the imperfections of the teacher, it will also have the spirit of practical teaching, and prove suggestive and helpful to a large number of students, and meet a great variety of needs.

S. S. C.

Boston, Massachusetts,
September, 1896.

CONTENTS.

II.

ASSIMILATION, OR THE DRAMATIC INSTINCT.

INTRODUCTION.

WHAT is the imagination? Is it of any use? Can it be trained?
Is it not a merely ornamental appendage to human nature, imprac-
tical and untruthful? Unfortunately, such questions are common,
and indicate widespread misconception of the faculty.

The relation of education to imagination has hitherto received
slight attention at the hands of educators in general. The development of the imagination has been given little or no place in
the courses of study in our schools, nor has it been regarded as
worthy of any distinctive attention in college training. "In the
curriculums of most of our higher institutions of learning in
America and England," says Professor Charles Eliot Norton,
"no place is given to that instruction which has for its end the
cultivation of the imagination and the sentiments, through the refining of the perceptions and the quickening of the love of beauty."
Education, say some of our legislators, must give a man the
means of making a living; our public schools must train up practical citizens; boys and girls must be educated in the practical
arts of life; the ornamental has no place in the school-room.

Such views of education utterly fail to grasp the nature of
the imagination and its relation to daily life. They overlook the
need of securing the right action of all the faculties, and do not
perceive that the harmonious development of the whole man is
necessary to the adequate performance of the simplest and most
practical business of life. Work without imagination is drudgery,
but with it the humblest employment is lifted into the realm of
beauty and art. "Whatever is worth doing at all is worth doing
well." The imagination is the source of all inspiration and interest
in life; its activity creates beauty in the commonest objects of
handicraft, and gives charm to the humblest home.

But why should the imagination be trained? Because its perversion or abnormal action is one of the leading causes of the degradation of character, while its right use is one of the highest characteristics of the normal human being. It should be developed because it is the chief creative faculty. It is this which gives man taste and refinement; which raises him out of a narrow prison into communion with the universe; which lifts him from a groove into relation with all things and all men; which develops the comprehension of universal principles; which prevents man from regarding Nature as a mere mechanical product, and enables him to feel it as a process, and consciously to follow that process in his own art.

Imagination should be developed because all true appreciation of art and literature is dependent upon its exercise. Man can appreciate art only by the same faculty which creates it. That which is awake in the artist in the act of production must be awakened in the beholder, or there can be no genuine realization. In short, imagination not only creates all art, but it appreciates art. Without its presence there can be no genuine love of art; without it, the language of art is unintelligible, its voice unheard, its spirit unfelt.

Imagination makes the individual a citizen of the world, an heir to all the ages; it enables him to appreciate not only the art of his own age and his own country, but that of all other lands and times. By its power he can become a Greek, and see as the Greeks saw, and feel as the Greeks felt.

Imagination lies at the foundation of all altruistic instinct, whether of art or ethics. Unless it is developed, there can be little improvement in the ideals of a man or a nation. No man has ever become great without an ideal, and the faculty which gives birth to ideals is imagination. This is the prophetic faculty of the soul, which gives hope, and which enables us to see a new and better world in the midst of the old, a new life in the midst of death, a new character in the midst of degradation. No man can ever rise higher than his ideal; but without an ideal, no man can ever rise at all. No age, no nation, no individual, can ever be elevated except by elevating its ideals.

Imagination is the faculty which enables us to enter into sympathy with our fellow-men. By its power alone can we appreciate the point of view of those different from ourselves. Without imagination, each of us would be alone; each of us would be cold and selfish.

Imagination gives us the power to penetrate to the heart of Nature; it is the faculty which sees beauty and loveliness; which discovers grace in the motion of the storm; "that leans her ear in many a secret place," until "beauty born of murmuring sound shall pass into her face."

Imagination is the faculty which enables man to realize eternity. The ordinary conceptions of the mind cannot embrace infinity, or God. Imagination alone enables man to transcend the fetters of time and space, to see the eternal through the temporal, the spiritual beneath the physical, the soul underlying all. It is imagination which penetrates through all seeming, through the wild whirlwind and storm which are part of every life and every human soul, to "the central peace existing at the heart of endless agitation."

The imagination should be trained because the whole man should be trained, because it is the fountain-head of all noble feeling, and upon its discipline depends any true education of the emotions.

Dramatic instinct has received even less recognition than imagination. All men more or less admire imagination, though they may not think of it as an object of education; but few persons regard dramatic power as a characteristic of a strong and noble human being. It is frequently considered an unnatural, if not an abnormal power. Nor do many consider it capable of education, but due to some accident of temperament peculiar to a few; while even those who regard its education as possible, look upon its development as on the same plane as the practice of sleight-of-hand.

There are some exceptions, however, to this superficial view. A prominent judge, at a dinner of the alumni of his college, is reported to have said that if he were a rich man he would endow a chair in all the colleges for the development of the dramatic instinct. Upon this instinct, he held, success in every walk of life depends. The teacher cannot teach unless he sees as the student sees; the preacher cannot preach without the power of putting himself in another man's place; the merchant succeeds on account of the ability to read the wishes and needs of his customers. And so it is throughout all human experience and endeavor: an instinctive knowledge of human nature is the basis of success. All men are great in proportion to their ability to get outside of themselves.

A proper conception of dramatic instinct must be gained apart from the stage. Many of the exhibitions upon the stage are devoid of anything essentially dramatic. If the stage were a place for the pure and noble representation of dramatic instinct, there would be few who would have any objection to it. The men with the strongest dramatic instinct whom it has been my privilege to meet or hear have not been actors, — such men as Beecher and Gough.

Dramatic instinct should be trained because it is a part of the imagination, because it gives us practical steps towards the development of the imagination, because it is the means of securing discipline and power over feeling. Dramatic instinct should be trained because it is the insight of one mind into another. The man who has killed his dramatic instinct has become unsympathetic, and can never appreciate any one's point of view but his own. Dramatic instinct endows us with broad conceptions of the idiosyncrasies, beliefs, and convictions of men. It trains us to unconscious reasoning, to a deep insight into the motives of man. It is universally felt that one's power to "other himself" is the measure of the greatness of his personality. All sympathy, all union of ourselves with the ideals and struggles of our race, are traceable to imagination and dramatic instinct.

The relation of imagination to dramatic instinct has not been sufficiently appreciated. Many years ago the editor of the "North American Review" published a symposium from various actors upon the nature of dramatic instinct. It is curious to note that nearly all these said that dramatic instinct had two elements, —

imagination and sympathy. Imagination affords insight into character; sympathy enables us to identify ourselves with it. Thus, imagination and dramatic instinct are essentially united. The little child who is imaginative always shows it by dramatic actions in his play.

While imagination and dramatic instinct may be separated in conception, while the difference in their actions may be distinguished, practically they are always united, especially in their higher actions. Together they form the chief elements of altruism. They redeem the mind from narrowness and selfishness; they enable the individual to appreciate the point of view, the feelings, motives, and characters of his fellow-men; they open his eyes to read the various languages of human art; they enable him to commune with his kind on a higher plane than that of commonplace facts; they lift him into communion with the art and spirit of every age and nation. Without their development man is excluded from the highest enjoyment, the highest communion with his kind, and from the highest success in every walk of life.

One of the chief needs of the education of our time is a practical method for the development of the imagination and the dramatic instinct, — a method which will prevent their abuse, bring the mind into direct contact with the greatest products of the imagination, and train students to appreciate the highest literature and art. There are many methods of studying and training these powers, but the one here to be indicated has proved successful through many years of experience, and is essentially the same as that adopted in the schools of the Greeks, whose development of the artistic nature is universally considered to have been the highest ever known.

The best method of developing the imagination is by the study of Nature and poetic expression. A sympathetic love of the beautiful in Nature is characteristic of noble imagination. Even in the study of art there must ever be a comparison with Nature. George F. Watts once said, "People must be trained to a higher appreciation of art by being led to see what a great artist Nature is."

The influence of Nature in the education of the human mind cannot be over-estimated. Wordsworth has taught us to realize the power of Nature to stimulate and unfold the energies of the soul. All art proceeds from wonder. A sympathetic observation of life has been instrumental in every age in stimulating the mental and artistic faculties.

Nature alone, however, is inadequate to secure the full power of imagination. Thousands have grown up in the midst of the greatest beauty of Nature with low and sensuous ideals, and without having their sense of beauty awakened. Art is therefore needed to show us Nature's subtleties, to give us a right attitude of mind towards her, and to awaken sympathetic attention to her revelations.

What form of art should be studied? Every form as far as possible; for each art is a distinct language, which expresses some aspect of the human soul and realizes some truth apprehended in no other way. Music and poetry are "arts in time," and can reveal the sequence of ideas and the movement of life; but painting works in space, and is confined to the intense realization of one moment. It is intensive, where other arts are extensive. Both are needed for adequate expression.

Any one of these arts — even poetry, the highest of all, and the most capable of being used as a means of developing the imagination — may, when studied alone, cause the student to become one-sided. The painter who never studies anything but his own art becomes superficial. The poet who fails to see the depth and force in plastic and pictorial art becomes merely literary. Painters condemn a picture which is too "literary," — this use of the word indicating those who merely write, who merely look at Nature as a means of literary description. On the other hand, the painter who never studies books or other arts almost ceases to think; some have even gone so far as to say "the painter has no business to think at all."

Every great art is a special language of the human spirit, and he who desires to awaken his artistic nature will learn to read all these languages. The possession of merely literary and artistic knowledge does not imply culture; for this results from the harmonious activity of all the faculties of the mind. It is dependent upon appreciation, upon insight into art and poetry, upon sympathy with the ideals of humanity.

Too much cannot be said in favor of the erection of beautiful public buildings, and of museums of art. It is to be hoped that the time is not far distant when every village will have its art collections, when every school-room and every home will be filled with objects of art.

Art which has to do with imagination is called poetry; and while poetry belongs to painting, sculpture, music, and architecture, its chief expression is in certain forms of literary composition. A love of poetic literature has nearly always preceded a desire for other forms of art. It is always associated with a love of the beautiful in Nature; its greatest masterpieces can become the possession of all, and hence it must serve as the chief means of educating the imagination.

Again, poetry is fullest of imaginative life and energy. In every poem there are possibilities of innumerable paintings, if only the artistic nature can intensely realize each successive picture. Its materials are the simple words of common minds; its form or body is simply an orderly or rhythmic arrangement of human speech.

Taking for granted, then, that literature will best educate the imagination, the question arises, What methods of studying it are best adapted to exercise this faculty?

Until comparatively recent times, the highest culture was supposed to be embodied in the Greek and Latin languages. The study of these constituted for centuries the chief means of literary training. But the great discoveries in every field of scientific investigation, during the present century, have led many to doubt the power of Greek and Latin to furnish the broadest possible education. With this tendency to doubt the advantage of studying these languages, there has grown up also a neglect of all literary culture. At the present time, a majority of the studies in all grades of schools concern themselves chiefly with the acquisition of knowledge.

The too exclusive study of science, however, is in turn slowly leading to the realization of the inadequacy of facts to develop the whole man harmoniously and completely. Slowly but surely our leading educators are coming to feel that science alone is insufficient for the complete development of the whole man. A great scientist of our age, Charles Darwin, has said: "I used to sit for hours reading the historical plays of Shakespeare, generally in an old window in the thick walls of the school. I read also other poetry, such as Thomson's 'Seasons,' and the recently published poems of Byron and Scott. I mention this, because later in life I wholly lost, to my great regret, all pleasure from poetry of any kind, including Shakespeare."

In another part of the biography from which this extract is taken, he adds: "Up to the age of thirty, or beyond it, poetry of many kinds — such as the works of Milton, Gray, Byron, Wordsworth, Coleridge, and Shelley — gave me great pleasure; and even as a schoolboy I took intense delight in Shakespeare, especially in the historical plays. I have also said that formerly pictures gave me considerable, and music very great, delight. But now for many years I cannot endure to read a line of poetry: I have tried lately to read Shakespeare, and found it so intolerably dull that it nauseated me. I have also almost lost my taste for pictures or music. Music generally sets me thinking too energetically on what I have been at work upon, instead of giving me pleasure. . . . My mind seems to have become a machine for grinding general laws out of large collections of facts; but why this should have caused the atrophy of that part of the brain alone on which the higher tastes depend, I cannot conceive. . . . If I had to live my life again, I would have made a rule to read some poetry and listen to some music at least once a week; for perhaps the parts of my brain now atrophied would thus have been kept active through use. The loss of these tastes is a loss of happiness, and may possibly be injurious to the intellect, and more probably to the moral character, by enfeebling the emotional part of our nature." [1]

[1] Life and Letters of Charles Darwin, i. 30, 81.

So innumerable have modern discoveries been, that it is almost impossible for any human being to acquire a mastery of all the facts in every department of human knowledge. Hence, there is a renewed disposition among some educators to defend the true principle of education; namely, mental discipline, rather than dependence upon the acquisition of unrelated facts.

This disposition, however, has not been shown in a renewal of interest in the study of Greek and Latin, but in the study of one's own language and literature. This is the most hopeful sign in modern education. It is a man's native literature which lies nearest his heart. It is upon this that the creative energy of the imagination must be exercised. "The highest mark of culture in any man is shown by his ability to speak and write his own language with accuracy, ease, and elegance."

In turning to the study of our own language, however, the true method of using it for the stimulation of the artistic nature has hardly been reached. Two influences have made the first method in the study of literature largely a study of philology. In the first place, the reverence given to Latin and Greek has led us to trace the origin of our words. In the second place, the scientific spirit of the age has affected even the study of literature; so that the courses of studies in literature in our different colleges have been chiefly studies in philology.

The study of literature, however, could not long remain thus limited. Such courses were presently felt to be a study, not of literature, but of words; and while etymology and philology are very important, they are simply aspects of scientific study, and have little to do with the development of the artistic nature. Everything may be studied both scientifically and artistically. The difference in training is not in the subject, but in the method of procedure and the faculties which are called into exercise.

The next step was the study of the facts of literature. This is at present regarded as a great advance in the study of literature. That it is a gain, no one will deny; but the method is still scientific. The facts about a poem — the aim, the subject, and the language used — are all analyzed and discussed. I have known many students to say that they never desired to recite or study or even read again those poems which they have analyzed during their college course. A great advantage, however, has come about by this method. Poetry and general literature are studied, and the fact that the student's attention is turned to them, even though in the wrong way, has the effect of stimulating him to some appreciation of their value.

Still, the problem of the practical development of the imagination has not yet been solved by either of these methods. Art can be studied only as art and by means of art. It is not science, nor can it be studied as science, or by exercising merely the analytical faculties of the mind. All art is a form of poetic expression, and the artistic nature can be awakened only by exercise in poetic expression in some of its forms.

The lessons in this book are arranged according to the principle that the artistic nature must be developed by being brought into active exercise, and that this can be achieved by using the simplest and most natural form of art, — that of *the spoken word.*

It was the attention given by the Greeks to the spoken word that caused them to be the most artistic of peoples. By far the most of the work of their schools was the study and recitation of the works of their poets. While they may have slighted the written word, and exaggerated too much the importance of speech, we in our day have gone to the other extreme, and are exaggerating the importance of writing as an agent of education, to the exclusion of the earlier and more simple and natural method of the human voice. The voice is the little child's first conscious agent of expression; it is man's chief means of communication; it is fullest of the life and energy of the human soul; it is the simplest and most natural agent of the faculties of the mind. Some may consider the Greeks to have been the greatest masters of writing in the world, and this is true; but their writing was great because founded upon and developed by their speech.

It is a well-known fact that all poetry was first written with reference to delivery; and many of our greatest poets have felt that the higher development of poetry cannot come until it is once more written with reference to its vocal expression. Milton has said, —

"Blest pair of Sirens, pledges of Heaven's joy,
 Sphere-born harmonious Sisters, Voice and Verse !
 Wed your divine sounds, and mixt power employ
 Dead things with imbreathed sense able to pierce."

Be this as it may, the most adequate method of studying literature and of developing the imagination and artistic nature is by
means of the spoken word; and for this there are many reasons.

Vocal expression is the most direct revelation of the processes
of thought and emotion. It is the most immediate manifestation
of the living activity of the soul, of which literature is the embodiment. Matthew Arnold called literature "the criticism of
life." The higher the literature, the more it embodies and suggests life; hence the more immediately is it related to the natural
languages, and the more capable of being interpreted by them.

The study of vocal expression furnishes a means of following
the processes of thought. The most subtle movements of the
imagination and feeling can be studied in connection with their
vocal response, and this response can be used also as an agent in
developing right imaginative and emotional action. If education
is "learning the use of tools," and if the exercise of the higher
faculties depends upon the use of a tool, then the voice furnishes
the simplest of tools for testing and exercising them.

Again, imagination and the artistic nature can be exercised only
by means of the most familiar agents. The artist can express
only what is native and inherent to his heart. Millet, the painter,
is said to have paused in the midst of his early work, on over-
hearing a remark about its character, to ask himself what really
was the most intense affection of his heart. It was because of
this that he turned to the portrayal of French peas-nts, and the
interpretation of the life of the poor. He thus led a new movement in art; the real spirit of the poor, their heroic devotion,
their tenderness, their pain, had never before been made the subject of art. No amount of contempt on the part of the critics
nor neglect on the part of the public could ever turn him from
his conviction that art can portray only the central affection of
the heart of the artist. The greatest artists of every age have
used the simple means which lay near to their hands.

Now, the native speech of every man lies nearest to his imagination and creative instinct. Vocal expression furnishes a simple and universal means of awakening the artistic nature. Speech is the primary, the most natural, language, and can be filled fullest of the life and spirit of man. The use of his native language carries him farther away from the dominion of mechanical rules. It is the most spontaneous and unconscious manifestation of the natural action of all his faculties. Before the imagination can show itself in painting, sculpture, or music, the student must have thoroughly mastered its mechanism; but the student's native tongue requires least of such mechanical and artificial mastery, and hence can most easily become the agent for the expression and testing of imaginative action.

"Style is the man himself." This statement has received careless acceptance, with very little realization of its truth, or of the postulates of such a truth. If style be the man, then artistic training must begin with disciplining his powers, and not with the external mechanical acquisition of certain facts or artificial rules. The *cause* of expression must be awakened; imagination and instinct must be quickened.

The study of general literature must begin by awakening those faculties and powers in ourselves which in another created the literature. Speech is the first form of expression. We talk before we write or draw or paint or model. Hence, the first language is the chief one to be used.

Of course, the objection will be urged that elocution is at present the most degraded of the arts; that the recitation of a poem frequently perverts its spirit,—and this is true. But the power of vocal expression to pervert literature or to destroy imaginative action only shows its influence. Its power may be used to elevate as well as to destroy.

Two methods of developing vocal expression grow out of two diverse views regarding the nature of delivery.

The advocates of one method consider vocal expression as a matter of pronunciation; and delivery a mechanical act having little, if any, relation to thinking. A few rules for inflection based upon phraseology, some mechanical directions for stress or pausing, according to grammatical structure, and for the " tone " to use for a given emotion, form, unfortunately, the common conception of vocal expression. According to this method, thought and imagination belong only to the author. The reader must not interpose his mental action between the author and the auditor: he must present correctly the form of the author's words. Exactly as the printed page presents the language of the author to the eye, so the reader must present the words of the author to the ear.

The other method regards vocal expression as the manifestation of the processes of thought and feeling; that it conveys these by natural signs in speaking the words which are only symbols, or conventional representatives, of thought. Vocal expression is the giving of thought with its associated experience. It presents thoughts in such a way as to make another mind realize in the fullest possible degree their nature and relations. This view holds also that if vocal expression be the translation, the re-incarnation of thought and feeling, then the reader must re-think the thought; must reproduce its processes and the feeling it awakens, according to the laws and associations of his own mind.

According to this theory, vocal expression is regarded as an interpretative art, whose exercise requires the direct action of imagination and feeling. Reading is not only an art, but the interpretation of the most exalted forms of art and literature. Though delivery has a physical and mechanical side; though enunciation is necessary and cannot be done too well, — this is not the most important element in vocal expression. Vocal expression is the direct manifestation of thought and feeling. It is the translation into natural language of ideas expressed in words. It is the interpretation, or the bringing to life, of the first processes of thought and emotion as suggested by the language of words, and manifesting these by means of the other co-ordinate languages or modulations of voice and body. Vocal expression manifests the speaker's own thought and feeling, or his assimilation and realization of that of others.

Again, the action of the mind in writing is not the same as that in reading and speaking. The reader uses the natural languages as his medium, not the pen; hence, he must think and feel with greater intensity than the writer. By him the ideas of the writer are made salient, their movement more natural, their realization more vivid.

According to any adequate view of the nature of vocal expression and delivery there must, therefore, be a definite training of those faculties concerned with the realization of truth. The development of vocal expression is dependent upon and simultaneous with the acquisition of literary taste. A man cannot express what he does not possess. The refinement of feeling, the intense realization of ideas, is fundamentally necessary.

Right vocal expression, then, is dependent upon the realization of truth; and the faculty most concerned with this is imagination. Where the imagination is inactive, all expression is mechanical and cold. "Imagination," says Fénelon, "is the only creative faculty of the human mind." It is the faculty which lies at the fountain-head of all art. Hence, that faculty which enables man to live in a mental world, to hold such an ideal before his mind that he can rise out of the literal and the actual; that faculty which enables him to live in a process of thought, to see and hear whatever is conceived by the mind as if it had real existence, — is especially necessary in vocal expression.

Again, the mind must continually change its point of view. There must be insight not only into truth and Nature, but into men. The reader, speaker, or actor must have quick and instinctive insight into character. He must see as others see, and feel as others feel. He must have that sympathy which will enable him to identify himself with all situations.

Sympathy, it has been said, is synonymous with insight. A lack of sympathy is a lack of imagination. Without imagination there can be no true appreciation, no earnest feeling.

Imagination appeals to imagination. Literature and poetry cannot be interpreted without the help of imagination to appreciate the highest ideals and most poetic visions. An interpretative art must accentuate the deepest and most fundamental elements in the matter interpreted. Imagination is needed to stimulate the deeper impulses, and to bring voice and body into unity. It alone can give such a vivid realization of ideas as to awaken all the complex impulses and languages of man. It is needed to prevent isolation of ideas, and the hardening of truths into mere facts. It is needed to place ideas and facts in sympathetic relationship with one another; to give the spirit and not the letter, truth and not mere fact, the soul and not the mere body.

Vocal expression is the direct result of the free, spontaneous impulses of mind and heart. The actions and characteristics of the imagination furnish the most essential qualities of vocal expression. No form of art is more intuitive and immediate; nowhere are rules so impossible as in its sphere. All actions in vocal expression are the direct and immediate result of insight. Nowhere is there needed more penetration, more stimulus to feeling; nowhere is there such need to awaken a play of free and spontaneous activity.

The object of rendering a passage of poetry, the function of delivery in oratory, is to make truth more vivid; to give it the life of a personality; to bring unity out of diversity; to change abstractions into living and moving creations. All these fundamental requisites of oratory, of eloquence, of poetry, are the direct product of imagination. Hence, this faculty is the chief characteristic of right delivery. Its development will secure naturalness and effectiveness, and prevent artificiality and affectation.

THE world is too much with us ; late and soon,
Getting and spending, we lay waste our powers ;
Little we see in Nature that is ours:
We have given our hearts away, a sordid boon !
This sea that bares her bosom to the moon ;
The winds that will be howling at all hours,
And are up-gathered now like sleeping flowers, —
For this, for everything, we are out of tune ;
It moves us not. — Great God ! I 'd rather be
A pagan suckled in a creed outworn,
So might I, standing on this pleasant lea,
Have glimpses that would make me less forlorn ;
Have sight of Proteus rising from the sea,
Or hear old Triton blow his wreathèd horn.

Wordsworth

BEAUTY — a living Presence of the earth,
Surpassing the most fair ideal Forms
Which craft of delicate Spirits hath composed
From earth's materials — waits upon my steps ;
Pitches her tent before me as I move,
An hourly neighbor.   Paradise, and groves
Elysian, Fortunate Fields — like those of old
Sought in the Atlantic Main — why should they be
A history only of departed things,
Or a mere fiction of what never was?
For the discerning intellect of Man,
When wedded to this goodly universe
In love and holy passion, shall find these
A simple produce of the common day.
— I, long before the blissful hour arrives,
Would chant, in lonely peace, the spousal verse
Of this great consummation : —and, by words
Which speak of nothing more than what we are,
Would I arouse the sensual from their sleep
Of Death, and win the vacant and the vain
To noble raptures ; while my voice proclaims
How exquisitely the individual Mind
(And the progressive powers perhaps no less
Of the whole species) to the external World
Is fitted : — and how exquisitely, too —
The external World is fitted to the Mind ;
And the creation (by no lower name
Can it be called) which they with blended might
Accomplish : — this is our high argument.
— Such grateful haunts foregoing, if I oft
Must turn elsewhere — travel and see ill sights
Of madding passions mutually inflamed ;
Must hear humanity in fields and groves
Pipe solitary anguish ; or must hang
Brooding above the fierce confederate storm
Of sorrow, barricadoed evermore
Within the walls of cities — may these sounds
Have their authentic comment ; that even these
Hearing, I be not downcast or forlorn ! —
Descend, prophetic Spirit ! that inspir'st
The human Soul of universal earth,
Dreaming on things to come ; and dost possess
A metropolitan temple in the hearts
Of mighty Poets.

The Recluse.

I.

IMAGINATION, OR THE CREATIVE INSTINCT.

I. CONCEPTION AND IMAGINATION.

In a valiant suffering for others, not in a slothful making of others suffer for us, did nobleness ever lie.   Every noble crown is, and on Earth will ever be, a crown of thorns.   *Carlyle.*

> Music, when soft voices die,
> Vibrates in the memory;
> Odours, when sweet violets sicken,
> Live within the sense they quicken;
> Rose-leaves, when the rose is dead,
> Are heap'd for the beloved's bed :
> And so thy thoughts, when thou art gone,
> Love itself shall slumber on.   *Shelley.*

In the first of the two sentences of the first extract a truth is stated plainly. In the second, the mind is made to realize the same idea with ten-fold force. What causes the difference? In the first there is a sequence of simple conceptions; in the second the mind suddenly and spontaneously discovers unity and relationship among diverse ideas. In the first clause a plain truth is stated in a simple and direct way; in the second, a concrete picture is made to stand for a universal truth.

> In the far North stands a Pine-tree, lone, upon a wintry height;
> It sleeps : around it snows have thrown a covering of white.
> It dreams forever of a Palm that, far i' the Morning-land,
> Stands silent in a most sad calm midst heaps of burning sand.
>
> *From Heine.*   *Lanier.*

Diverse objects and situations are here brought into direct and vivid contrast, while unity is discovered between them. The attention is so attracted by living images that the powers of the mind are quickened and made to realize a thought intensely. The importance of vivid conceptions and their relations to vocal expression has already been explained; but in such extracts and selections as the two preceding we find something more than isolated ideas or logical relations. Here are higher relations of ideas to one another and more complex conceptions. A peculiar faculty is found active, which contemplates objects and penetrates through all superficial relations to ideas which are more central and ideal; and which also brings together two more or less commonplace conceptions into such organic unity as to suggest and awaken interest in an exalted truth. It discovers, not by reasoning or conscious comparison, but by an intuitive, spontaneous, prophetical vision a hidden truth or unity amid seemingly diverse ideas. The power concerned in this process is usually called the imagination.

Poetry was defined by Aristotle as the universal element in human life. The imagination has always something of this universalizing tendency. It is the faculty which gives universal truth by presenting concrete conceptions.

Poetry, however, has never been defined by prose: otherwise prose would be superior to poetry. Neither has imagination ever been adequately defined by reason. Imagination is the transcendent faculty of the human mind. It is a power by which the mind arrives at truth through an immediate process. It is unconscious reason. It sees truth from the heart, and not by external and objective comparison; hence, reason cannot adequately define it.

" If asked," says Mr. Shairp, " what imagination is, who can tell? If we turn to the psychologists, — the men who busy themselves with labelling and ticketing the mental faculties, — they do not help us. Scattered through the poets, here and there, and in some writers on æsthetic subjects, notably in the works of Mr. Ruskin, we find thoughts which are more suggestive." There will be here, therefore, no effort made to analyze this faculty; but certain illustrations will be given of some of its actions, so that its presence and the conditions of its exercise may be recognized.

One of the most common notions regarding the imagination is that it pictures for the mind that which is not an object of sense. It is the image-making faculty: this gives it its name. It is regarded as one of the reproductive faculties, the memory being the other. This definition, however, confuses imagination with conception.

It is well carefully to distinguish imagination from conception. In general, conception has reference to single objects or ideas: imagination to their relation. An idea to be conceived is more or less isolated. Imagination, on the other hand, has a vision of an organic whole, composed of dissimilar objects or ideas. Imagination does not perceive mere fragments: it sees the whole at once. Its action is free and untrammelled. It never repeats itself. It never constructs by patchwork or by process of aggregation. It creates, as Nature does, from the centre outward; its visions grow. It is always characterized by simplicity, by unity and truth. The imagination creates all our ideals, and is the soul of all inspiration. Conceptions may weary, memory may pall upon our attention; but imagination, never.

Conception may be vivid, and imagination dim; for conception deals with distinct features, with things which lie on the plane of sense; whereas imagination may rise into the realm of pure spirit. The difference between conception and imagination has been very simply and plainly stated by Professor Shairp: "To a man's ordinary conception of things imagination adds force, clearness, distinction of outline, vividness of coloring." Imagination vitalizes all knowledge, shows us the kinship of things, gives to every object a situation or background, and so prevents knowledge from becoming isolated or disconnected; enables the soul to feel the life of the universe permeating every object.

We can analyze and read the following Shakespearian lyric so as to destroy all its poetry. A mere lark, or a mere gate, or even the flowers, or sunbeams in isolation, furnish no clew whatever to the thought or beauty of the poem. It is only when we take all these together, give vivid coloring and atmosphere, and idealize them into parts of one beautiful picture of morning, that we have the spirit of the poem: —

Hark ! hark ! the lark at Heaven's gate sings,
    And Phœbus 'gins arise,
His steeds to water at those springs
    On chaliced flowers that lies ;
And winking Mary-buds begin
    To ope their golden eyes ;
With everything that pretty bin,
    My lady sweet, arise !
        Arise ! arise !

Cymbeline.   *Shakespeare.*

Imagination does not isolate conceptions: it not only conceives ideas and makes them clearer, but creates vital relations and restores normal situations and environment. Beauty and art deal with relation. Art is the creation of the right relation of objects. As life depends on environment, so do beauty, truth, and religion. The highest judgment of the human mind is a proper co-ordination of different ideas.

THE HOUSE BEAUTIFUL.

A naked house, a naked moor,
A shivering pool before the door,
A garden bare of flowers and fruit,
And poplars at the garden foot, —
Such is the place that I live in,
Bleak without and bare within.

Yet shall your ragged moor receive
The incomparable pomp of eve,
And the cold glories of the dawn
Behind your shivering trees be drawn ;
And when the wind from place to place
Doth the unmoored cloud-galleons chase,
Your garden gloom and gleam again,
With leaping sun, with dancing rain.
Here shall the wizard moon ascend
The heavens, in the crimson end
Of day's declining splendor ; here
The army of the stars appear.
The neighbor hollows dry or wet,
Spring shall with tender flowers beset ;
And oft the morning muser see
Larks rising from the broomy lea,

> And every fairy wheel and thread
> Of cobweb dew-bediamondèd.
> When daisies go, shall winter time
> Silver the simple grass with rime,
> Autumnal frosts enchant the pool
> And make the cart-ruts beautiful.
> And when snow-bright the moor expands,
> How shall your children clap their hands !
> To make this earth, our hermitage,
> A cheerful and a pleasaut page,
> God's bright and iutricate device
> Of days and seasons doth suffice.　*Robert Louis Stevenson.*

In the first six lines of the foregoing extract we find simple conceptions, given without atmosphere, or without any feeling of connection with other objects. In the next few lines the very same objects are taken up uuder the dominion of the imagiuation. Here there is iusight into the relation or fellowship of things. Pictures of the simplest and plainest objects are filled by the imagination with all the beauty of light aud atmosphere. In the first part, the house and objects are given literally. In the second, we have their fellowship with the sun and sky, with wind and weather. Things are painted as they exist in Nature, sharing in one another's life, reflecting and changing one another's appearance, as they have done every moment through all the history of the ages; and thus they are contemplated and conceived by a sympathetic mind that perceives from the heart.

PROBLEM I. *Read a passage with definite, vivid conceptions, but without imaginative action; and then read the same with vivid conceptions related to one another by the imagination, and note the difference in effect upon the voice.*

PROBLEM II. *Read an imaginative passage with definite, clear, but isolated conceptions, and notice how the spirit of the passage is degraded.*

PROBLEM III. *Read a beautiful passage with, and then without, any background, and note the difference in expression.*

PROBLEM IV. *Distinguish between analytic and synthetic actions of the mind, and their effect upon the voice.*

NEW voices come to me where'er I roam;
My heart, too, widens with its widening home :
The former songs seem little ; yet no more
Can soul, hand, voice, with interchanging lore,
Tell what the earth is saying unto me :
The secret is too great.

George Eliot

THE HOUSE OF THE TREES.

OPE your doors and take me in, spirit of the wood !
Wash me clean of dust and din, clothe me in your mood.
Take me from the noisy light to the sunless peace,
Where at midday standeth Night singing Toil's release.
All your dusky twilight stores to my senses give ;
Take me in and lock the doors, show me how to live.
Lift your leafy roof for me, part your yielding walls :
Let me wander lingeringly through your scented halls.
Ope your doors and take me in, spirit of the wood !
Take me — make me next of kin to your leafy brood.

Ethelwyn Wetherald

FULL many a glorious morning have I seen
Flatter the mountain-tops with sovereign eye,
Kissing with golden face the meadows green,
Gilding pale streams with heavenly alchemy ;
Anon permit the basest clouds to ride
With ugly rack on his celestial face,
And from the forlorn world his visage hide,
Stealing unseen to west with this disgrace :
Even so my sun one early morn did shine,
With all triumphant splendor on my brow ;
But out ! alack ! he was but one hour mine, —
The regent cloud hath masked him from me now.
Yet him for this my love no whit disdaineth ;
Suns of the world may stain, when heaven's sun staineth.

Shakespeare.

SUCH a starved bank of moss till that May-morn,
Blue ran the flash across : violets were born !
Sky — what a scowl of cloud till, near and far,
Ray on ray split the shroud : splendid, a star !
World — how it walled about life with disgrace
Till God's own smile came out : that was thy face !

Browning.

Not only around our infancy
Doth heaven with all its splendors lie:
Daily, with souls that cringe and plot,
We Sinais climb, and know it not.
Over our manhood bend the skies;
Against our fallen and traitor lives
The great winds utter prophecies;
With our faint hearts the mountain strives;
Its arms outstretched, the Druid wood
Waits with its benedicite;
And to our age's drowsy blood
Still shouts the inspiring sea.

Lowell

II. IMAGINATIVE ATTENTION.

The eye — it cannot choose but see; we cannot bid the ear be still;
Our bodies feel, where'er they be, against or with our will.
Nor less I deem that there are Powers which of themselves our minds impress,
That we can feed this mind of ours in a wise passiveness.

One impulse from a vernal wood may teach you more of man,
Of moral evil and of good, than all the sages can.
Sweet is the lore which Nature brings; our meddling intellect
Mis-shapes the beauteous forms of things: we murder to dissect.

One moment now may give us more than years of toiling reason:
Our minds shall drink at every pore the spirit of the season.

Wordsworth.

If you ask any one whether attention is active or passive, he will be sure to answer, "It is active, of course." The reason for this is on account of the emphasis that is usually placed upon rational analysis, upon intellectual concentration, upon one fact or object or idea, to the exclusion of all others. By attention, most persons mean the concentration of the mind upon one thing to the exclusion of all others. But when we come to observe more carefully, we find that this is not the whole of attention. If at a symphony concert we give our attention to one man only in the orchestra, or to one instrument, excluding by the action of our mind the effect of others, we do not enjoy the music. Again, if we enter a gallery and observe one little detail in a picture, we shall not get the true impression which the picture is meant to create. The same is true of a poem. We must contemplate the whole. Thus there is an analytic attention which is more active, and an artistic or synthetic attention which is more passive.

To enjoy music, we must hold ourselves in a responsive attitude toward the whole orchestra. To enjoy a painting, we must stand away from it, and allow the unity of the whole to impress us; allow the rhythm, consciously or unconsciously, to dominate us,— until the situation of the whole has been created. Then, and then only, does the true feeling arise which the picture was intended to awaken.

The same mental attitude is needful not only for appreciation of every object of art, but in regard to Nature herself. Even when we listen to a bird, a certain sympathetic or impressionable, not a mechanical or analytic, attention is requisite. In looking upon a flower or beautiful landscape, it is only when we feel the relation of the whole that we get a sense of beauty or loveliness.

Art has been defined as relation; hence, the artistic nature demands the development of contemplative attention. According to Delsarte, contemplation is the most exalted faculty of art. We must gaze upon the face of Nature, or upon a work of art, our whole nature being co-ordinate, and with such intensity as to cause a sympathetic response; only thus do appreciation and comprehension become possible.

In the study of our conceptions, we find, that, in attempting to vivify and make clear our ideas, there is a natural tendency to isolate conceptions from one another. As we think one thing, we exclude all else, that our ideas may be distinct and adequate. But in any work of art, ideas or objects, on the contrary, are brought into such living relation as will produce a general impression rather than a specific conception of details.

Some one has said that the supreme faculty of art is the faculty of generalization. There is a great difference between a picture and a statue. A statue is simply a representation of the object,— it corresponds with the conception; but when an artist paints a picture, his greatest problem is to generalize the details of his work so as to give oneness of impression, and to awaken definite feeling.

All art is expression; and expression is an equivalent that can exist out of the mind. Art is not a representation of objects, or even of the conception of objects: it is the intervention of personality; it is the revelation of the feeling soul; it is the expression of the man. It has been said that one of Corot's paintings of Morning "contains in it something of all the mornings that have ever been." It is not a literal photograph of some specific facts or details of one particular morning, or of certain trees or leaves or colors which he saw, but an impression so given as to awaken the right attitude of the man towards morning. It appeals to the universal human heart, and calls forth the same feeling as the morning itself.

Two forms of attention are therefore necessary. Contemplative attention is just as necessary as active attention. In fact, a failure to change our point of view, and to exercise sympathetic attention, is the chief cause of a lack of love for Nature, music, painting, or art.

We often fail to realize the character of human language. We look upon it as all upon the plane of commonplace or rational action. We do not perceive that every art has a specific nature distinct from every other; that a painting expresses something which can never be told by a poem; that music reveals an aspect of the human spirit which can hardly be suggested by a statue; and that to read the language of art, the attention of the human being must be trained to act in different ways, — passively and responsively as well as actively. At all times the man must be able to vary his point of view, and especially never to lose the fundamental character of realistic attention.

The highest mark of culture is the ability to read all languages of the human soul. This ability is not dependent merely upon knowledge, which may sometimes arouse prejudice or prevent teachableness. To know too much of some period of art may cause us to make this a standard for the judgment of every other movement in art. However much we know about any one form or any one period of art, we must be careful to remain passive and contemplative in attending to new movements and other forms of art, or to the art of different peoples.

Such passive responsiveness, such reposeful and unprejudiced attitudes of receptivity, are not only necessary to the appreciation of art, but to any exercise of the imagination. The reason may pre-judge, may mechanically compare, may be unreceptive and unresponsive; but not so with the imagination. Intellectual or commonplace attention may dwell upon accidents, but imagination looks to the heart. Imagination is the spontaneous result of sympathetic contemplative attention.

PROBLEM V. — *Read a passage, first with analytic attention, and then with contemplative attention, and note the difference in action.*

> My soul is an enchanted boat,
> Which, like a sleeping swan, doth float
> Upon the silver waves of thy sweet singing;
>   And thine doth like an angel sit
>   Beside a helm conducting it,
> Whilst all the winds with melody are ringing.
>   It seems to float ever, forever,
>   Upon that many-winding river,
>   Between mountains, woods, abysses, —
>   A paradise of wildernesses!
> Till, like one in slumber bound,
> Borne to the ocean, I float down, around,
> Into a sea profound of ever-spreading sound.
>
>   Meanwhile thy spirit lifts its pinions
>   In music's most serene dominions;
> Catching the winds that fan that happy heaven.
>   And we sail on, away, afar,
>   Without a course, without a star,
> But by the instinct of sweet music driven, —
>   Till through Elysian garden islets
>   By thee, most beautiful of pilots,
>   Where never mortal pinnace glided,
>   The boat of my desire is guided:
> Realms where the air we breathe is love,
> Which in the winds and on the waves doth move,
> Harmonizing this earth with what we feel above.

THE CUCKOO.

HAIL, beauteous stranger of the grove ! Thou messenger of spring !
Now heaven repairs thy rural seat, and woods thy welcome sing.
What time the daisy decks the green, thy certain voice we hear :
Hast thou a star to guide thy path, or mark the rolling year ?
Delightful visitant ! with thee I hail the time of flowers,
And hear the sound of music sweet from birds among the bowers.
The schoolboy, wandering through the wood to pull the primrose gay,
Starts, the new voice of spring to hear, and imitates thy lay.
What time the pea puts on the bloom, thou fliest thy vocal vale,
An annual guest in other lands, another spring to hail.
Sweet bird ! thy bower is ever green, thy sky is ever clear ;
Thou hast no sorrow in thy song, no winter in thy year !
Oh could I fly, I 'd fly with thee ! We 'd make, with joyful wing,
Our annual visit o'er the globe, companions of the spring.

John Logan.

———

LOVERS AND MUSIC.

Lorenzo.   The moon shines bright.   *In such a night as this,*[1]
When the sweet wind did gently kiss the trees,
And they did make no noise, — in such a night
Troilus, methinks, mounted the Trojan walls,
And sigh'd his soul towards the Grecian tents,
Where Cressid lay that night.
   Jessica.   *In such a night*
Did Thisbe fearfully o'ertrip the dew,
And saw the lion's shadow ere himself,
And ran dismay'd away.
   Lor.   *In such a night*
Stood Dido with a willow in her hand
Upon the wild sea-banks, and wav'd her love
To come again to Carthage.
   Jes.   *In such a night*
Medea gather'd the enchanted herbs
That did renew old Æson.
   Lor.   *In such a night*
Did Jessica steal from the wealthy Jew ;
And with an unthrift love did run from Venice,
As far as Belmont.

[1] The passages printed in Italics were so marked by Leigh Hunt, to indicate the presence of imagination.

Jes.   *And in such a night*
Did young Lorenzo swear he lov'd her well ;
Stealing her soul with many vows of faith,
And ne'er a true one.
   Lor.   *And in such a night*
Did pretty Jessica, like a little shrew,
Slander her love, *and he forgave it her.*
   Jes.   I would out-night you, did nobody come ;
But, hark! I hear the footing of a man.   [*Enter* STEPHANO.
   Lor.   Who comes so fast in silence of the night ?
   Steph.   A friend.
   Lor.   A friend ! what friend ?   Your name, I pray you, friend ?
   Steph.   Stephano is my name : and I bring word
My mistress will, before the break of day,
Be here at Belmont : she doth stray about
By holy crosses, where she kneels and prays
For happy wedlock hours.
   Lor.   Who comes with her ?
   Steph.   None but a holy hermit and her maid.
   Lor.   Sweet soul, let 's in, and there expect their coming.
And yet no matter : why should we go in ?
My friend Stephano, signify, I pray you,
Within the house, your mistress is at hand ;
And bring your music forth into the air.   [*Exit* STEPHANO.
How sweet the moonlight sleeps upon this bank !
Here will we sit, and let the sounds of music
Creep into our ears ; *soft stillness and the night*
Become the touches of sweet harmony.
Sit, Jessica.   Look, how the floor of heaven
Is thick inlaid with patines of bright gold ;
There 's not the smallest orb which thou behold'st,
But in his motion *like an angel sings,*
Still quiring to the young-eyed cherubims.
Such harmony is in immortal souls ;
But whilst this muddy vesture of decay
Doth grossly close us in, we cannot hear it.   [*Enter Musicians.*
Come, ho ! and wake Diana with a hymn ;
With sweetest touches pierce your mistress' ear,
And draw her home with music.   (*Music.*)
   Jes.   I am never merry when I hear sweet music.
   Lor.   The reason is, your spirits are attentive :
For do but note a wild and wanton herd,
A race of youthful and unhandled colts,
Fetching mad bounds, — bellowing and neighing loud,

Which is the hot condition of their blood :
If they but hear, perchance, a trumpet sound,
Or any air of music touch their ears,
You shall perceive them make a mutual stand, —
Their savage eyes turned to a modest gaze
By the sweet power of music.   Therefore the poet
Did feign that Orpheus drew trees, stones, and floods,
Since naught so stockish, hard, and full of rage,
But music for the time doth change his nature.
The man that hath no music in himself,
Nor is not mov'd by concord of sweet sounds,
Is fit for treasons, stratagems, and spoils ;
The motions of his spirit are dull as night,
And his affections dark as Erebus.
Let no such man be trusted.   Mark the music.

                [*Enter* PORTIA *and* NERISSA *at distance.*

   Por.   That light we see is burning in my hall ;
How far that little candle throws its beams !
So shines a good deed in a naughty world.

   Ner.   When the moon shone, we did not see the candle.

   Por.   So doth the greater glory dim the less ;
A substitute shines brightly as a king,
Until a king be by ; *and then his state*
Empties itself, as doth an inland brook
Into the main of waters.   Music ! hark !

   Ner.   It is your music, madam, of the house.

   Por.   Nothing is good, I see, without respect ;
Methinks it sounds much sweeter than by day.

   Ner.   Silence bestows that virtue on it, madam.

   Por.   The crow doth sing as sweetly as the lark,
When neither is attended ; and, I think,
The nightingale, if she should sing by day,
When every goose is cackling, would be thought
No better a musician than the wren.
How many things by season season'd are
To their right praise and true perfection !
Peace, hoa ! the moon sleeps with Endymion,
And would not be awak'd !   (*Music ceases.*)

   Lor.   That is the voice,
Or I am much deceiv'd, of Portia.

   Por.   He knows me as the blind man knows the cuckoo, —
By the bad voice.

   Lor.   Dear lady, welcome home.

> THE champaign with its endless fleece
>   Of feathery grasses everywhere !
> Silence and passion, joy and peace,
>   An everlasting wash of air, — . . .
> Such life here, through such length of hours,
>   Such miracles performed in play,
> Such primal naked forms of flowers,
>   Such letting Nature have her way.   *Browning*

III. IMAGINATION AND MEMORY.

> IN front the awful Alpine track
> Crawls up its rocky stair ;
> The autumn storm-winds drive the rack
> Close o'er it in the air.
>
> Behind are the abandoned baths
> Mute in their meadows lone ;
> The leaves are on the valley paths,
> The mists are on the Rhone, —
>
> The white mists rolling like a sea !
> I hear the torrents roar.
> Yes, Obermann ! all speaks of thee ;
> I feel thee near once more !   *Matthew Arnold.*

IN reading these lines by Matthew Arnold, a number of questions naturally spring up in the mind. What is meant by Obermann; what baths are referred to; what special place is in the mind of the poet? We read the whole poem, and find from the poet's notes that it was written after the death of Senancour, the author of " Obermann," and that the sympathies of Matthew Arnold have been deeply stirred. We find also that the " abandoned baths " are the baths of Leuk, and that the " poem was conceived, and partly composed, in the valley going down from the foot of the Gemmi Pass towards the Rhone."

On reading these facts, those who have visited the place may remember the scene; but if they enjoy the poem, though they may begin with memory, the whole situation will be very soon transformed in their minds. They will read the poem, not with an act of memory, but with the aid of imagination. Poetry expresses the universal element in human nature. Arnold's words do not appeal to memory, but to a higher faculty. He meant to place in every reader's mind a background for certain feelings. The poem is not a literal description of what he himself saw.

Some one prepared a book, locating all the events referred to in Tennyson's "Idyls of the King;" but the poet was displeased,—it was foreign to the true spirit of poetry. Tennyson had endeavored to appeal to the universal heart and imagination of mankind. He had written no book of description or travel, and any attempt to locate literally the scenes would be only a hindrance to the universal appreciation or true realization of the poetry.

Poetry appeals to the imagination; memory and conception may furnish the materials, but imagination idealizes and universalizes them. True poetry is but suggestion. This is the function of poetry and art. Before a literal object, no two minds have the same impression. Art alone can awaken a corresponding feeling and impression in different hearts. It does this by an appeal to the imagination. This is the creative power, the faculty which conceives essentials rather than accidentals, and realizes the relations of objects to one another and to human feeling.

Imagination is most active in that which is familiar. It uses the simplest, the most insignificant objects and the most familiar scenes as the material for its exalted flights. Notice in illustration of this the following translation of a poem in which the writer speaks of her own home: —

MY REST.

Round yon snowy house green woods dream ;
'Twixt the giant boughs moonbeams stream.
Ah ! fain I 'd adore ev'ry tree ;
Here dreamt I of yore happily.
All my many songs found I here,
'Mid thy branches heard, woodland dear !

In my tiny room, vine entwin'd,
Can I those sweet thoughts once more find ?
Here the Rhine like to silv'ry band,
Like to sunbeam, flows o'er the land.
Wind, which 'mid green boughs o'er me blows,
Once thy lullaby brought repose.　　　　*Carmen Sylva.*

Of nearly every great scene,—Mont Blanc or Niagara, for instance,— most persons' carry an imaginary picture as well as a memory of the place itself. In reading a poem describing such objects, it is the imagined scene which is foremost. After long familiarity with some locality, the imagination and memory tend to become one. But even in this case there are a thousand memories of different sunrises and sunsets, of different aspects of light, of various conditions of atmosphere; and in reading, it is hardly possible to apply any one of these specially. In nearly all cases the scene is imagined to suit the mental attitude of the moment.

Many persons in travelling see nothing, because they do not use the imagination. A mere superficial glancing at some scene, a rushing through a country on an express train, gives very little food for imagination. The true traveller endeavors to blend his imaginative conception with the observation of the scene itself.

Imagination is not antagonistic to observation. In order to read a poem well, we analyze it, we study all possible references, we look up facts regarding places mentioned, we refer to events of history, we study the lives of any historical characters which may be referred to; but in the act of reading, all this knowledge is so assimilated that it furnishes only a background or material for imaginative conception.

Memory recalls specific facts and objects; but imagination supplies situations and living relations. Imagination takes facts, and gives them vital kinship to other facts. It deals not with the letter, but with the spirit. " Imagination," says Wordsworth, " has no reference to images that are merely a faithful copy, existing in the mind, of absent external objects; but is a word of higher import, denoting operations of the mind upon those objects, and processes of creation or of composition.

> " 'half way down
> Hangs one who gathers samphire,'

is the well-known expression of Shakespeare, delineating an ordinary image upon the cliffs of Dover." Here is found "a slight exertion of the faculty which I denominate imagination, in the use of one word: neither the goats nor the samphire-gatherer do literally hang, as does the parrot or the monkey; but, presenting to the senses something of such an appearance, the mind in its activity, for its own gratification, contemplates them as hanging.

> " ' As when far off at sea a fleet descried
>   Hangs in the clouds : . . . . so seemed
>   Far off the flying Fiend.'

Here is the full strength of the imagination involved in the word *hangs*, and exerted upon the whole image. First, the fleet, an aggregate of many ships, is represented as one mighty person, whose track, we know and feel, is upon the waters; but, taking advantage of its appearance to the senses, the Poet dares to represent it as hanging in the clouds, both for the gratification of the mind in contemplating the image itself, and in reference to the motion and appearance of the sublime objects to which it is compared. "

PROBLEM VI. *Read an extract, and call into exercise simply the memory: then read the same extract with an imaginative atmosphere, without perverting memory.*

> THE old trees
> Which grew by our youth's home ; the waving mass
> Of climbing plants, heavy with bloom and dew ;
> The morning swallows with their songs like words, —
> All these seem clear and most distinct amid
> The fever and the stir of after years.   *Browning.*

PROBLEM VII. *Read a description of some place, and show how the imagination can build upon memory, and act without perverting it.*

> O ROME ! my country ! city of the soul !
> The orphans of the heart must turn to thee,
> Lone Mother of dead empires ! and control
> In their shut breasts their petty misery.
> What are our woes and sufferance ?   Come and see
> The cypress, hear the owl, and plod your way
> O'er steps of broken thrones and temples, ye
> Whose agonies are evils of a day !
> A world is at our feet as fragile as our clay.

The Niobe of nations! there she stands,
Childless and crownless, in her voiceless woe,
An empty urn within her withered hands,
Whose holy dust was scattered long ago.
The Scipios' tomb contains no ashes now;
The very sepulchres lie tenantless
Of their heroic dwellers: dost thou flow,
Old Tiber, through a marble wilderness?
Rise, with thy yellow waves, and mantle her distress!

Byron.

MONT BLANC BEFORE SUNRISE.[1]

HAST thou a charm to stay the Morning-star
In his steep course?   So long he seems to pause
On thy bald, awful head, O sovereign Blanc!
The Arvé and the Arveiron at thy base
Rave ceaselessly ; but thou, most awful form,
Risest from forth thy silent sea of pines,
How silently !   Around thee, and above,
Deep is the air and dark, substantial, black,
An ebon mass: methinks thou piercest it
As with a wedge.   But when I look again
It is thine own calm home, thy crystal shrine,
Thy habitation from eternity.

O dread and silent Mount !   I gazed upon thee
Till thou, still present to the bodily sense,
Didst vanish from my thought ! entranced in prayer
I worshipped the Invisible alone.
Yet, like some sweet beguiling melody, —
So sweet we know not we are listening to it, —
Thou, the mean while wast blending with my thought,
Yea, with my life, and life's own secret joy ;
Till the dilating soul, enrapt, transfused,
Into the mighty vision passing — there,
As in her natural form, swelled vast to heaven.

Awake, my soul ! not only passive praise
Thou owest ! not alone these swelling tears,
Mute thanks, and secret ecstasy !   Awake,
Voice of sweet song !   Awake, my heart, awake !
Green vales and icy cliffs ! all join my hymn !

[1] In parts, a paraphrase of Fredrike Brün's poem, p. 222.

Thou first and chief, sole sovereign of the vale !
Oh, struggling with the darkness all the night,
And visited all night by troops of stars,
Or when they climb the sky, or when they sink, —
Companion of the Morning-star at dawn,
Thyself earth's rosy star, and of the dawn
Co-herald — wake ! oh, wake ! and utter praise !
Who sank thy sunless pillars deep in earth ?
Who filled thy countenance with rosy light ?
Who made thee parent of perpetual streams ?

And you, ye five wild torrents fiercely glad !
Who called you forth from night and utter death,
From dark and icy caverns called you forth,
Down those precipitous, black, jaggèd rocks,
Forever shattered, and the same forever ?
Who gave you your invulnerable life,
Your strength, your speed, your fury, and your joy,
Unceasing thunder, and eternal foam ?
And who commanded, — and the silence came, —
" Here let the billows stiffen and have rest " ?

Ye ice-falls ! ye that from the mountain's brow
Adown enormous ravines slope amain, —
Torrents, methinks, that heard a mighty voice,
And stopped at once amid their maddest plunge !
Motionless torrents ! silent cataracts !
Who made you glorious as the gates of heaven
Beneath the keen full moon ?   Who bade the sun
Clothe you with rainbows ?   Who, with living flowers
Of loveliest blue, spread garlands at your feet ?

" God ! " let the torrents, like a shout of nations,
Answer ! and let the ice-plain echo, " God ! "
" God ! " sing, ye meadow streams, with gladsome voice !
Ye pine groves, with your soft and soul-like sounds !   .
And they, too, have a voice, yon piles of snow,
And in their perilous fall shall thunder, " God ! "
Ye living flowers that skirt the eternal frost !
Ye wild goats sporting round the eagle's nest !
Ye eagles, playmates of the mountain storm !
Ye lightnings, the dread arrows of the clouds !
Ye signs and wonders of the elements !
Utter forth " God ! " and fill the hills with praise !

Thou too, hoar Mount! with thy sky-pointing peaks,
Oft from whose feet the avalanche, unheard,
Shoots downward, glittering through the pure serene
Into the depth of clouds that veil thy breast, —
Thou too, again, stupendous mountain! thou
That, as I raise my head, awhile bowed low
In adoration, upward from thy base
Slow travelling, with dim eyes suffused with tears,
Solemnly seemest, like a vapory cloud,
To rise before me, — rise, oh, ever rise!
Rise, like a cloud of incense, from the earth!
Thou kingly spirit, throned among the hills,
Thou dread ambassador from earth to heaven,
Great Hierarch! tell thou the silent sky,
And tell the stars, and tell yon rising sun,
Earth, with her thousand voices, praises God.   *Coleridge.*

PROBLEM VIII. *Read an account of some historic event, and show how the imagination may be used to realize its significance more vividly.*

THE CONCORD HYMN.

By the rude bridge that arched the flood,
    Their flag to April's breeze unfurled,
Here once the embattled farmers stood,
    And fired the shot heard round the world.

The foe long since in silence slept;
    Alike the conqueror silent sleeps;
And Time the ruined bridge has swept
    Down the dark stream which seaward creeps.

On this green bank, by this soft stream,
    We set to-day a votive stone,
That memory may their deed redeem,
    When, like our sires, our sons are gone.

Spirit, that made those heroes dare
    To die, or leave their children free!
Bid Time and Nature gently spare
    The shaft we raise to them and thee.   *Emerson.*

THIS precious stone set in a silver sea,
Which serves it in the office of a wall,
Or as a moat defensive of a house
Against the enemy of less happier lands:

> This blessèd plot, this earth, this realm, this England ! —
> This England never did, nor never shall,
> Lie at the proud foot of a conqueror
> But when it first did help to wound itself,
> Come the three corners of the world in arms,
> And we shall shock them : nought shall make us rue,
> If England to itself do rest but true.

Richard II.   *Shakespeare.*

IV. IMAGINATION AND SCIENCE.

IMAGINATION is not a wild departure from truth. Truth is its material, its life and soul. It uses all the facts of science. Poetry in every age employs discoveries as the rounds of a ladder up which it climbs to a higher outlook upon the mystery of the universe. No age has equalled our own in scientific investigations. These have furnished Tennyson with some of his greatest inspirations; and the deepest philosophical thought of our speculative age has been the theme of Browning. Bacon, the father of all modern science, was contemporaneous with Shakespeare. In our greatest era of poetry the foundations of science were laid. Poetry and science are not antagonistic. In fact, imagination is an agent in scientific investigation; it is part of the initiatory step of the true scientific method. The scientific method begins with preliminary observation or formation of hypothesis; and to this succeeds experiment and observation, to prove or disprove this hypothesis; then follows generalization. Thus imagination precedes and inspires scientific investigation, and true scientific attainment awakens a struggle for higher realization of the new truth.

Imagination goes beyond science; it supplies what science lacks; it brings the facts discovered by science into living unity.

As truth is not antagonistic to fact, so imagination is not antagonistic to reason. Indeed, imagination gives careful observation, and is helpful to reception: as Wordsworth has said, " Poetry is the breath and finer spirit of all knowledge."

Imagination has a sphere peculiarly her own. She refuses to become the handmaid or servant of any science, philosophy, creed, or

view of life; and yet she sheds light on all.   She does not supply
or pervert facts, nor is she subservient to them.   She unites facts,
and discovers higher relations, beauties, and truths.   She often
points out the path where reason and experiment must walk, and
always precedes rather than follows.   She transcends external relations, but never warps or acts inconsistently with truth.

In the following illustration, notice with what scientific accuracy
Tennyson describes the coming on of night and the rising moon.
Nor is the passage any less poetic for its scientific basis.

> MOVE eastward, happy Earth ! and leave
>   Yon orange sunset waning slow :
> From fringes of the faded eve,
>   O happy planet ! eastward go ;
> Till over thy dark shoulder glow
>   Thy silver sister-world, and rise
>   To glass herself in dewy eyes
> That watch me from the glen below.

In the same way, note the scientific facts hinted at in the next
illustration from " In Memoriam."   The ideas of Tennyson are
here also scientifically accurate; he gives established facts, and
the poetry is all the more sublime and imaginative from its
truthfulness.

> THERE rolls the deep where grew the tree.
>   O Earth, what changes hast thou seen !
>   There where the long street roars, hath been
> The stillness of the central sea.
> The hills are shadows, and they flow
>   From form to form, and nothing stands ;
>   They melt like mist, the solid lands,
> Like clouds they shape themselves and go.

PROBLEM IX.   *State in plain prose the scientific facts referred to in one
of the following poems; then read the poem, and observe the uses made of such
facts by the imagination.   Are the facts perverted by being idealized, or only
more intensely realized ?*

> ROLL on, and with thy rolling crust
>   That round thy poles thou twirlest,
> Roll with thee, Earth! this grain of dust,
>   As through the Vast thou whirlest :

On, on through zones of dark and light
  Still waft me, blind and reeling,
Around the Sun, and with his flight
  In wilder orbits wheeling.

THE CHAMBERED NAUTILUS.

THIS is the ship of pearl, which, poets feign,
  Sails the unshadowed main, —
  The venturous bark that flings
On the sweet summer wind its purpled wings
In gulfs enchanted, where the siren sings,
  And coral reefs lie bare ;
Where the cold sea-maids rise to sun their streaming hair.

Its webs of living gauze no more unfurl, —
  Wrecked is the ship of pearl !
  And every chambered cell,
Where its dim dreaming life was wont to dwell,
As the frail tenant shaped his growing shell,
  Before thee lies revealed, —
Its irised ceiling rent, its sunless crypt unsealed !

Year after year beheld the silent toil
  That spread his lustrous coil !
  Still, as the spiral grew,
He left the past year's dwelling for the new,
Stole with soft step its shining archway through,
  Built up its idle door,
Stretched in his last-found home, and knew the old no more.

Thanks for the heavenly message brought by thee,
  Child of the wandering sea,
  Cast from her lap forlorn !
From thy dead lips a clearer note is borne
Than ever Triton blew from wreathèd horn !
  While on mine ear it rings,
Through the deep caves of thought I hear a voice that sings :

Build thee more stately mansions, O my soul,
  As the swift seasons roll !
  Leave thy low-vaulted past !
Let each new temple, nobler than the last,
Shut thee from heaven with a dome more vast,
  Till thou at length art free,
Leaving thine outgrown shell by life's unresting sea !

O. W. Holmes.

THE RISING OF THE HILLS.

SINKING, sinking, all the country slowly sank beneath the waves;
And the ocean swept the forests, reptiles, dragons, to their graves;
Afterwards with shells old Ocean all the conquered country paves, —

Singing, "It is mine forever!" — Not forever, not for long,
For the subterranean forces laughed at Ocean's boastful song,
Lifting up the sunken country, for their backs were broad and strong,

Till the sea-shells were uplifted even to the mountain peak.
Far below the waves are moaning, but with voices faint and weak,
Sorrowing for their lost dominion and the toys they vainly seek.

Hamerton

THE PETRIFIED FERN.

IN a valley, centuries ago,
   Grew a little fern-leaf, green and slender,
   Veining delicate and fibres tender;
Waving when the wind crept down so low.
   Rushes tall, and moss, and grass grew round it,
   Playful sunbeams darted in and found it,
   Drops of dew stole in by night and crowned it,
   But no foot of man e'er trod that way:
   Earth was young, and keeping holiday.

Monster fishes swam the silent main,
   Stately forests waved their giant branches,
   Mountains hurled their snowy avalanches,
Mammoth creatures stalked across the plain:
   Nature revelled in grand mysteries.
   But the little fern was not of these,
   Did not number with the hills and trees;
   Only grew and waved its wild sweet way,
   None ever came to note it day by day.

Earth one time put on a frolic mood,
   Heaved the rocks, and changed the mighty motion
   Of the deep, strong currents of the ocean,
Moved the plain and shook the haughty wood,
   Crushed the little fern in soft moist clay, —
   Covered it, and hid it safe away.
   Oh, the long, long centuries since that day!
   Oh, the agony! Oh, life's bitter cost,
   Since that useless little fern was lost!

Useless ? Lost ? There came a thoughtful man,
  Searching Nature's secrets, far and deep ;
  From a fissure in a rocky steep
He withdrew a stone, o'er which there ran
  Fairy pencillings, a quaint design, —
  Veinings, leafage, fibres clear and fine, —
  And the fern's life lay in every line !
  So, I think, God hides some souls away,
  Sweetly to surprise us, the last day.   *Mary Bolles Branch.*

V. THE IDEAL AND THE REAL.

IT is the usual opinion that the imagination is concerned with the ideal; that it creates the ideal. This is true; but this is only one function of the imagination. All great art is either a realization of the ideal, or an idealization of the real. In fact, it is usually both.

When we look at the statue in the west pediment of the Parthenon, representing the river Cephissos, we are tempted to call Phidias a realist. The cloth which hangs over the arm is rendered with literal accuracy; only a wet cloth could hang in this position. Yet Phidias is considered the idealist of the idealists.

Ideal art does not mean that form of art which is above or contrary to the facts of Nature, or even that which is obtained by a process of abstraction, but refers to an art product which is an embodiment of the conceptions of the human mind. That is to say, ideal art is a realization in natural form of an imaginative conception. Phidias, therefore, was an idealist because he embodied a mental conception in a statue; the fact that he adopted literal details true to Nature did not make him a realist.

Realism, on the contrary, is the idealization of the real. The imagination is perhaps as much concerned with realistic art as with idealistic art. Rembrandt had a positive imaginative delight in every wrinkle of the old faces whose portraits he has painted. Zorn can give imaginative feeling in the most simple and realistic touch. F. H. Tompkins shows imaginative delight in the simplest shadow.

In fact, realism and idealism are two modes of artistic endeavor. Idealism begins with mental conception, and brings it into the realm of real objects, and makes that an object of sense which was only a dim dream. Realism begins with the physical object, with the definite literal fact; brings imagination to bear upon it; paints the spirit beneath the surface, and so lifts it into the realm of poetry and of beautiful truth. In both the idealistic and the realistic processes a coloring is received from personality. Thus art in each case is " the intervention of personality."

There may, therefore, be unimaginative realistic art. Where there is no intervention of personality, no " conforming of the shows of things to the desires and feelings of the mind," all is a mere copy and reproduction of the literal object. But there may be also unimaginative idealism. The artist has merely reproduced conventional conceptions received from others. He may have even an original conception of the object, and paint it in an artificial, conventional way with total absence of imagination. Some of the most conventional forms, some of the most academic products of art students, are in the line of idealism.

True art, or genuine work of the imagination, — whether it is the embodiment of the mental conceptions in objective form, or a truthful rendering of the simple facts of Nature, — is a union of something which belongs to the feeling heart with something which belongs to objective Nature. Coleridge once said of painting, that it was something between a thought and a thing, " a union of that which is human with that which is natural."

This principle applies also to poetry. Many poems are mere mental conceptions, and seem to have no correspondent existence in the actual world; but they are embodied in conceivable forms, and are communicated from mind to mind by suggestion. Such poems are ideal. But there are also poems which deal faithfully and definitely with the simplest facts of Nature, with the simplest occurrences in human life. Here the imagination is none the less present, having lent its services to the idealization, to the giving of environment and atmosphere.

Nothing is more important than to have an adequate conception of the wide range of imaginative action. Imagination is not the slave of any theory of art; it is not subservient to any one age, class of men, or view of art. He who tries to decide upon the presence of imagination in any artistic production, on the basis of his own theory or definition of art, is very sure to make a mistake, since the appreciation of poetry and music demands the broadest sympathy. Imagination has been different in every age, and yet the same. It has aided not only the sublimest work, but has lent its charm to the simplest production of human hands.

It must be recognized, in short, that no class of subjects, no class of human beings, no peculiar theory of art or poetry, has a monopoly of imagination. Anything may be made a subject of imaginative contemplation; anything may become poetic by being "intensely realized."

PROBLEM X. *Read a passage describing some real object or scene, and also some passage involving the most ideal thought, and note the action of the imagination in each case, and express this as far as possible by the voice: in other words, idealize the real, and realize the ideal.*

ON WESTMINSTER BRIDGE.

EARTH has not anything to show more fair :
    Dull would he be of soul who could pass by
    A sight so touching in its majesty :
This city now doth, like a garment, wear
The beauty of the morning ; silent, bare,
    Ships, towers, domes, theatres, and temples lie
    Open unto the fields and to the sky,
All bright and glittering in the smokeless air.
Never did sun more beautifully steep
    In his first splendor valley, rock, or hill ;
Ne'er saw I, never felt, a calm so deep.
    The river glideth at his own sweet will.
Dear God, the very houses seem asleep ;
    And all that mighty heart is lying still.

Wordsworth.

KUBLA KHAN.

IN Xanadu did Kubla Khan
    A stately pleasure-dome decree,
Where Alph, the sacred river, ran
Through caverns measureless to man
    Down to a sunless sea.

So twice five miles of fertile ground
With walls and towers were girdled round :
And there were gardens bright with sinuous rills
Where blossomed many an incense-bearing tree ;
And here were forests ancient as the hills,
Enfolding sunny spots of greenery.
But oh that deep romantic chasm which slanted
Down the green hill athwart a cedarn cover !
A savage place ! as holy and enchanted
As e'er beneath a waning moon was haunted
By woman wailing for her demon-lover !
And from this chasm, with ceaseless turmoil seething,
As if this earth in fast thick pants were breathing,
A mighty fountain momently was forced,
Amid whose swift, half-intermitted burst
Huge fragments vaulted like rebounding hail,
Or chaffy grain beneath the thresher's flail ;
And 'mid these dancing rocks at once and ever
It flung up momently the sacred river.
Five miles meandering with a mazy motion
Through wood and dale the sacred river ran,
Then reached the caverns measureless to man,
And sank in tumult to a lifeless ocean ;
And 'mid this tumult Kubla heard from far
Ancestral voices prophesying war !

    The shadow of the dome of pleasure
        Floated midway on the waves,
    Where was heard the mingled measure
        From the fountain and the caves.
It was a miracle of rare device,
A sunny pleasure-dome with caves of ice !
    A damsel with a dulcimer
        In a vision once I saw :
    It was an Abyssinian maid,
    And on her dulcimer she played,
        Singing of Mount Abora.
    Could I revive within me
        Her symphony and song,
    To such a deep delight 't would win me,
        That with music loud and long
I would build that dome in air, —
    That sunny dome ! those caves of ice !
And all who heard should see them there,

And all should cry, Beware ! beware!
His flashing eyes, his floating hair !
  Weave a circle round him thrice,
And close your eyes with holy dread,
For he on honey-dew hath fed,
  And drunk the milk of Paradise.

FROM POESY.

She doth tell me where to borrow
Comfort in the midst of sorrow ;
Makes the desolatest place
To her presence be a grace,
And the blackest discontents
Be her fairest ornaments.
In my former days of bliss
Her divine skill taught me this:
That from everything I saw
I could some invention draw,
And raise pleasure to her height
By the meanest object's sight, —
By the murmur of a spring,
Or the least bough's rustling,
Or a daisy whose leaves spread,
Shut when Titan goes to bed,
Or a shady bush or tree.
She could more infuse in me
Than all Nature's beauties can
In some other wiser man ;
By her help I also now
Make this churlish place allow
Some things that may sweeten gladness
In the very gall of sadness.
The dull lowness, the black shade,
That these hanging vaults have made ;
The strange music of the waves
Beating on these hollow caves ;
This black den which rocks emboss,
Overgrown with eldest moss ;
The rude portals that give light
More to Terror than Delight ;
This my chamber of Neglect,
Walled about with Disrespect,—

> From all these, and this dull air,
> A fit object for Despair,
> She hath taught me by her might
> To draw comfort and delight.
> Therefore, thou best earthly bliss,
> I will cherish thee for this.
> Poesy, thou sweet'st content
> That e'er Heaven to mortals lent,
> Though they as a trifle leave thee,
> Whose dull thoughts cannot conceive thee,
> Thou then be to them a scorn,
> That to naught but earth are born,—
> Let my life no longer be
> Than I am in love with thee.

Written in Marshalsea Prison.   *George Wither.*

VI. IMAGINATION AND FANCY.

The harmonious nave of the cathedral fell asleep, with its arms extended in the shape of a cross.   *Louis Bertrand.*

> "She comes like the husht beauty of the night,
> But sees too deep for laughter;
> Her touch is a vibration and a light
> From worlds before and after."

One important function of the imagination is to retain the attention in the study of the simplest objects or events. It can not only penetrate to the depth, but contemplate the simplest aspects of Nature and life. In its workings we often find a conscious or unconscious comparison. There is an unconscious union of conceptions which are remotely separated; but all differences are brought into a harmonious union.

All actions of the imagination are complex; it unites the most diverse ideas; it harmonizes antithetic conceptions; it reconciles opposites, and produces a living, organic unity.

One definition of beauty is "unity in the midst of variety." It is the function of the imagination to discover this unity. It can hold many conceptions simultaneously, and unite them by discovering a central idea.

The combination or comparison of complex conceptions must be immediate and spontaneous, or the result will be the action of fancy, if not of a still lower mental power. The contemplation, too, must be simple and sincere, if not unconscious. Where the comparison is conscious, the process is more the work of fancy; but where contemplation is concentrated at the heart of the object, the union of complex conceptions natural and spontaneous, the relation sincere and sympathetic, then imagination is dominant.

Imagination is often confounded with fancy. To distinguish between them is one of the most helpful means of appreciating the highest action of the imagination.

Fancy has more to do with the playful comparison of objects, with apparent or superficial relation, with the discovery of odd images and illustrations. It is wilder and more extravagant. Imagination deals with the essential nature of objects; fancy, with curious and unexpected resemblances. Imagination is the source of sympathy and insight, and is therefore far more intimately related to feeling than fancy. Fancy is playful and mischievous; it is not the result of a serious mood of mind and heart. Imagination, on the contrary, sees to the depth of things; it is serious, sincere, and truthful. Fancy is often exaggerated and untruthful; it imitates and mocks. Imagination sees things in relation to the heart; it touches the deepest chords of feeling; it is the one faculty which sees the life of things. Without imagination the human soul is imprisoned in a narrow cell, the mind has but one point of view, — never sees with other eyes, catches no gleam of the eternal morning, feels no future in the present.

The difference between fancy and imagination can be better illustrated than defined. Let us take two extracts from Shelley. His poem upon "The Cloud" is popular. It is easy for the mind to carry on its playful and beautiful comparison: —

I WIELD the flail of the lashing hail,
    And whiten the green plains under;
And then again I dissolve it in rain,
    And laugh as I pass in thunder.

> The sanguine Sunrise, with his meteor eyes,
>   And his burning plumes outspread,
> Leaps on the back of my sailing rack
>   When the morning star shines dead ;
> As on the jag of a mountain crag
>   Which an earthquake rocks and swings,
> An eagle alit one moment may sit
>   In the light of its golden wings.
> And when sunset may breathe, from the lit sea beneath,
>   Its ardors of rest and of love,
> And the crimson pall of eve may fall
>   From the depth of heaven above,
> With wings folded I rest on my airy nest,
>   As still as a brooding dove.

The variety of images in this poem is often mistaken for imagination. But it is not highly imaginative; the heart is not touched; there is no deep insight into the beauty of the cloud and its relations to the Infinite, or to the soul of man. Hence, it is one of the weakest of Shelley's poems.

There is more imagination in the following four lines from "Prometheus Unbound" than in the whole poem of "The Cloud;" more insight, more suggestion of feeling, more realization of the truth of Nature. The subject is the same, but much more simply, sincerely, and sympathetically treated. The mind identifies human experience with Nature, but there is no external comparison.

> WE wander'd underneath the young gray dawn,
> And multitudes of dense white fleecy clouds
> Were wandering in thick flocks along the mountains,
> Shepherded by the slow, unwilling wind.

Contrast also with "The Cloud" — his masterpiece, if not the greatest masterpiece of lyric poetry — the "Prometheus Unbound." This poem is not popular; unfortunately, it is rarely read, even by professed lovers of poetry. It demands the highest activity of the imagination for its comprehension. There is little of fancy, but much of imagination. It is not merely a difference of subject, but a difference of insight, a difference of ideal exaltation.

Take, for example, the scene where the spirits speak to Prometheus; that is, where are represented the arts that minister to the human mind; or this where Panthea and Asia, commonly understood in the language of prose to be Faith and Love, make their journey to the far-off cave of Demogorgon, — a journey which suggests the long struggles and progress of the human race through the different ages of gloom to the far-off realization of its ideal.   During this journey, delicate voices or echoes ever call them onward and upward, inspiring them with patience and perseverance.

THE JOURNEY OF FAITH AND LOVE.

Morning.   A lovely Vale in the Indian Caucasus.

Asia (alone). From all the blasts of heaven thou hast descended:
Yes, like a spirit, like a thought, which makes
Unwonted tears throng to the horny eyes,
And beatings haunt the desolated heart,
Which should have learnt repose : thou hast descended
Cradled in tempests ; thou dost wake, O Spring !
A child of many winds !   As suddenly
Thou comest as the memory of a dream,
Which now is sad because it hath been sweet.
This is the season, this the day, the hour ;
At sunrise thou shouldst come, sweet sister mine,
Too long desired, too long delaying, come !
How like death-worms the wingless moments crawl !
The point of one white star is quivering still
Deep in the orange light of widening morn
Beyond the purple mountains : through a chasm
Of wind-divided mist the darker lake
Reflects it : now it wanes ; it gleams again
As the waves fade, and as the burning threads
Of woven cloud unravel in the pale air :
'T is lost ! and through yon peaks of cloud-like snow
The roseate sunlight quivers : hear I not
The Æolian music of her sea-green plumes
Winnowing the crimson dawn ?
    (*To Panthea entering.*)   I feel, I see
Those eyes which burn through smiles that fade in tears,
Like stars half quenched in mists of silver dew.
Belovèd and most beautiful, who wearest
The shadow of that soul by which I live,

How late thou art ! the spherèd sun had climbed
The sea ; my heart was sick with hope, before
The printless air felt thy belated plumes.
   Pan.   Pardon, great sister ! but my wings were faint
With the delight of a remembered dream,
As are the noontide plumes of summer winds
Satiate with sweet flowers.
   Asia.   Lift up thine eyes,
And let me read thy dream.
   Pan.   As I have said,
With our sea-sister at his feet I slept.
The mountain mists, condensing at our voice
Under the moon, had spread their snowy flakes,
From the keen ice shielding our linkèd sleep.
Then two dreams came.   One I remember not ;
But in the other his pale wound-worn limbs
Fell from Prometheus, and the azure night
Grew radiant with the glory of that form
Which lives unchanged within, and his voice fell
Like music which makes giddy the dim brain,
Faint with intoxication of keen joy :
" Sister of her whose footsteps pave the world
With loveliness, — more fair than aught but her
Whose shadow thou art, — lift thine eyes on me."
I lifted them : the overpowering light
Of that immortal shape was shadowed o'er
By love, which, from his soft and flowing limbs,
And passion-parted lips, and keen, faint eyes,
Steamed forth like vaporous fire, — an atmosphere
Which wrapt me in its all-dissolving power,
As the warm ether of the morning sun
Wraps ere it drinks some cloud of wandering dew.
   Asia.   Thou speakest, but thy words
Are as the air : I feel them not : oh, lift
Thine eyes, that I may read his written soul !
   Pan.   I lift them, though they droop beneath the load
Of that they would express : what canst thou see
But thine own fairest shadow imaged there ?
   Asia.   Thine eyes are like the deep, blue, boundless heaven
Contracted to two circles underneath
Their long, fine lashes ; dark, far, measureless,
Orb within orb, and line through line inwoven.
   Pan.   Why lookest thou as if a spirit past ?
   Asia.   There is a change ; beyond their inmost depth

I see a shade, a shape : 't is he, arrayed
In the soft light of his own smiles, which spread
Like radiance from the cloud-surrounded morn.
Prometheus, it is thine ! depart not yet !
Say not those smiles that we shall meet again
Within that bright pavilion which their beams
Shall build on the waste world ?   The dream is told.
What shape is that between us ?   Its rude hair
Roughens the wind that lifts it ; its regard
Is wild and quick, yet 't is a thing of air,
For through its grey robe gleams the golden dew
Whose stars the noon has quenched not.

    Dream.   Follow ! Follow !

    Pan.   It is mine other dream.

    Asia.   It disappears.

    Pan.   It passes now into my mind.   Methought,
As we sate here, the flower-enfolding buds
Burst on yon lightning-blasted almond-tree,
When swift from the white Scythian wilderness
A wind swept forth wrinkling the earth with frost :
I looked, and all the blossoms were blown down ;
But on each leaf was stamped, as the blue-bells
Of Hyacinth tell Apollo's written grief,
OH, FOLLOW, FOLLOW !

    Asia.   As you speak, your words
Fill, pause by pause, my own forgotten sleep
With shapes.   Methought among the lawns together
We wandered, underneath the young grey dawn,
And multitudes of dense, white, fleecy clouds
Were wandering in thick flocks along the mountains
Shepherded by the slow, unwilling wind ;
And the white dew on the new-bladed grass,
Just piercing the dark earth, hung silently ;
And there was more which I remember not ;
But on the shadows of the morning clouds,
Athwart the purple mountain slope, was written
FOLLOW, OH, FOLLOW !   As they vanished by,
And on each herb from which heaven's dew had fallen
The like was stamped, as with a withering fire,
A wind arose among the pines : it shook
The clinging music from their boughs, and then
Low, sweet, faint sounds, like the farewell of ghosts,
Were heard : OH, FOLLOW, FOLLOW, FOLLOW ME !
And then I said, "Panthea, look on me."

But in the depth of those belovèd eyes
Still I saw, FOLLOW, FOLLOW !
   Echo.   Follow ! Follow !
   Pan.   The crags, this clear spring morning, mock our voices
As they were spirit-tongued.
   Asia.   It is some being
Around the crags.   What fine clear sounds !   Oh, list !
   Echoes (unseen).   Echoes we: listen !
                  We cannot stay :
                  As dew-stars glisten,
                    Then fade away —
                        Child of Ocean !
   Asia.   Hark ! Spirits speak.   The liquid responses
Of their aërial tongues yet sound.
   Pan.   I hear.
   Echoes.   Oh, follow, follow,
             As our voice recedeth
          Through the caverns hollow,
             Where the forest spreadeth ; (*More distant.*)
        Oh, follow, follow !
        Through the caverns hollow,
        As the song floats thou pursue
        Where the wild bee never flew,
        Through the noontide darkness deep,
        By the odour-breathing sleep
        Of faint night-flowers, and the waves
        At the fountain-lighted caves.
        While our music, wild and sweet,
        Mocks thy gently-falling feet,
           Child of Ocean !
   Asia.   Shall we pursue the sound ?   It grows more faint
And distant.
   Pan.   List ! the strain floats nearer now.
   Echoes.   In the world unknown
            Sleeps a voice unspoken ;
        By thy step alone
          Can its rest be broken,
           Child of Ocean !
   Asia.   How the notes sink upon the ebbing wind !
   Echoes.   Oh, follow, follow !
          Through the caverns hollow ;
       As the song floats thou pursue,
       By the woodland noontide dew ;
       By the forests, lakes, and fountains,

> Through the many-folded mountains ;
> To the rents and gulfs and chasms,
> Where the earth repo<ed from spasms,
> On the day when he and thou
> Parted, to commingle now,
>   Child of Ocean !
> *Asia.*   Come, sweet Panthea, link thy hand in mine,
> And follow, ere the voices fade away.

Shelley.

One of the first to make a distinction between fancy and imagination was Wordsworth, in one of his famous prefaces to his poems.   No better words can be found to explain their differences than a few sentences from this famous Essay: " Fancy," he says, " does not require that the materials which she makes use of should be susceptible of change in their constitution from her touch; and, where they admit of modification, it is enough for her purpose if it be slight, limited, and evanescent.   Directly the reverse of these are the desires and demands of the Imagination.   She recoils from everything but the plastic, the pliant, and the indefinite. When the Imagination frames a comparison, if it does not strike on the first presentation, a sense of the truth of the likeness, from the moment that is perceived, grows, and continues to grow, upon the mind, — the resemblance depending less upon outline of form and feature than upon expression and effect; less upon casual and outstanding than upon inherent and internal properties: moreover, the images invariably modify each other.   The law under which the processes of Fancy are carried on is as capricious as the accidents of things; and the effects are surprising, playful, ludicrous, amusing, tender, or pathetic, as the objects happen to be appositely produced or fortunately combined.   Fancy depends upon the rapidity and profusion with which she scatters her thoughts and images; trusting that their number, and the felicity with which they are linked together, will make amends for the want of individual value: or she prides herself upon the curious subtilty and the successful elaboration with which she can detect their lurking affinities.   If she can win you over to her purpose, and impart to you her feelings, she cares not how unstable or transitory may be her influence, knowing that it will not be out of her power to resume it upon an apt occasion.   But the Imagination is conscious of an indestructible dominion: the Soul may fall away from it, not being able to sustain its grandeur; but if once felt and acknowledged, by no act of any other faculty of the mind can it be relaxed, impaired, or diminished. Fancy is given to quicken and to beguile the temporal part of our nature, Imagination to incite and to support the eternal."

Another writer who has done much to awaken a true appreciation of the exalted function of imagination as distinguished from fancy is Ruskin.   The student cannot do better than to take a few of his illustrations and test them by vocal expression.

> "WHERE the Norweyan banners flout the sky
> And fan our people cold."

"WHO is she that looketh forth as the morning, — fair as the moon, clear as the sun, and terrible as an army with banners ?"

Of the first of these extracts, Ruskin says: "The outward shiver and coldness of fear is seized on, and irregularly but admirably attributed by the fancy to the drift of the banners." Of the second: "The imagination stays not at the outside, but dwells on the fearful emotion itself."

A NUN demure of lowly port ; or sprightly maiden, of Love's court, in thy simplicity the sport of all temptations ; a queen in crown of rubies drest ; a starveling in a scanty vest, — are all, as seems to suit thee best, thy appellations.

A little cyclops, with one eye staring to threaten and defy, — that thought comes next ; and instantly the freak is over, the shape will vanish — and behold a silver shield with boss of gold, that spreads itself, some faery bold in fight to cover.

I see thee glittering from afar — and then thou art a pretty star ; not quite so fair as many are in heaven above thee ! Yet like a star, with glittering crest, self-poised in air thou seem'st to rest : may peace come never to his nest, who shall reprove thee !

Bright Flower ! for by that name at last, when all my reveries are past, I call thee, — and to that cleave fast, sweet silent creature ! that breath'st with me in sun and air, do thou, as thou art wont, repair my heart with gladness and a share of thy meek nature !

From " To a Daisy."   *Wordsworth.*

Which stanza here is the most imaginative? Ruskin says: "Observe how spiritual, yet how wandering and playful the fancy is in the first stanzas, and how far she flies from the matter in hand, never stopping to brood on the character of any one of the images she summons, and yet for a moment truly seeing and believing in them all; while in the last stanza the imagination returns with its deep feeling to the heart of the flower and 'cleaves fast' to that." There is more imagination in the last, because it is more simple, more genuine, truer to human experience, and centres the mind's attention, as the imagination always does, at the heart of things.

BRING the rathe primrose, that forsaken dies;	(Imag.)
The tufted crow-toe and pale jessamine,	(Nugatory.)
The white pink and the pansy freaked with jet,	(Fancy.)
The glowing violet,	(Imag.)
The musk-rose and the well-attired woodbine,	(Fancy, vulgar.)
With cowslips wan, that hang the pensive head,	(Imag.)
And every flower that sad embroidery wears.	(Mixed.)

Milton.

O, PROSERPINA,
For the flowers now, that frighted thou let'st fall
From Dis's wagon: Daffodils
That come before the swallow dares, and take
The winds of March with beauty. Violets, dim,
But sweeter than the lids of Juno's eyes
Or Cytherea's breath; pale primroses
That die unmarried, ere they can behold
Bright Phœbus in his strength, a malady
Most incident to maids.

Shakespeare.

Ruskin contrasts these extracts from Milton and Shakespeare. "Observe," he says, "how the imagination in these last lines goes into the very inmost soul of every flower, after having touched them all at first with that heavenly timidity, the shadow of Proserpine's, and gilded them with celestial gathering, and never stops on their spots or their bodily shape; while Milton sticks in the stains upon them, and puts us off with that unhappy freak of jet in the very flower that without this bit of paper-staining would have been the most precious to us of all. 'There is pansies, that's for thoughts.'"

While the imagination is superior to fancy, it must be borne in mind that fancy is not to be despised. It has a high and important function, though one distinct from imagination. The true office of each of these is best illustrated by Shakespeare. He gives the greatest variety, as well as the highest action, of both of these faculties.

PROBLEM XI. *Contrast the play of fancy with imagination; note the difference in mental action, and in the effect upon the voice.*

> O, THEN, I see, Queen Mab hath been with you.
> She is the fairy midwife; and she comes
> In shape no bigger than an agate-stone
> On the fore-finger of an alderman,
> Drawn with a team of little atomies
> Athwart men's noses as they lie asleep.
> Her chariot is an empty hazel-nut,
> Made by the joiner squirrel or old grub,
> Time out o' mind the fairies' coachmakers:
> Her wagon-spokes made of long spinner's legs;
> The cover, of the wings of grasshoppers;
> The traces, of the smallest spider's web;
> The collars, of the moonshine's watery beams;
> Her whip, of cricket's bone; the lash, of film;
> Her wagoner, a small grey-coated gnat.
> And in this state, she gallops night by night
> Though lovers' brains, and then they dream of love;
> O'er courtiers knees, that dream on curtsies straight;
> O'er lawyers' fingers, who straight dream on fees;
> O'er ladies' lips, who straight on kisses dream:
> Sometimes she gallops o'er a courtier's nose,
> And then dreams he of smelling out a suit;
> And sometimes comes she with a tithe-pig's tail
> Tickling a parson's nose that lies asleep,
> Then dreams he of another benefice:
> Sometimes she driveth o'er a soldier's neck,
> And then dreams he of cutting foreign throats,
> Of breaches, ambuscadoes, Spanish blades,
> Of healths five-fathom deep; and then anon
> Drums in his ear, at which he starts, and wakes;
> And, being thus frighted, swears a prayer or two,
> And sleeps again.   *Shakespeare.*

WHEN to the sessions of sweet silent thought
I summon up remembrance of things past,
I sigh the lack of many a thing I sought,
And with old woes new wail my dear time's waste ;
Then can I drown an eye, unused to flow,
For precious friends hid in death's dateless night,
And weep afresh love's long-since-cancell'd woe,
And moan the expense of many a vanish'd sight.
Then can I grieve at grievances foregone,
And heavily from woe to woe tell o'er
The sad account fore-bemoanèd moan,
Which I new pay as if not paid before :
But if the while I think on thee, dear friend,
All losses are restored, and sorrows end.

Shakespeare.

By wells and rills, in medowes greene,
We nightly sing our heydey guise ;
And to onr fairy king and queene
We chant our moonlight minstrelsies :
When larks 'gan sing, away we fling ;
And babes new-borne steal as we go,
And elfe in bed we leave instead,
And wend us laughing, ho, ho, ho !

Shakespeare.

THERE is an eminence of these our hills,
The last that parleys with the setting sun.

Wordsworth.

AMONG THE ROCKS.

OH, good gigantic smile o' the brown old Earth,
  This autumn morning ! How he sets his bones
To bask i' the sun, and thrusts out knees and feet
For the ripple to run over in its mirth ;
  Listening the while, where on the heap of stones
The white breast of the sea-lark twitters sweet !

That is the doctrine, simple, ancient, true ;
  Such is life's trial, as old Earth smiles and knows.
If you loved only what were worth your love,
Love were clear gain, and wholly well for you :
  Make the low nature better by your throes !
Give Earth yourself, go up for gain above !

Browning.

THERE's one great bunch of stars in heaven
  That shines so sturdily,
Where good Saint Peter's sinewy hand
  Holds up the dull gold-wroughten key.

And also there 's a little star
  So white, a virgin's it must be, —
Perhaps the lamp my love in heaven
  Hangs out to light the way for me.

Theophile Marzials.

NIGHT AND MORNING.

Low hanging in a cloud of burnished gold,
  The sleepy sun lay dreaming ;
And where, pearl-wrought, the Orient gates unfold,
  Wide ocean realms were gleaming.
Within the night he rose and stole away,
  And, like a gem adorning,
Blazed o'er the sea upon the breast of day, —
  And everywhere was morning.

Eugene Field.

VII. ACTIONS OF THE IMAGINATION.

THE Poet should communicate an Infinitude to his delineation. By intensity of conception, by that gift of transcendental Thought which is fitly named *genius* and inspiration, he should *inform* the Finite with a certain Infinitude of significance; or, as they sometimes say, ennoble the Actual into Idealness.

Carlyle.

THE outward shows of sky and earth,
  Of hill and valley, he has viewed ;
And impulses of deeper birth
  Have come to him in solitude.

In common things that round us lie
  Some random truths he can impart, —
The harvest of a quiet eye
  That broods and sleeps on his own heart.

Wordsworth.

THE most diverse opinions are held regarding the imagination. One of the latest theories is that there is no such faculty, but that the human mind is full of "imaginations." According to this view, the imagination is simply a general word for perceptive action. Another theory is that the imagination is not a separate faculty, but is the spontaneous and harmonious union of all the faculties and powers of the mind acting together contemplatively or creatively.

Theories, however, are of little value in comparison with the direct study of the action and products of the faculty itself. What are some of the simplest and most elemental actions of the imagination?

Imagination can unite a general idea to an individual conception. According to logic, a general idea has greater " extension," and an individual idea greater intension. The word *tree*, for example, covers far more objects than *oak*. There is a less number of marks characteristic of the conception awakened in the mind by the word *tree*, and a greater number by the word *oak*. Extension and intension are thus in direct opposition. Now, observe the imagination: —

> They lay along the battery's side,
> Below the smoking cannon ;
> Brave hearts, from Severn and from Clyde,
> And from the banks of Shannon.

Song of the Camp. *Bayard Taylor.*

The thought expressed in plain prose in these lines is simply that there lay on the battle-field soldiers from England, Scotland, and Ireland; but this general thought is stated imaginatively. The poet names or suggests each place by a characteristic which awakens a vivid picture and sympathetic feeling. He does not suggest a map of the regions, but brings before us three rivers. "Brave hearts" names not only soldiers, but suggests also the thought which he wishes to emphasize in his poem. Thus he leads us to realize that the soldiers are living men, with homes and affections. The picture of the river is in the foreground of each conception, while the general thought of the country is in the background. The truth is stated not only clearly and adequately, but with far greater force. It brings mutual facts into the realm of feeling; it makes everything living and human.

Logic and reason secure a universal by eliminating the specific and concrete marks; the result is an abstraction. But the imagination secures a universal in exactly the opposite way. It penetrates beneath the accidents, and fixes the attention upon the essential elements; and by vivid realization and by getting at the heart of objects, or the distinct character of a scene, it chooses such an expression that a specific and concrete fact becomes a suggestion of a universal truth. It unites a specific and definite image with all the marks of intension, and gives it in such a way as to suggest extension. The imagination is thus a power that can unite intension and extension in conception; and this explains, partly at least, why reason and imagination, poetry and science, are so antithetic to each other.

The imagination realizes ideas. It translates abstractions into more conceivable forms. Out of vague and chaotic ideas, it creates an organic unity; out of the dryest abstractions, it makes vivid pictures. It brings the coldest conceptions of the intellect into sympathy with the heart; it turns dry facts into living truth. It sees the life in all the operations of Nature, and creates a new world.

L'ESPÉRANCE.

ONLY a brave old maple,
   Shorn of its scarlet and gold,
And traced in the scroll of sunset
   As a handwriting — black and bold.

A low, wailing wind frets the branches,
   The dead leaves start up in surprise,
Till, in the hush of the gloaming,
   The dryad's sad monody dies.

O desolate tree in the meadow,
   With pleading hands stretched to the sky !
Do you know the glad hopes of the springtide
   Asleep in your folded arms lie ?

And never a breath of the storm-king,
   And never a waft of the snow,
Can snatch the frail bud from its casket,
   Or loose the firm anchor below ?

> 'Bide patiently, then, the bleak winter,
> And change the sad wail to a song :
> Bear up, for the robins and bluebirds
> And south winds are coming ere long.
>
> *Anon.*

Again, the imagination elevates or idealizes the simplest objects, scenes, or events. "The ideal," says Charles Blanc, "is the primitive divine exemplar of all things; it is, so to speak, a reminiscence of having already witnessed perfection, and the hope of seeing it once again." This is but one of the many echoes of the greatest of all definitions of the ideal. "It is," says Plato, "a recollection of those things our soul formerly beheld when in company with God, despising the things that we now say are, and looking upward towards that which really is."

Bacon expresses what is perhaps the most prevalent modern view regarding the idealizing action of the mind. "Poetry," says he, "has something divine in it, because it raises the mind and hurries it into sublimity by conforming the shows of things to the desires of the soul, instead of subjecting the soul to external things, as reason and history do."

What more simple and more familiar experience than falling asleep! To many it is in the highest degree commonplace, but notice how the imagination may lift it into the realm of interest and beauty : —

> Soon trembling in her soft and chilly nest,
> In sort of wakeful swoon, perplex'd she lay,
> Until the poppied warmth of sleep oppress'd
> Her smoothèd limbs, and soul, fatigued away,
> Flown, like a thought, until the morrow day ;
> Blissfully haven'd both from joy and pain ;
> Clasp'd like a missal, where swart Paynims pray;
> Blinded alike from sunshine and from rain,
> As though a rose should shut and be a bud again.

Eve of St. Agnes.   *Keats.*

Every one will speak of the silent sky and the lonely hills, but notice how the imagination of the poet seizes the characteristic which brings these two objects of human attention together,

creating in the mind a perfect picture and awakening noble
feeling with the simplest words. We can read the following lines
so as to make them seem commonplace and lacking in poetry;
but when we give up our imagination to the suggestions of the
author, we realize how superficial was our first impression:—

> Love had he found in huts where poor men lie ;
> His daily teachers had been woods and rills,
> The silence that is in the starry sky,
> The sleep that is among the lonely hills.

Brougham Castle.   *Wordsworth.*

Imagination, as already implied, penetrates to the depth; it does
not deal in external accidents and mechanical relations, but sees
the heart of the object, or its relations, act, or character; it finds
the elements and the cause in everything which it touches, and
goes to the true fountain-head of expression. Witness in this
extract how forcible simple ideas and simple words may become:

> WEARINESS
> Can snore upon the flint, when resty sloth
> Finds the down-pillow hard.

Cymbeline.   *Shakespeare.*

Here Shakespeare does not say sleeps soundly, peacefully slumbers, or rests in repose; he uses only one word, but it is the one
word that can give the most definite impression. He does not say
hardest bed, nor floor, nor ground, nor even stone, but " flint; "
and then he contrasts with this, not bed, but something more specific, a " down-pillow. " Thus the imagination reaches to that
which is most simple and fundamental. It gives the one object
and finds the one word which will suggest by one image, without
detail, the deepest idea and most definite contrast.

BEFORE the dawn, comes the marginal minute of the dark, when the
grove is still mute, save for one prophetic bird, who sings with a clear-
voiced conviction that he at least knows the correct time of day, — the
rest preserving silence, as if equally convinced that he is mistaken.

Thomas Hardy.

Plain prose will tell us that a guitar is made of wood, and the ordinary mind will go no further than to look simply at the accidentals, and perhaps wonder at the texture of the wood and its resonance. Now listen to Shelley. He sent this poem, with an instrument, as a present, to Mrs. Williams. Here is the very soul of music. All the history, the breezes, and the storms which have passed over the tree are imprisoned in the wood, and can only be set free by the master hand: —

TO A LADY, WITH A GUITAR.

ARIEL to Miranda : — Take
This slave of music, for the sake
Of him who is the slave of thee ;
And teach it all the harmony
In which thou canst, and only thou,
Make the delighted spirit glow,
Till joy denies itself again,
And, too intense, is turn'd to pain.
For by permission and command
Of thine own Prince Ferdinand,
Poor Ariel sends this silent token
Of more than ever can be spoken :
Your guardian spirit, Ariel, who
From life to life must still pursue
Your happiness, for thus alone
Can Ariel ever find his own ;
From Prospero's enchanted cell,
As the mighty verses tell,
To the throne of Naples he
Lit you o'er the trackless sea,
Flitting on, your prow before,
Like a living meteor.
When you die, the silent Moon
In her interlunar swoon
Is not sadder in her cell
Than deserted Ariel ;
When you live again on earth,
Like an unseen Star of birth
Ariel guides you o'er the sea
Of life from your nativity.
Many changes have been run
Since Ferdinand and you begun

Your course of love, and Ariel still
Has track'd your steps and served your will.
Now in humbler, happier lot
This is all remember'd not ;
And now, alas! the poor sprite is
Imprison'd for some fault of his,
In a body like a grave —
From you he only dares to crave
For his service and his sorrow
A smile to-day, a song to-morrow.

The artist who this idol wrought
To echo all harmonious thought,
Fell'd a tree, while on the steep
The woods were in their winter sleep,
Rock'd in that repose divine
On the wind-swept Apennine ;
And dreaming, some of autumn past,
And some of spring approaching fast,
And some of April buds and showers,
And some of songs in July bowers,
And all of love ; and so this tree —
Oh that such our death may be ! —
Died in sleep, and felt no pain,
To live in happier form again :
From which, beneath Heaven's fairest star,
The artist wrought this loved Guitar ;
And taught it justly to reply
To all who question skilfully
In language gentle as thine own ;
Whispering in enamour'd tone
Sweet oracles of woods and dells,
And summer winds in sylvan cells :
For it had learnt all harmonies
Of the plains and of the skies,
Of the forests and the mountains,
And the many-voicèd fountains,
The clearest echoes of the hills,
The softest notes of falling rills,
The melodies of birds and bees,
The murmuring of summer seas,
And pattering rain and breathing dew,
And airs of evening ; and it knew
That seldom-heard mysterious sound

> Which, driven on its diurnal round,
> As it floats through boundless day,
> Our world enkindles on its way :
> All this it knows, but will not tell
> To those who cannot question well
> The spirit that inhabits it ;
> It talks according to the wit
> Of its companions ; and no more
> Is heard than has been felt before
> By those who tempt it to betray
> These secrets of an elder day.
> But, sweetly as it answers will
> Flatter hands of perfect skill,
> It keeps its highest holiest tone
> For our belovèd Friend alone.   *Shelley.*

Thus the imagination sees, contemplates, and creates such an individual conception that it can stand for a most general truth. It idealizes, it gives life and feeling to every object. It compares the unknown with the known; makes the seen a window through which the mind beholds the unseen. It surrounds or environs ; it shows the kinship of things; it paints a picture which blends harmoniously into one vision; it makes the desert a dwelling-place; it fathoms the life of the universe, and enters the most secret chambers of the human soul.

PROBLEM XII. *Read a variety of passages, and exercise the many diverse actions of the imagination.*

> THE mountains rose, — the valleys sank
> Unto the place which thou hadst founded for them.

> THE moon doth with delight
> Look round her when the heavens are bare.

> SWEET as the primrose peeps beneath the thorn.

> LIFE, like a dome of many-coloured glass,
> Stains the white radiance of eternity.
>   *Shelley.*

> THE bees are stirring — birds are on the wing —
> And Winter, slumbering in the open air,
> Wears on his smiling face a dream of Spring !
>   *Coleridge*

THE stars of midnight shall be dear
To her; and she shall lean her ear
In many a secret place
Where rivulets dance their wayward round,
And beauty born of murmuring sound
Shall pass into her face.

———

. . . THOU dost preserve the stars from wrong,
And the most ancient heavens through thee are fresh and strong.

THE winds come to me from the fields of sleep.

Wordsworth.

———

THERE is a budding morrow in midnight.

Keats.

———

THIS is the very heart of the woods all round
Mountain-like heaped above us; yet even here
One pond of water gleams; far off the river
Sweeps like a sea, barred out from land; but one,—
One thin, clear sheet has over-leaped and wound
Into this silent depth, which gained, it lies
Still, as but let by sufferance; the trees bend
O'er it as wild men watch a sleeping girl.

Browning.

———

THE LOST CHURCH.

OFT in the forest far one hears
 A passing sound of distant bells;
Nor legends old nor human wit
 Can tell us whence the music swells.
From the Lost Church, 't is thought, that soft
 Faint ringing cometh on the wind;
Once many pilgrims trod the path,
 But no one now the way can find.

Not long since, deep into the wood
 I stray'd, where path was none to see:
Weary of human wickedness,
 My heart to God yearn'd longingly.
There, through the silent wilderness,
 Again I heard the sweet bells stealing,
Ever, as higher yearn'd my heart,
 The nearer and the louder pealing.

My spirit was so self-indrawn,
  My sense with sweetness rapt so high,
That how those sounds within me wrought
  Remaineth yet a mystery.
It seem'd as if a hundred years
  Had laps'd while thus I had been dreaming,
When, lo ! above the clouds a space
  Free opened out, in sunshine gleaming.

The heaven was so darkly blue,
  The sun so full and glowing bright —
And rose a minster's stately pile,
  Expanding in the golden light.
Seemed the clouds resplendently,
  Like wings, to bear it up alway,
And in the blessed depths of heaven
  Its spired tower to melt away.

The bells' delicious harmony
  Down from the tower in quiverings flow'd,
Yet drew not hand of man the strings, —
  They moved but to the Breath of God.
As if upon my throbbing heart
  That self-same Breath its influence shed,
So entered I that minster high
  With timorous joy and faltering tread.

Words cannot paint what there-within
  Awoke my spirit's ecstasies ;
The darkly-brilliant windows glow'd
  With martyrs' pious effigies ;
Into a new and living world,
  Rich imag'd forth, I gaz'd abroad, —
A world of holy women and
  Of warriors of the host of God.

Down at the altar low I knelt,
  Thrilling with awe and holy love —
Heaven and its glorious mysteries
  Were pictur'd on the vault above.
But when again I lookèd up,
  Roof, arch, and pictur'd vault were gone —
Full opened was the door of heaven,
  And every veil had been withdrawn.

> What then, in silent prayerful awe,
>   Of majesty I saw reveal'd,
> What heard of sound more blissful far
>   Than aught to human ear unseal'd,
> Lies not within the might of words;
>   Yet whoso longeth for such good,
> Let him take heed unto the bells
>   That ring in whispers through the wood.
>
> *Uhland.*

VIII. CHARACTERISTICS OF THE IMAGINATION.

THE most imaginative poem may be turned into commonplace prose if read without a proper realization of its spirit. The imagination does not act mechanically or by artificial analysis. It is synthetic, natural, and simple. No rules can be framed to interpret poetry, or to understand its nature, without proper imaginative and emotional exercise. <u>Imagination appeals to imagination, and can be interpreted only by imagination.</u> <u>It acts by intuition and intensity of gaze, not by reasoning.</u> It gives a more essential truth than can be seized by the eye. It does not accumulate accidents or multiply details, but penetrates immediately to the life and soul.

> . . . SWEET bird, that shunn'st the noise of folly,
> Most musical, most melancholy !
> Thee, chauntress, oft the woods among
> I woo, to hear thy even-song;
> And missing thee, I walk unseen
> On the dry, smooth-shaven green,
> To behold the wandering Moon
> Riding near her highest noon,
> Like one that had been led astray
> Through the heaven's wide, pathless way,
> And oft, as if her head she bow'd,
> Stooping through a fleecy cloud.
>
> *Il Penseroso.*   *Milton.*

Here we perceive no process of reasoning about the moon being lost in heaven; we feel the immediate creative action of the mind.

Imagination never goes by rule, or by experiments, by accumulation or by aggregation of facts; it acts *spontaneously*. We never know the process by which it arrives at its pictures, or the road it travels. We are brought face to face with a truth which exists at the heart of things.

> IT winds all noiselessly through the deep wood,
> Till thro' a cleft way, thro' the moss and stone,
> It joins its parent-river with a shout.
>
> *Browning.*

Again, imagination acts *immediately*. It moves with the vigor of life and at once, without deliberation, conscious medium, or chosen by-paths, and causes the soul of the hearer to vibrate in response. As Fuseli has said: "Invention never suffers the action to expire, nor the spectator's fancy to consume itself in preparation, or stagnate into repose. It neither begins from the egg, nor coldly gathers the remains." As Athena was born fully grown from the brain of Zeus, so the creations of the imagination spring into the highest vigor of life. Imagination realizes life in everything. It is the outgoing of the living, unconscious energy of one mind and awakens the life of another. It is the faculty that brings the soul into most immediate contact with ideas, feelings, or objects, and with other minds or beings.

Again, the imagination acts *simply*; it is never stilted or affected; it sees things as they are. It is by this simplicity that the greatest masters of the imagination are recognized. Simplicity is the climax of art. Homer, Phidias, Virgil, Dante, Cervantes, and Shakespeare, — the greatest masters of simplicity can be counted upon the fingers. Simplicity and truthfulness are conditions without which imagination can hardly act. Imagination is the centring of the human soul in the midst of the universe. It is the seeing eye that looks deepest into Nature's heart, and the hearing ear that catches her simplest and most delicate tones.

> BENEATH those rugged elms, that yew-tree's shade,
> Where heaves the turf in many a mouldering heap,
> Each in his narrow cell forever laid,
> The rude Forefathers of the hamlet sleep.

> The breezy call of incense-breathing morn,
> The swallow twittering from the straw-built shed,
> The cock's shrill clarion, or the echoing horn,
> No more shall rouse them from their lowly bed.
>
> *Gray.*

The imagination acts *freely.*   Not only must the mind in conception, but still more must the imagination obey its own law of action.   For example, in reading, while we use the words of the author, the ideas must be our own.

> Boughs are daily rifled by the gusty thieves,
> And the book of Nature getteth short of leaves.
>
> *Seasons.*   *Hood.*

In this play of fancy from Hood's " Seasons," what particular place, or kind of trees or leaves, come before the mind of the reader? These vary with every individual mind.   The pictures may be vivid, but the imagination creates freely; it is governed only by association of ideas.

> I SAW two clouds at morning, tinged by the rising sun,
> And in the dawn they floated on, and mingled into one.
>
> *Brainard.*

Here is stated one of the most familiar facts regarding clouds; but imagination rather than memory is awakened in the reader's mind, and the kind of cloud, the size, the form, the color, and the light and shade are the spontaneous results of processes of which the man himself is not conscious.   Poetry and art are great in proportion as they stimulate this free, spontaneous creation of the mind.

The imagination always acts *easily;* it is never labored.   Physical labor not only constricts the body, but the normal action of the higher faculties as well.   The development, therefore, of the imagination must differ essentially from the development of other powers of the mind.   It calls for simple contemplation, reposeful observation, and the free and easy giving of ourselves to the objects around us.

Again, the imagination does not act literally, but *suggestively ;* it does not dictate, but hints and intimates.   Sometimes a single word suggests a whole situation, awakens a conception of a whole life or character, and gives sympathetic insight into feelings which are too delicate almost for expression. Notice the use of the word "alien" in the following stanza from the "Nightingale":—

> Thou wast not born for death, immortal Bird!
> No hungry generations tread thee down;
> The voice I hear this passing night was heard
> In ancient days by emperor and clown:
> Perhaps the self-same song that found a path
> Through the sad heart of Ruth, when, sick for home,
> She stood in tears amid the alien corn;
> The same that oft-times hath
> Charm'd magic casements, opening on the foam
> Of perilous seas, in faery lands forlorn.

From " The Nightingale."   *Keats.*

Does not the expression "found a path" impart a sense of Ruth's homelessness, of the vague dread she had in the midst of a foreign nation, and the confusion and conflict of emotions which made her almost doubt the course she had taken, and feel like one lost in a forest? With her heart in this condition, the sweet song of the bird makes a path for hope. Or we may imagine the alien looks and suspicious glances of strangers, their silent contempt, that shut the doors to her heart. But through these the song, which she had heard in childhood, finds a path and awakens a response.

Such discussions of poetry are perhaps useless. It is impossible to interpret in prose these delicate touches, — they are only apprehended by imagination; but we all delight to hear another's honest opinion of the meaning of a poem. We must not, however, allow prosy explanations to fetter our own imaginative action and thorough study. A work of art means something peculiar to every individual soul. It is strong, not for what it communicates, but for what it evokes.

The characteristics of the imagination have been well stated by Ruskin in his famous section on the Imagination in "Modern Painters." The whole deserves careful attention; but a few paragraphs are reproduced here for convenience of study:—

"It is the power that works into the very rock heart, no matter what may be the subject submitted to it; substance or spirit, all is alike divided asunder, joint and marrow, whatever utmost truth, life, principle it has, laid bare, and that which has no truth, life, nor principle dissipated into its original smoke at a touch. The whispers at men's ears it lifts into visible angels. Vials that have lain sealed in the deep sea a thousand years it unseals, and brings out of them Genii.

"Every great conception of poet or painter is held and treated by this faculty. Every character that is so much as touched by men like Eschylus, Homer, Dante, or Shakespeare is by them held by the heart; and every circumstance or sentence of their being, speaking or seeming, is seized by process from within, and is referred to that inner secret spring of which the hold is never lost for an instant, — so that every sentence, as it has been thought out from the heart, leads us to the centre, and then leaves us to gather what more we may. It is the open sesame of a huge, endless cave, with inexhaustible treasure of pure gold scattered in it. The wandering about and gathering the pieces may be left to any of us, — all can accomplish that; but the first opening of that invisible door in the rock is of the imagination only.

"The unimaginative writer, on the other hand, as he has never pierced to the heart, so he can never touch it. If he has to paint a passion, he remembers the external signs of it; he collects expressions of it from other writers, he searches for similes; he composes, exaggerates, heaps term on term, figure on figure, till we groan beneath the cold, disjointed heap : but it is all faggot and no fire; the life breath is not in it. His passion has the form of the Leviathan, but it never makes the deep boil; he fastens us all at anchor in the scaly rind of it; our sympathies remain as idle as 'a painted ship upon a painted ocean.'

"A writer with neither imagination nor fancy, describing a fair lip, does not see it, but thinks about it, and about what is said of it, and calls it well-turned or rosy or delicate or lovely, or afflicts us with some other quenching and chilling epithet. Now hear fancy speak: —

> "'Her lips were red, and one was thin;
> Compared with that was next her chin :
> Some bee had stung it newly.'

"The real, red, bright being of the lip is there in a moment; but it is all outside, — no expression yet, no mind. Let us go a step farther with Warner, of fair Rosamond struck by Eleanor: —

> " ' With that she dashed her on the lips,
>   So dyed double red ;
>   Hard was the heart that gave the blow,
>   Soft were those lips that bled.'

" The tenderness of mind begins to mingle with the outside color ; the imagination is seen in its awakening.   Next Shelley: —

> " ' Lamp of life, thy lips [1] are burning
>   Through the veil that seems to hide them,
>   As the radiant lines of morning
>   Through thin clouds, ere they divide them.'

" There dawns the entire soul in that morning ; yet we may stop, if we choose, at the image still external, — at the crimson clouds. The imagination is contemplative rather than penetrative. Last, hear Hamlet: —

> " ' Here hung those lips that I have kissed, I know not how oft. Where be your gibes now, your gambols, your songs, your flashes of merriment that were wont to set the table on a roar ? '

" Here is the essence of lip, and the full power of the imagination."

Problem XIII. — *Find some of the characteristics of the action of the imagination, and simply and naturally apply these to the vocal rendering of the passages where they are found.*

MISCONCEPTIONS.

This is a spray the bird clung to,
    Making it blossom with pleasure,
Ere the high tree-top she sprung to,
    Fit for her nest and her treasure :
    Oh, what a hope beyond measure
Was the poor spray's, which the flying feet hung to, —
So to be singled out, built in, and sung to !

This is a heart the queen leant on,
    Thrill'd in a minute erratic,
Ere the true bosom she bent on,
    Meet for love's regal dalmatic.
    Oh, what a fancy ecstatic
Was the poor heart's, ere the wanderer went on, —
Love to be sav'd for it, proffer'd to, spent on !

Robert Browning.

---

[1] Ruskin here prints "lips" for "limbs," — doubtless a slip of memory.

THEN rode Geraint into the castle court,
His charger trampling many a prickly star
Of sprouted thistle on the broken stones.
    He look'd and saw that all was ruinous.
Here stood a shatter'd archway plumed with fern ;
And here had fall'n a great part of the tower,
Whole, like a crag that tumbles from the cliff,
And like a crag was gay with wilding flowers :
And high above a piece of turret stair,
Worn by the feet that now were silent, wound
Bare to the sun, and monstrous ivy-stems
Claspt the gray walls with hairy-fibred arms,
And suck'd the joining of the stones, and look'd
A knot beneath of snakes ; aloft, a grove.

    And while he waited in the castle court,
The voice of Enid, Yniol's daughter, rang
Clear thro' the open casement of the hall,
Singing ; and as the sweet voice of a bird,
Heard by the lander in a lonely isle,
Moves him to think what kind of bird it is
That sings so delicately clear, and make
Conjecture of the plumage and the form, —
So the sweet voice of Enid moved Geraint,
And made him, like a man abroad at morn,
When first the liquid note beloved of men
Comes flying over many a windy wave
To Britain, and in April suddenly
Breaks from a coppice gemm'd with green and red,
And he suspends his converse with a friend,
Or it may be the labour of his hands,
To think or say, "There is the nightingale !"
So fared it with Geraint, who thought and said,
"Here, by God's grace, is the one voice for me."

It chanced the song that Enid sang was one
Of Fortune and her wheel ; and Enid sang :

    "Turn, Fortune, turn thy wheel and lower the proud ;
Turn that wild wheel thro' sunshine, storm, and cloud :
Thy wheel and thee we neither love nor hate.

    "Turn, Fortune, turn thy wheel with smile or frown :
With that wild wheel we go not up or down ;
Our hoard is little, but our hearts are great.

> "Smile and we smile, the lords of many lands ;
> Frown and we smile, the lords of our own hands ;
> For man is man, and master of his fate.
>
> "Turn, turn thy wheel above the staring crowd :
> Thy wheel and thou are shadows in the cloud ;
> Thy wheel and thee we neither love nor hate."

The Marriage of Geraint. ——— *Tennyson.*

> THY voice is heard thro' rolling drums
>   That beat to battle where he stands;
> Thy face across his fancy comes,
>   And gives the battle to his hands :
> A moment, while the trumpets blow,
>   He sees his brood about thy knee;
> The next, like fire he meets the foe,
>   And strikes him dead for thine and thee.

Tennyson.

———

IX. SITUATION AND BACKGROUND.

ONE of the most important functions of the imagination is its power to supply the natural surroundings of an object, action, or conception. Ordinary thinking, as has been shown, on account of the necessity of definite concentration, is apt to conceive ideas in isolation; but however adequate a conception may be, it cannot be truthfully expressed in isolation. Expression results from a synthetic product of the imagination. Natural expression is hardly possible without *situation*. The power of conceiving and feeling a background is most important; the most isolated fact must be brought into sympathetic relation with other things, and with the human soul,— then expression becomes possible.

The power to conceive a situation is the chief characteristic of a natural, effective reader or speaker. The expression of any truth must lift it into the realm of interest. Hence the relations of the human soul to the thought it conceives, and to the feeling of its life and kinship with other things, are the soul of all artistic expression. "It is where the bird is that makes the bird," said William M. Hunt. Certainly if science endeavors to tell *what* a thing is, art shows *where* it is. The elliptic relations of an object, or those which cannot be expressed in words, are the chief elements in all imaginative or dramatic power. These elements give any truth its interest and its influence over the human mind. Where these are lacking, everything is untruthful, unnatural, artificial, and dead.

A situation or background in some form, or with some degree of vividness, is present in every act of the mind. If we read the simplest phrase, we find that there is not only an idea suggested, but that this idea is located or environed.

The background, however, is especially important in poetry; it is the primary function of poetry to suggest and create a right background or relation for truth. Read, for example, some lines from one of the simplest and most popular of poems; and we find from first to last, not an isolated conception, but a vivid picture of every object as a part of a living scene: —

> At eve they all assembled : then care and doubt were fled ;
> With jovial laugh they feasted, the board was nobly spread.
> The elder of the village rose up, his glass in hand,
> And cried, " We drink the downfall of an accursèd land !
>
> " The night is growing darker, ere one more day is flown,
> Bregenz, our foeman's stronghold, Bregenz shall be our own ! "
> The women shrank in terror (yet pride, too, had her part),
> But one poor Tyrol maiden felt death within her heart.
>
> Nothing she heard around her (though shouts rang forth again);
> Gone were the green Swiss valleys, the pasture and the plain ;
> Before her eyes one vision, and in her heart one cry,
> That said, " Go forth, save Bregenz ; and then, if need be, die ! "
>
> With trembling haste and breathless, with noiseless step she sped ;
> Horses and weary cattle were standing in the shed ;
> She loosed the strong white charger that fed from out her hand,
> She mounted, and she turned his head toward her native land.
>
> Out — out into the darkness — faster, and still more fast!
> The smooth grass flies behind her, the chestnut wood is passed ;
> She looks up : the clouds are heavy : why is her steed so slow ?
> Scarcely the wind beside them can pass them as they go.

Legend of Bregenz.   *Adelaide Procter.*

Now, if in reading these lines we present mere facts, the effect is tame. Every fact must be given, but it must become an event in a series. The spirit of the time and place must rise in our mind as a background. The imagination must penetrate to the heart of the girl, and realize her resolution, her patriotism, her heroism. The reader must perceive her deliberation and her decision; in short, he must re-create all the workings of her mind: the events described are but a means of manifesting her mind and heart. Expression is concerned primarily with the human soul. A fact in itself is dead; it must be assimilated; it must be seen; it must become food for the imagination, before it becomes a living truth.

Thus, imagination in conceiving the smallest event makes it a part of a complete whole: the whole poem, the whole history, the whole situation is held and sustained by the mind, as each idea unfolds itself. The mental conception of the age gives atmosphere and character to the expression of the individual event. The study of a specific object, or even of a scene in its isolation, is called by the artist a sketch or study. A picture is the bringing of all the facts or objects into one degree of light, one color, one tone, one complete whole. Unity is the fundamental law of all art, and it is not a human invention, — it is the expression of the relation of things in Nature.

The situation, or background, must be intuitively and instinctively conceived; it cannot be reasoned out, it cannot be produced by mechanical adjustment. This process is called composition, and is not imagination. The proper apprehension of situation must come from dramatic instinct, from imaginative intuition.

One of the most common violations of this function of the imagination is found in the public reading of the Scriptures. Much of the Bible is poetry, and belongs to the realm of the sublimest art; but passages are often rendered with an entire disregard of any imaginative situation. Objection is even made to studies which endeavor to give the sublime, poetic passages in the Prophets or the Psalms any specific background; and often many passages of the highest exaltation are given in a vague, sad, mournful, or didactic manner, with no situation of any kind.

To read appreciatively the poetry of the Prophets or of the Psalms, there must be study to find the historical situation. The imagination must create an environment. What was the occasion? What was in the mind of the poet? In many cases, of course, it will be impossible to find the historic situation; but the attempt to do so brings a deeper comprehension of the poem: the mind will seize upon some conception which will approximate to the right one, so as to give specific feeling to the passage. Even a wrong situation is better than none. Dr. Cheyne, than whom there is no better authority, says: "The historical occasions of the Psalms are not to be determined by a dictatorial assertion;" and in speaking of two views of Psalm L. he says: "Neither view do I myself hold; but I would rather that my readers adopted one or the other than that they rejected all attempts to find historical situations for the sacred lyrics. Without reconstructing the porticoes, we shall not be in a position to do full justice to the inner glories of the palaces of the Psalter."

The conception of a situation by a critic colors even his translation of specific words. For example, Ewald thinks that verses 7 and 8 of Psalm CIV. refer to the great earthquake which took place near the close of Uzziah's reign, — a calamity which made a deep impression on the national mind, as shown by the imagery of many prophets and psalmists; he therefore translates the passage thus : —

> AT thy rebuke the mountains flee ;
> At the voice of thy thunder they tremble away ;
> Mountains rise and valleys sink
> To the place which thou hast founded for them.

Most critics, however, think there is a reference here to creation, and so they give a different tense to the verbs; but the ordinary translation means little or nothing. It is foreign to the spirit of Hebrew poetry not to refer to definite places and events. In fact, it is untrue to the spirit of all poetry. The highest flights of the imagination, in dealing with a general truth, start from specific thought and a definite situation.

In speaking of the words of Jeremiah, "Oh that I had in the wilderness a lodging-place of wayfaring men, that I might leave my people and go from them!" Dr. Cheyne says that "one of the psalmists who thought themselves back into the soul of this prophet, was so moved by this passage that he amplified it in lyric verse." Psalm LV., at any rate, embodies the bitter experience of some soul in a similar situation; and if a reader, before reading the fifty-fifth Psalm, will make a thorough study of the whole life of Jeremiah, enter into imaginative sympathy with some one of his despondent moods in the midst of trickery and disappointment, and bring all his feeling to an intense realization of these lines, he will realize the true spirit of lyric poetry, and also the true nature of vocal expression and its use of the imagination.

> FEAR and trembling have come upon me,
> And horror overwhelmeth me ;
> And I say, Oh that I had wings like a dove !
> Then would I fly away, and be at rest :
> Lo, then would I wander far off,
> I would lodge in the wilderness ;
> I would haste me to my safe retreat
> From the stormy wind and the tempest.

Translated by De Witt. *Psalm lv. 5-8.*

The student must, in every way, endeavor to be accurate. He must consult many authorities, and, above all, from internal evidence judge for himself what was the real situation; but when he comes to read, he must give his imagination some freedom. For example, in this fifty-fifth Psalm, it makes little difference in the reading whether he considers the Psalm to have been written by Jeremiah, or by one of his contemporaries, or by a later psalmist "who thought himself back into the situation," — the feeling will be the same. The imagination will centre upon Jeremiah as the real situation, and the reader will think himself back into a realization of the great prophet and the spirit of his time.

At times a personal situation may be present. For example, in reading the ninety-first Psalm, one may see rising before him the worn face of some poor woman upon her dying bed, to whom he once read the words, "Under His wings shalt thou trust," which gave her hope. That event may take such hold upon his mind that it becomes a situation, or background of the Psalm. Such situations are in accordance with the true spirit of poetry, which is " the expression of the universal element in human nature." This universal element, however, will not be felt without the definite grasp by the imagination of a specific situation.

Poetry, wherever it may be found, is governed by the same laws. It is the product of the same faculties, and it can be interpreted only by the imagination. It is not primarily didactic; " it does the thing that breeds the thought." It deals with truth, not with falsehood. It is synthetic, and not analytic; but it is founded upon vivid ideas and specific thought. No poetry is founded upon confusion or misunderstanding or inadequacy of conception. The sublimest poem issues from a vivid and clear realization of truth.

Many persons, even clergymen, who would be ashamed not to be able to give the argument of Hamlet, or King Lear, or David Copperfield, or " Les Misérables," allow themselves to remain without any definite conception of the argument of the Book of Job, of the second Psalm, of the Book of Amos, or of the greatest Hebrew classic, Isaiah. Much of the Bible is vague and confused to many minds.

As an example of the imaginative use which may be made of the results of the most severe critical study, note how the fortieth chapter of Isaiah takes definite shape and awakens the most exalted feeling, when studied and read in the light of the situation which is now accepted by almost every one, — that the prophet was at Babylon in captivity, and was speaking to his fellow-captives of their return. The six hundred miles from Babylon to Jerusalem westward across the desert is " the wilderness " through which is to open " the way of the Lord." Through this is to be prepared a " highway " for God's deliverance of his people. Through this seemingly impassable region " every valley shall be exalted, and every mountain and hill be made low." The prophet sees far away on the hills of Judea his native country, idealized into an angelic form that looks out across the desert and beholds the returning wanderers, as a herald proclaims the good news to the desolated land; or, as others think, that calls the captives by their ancient name to awaken their patriotism, and to rouse them to proclaim to one another the fact that their bondage is over. The passage is inexplicable without some such situation which took hold of the ideas of a nation and became prophetic of even higher events. A reader should study such a passage with at least as much intensity and earnestness as he would give to a monologue of Browning or a play of Shakespeare. It is the sublimest poetry, and will inspire the dullest imagination.

THE VOICES.

COMFORT ye, comfort ye my people, saith your God.
Speak ye home to the heart of Jerusalem and call unto her,
That her affliction is ended, that her debt is paid ;
That she hath received from the hand of Jehovah double for all her sins.

Hark, one calling :
"In the wilderness prepare ye a way for Jehovah !
Make straight in the desert a highway for our God !
Let every valley be exalted,
And every mountain and hill be made low ;
And let the rugged be made a plain,
And the ledges of rocks a valley,
And the glory of Jehovah be revealed,
And all flesh shall see it together ;
For the mouth of Jehovah hath spoken it."

Hark ! one saying, "Cry !"
And I said :
          "What can I cry ?
All flesh is grass,
And all its beauty as a wild-flower.
Grass is withered, flower faded :
For the breath of Jehovah hath blown upon it.
Surely grass is the people."

"Grass withereth, flower fadeth :
Yet the word of our God will stand forever."

Up on a high mountain, get thee up,
O Evangelistess Zion !
Lift up thy voice with strength,
Evangelistess Jerusalem !
Lift up, be not afraid, say to the cities of Judah :
Behold your God.
Behold the Lord, Jehovah : as a mighty one will he come,

His arm ruling for Him ;
Behold, His reward is with Him,
And His recompence before Him.
He will feed His flock like a shepherd,
Gather the lambs with His right arm
And carry them in His bosom,
And tenderly lead the ewe-mothers.

Who hath measured the waters with the hollow of His hand, and regulated the heavens with a span, and taken up the dust of the earth in a third measure, and weighed the mountains with scales, and the hills in a balance?   Who hath directed the spirit of Jehovah, and instructed Him as His counsellor ?   With whom took He counsel, and who would have explained to Him and instructed Him in the path of judgment, and taught Him knowledge, and helped Him to know the way of intelligence?   Behold, nations! as a drop from a bucket, and like a grain of sand in a balance, are they esteemed ; behold, islands! like an atom of dust that rises in the air.   And Lebanon is not enough for burning, nor its game enough for an offering.   All the nations are as nothing before Him ; as spent and as waste are they regarded for Him.

To whom then can ye liken God, and what kind of image can ye place beside Him ?

The image !   A smith cast it, a smelter plates it with gold, and smelts for it silver chains.   He that is straightened for an offering, — he chooses a block of wood that will not rot ; he seeketh for himself a skilful carver to set up an image that will not totter.

Have ye not known ?   Have ye not heard ?   Hath it not been told you from the beginning ?   Have ye not understood from the foundations of the earth ?   He who is enthroned above the vault of the earth, and its dwellers are before him as grasshoppers ; who stretcheth the heavens as a fine veil, and spreadeth them like a dwelling tent.   He who bringeth great men to nothing, maketh judges of the earth like a desolation. They are hardly planted, hardly sown, their stem has hardly taken root in the earth, and he only blows upon them, and they dry up, and the storm carries them away like stubble.   " To whom then will ye liken me that I may match with him ?" saith the Holy One.

Lift up your eyes on high, and see !   Who hath created these ?   It is He who bringeth out their host by number, calleth them all by names, by the greatness of His might, for He is powerful in strength : there is not one that is missing.   Why sayest thou then, O Jacob, and speakest, O Israel, " My way is hidden from Jehovah, and my right is overlooked by my God" ?

Hast thou not known, hast thou not heard, that an everlasting God is Jehovah, Creator of the ends of the earth ? He fainteth not, neither becomes weary. His understanding is unsearchable. Giver to the weary of strength ! And upon him that is of no might He lavisheth power. Even youths may grow faint and weary, and young men utterly fall; but they who hope in Jehovah shall renew their strength; they shall mount up with wings as eagles ; they shall run, and not be weary ; they shall walk, and not faint.

X. IMAGINATION AND FEELING.

AND there was mounting in hot haste : the steed,
The mustering squadron, and the clattering car
Went pouring forward with impetuous speed,
And swiftly forming in the ranks of war ;
And the deep thunder peal on peal afar ;
And near, the beat of the alarming drum
Roused up the soldier ere the morning star ;
While thronged the citizens with terror dumb,
Or whispering, with white lips, "The foe ! They come ! they come !"

Byron.

SUDDENLY the pathway ends,
Sheer the precipice descends,
    Loud the torrent roars unseen ;
Thirty feet from side to side
Yawns the chasm ; on air must ride
    He who crosses this ravine.

Roushan Beg.   *Longfellow.*

THE first line of the second extract may be read in many ways. The reader may imagine a simple walk, a race for pleasure, or some game; the pathway may end so as to excite mere curiosity, pleasant surprise, simple disappointment; or its sudden ending on the brink of a precipice may mean life and death, as it does in the above illustration. If the passage is read abstractly or without relation to a specific situation, no feeling whatever can be awakened in reader or listener. Thus to read even one line with feeling, a definite situation must be conceived.

The first clause of the extract from Byron can also be read as the expression of entirely different situations. The mounting may be for a hunt, as an act in some comical story, to go for a physician, to escape danger, to save life, or to take a ride for pleasure. It may also be seen and felt as one act among thousands in preparation for the battle of Waterloo,—about this one act being gathered the situation and atmosphere of the whole event. Vocal expression can be still more definite. The mounting may be simply on the part of an individual, or it may be the whole army. Such variations can be applied to every phrase and sentence in both extracts.

From these illustrations it may be seen that feeling depends upon situation; that with every change of situation there is a change in emotion; and, in fact, that imaginative conception of a situation is the source of true emotion.

Feeling also results from the vivid realization of relations or associations. Here, for example, is a little coat. To the ordinary observer it is a mere rag; but the mother folds it away with tears, for it recalls a little form with the sunshine and tenderness, the joys and hopes, of other days. Memory thus plays an important part in awakening feeling; but the imagination uses the material furnished by memory and creates a background, gives relations and associations. Thus the most familiar objects or events are often so related or associated by the imagination as to awaken exalted emotion.

Here are a few scraps of cloth sewed together floating upon the breeze from the mast of a ship; but for this men will give their lives: it is the flag of their country.

Notice how the poet makes the season, the cold, leafless trees and the stillness, all co-operate to awaken feeling for the bird —

> A WIDOW bird sate mourning for her Love
>   Upon a wintry bough ;
> The frozen wind crept on above,
>   The freezing stream below.
>
> There was no leaf upon the forest bare,
>   No flower upon the ground,
> And little motion in the air
>   Except the mill-wheel's sound.
>
> Shelley.

One of the most important functions of imagination is to prevent the mind from forming a mere literal conception of any object or scene, and to connect it with deeper and more significant relations to life. Blood to the outer eye awakens horror; the imagination of a Shakespeare uses it so as to become the means of stimulating exalted feeling: —

> THROUGH this the well-belovèd Brutus stabb'd;
> And as he pluck'd his cursèd steel away,
> Mark how the blood of Cæsar follow'd it,
> As rushing out of doors, to be resolv'd
> If Brutus so unkindly knock'd, or no.

This passage is considered one of the most imaginative in the English language. Prose explanations of it only spoil it. By a simple, natural process, home-like images are drawn forth from every heart, and the observer does not see mere blood, but beholds a living embodiment of the love of Cæsar for Brutus.

Imagination lifts the commonplace into the realm of interest; it surrounds the smallest object with the atmosphere of infinity. It makes the most trivial event throb with the spirit of ages, and the life of the race thrill in an individual soul.

We are tempted to dwell merely upon the literal and commonplace. A drudge in any profession is one who works without imagination. Imagination exalts and ennobles all life; it awakens the mind to feel what will be in what is, — to see the ideal in the actual; it penetrates beneath the surface of mere sense-perception, and discovers hidden relations of the life which throbs at the heart of the universe, and thus awakens a thrill of feeling in the dullest breast.

The imagination also brings the individual mind into sympathy with the race. It creates the possibility of that true altruism by which each soul can appreciate the point of view of another soul, of another race or age. It enables man to realize that which can only be suggested or vaguely hinted at in language. It gives power to create art, and to read and feel the message of the art of every age.

Again, imagination arouses feeling by vividly conceiving ideas as present realities; by it the distant is made near, the past made present. The world of ideas becomes a living world, and every object is conceived in a natural, a living scene. " It is by means of ideal presence," says Lord Kames, "that our passions are excited; and till words produce that charm, they avail nothing; even real events entitled to our belief must be conceived present and passing in our sight, before they can move us. And this theory serves to explain several phenomena otherwise unaccountable. A misfortune happening to a stranger makes a less impression than one happening to a man we know, even where we are in no way interested in him; our acquaintance with this man, however slight, aids the conception of his suffering in our presence. Even genuine history has no command over our passions but by ideal presence only. Without it the finest speaker or writer would in vain attempt to move any passion; our sympathy would be confined to objects that are really present; and language would lose entirely its signal power of making us sympathize with beings removed at the greatest distance of time as well as of place."

These facts indicate that imagination and feeling are closely connected. Imagination has been defined as " the mind of passion, the thinking of the heart." " Imagination," says Professor Shairp, " seems to be a power intermediate between intellect and emotion, looking towards both, and partaking of the nature of both. In its highest form, it would seem to be based on ' moral intensity.' The emotional and the intellectual in it act and react on each other, — deep emotion kindling imagination, and expressing itself in imaginative form, while imaginative insight kindles and deepens emotion. Whenever the soul comes vividly in contact with any fact, truth, or existence; whenever it realizes and takes them home to itself with more than common intensity, — out of that meeting of the soul and its object there arises a thrill of joy, a glow of feeling. . . . Emotion, then, from first to last, inseparably attends the exercise of imagination, — pre-eminently in him who creates, in a lesser degree in those who enjoy his creations."

All this applies with double force to speaking, or to any form of vocal expression. It is the imagination which conceives an idea in its relation to others, and supplies the right background; which brings ideas or objects into sympathetic association with the human mind, and makes them live and act; it is the only faculty that can create ideal presence. Hence imagination is the chief cause of feeling in all forms of art, but especially in speaking.

It is only an unimaginative speaker who says he cannot read a poem or story because he never "saw the place" or experienced the emotion. Such a person entirely misunderstands the nature of feeling. Every scene in history, sacred or profane, is imaginary. Hardly a scene in the Bible can be definitely located; and even if the few scraggy trees called Gethsemane mark the real spot, what help are they to feeling? None. The imagination must create a Capernaum and a Calvary. In fact, without imagination, noble emotion is impossible.

Besides, emotion arises from an imaginative situation more than from a literal scene or object. When Mark Antony steps down from the rostrum, Shakespeare does not make him try to awaken feeling by showing Cæsar's body to the Roman populace. He displays at first only the mantle, and appeals to their memory and imagination, not to their eyes. He even carries them back to a great historical battle which was a part of their national pride. Even then he does not show them the body, but makes them feel Cæsar's death by showing the thrusts of the daggers through his mantle. He appeals to the imagination and not to the eye to awaken emotion. People have been so stunned, so shocked, by the sight of a dead body — of a father or a mother or a child — that no tear could be shed; but afterward the sight of a vacant chair, or a pair of little shoes, has wrung the heart and caused a flood of tears. The deepest passion is awakened by suggestion, because suggestion is associated with imagination. The higher the thought, the deeper the feeling, the more impossible it is for expression to be literal. "The art of expression," says Goethe, "is the art of intimation."

Without imagination there can be no genuineness in art. It is only by imagination that a speaker can make real the scenes of other days; it is only by imagination that we identify ourselves with the sorrows of our kind. Sympathy is insight, and insight is sympathy. The unsympathetic person is unimaginative and lacks feeling. He can sympathise only with experiences he has had himself. Hence, he measures all by himself; he is often unable to enter into sympathy with people of other ages, other lands, or other relations of life.

> Weep no more, lady, weep no more, thy sorrow is in vain :
> For violets plucked, the sweetest showers will ne'er make grow again.
>
> *Damon and Pythias.*

In the first of these lines there is an endeavour to produce sympathy; but it is in the infinite suggestion in the next line, by means of a specific imagination picture, that the deeper sentiment of the heart is reached.

> It was a lovely sight to see
> The lady Christabel, when she
> Was praying at the old oak-tree:
> Amid the jagged shadows
>   Of mossy leafless boughs,
> Kneeling in the moonlight
>   To make her gentle vows:
> Her slender palms together prest,
> Heaving sometimes on her breast;
> Her face resigned to bliss or bale —
> Her face, oh call it fair not pale!
> And both blue eyes more bright than clear,
> Each about to have a tear.
>
> *Coleridge.*

Experiences in emotion and vision are very important, because they develop imagination and dramatic instinct. They impart a sense of the value of emotion and surroundings in truth and emotion. They develop also that emotional response to ideas which lies at the foundation of all noble experience. Such experiences tend to correct narrowness, and that vague unreality and still artificiality which are so common. When the imagination is brought to bear upon a scene, it creates vivid interest; it makes everything live: it secures precision and definiteness of emotion, naturalness and variation of expression.

Students should practice reading aloud poems in which they genuinely delight. These should, however, be recitation with them: the pleasure must not be superficial. A selection which at first seems to create interest of[illegible] will grow uninteresting if it does not [call to itself] imagination of a [high] order. On the contrary, a selection which at the ordinary reading may be less well [interesting], when rightly studied will begin to grow in interest, and [strike] more and more appreciation. "A thing of beauty is a joy for ever." Imagination not only [supplies] [illegible] in the [illegible] — [but] [illegible] in senses that permanent [condition] of [thought] which is the chief joy and pleasure of the human soul.

Notice how the greatest of the masters in the portrayal of character makes successive bursts or scenes each display with conflicting passions. Does Tubal give these successive emotions immediately from careless [release], or gradually?

SHYLOCK AND TUBAL

Shylock. How now, Tubal, what news from Genoa? Hast thou found my daughter?

Tubal. I often came where I did hear of her, but cannot find her.

Shy. Why, there, there, there, there! a diamond gone, cost me two thousand ducats in Frankfort! The curse never fell upon our nation till now; I never felt it till now: two thousand ducats in that; and other precious, precious jewels. I would my daughter were dead at my foot, and the jewels in her ear! would she were hearsed at my foot, and the ducats in her coffin! No news of them? Why, so: and I know not what's spent in the search. Why, thou loss upon loss! the thief gone with so much, and so much to find the thief; and no satisfaction, no revenge: nor no ill luck stirring but what lights o' my shoulders, no sighs but o' my breathing, no tears but o' my shedding.

Tub. Yes, other men have ill luck too: Antonio, as I heard in Genoa —

Shy. What, what, what? ill luck, ill luck?

Tub. — hath an argosy cast away, coming from Tripolis.

Shy. I thank God, I thank God! — Is it true? is it true?

Tub. I spoke with some of the sailors that escaped the wreck.

Shy. I thank thee, good Tubal: — good news, good news! ha, ha! — Where? in Genoa?

Tub. Your daughter spent in Genoa, as I heard, one night, fourscore ducats.

Shy. Thou stick'st a dagger in me ; — I shall never see my gold again. Fourscore at a sitting! fourscore ducats!

Tub. There came divers of Antonio's creditors in my company to Venice, that swear he cannot choose but break.

Shy. I am very glad of it. I 'll plague him: I 'll torture him: I am glad of it.

Tub. One of them showed me a ring, that he had of your daughter for a monkey.

Shy. Out upon her! Thou torturest me, Tubal! It was my turquoise: I had it of Leah, when I was a bachelor. I would not have given it for a wilderness of monkeys.

Tub. But Antonio is certainly undone.

Shy. Nay, that 's true, that 's very true. Go, Tubal, fee me an officer ; bespeak him a fortnight before. I will have the heart of him, if he forfeit ; for were he out of Venice, I can make what merchandise I will. Go, Tubal, and meet me at our synagogue ; go, good Tubal ; at our synagogue, Tubal.

Shakespeare.

Again, in the speeches of Cassius, observe how imagination works upon feeling. His hatred becomes active as he recalls or creates a picture of Cæsar's weakness in the water, or when he had the fever in Spain.

CASSIUS INSTIGATING BRUTUS.

Cassius. Will you go see the order of the course ?
Brutus. Not I.
Cas. I pray you, do.
Bru. I am not gamesome : I do lack some part
Of that quick spirit that is in Antony.
Let me not hinder, Cassius, your desires ;
I 'll leave you.
    Cas. Brutus, I do observe you now of late
I have not from your eyes that gentleness
And show of love as I was wont to have :
You bear too stubborn and too strange a hand
Over your friend that loves you.
    Bru.   Cassius,
Be not deceived : if I have veil'd my look,
I turn the trouble of my countenance

Merely upon myself.   Vexèd I am
Of late with passions of some difference,
Conceptious only proper to myself,
Which give some soil perhaps to my behaviours ;
But let not therefore my good friends be grieved —
Among which number, Cassius, be you one —
Nor construe any further my neglect,
Than that poor Brutus, with himself at war,
Forgets the shows of love to other men.

  Cas.   Then, Brutus, I have much mistook your passion ;
By means whereof this breast of mine hath buried
Thoughts of great value, worthy cogitations.
Tell me, good Brutus, can you see your face ?

  Bru.   No, Cassius ; for the eye sees not itself,
But by reflection by some other things.

  Cas.   'T is just :
And it is very much lamented, Brutus,
That you have no such mirror as will turn
Your hidden worthiness into your eye,
That you might see your shadow.   I have heard,
Where many of the best respect in Rome,
Except immortal Cæsar, speaking of Brutus
And groaning underneath this age's yoke,
Have wish'd that noble Brutus had his eyes.

  Bru.   Into what dangers would you lead me, Cassius,
That you would have me seek into myself
For that which is not in me ?

  Cas.   Therefore, good Brutus, be prepared to hear :
And since you know you cannot see yourself
So well as by reflection, I, your glass,
Will modestly discover to yourself
That of yourself which you yet know not of.
And be not jealous on me, gentle Brutus :
Were I a common laugher, or did use
To stale with ordinary oaths my love
To every new protester ; if you know
That I do fawn on men and hug them hard,
And after scandal them ; or if you know
That I profess myself in banqueting
To all the rout, — then hold me dangerous.

                                    [Flourish and shout.

  Bru.   What means this shouting ?   I do fear, the people
Choose Cæsar for their king.

Cas.   Ay, do you fear it ?
Then must I think you would not have it so.
  Bru.   I would not, Cassius ; yet I love him well. —
But wherefore do you hold me here so long ?
What is it that you would impart to me ?
If it be aught toward the general good,
Set honour in one eye and death i' th' other,
And I will look on both indifferently;
For let the gods so speed me as I love
The name of honour more than I fear death.
  Cas.   I know that virtue to be in you, Brutus,
As well as I do know your outward favour.
Well, honour is the subject of my story.
I cannot tell what you and other men
Think of this life ; but, for my single self,
I had as lief not be, as live to be
In awe of such a thing as I myself.
I was born free as Cæsar ; so were you :
We both have fed as well ; and we can both
Endure the winter's cold as well as he :
For once, upon a raw and gusty day,
The troublèd Tiber chafing with her shores,
Cæsar said to me, "Dar'st thou, Cassius, now
Leap in with me into this angry flood,
And swim to yonder point?"   Upon the word,
Accoutrèd as I was, I plungèd in
And bade him follow : so indeed he did.
The torrent roar'd, and we did buffet it
With lusty sinews, throwing it aside
And stemming it with hearts of controversy.
But ere we could arrive the point proposed,
Cæsar cried, "Help me, Cassius, or I sink !"
I, as Æneas, our great ancestor,
Did from the flames of Troy upon his shoulder
The old Anchises bear, so from the waves of Tiber
Did I the tired Cæsar.   And this man
Is now become a god, and Cassius is
A wretched creature, and must bend his body
If Cæsar carelessly but nod on him.
He had a fever when he was in Spain,
And when the fit was on him, I did mark
How he did shake : 't is true, this god did shake :
His coward lips did from their colour fly;

And that same eye whose bend doth awe the world
Did lose his lustre. I did hear him groan :
Ay, and that tongue of his that bade the Romans
Mark him and write his speeches in their books,
Alas, it cried, "Give me some drink, Titinius,"
As a sick girl.   Ye gods! it doth amaze me,
A man of such a feeble temper should
So get the start of the majestic world,
And bear the palm alone.   [*Shout.*

   Bru.   Another general shout !
I do believe that these applauses are
For some new honours that are heap'd on Cæsar.
   Cas.   Why, man, he doth bestride the narrow world
Like a Colossus, and we petty men
Walk under his huge legs and peep about
To find ourselves dishonourable graves.
Men at some time are masters of their fates :
The fault, dear Brutus, is not in our stars,
But in ourselves, that we are underlings.
Brutus and Cæsar : what should be in that "Cæsar" !
Why should that name be sounded more than yours ?
Write them together : yours is as fair a name ;
Sound them: it doth become the mouth as well ;
Weigh them: it is as heavy ; conjure with 'em :
"Brutus" will start a spirit as soon as "Cæsar."   [*Shout.*
Now, in the names of all the gods at once,
Upon what meat doth this our Cæsar feed,
That he is grown so great ?   Age, thou art sham'd !
Rome, thou hast lost the breed of noble bloods !
When went there by an age, since the great flood,
But it was fam'd with more than with one man ?
When could they say till now, that talk'd of Rome,
That her wide walls encompass'd but one man ?
Now is it Rome indeed and room enough,
When there is in it but one only man.
Oh, you and I have heard our fathers say,
There was a Brutus once that would have brook'd
The eternal devil to keep his state in Rome
As easily as a king.
   Bru.   That you do love me, I am nothing jealous ;
What you would work me to, I have some aim.
How I have thought of this and of these times,
I shall recount hereafter ; for this present,
I would not, so with love I might entreat you,

Be any further movèd.   What you have said
I will consider ; what you have to say
I will with patience hear, and find a time
Both meet to hear and answer such high things.
Till then, my noble friend, chew upon this :
Brutus had rather be a villager
Than to repute himself a son of Rome
Under these hard conditions as this time
Is like to lay upon us.
    Cas.   I am glad that my weak words
Have struck but thus much show of fire from Brutus.

Shakespeare.

PROBLEM XIV. — *Read a poem referring to common objects or expressing
simple ideas, conceiving the ideas so vividly and uniting them so harmoniously as to awaken noble emotion.*

SOMETIMES with secure delight
The upland hamlets will invite,
When the merry bells ring round,
And the jocund rebeks sound
To many a youth and many a maid,
Dancing in the chequered shade.

TO MARGUERITE.

YES : in the sea of life enisl'd,
  With echoing straits between us thrown,
Dotting the shoreless watery wild,
  We mortal millions live *alone*.
    The islands feel the enclasping flow,
    And then their endless bounds they know.

But when the moon their hollows light,
  And they are swept by balms of spring ;
And in their glens, on starry nights,
  The nightingales divinely sing ;
    And lovely notes, from shore to shore,
    Across the sounds and channels pour, —

Oh then a longing like despair
  Is to their farthest caverns sent ;
For surely once, they feel we were
  Parts of a single continent.
    Now round us spreads the watery plain —
    Oh might our marges meet again !

> Who order'd that their longing's fire
>   Should be, as soon as kindled, cool'd ?
> Who renders vain their deep desire ?—
>   A God, a God their severance rul'd ;
>   And bade betwixt their shores to be
>   The unplumb'd, salt, estranging sea.

Matthew Arnold.

XI. EFFECT OF PASSION UPON IMAGINATION.

> " BETWEEN the acting of a dreadful thing
> And the first motion, all the interim is
> Like a phantasma or a hideous dream.
> The mortal instruments are then in council ;
> And the state of man, like to a little kingdom
> Suffers then the nature of an insurrection."

NOT only does imagination awaken feeling, but feeling arouses imagination. After Horatio and his companions have seen the ghost at the close of the first scene in " Hamlet," their talk rises to a much higher plane. " The morn with russet mantle clad, walks o'er the dew of yon high eastern hill." Some have considered this as being untrue to Nature; but these men have seen the ghost, and their imaginations have been aroused.

Macbeth after the murder of Duncan, with conscience quickened and every feeling awake, reveals great activity of imagination. His metaphors are more or less mixed, but their vigor and force manifest the excitement of his mind. The activity of his imagination is the direct effect of the activity of passion.

Notice how Othello, about to strangle Desdemona, sees the little candle, and his awakened feeling impels the imagination to create images and analogies : —

> IF I quench thee, thou flaming minister,
> I can again thy former light restore,
> Should I repent me ; but once put out thine,
> Thou cunning'st pattern of excelling nature,
> I know not where is that Promethean heat
> That can thy light relume : when I have pluck'd thy rose,
> I cannot give it vital breath again ;
> It needs must wither.

Othello. *Shakespeare.*

The emotions of Romeo in the garden are stirred by the sight of Juliet at the window, and the result is vivid and complex figures.   His imagination is intensely, " passionately active."

> *Romeo.*   He jests at scars, that never felt a wound.
>   [*Juliet appears above at a window.*
> But, soft ! what light through yonder window breaks ?
> It is the east, and Juliet is the sun.
> Arise, fair sun, and kill the envious moon,
> Who is already sick and pale with grief,
> That thou, her maid, art far more fair than she :
> Be not her maid, since she is envious ;
> Her vestal livery is but sick and green,
> And none but fools do wear it : cast it off.
> It is my lady ; oh, it is my love !
> Oh that she knew she were !
> She speaks, yet she says nothing : what of that ?
> Her eye discourses, I will answer it. —
> I am too bold, 't is not to me she speaks :
> Two of the fairest stars in all the heaven,
> Having some business, do entreat her eyes
> To twinkle in their spheres till they return.
> What if her eyes were there, they in her head ?
> The brightness of her cheek would shame those stars,
> As daylight doth a lamp ; her eyes in heaven
> Would through the airy region stream so bright
> That birds would sing and think it were not night.
> As silver-voiced ; her eyes as jewel-like,
> And cased as richly ; in face another Juno ;
> Who starves the ears she feeds, and makes them hungry
> The more she gives them speech.

Romeo and Juliet.   *Shakespeare.*

Intensity of feeling arouses and stimulates the imagination.   It has been said by some one that the " literary language is a stagnant pool."   The words which men use under pressure of real emotion, these are the running stream, the living spring.   That is to say, the domination of passion and imagination are necessary to any effective use of figurative language or literary style.   Man must give himself up to feeling, to have any true use of his imagination.   Imagination is a spontaneous faculty which cannot be governed or guided in any deliberative manner. No one can use illustrations by rule, or by any mechanical or artificial process; they must result from abandon to feeling and imagination; they must be dictated by spontaneous impulse.

This is not only true of words in literary composition; it is still more true of the modulations of the voice and the body in reading, acting, or speaking. If words to be living must be dominated by imagination and feeling, how much more must the inflections and textures of the voice and the actions of the body, which belong to natural and more spontaneous modes of expression.

The necessity of abandon has already been shown;[1] but the more fully we pass into the realm of imagination, the more exalted the form of poetry that we read, the more we find mere mechanical or deliberative action inadequate for any effective and natural expression. We must abandon ourselves to the free and spontaneous sway of imagination and feeling.

Imagination and feeling are thus always connected. To awaken imagination we must sympathetically contemplate an object. To read a poem we must meditate upon it quietly, and assimilate every situation. Imagination cannot act without emotion. It refines and ennobles feeling; but feeling in its turn is the motive power of imagination.

WE parted: sweetly gleam'd the stars,
And sweet the vapour-braided blue,
Low breezes fann'd the belfry bars,
As homeward by the church I drew.

Tennyson.

OH, it is monstrous, monstrous!
Methought the billows spoke and told me of it;
The winds did sing it to me; and the thunder,
That deep and dreadful organ-pipe, pronounced
The name of Prosper: it did bass my trespass;
Therefore my son i' the ooze is bedded, and
I'll seek him deeper than e'er plummet sounded,
And with him there lie mudded.

Tempest. *Shakespeare.*

[1] See lessons in Vocal Expression, pp. 35–41, and Province of Expression, pp. 184–189.

My wind, cooling my broth,
Would blow me to an ague, when I thought
What harm a wind too great might do at sea.
I should not see the sandy hour-glass run,
But I should think of shallows and of flats;
And see my wealthy Andrew dock'd in sand,
Vailing her high-top lower than her ribs,
To kiss her burial.   Should I go to church,
And see the holy edifice of stone,
And not bethink me straight of dangerous rocks,
Which, touching but my gentle vessel's side,
Would scatter all her spices on the stream,
Enrobe the roaring waters with my silks;
And, in a word, but even now worth this,
And now worth nothing.

Gratiano in " Merchant of Venice."   *Shakespeare.*

THE MURDER OF DUNCAN.

Macbeth.   Go bid thy mistress, when my drink is ready,
She strike upon the bell.   Get thee to bed. —   *[Exit Servant.*
Is this a dagger which I see before me,
The handle toward my hand ?   Come, let me clutch thee :—
I have thee not, and yet I see thee still.
Art thou not, fatal vision, sensible
To feeling as to sight ? or art thou but
A dagger of the mind, a false creation,
Proceeding from the heat-oppressèd brain ?
I see thee yet, in form as palpable
As this which now I draw.
Thou marshall'st me the way that I was going;
And such an instrument I was to use. —
Mine eyes are made the fools o' the other senses,
Or else worth all the rest : I see thee still,
And on thy blade and dudgeon gouts of blood,
Which was not so before. — There 's no such thing :
It is the bloody business which informs
Thus to mine eyes. — Now o'er the one half-world
Nature seems dead, and wicked dreams abuse
The curtain'd sleep ; now witchcraft celebrates
Pale Hecate's offerings ; and wither'd Murder,
Alarum'd by his sentinel, the wolf,
Whose howl 's his watch, thus with his stealthy pace,
With Tarquin's ravishing strides, toward his designs

Moves like a ghost. — Thou sure and firm-set earth,
Hear not my steps, which way they take, for fear
The very stones prate of my whereabout,
And take the present horror from the time,
Which now suits with it. — Whiles I threat, he lives :
Words to the heat of deeds too cold breath gives.   *[A bell rings.*
I go, and it is done ; the bell invites me.
Hear it not, Duncan ; for it is a knell
That summons thee to Heaven or to Hell.   *[Exit.*
  Lady Macbeth (entering).   That which hath made them drunk hath made
    me bold ;
What hath quench'd them, hath given me fire. — Hark ! — Peace !
It was the owl that shriek'd, the fatal bellman,
Which gives the stern'st good-night.   He is about it :
The doors are open ; and the surfeited grooms
Do mock their charge with snores.   I have drugg'd their possets,
That death and nature do contend about them,
Whether they live or die.
  Macbeth (within).   Who's there ? — what, ho !
  L. Macb.   Alack ! I am afraid they have awak'd,
And 't is not done : — the attempt, and not the deed,
Confounds us. — Hark ! — I laid their daggers ready ;
He could not miss them. — Had he not resembled
My father as he slept, I had done 't. — My husband !   *[Enter* Macb.
  Macb.   I have done the deed.   Didst thou not hear a noise ?
  L. Macb.   I heard the owl scream, and the cricket cry.
Did you not speak ?
  Macb.   When ?
  L. Macb.   Now.
  Macb.   As I descended ?
  L. Macb.   Ay.
  Macb.   Hark ! —
Who lies i' the second chamber ?
  L. Macb.   Donalbain.
  Macb.   This is a sorry sight.   *[Looking on his hands.*
  L. Macb.   A foolish thought, to say a sorry sight.
  Macb.   There's one did laugh in his sleep, and one cried, " Murder ! "
That they did wake each other : I stood and heard them ;
But they did say their prayers, and address'd them
Again to sleep.
  L. Macb.   There are two lodged together.
  Macb.   One cried " God bless us ! " and " Amen," the other ;
As they had seen me, with these hangman's hands.

Listening their fear, I could not say, "Amen,"
When they did say, "God bless us!"
   L. Macb.   Consider it not so deeply.
   Macb. But wherefore could not I pronounce, "Amen"?
I had most need of blessing, and "Amen"
Stuck in my throat.
   L. Macb. These deeds must not be thought
After these ways; so, it will make us mad.
   Macb. Methought I heard a voice cry, "Sleep no more!
Macbeth does murder sleep!" the innocent sleep;
Sleep, that knits up the ravell'd sleave of care,
The death of each day's life, sore labor's bath,
Balm of hurt minds, great nature's second course,
Chief nourisher in life's feast —
   L. Macb.   What do you mean?
   Macb. Still it cried, "Sleep no more!" to all the house:
"Glamis hath murder'd sleep, and therefore Cawdor
Shall sleep no more; Macbeth shall sleep no more!"
   L. Macb. Who was it that thus cried? Why, worthy thane,
You do unbend your noble strength, to think
So brain-sickly of things. Go, get some water,
And wash this filthy witness from your hand. —
Why did you bring these daggers from the place?
They must lie there : go, carry them ; and smear
The sleepy grooms with blood.
   Macb.   I 'll go no more :
I am afraid to think what I have done ;
Look on 't again I dare not.
   L. Macb.   Infirm of purpose!
Give me the daggers : the sleeping and the dead
Are but as pictures : 't is the eye of childhood
That fears a painted devil. If he do bleed,
I 'll gild the faces of the grooms withal,
For it must seem their guilt.   *[Exit. Knocking within.*
   Macb.   Whence is that knocking?
How is 't with me, when every noise appals me?
What hands are here? Ha! They pluck out mine eyes!
Will all great Neptune's ocean wash this blood
Clean from my hand? No; this my hand will rather
The multitudinous seas incarnadine,
Making the green one red.   *[Re-enter Lady Macbeth.*
   L. Macb. My hands are of your color, but I shame
To wear a heart so white. (*Knock.*) I hear a knocking

At the south entry : — retire we to our chamber :
A little water clears us of this deed :
How easy it is then ! Your constancy
Hath left you unattended. — (*Knocking.*) Hark ! more knocking.
Get on your night-gown, lest occasion call us,
And show us to be watchers.   Be not lost
So poorly in your thoughts.
   Macb.   To know my deed, 't were best not know myself (*knock*).
Wake Duncan with thy knocking ! I would thou couldst !

Macbeth.   *Shakespeare.*

XII. IMAGINATION AND FIGURATIVE LANGUAGE.

IMAGINATION affects every form of expression, but its action is
especially apparent in its modification of written language.   It is
the chief cause of figures of speech.   A figure of speech is a departure from plain language, to express higher associations and
relations of ideas, to awaken more vivid images, and to stimulate
deeper feeling.

This figurative action of the mind is manifest in the most familiar words.   "Words are fossil poetry."   Nearly all our words
have been derived from some action of the imagination, and hold
still an element of poetic expression.   "He who first spake of a
dilapidated fortune," says Archbishop Trench, "what an image
must have risen up before his mind's eye of some falling house
or palace, stone detaching itself from stone, till all had gradually
sunk into desolation and ruin ! Or he who to that Greek word
which signifies 'that which will endure to be held up to and
judged by sunlight,' gave first its ethical signification of 'sincere,'
'truthful,' or, as we sometimes say, 'transparent,' can we deny
to him the poet's feeling and eye?   Many a man had gazed, we
are sure, at the jagged and indented mountain ridges of Spain,
before one called them 'sierras,' or 'saws,' — the name by which
now they are known, as Sierra Morena, Sierra Nevada; but that
man coined his imagination into a word which will endure as long
as the everlasting hills which he named."   Take the names of
flowers or of animals, or almost any class of words, and from
their etymology it can be easily seen that they have been derived
from imaginative conceptions.

A more apparent effect of imagination on language is seen in the various rhetorical figures which especially characterize all poetic verbal expression.

There have been many attempts to find a common principle underlying all figures. Without reviewing the many speculations, possibly the chief figures are due to two mental acts which are more or less the result of imagination. One is comparison. We compare the unknown with the known, and find a deeper principle of explanation, and so enlarge the scope of our minds. We discover unity in the midst of variety, and this is the secret of beauty. The act of discrimination is one of the most fundamental in the mind. The discovery of analogy, and of the kinship of things, is implied more or less in all thinking or expression.

The other principle is personification. Imagination makes objects live. In our every-day speech, we are continually giving living attributes to physical things. To a vivid imagination nothing is dead. Many figures are at heart personifications, though we do not at first think of putting them under this name.

The associative or comparative action of the imagination gives rise to simile, metaphor, contrast, antithesis, and many other figures. The other action of the mind — the power that makes things live — gives rise to personification, vision, apostrophe, allegory, and the like.

The imagination is not present in the same degree in all figures. In some, it is hardly present at all; in others, it is almost the only element. For example, in the comparison of images, — the more complete the union, the greater will be the abandon to the imagination. For this reason, there is usually more imaginative action in metaphors than in similes; the union is more immediate, and the identification more complete.

Again, the imagination is more active where there is delicate allusion, or suggestion of some pictures, which brings about a union of the most complex ideas, suddenly discovers similarity, and causes great pleasure.

> THE healing of the seamless dress is by our beds of pain ;
> We touch him in life's throng and press, and we are whole again.
>
> *Our Master.*   *Whittier.*

The figures of speech have been so carefully defined and so often illustrated that the student need only refer to his rhetoric for information. While it is very important to analyze and be able to recognize all rhetorical figures, the student should remember that the power to do so does not presuppose any imaginative action, or any power to use such figures.

There should not be too much analysis and naming of figures. A certain amount of this work is helpful, but too much may make the study mechanical.

The best way to simplify or to understand figures, is to study the action of the imagination which creates them. The means of developing the power to use them consist in stimulating the creative and artistic faculties of the mind, to cause their use in speaking or writing, and such an appreciation of their force as will enable them to be rendered by the voice.

PROBLEM XV. *Arrange short illustrations of all the rhetorical figures, and render their spirit by vocal expression.*

> INTO her dream he melted, as the rose
> Blendeth its odours with the violet.
>
> *Keats.*

ONE night, after ten hours' walking, I reached a little dwelling quite by itself at the bottom of a narrow valley which was about to throw itself into the sea a league farther on.

> *Guy de Maupassant.*

> E'EN at the last I have her still,
> With her delicious eyes as clear as heaven
> When rain in a quick shower has beat down mist,
> And clouds float white in the sun like broods of swans.
>
> *Browning.*

> ON poured the Trojan masses ; in the van
> Hector straight forward drove in full career, —
> As some huge bowlder, from its rocky bed
> Detached, and by the wintry torrent's force
> Hurled down the steep cliff's face, when constant rains
> The massive rock's firm hold have undermined :
> With giant bounds it flies ; the crashing wood
> Resounds beneath it ; still it hurries on,
> Until, arriving at the level plain,
> Its headlong impulse checked, it rolls no more.
>
> *Homer.*

For the main criminal I have no hope
Except in such a suddenness of fate.
I stood at Naples once, a night so dark
I could have scarce conjectured there was earth
Anywhere, sky or sea or world at all :
But the night's black was burst through by a blaze —
Thunder struck blow on blow, earth groaned and bore,
Through her whole length of mountain visible :
There lay the city thick and plain with spires,
And, like a ghost disshrouded, white the sea.
So may the truth be flashed out by one blow,
And Guido see, one instant, and be saved.

Browning.

As the earth bringeth forth her bud, and as the garden causeth the things that are sown in it to spring forth : so the Lord God will cause righteousness and praise to spring forth before all the nations.

'T is her breathing that
Perfumes the chamber thus : the flame o' the taper
Bows toward her, and would under-peep her lids
To see th' enclosèd lights, now canopied
Under these windows — white and azure — laced
With blue of heaven's own tint.

Cymbeline.   *Shakespeare.*

In yonder grave a Druid lies,
    Where slowly winds the stealing wave,
The year's best sweets shall duteous rise
    To deck its poet's sylvan grave. . . . .
Remembrance oft shall haunt the shore,
    When Thames in summer wreaths is drest,
And oft suspend the dashing oar
    To bid his gentle spirit rest.

Collins.

She dwelt among the untrodden ways beside the springs of Dove ;
A maid whom there were none to praise, and very few to love.
A violet by a mossy stone half-hidden from the eye !
Fair as a star, when only one is shining in the sky.
She lived unknown, and few could know when Lucy ceased to be ;
But she is in her grave, and oh the difference to me !

Wordsworth.

SEE this our new retreat
Walled in with a sloped mound of matted shrubs,
Dark, tangled, old, and green, still sloping down
To a small pool whose waters lie asleep
Amid the trailing boughs turned water-plants:
And tall trees over-arch to keep us in,
Breaking the sunbeams into emerald shafts;
And in the dreamy water one small group
Of two or three strange trees are got together
Wondering at all around, as strange beasts herd
Together far from their own land : all wildness,
No turf nor moss, for boughs and plants pave all,
And tongues of bank go shelving in the waters.

Pauline.   *Browning.*

———

AH, well ! for us all some sweet hope lies
Deeply buried from human eyes ;
And in the hereafter, angels may
Roll the stone from its grave away.

                                                          Whittier.

———

AND the most ancient heavens through thee are fresh and strong.

THE member did his party all the harm in his power: he spoke for it, and voted against it.

WHERE snow falls, there is freedom.

HE cannot see the wood for trees.

DAUGHTER of heaven, fair art thou ! The silence of thy face is pleasant. Thou comest forth in loveliness. The stars attend thy blue course in the east. The clouds rejoice in thy presence, O Moon!

                                                          Ossian.

———

A-FLOATING, a-floating across the sleepless sea,
All night I heard a singing bird upon the topmost tree.
"Oh, came you from the isles of Greece or from the banks of Seine ;
Or off some tree in forests free, which fringe the western main ?"
" I came not of the old world, nor yet from off the new ;
But I am one of the birds of God which sing the whole night through."
"Oh, sing and wake the dawning ! Oh. whistle for the wind !
The night is long, the current strong, my boat it lags behind."
" The current sweeps the old world, the current sweeps the new ;
The wind will blow, the dawn will glow, ere thou hast sailed them through."

A Myth.   *Charles Kingsley*

A GOOD method of studying figures is to take some great poem, such as Wordsworth's " Ode on Immortality," and read it many times. On the first reading, note the beauty of the entire poem; then meditate over every line and phrase, seeing and realizing the process of the author's mind in each specific picture; then afterwards it may be well to go over the whole, and mark or name as far as possible the various figures. It is important to study a poem from as many points of view as possible. Careful study of the figures may bring us into contact with new beauties. The poem should be learned, and its every picture contemplated and medi-tated over, till its real beauties dawn upon the mind, till the imagination has recreated its life and spirit. Lines and images of the poem will haunt the mind for years, continually growing in beauty and depth of meaning.

INTIMATIONS OF IMMORTALITY.

THERE was a time when meadow, grove, and stream,
The earth, and every common sight
  To me did seem
  Apparelled in celestial light,
The glory and the freshness of a dream.
It is not now as it hath been of yore ; —
  Turn wheresoe'er I may,
   By night or day,
The things which I have seen, I now can see no more.

The rainbow comes and goes, and lovely is the rose ;
  The moon doth with delight
Look round her when the heavens are bare ;
  Waters on a starry night
  Are beautiful and fair ;
 The sunshine is a glorious birth ;
 But yet I know, where'er I go,
That there hath passed away a glory from the earth.

Now, while the birds thus sing a joyous song,
  And while the young lambs bound
  As to the tabor's sound,
To me alone there came a thought of grief :
A timely utterance gave that thought relief,
  And I again am strong.
The cataracts blow their trumpets from the steep ; —
No more shall grief of mine the season wrong :

I hear the echoes through the mountains throng,
The winds come to me from the fields of sleep,
      And all the earth is gay ;
        Land and sea
     Give themselves up to jollity,
       And with the heart of May
    Doth every beast keep holiday ; —
      Thou child of joy,
Shout round me, let me hear thy shouts, thou happy Shepherd-boy !

Ye blessèd Creatures, I have heard the call
     Ye to each other make ; I see
The heavens laugh with you in your jubilee ;
     My heart is at your festival,
      My head hath its coronal —
The fullness of your bliss, I feel, I feel it all.
      O evil day ! if I were sullen
      While Earth herself is adorning,
        This sweet May-morning,
     And the children are culling
        On every side
     In a thousand valleys far and wide
    Fresh flowers ; while the sun shines warm,
And the babe leaps up on his mother's arm : —
     I hear, I hear, with joy I hear !
     — But there 's a tree, of many one,
A single field which I have looked upon, —
Both of them speak of something that is gone :
      The pansy at my feet
      Doth the same tale repeat :
Whither is fled the visionary gleam ?
Where is it now, the glory and the dream ?

Our birth is but a sleep and a forgetting ;
The Soul that rises with us, our life's Star,
     Hath had elsewhere its setting,
      And cometh from afar ;
     Not in entire forgetfulness,
     And not in utter nakedness,
But trailing clouds of glory, do we come
     From God, who is our home :
Heaven lies about us in our infancy !
Shades of the prison-house begin to close
     Upon the growing Boy,
But he beholds the light, and whence it flows,
     He sees it in his joy :

The Youth, who daily farther from the east
  Must travel, still is Nature's priest,
  And by the vision splendid
  Is on his way attended :
At length the Man perceives it die away,
And fade into the light of common day.

Earth fills her lap with pleasures of her own ;
Yearnings she hath in her own natural kind,
And, even with something of a mother's mind
  And no unworthy aim,
  The homely nurse doth all she can
To make her foster-child, her inmate, Man,
  Forget the glories he hath known,
And that imperial palace whence he came.

Behold the Child among his new-born blisses,
A six years' darling of a pigmy size !
See, where 'mid work of his own hand he lies,
Fretted by sallies of his mother's kisses,
With light upon him from his father's eyes !
See, at his feet, some little plan or chart,
Some fragment from his dream of human life,
Shaped by himself with newly-learnèd art ;
  A wedding or a festival,
  A mourning or a funeral ;
   And this hath now his heart,
  And unto this he frames his song :
   Then will he fit his tongue
To dialogues of business, love, or strife ;
  But it will not be long
  Ere this be thrown aside,
  And with new joy and pride
The little actor cons another part ;
Filling from time to time his "humorous stage"
With all the Persons, down to palsied Age,
That life brings with her in her equipage ;
  As if his whole vocation
  Were endless imitation.

Thou, whose exterior semblance doth belie
  Thy soul's immensity !
Thou best philosopher, who yet dost keep
Thy heritage ! thou eye among the blind,
That, deaf and silent, read'st the eternal deep,
Haunted for ever by the eternal mind, —

Mighty Prophet !   Seer blest !
On whom those truths do rest
Which we are toiling all our lives to find,
In darkness lost, the darkness of the grave !
Thou, over whom thy Immortality
Broods like the day, a master o'er a slave,
A Presence which is not to be put by !
Thou little child, yet glorious in the might
Of heaven-born freedom on thy being's height,
Why with such earnest pains dost thou provoke
The years to bring the inevitable yoke,
Thus blindly with thy blessedness at strife ?
Full soon thy soul shall have her earthly freight,
And custom lie upon thee with a weight
Heavy as frost, and deep almost as life !

O joy ! that in our embers
Is something that doth live,
That Nature yet remembers
What was so fugitive !
The thought of our past years in me doth breed
Perpetual benediction : not indeed
For that which is most worthy to be blest,
Delight and liberty, the simple creed
Of childhood, whether busy or at rest,
With new-fledged hope still fluttering in his breast : —
— Not for these I raise the song of thanks and praise ;
But for those obstinate questionings
Of sense and outward things,
Fallings from us, vanishings ;
Blank misgivings of a creature
Moving about in worlds not realized,
High instincts, before which our mortal nature
Did tremble like a guilty thing surprised :
But for those first affections,
Those shadowy recollections,
Which, be they what they may,
Are yet the fountain-light of all our day,
Are yet a master light of all our seeing ;
Uphold us, cherish, and have power to make
Our noisy years seem moments in the being
Of the eternal Silence : truths that wake,
To perish never ;
Which neither listlessness, nor mad endeavor,
Nor man nor boy,
Nor all that is at enmity with joy,
Can utterly abolish or destroy !

Hence in a season of calm weather
  Though inland far we be,
Our souls have sight of that immortal sea
  Which brought us hither —
  Can in a moment travel thither,
And see the children sport upon the shore,
And hear the mighty waters rolling evermore.

Then sing, ye birds, sing, sing a joyous song!
  And let the young lambs bound
  As to the tabor's sound!
We in thought will join your throng,
  Ye that pipe and ye that play,
  Ye that through your hearts to-day
  Feel the gladness of the May!
What though the radiance which was once so bright
Be now for ever taken from my sight,
Though nothing can bring back the hour
Of splendor in the grass, of glory in the flower;
  We will grieve not, rather find
  Strength in what remains behind;
  In the primal sympathy
  Which, having been, must ever be;
  In the soothing thoughts that spring
  Out of human suffering;
  In the faith that looks through death,
In years that bring the philosophic mind.

And O, ye Fountains, Meadows, Hills, and Groves,
Forebode not any severing of our loves!
Yet in my heart of hearts I feel your might;
I only have relinquished one delight
To live beneath your more habitual sway:
I love the brooks which down their channels fret,
Even more than when I tripped lightly as they;
The innocent brightness of a new-born day
  Is lovely yet;
The clouds that gather round the setting sun
Do take a sober coloring from an eye
That hath kept watch o'er man's mortality;
Another race hath been, and other palms are won.
Thanks to the human heart by which we live,
Thanks to its tenderness, its joys, and fears —
To me the meanest flower that blows can give
Thoughts that do often lie too deep for tears.

Wordsworth.

> HE, above the rest
> In shape and gesture proudly eminent,
> Stood like a tower : his form had yet not lost
> All her original brightness ; nor appear'd
> Less than arch-angel ruin'd, and the excess
> Of glory obscur'd : as when the sun, new risen,
> Looks through the horizontal misty air
> Shorn of his beams ; or from behind the moon,
> In dim eclipse, disastrous twilight sheds
> On half the nations, and with fear of change
> Perplexes monarchs.   Darken'd so, yet shone
> Above them all the arch-angel : but his face
> Deep scars of thunder had intrench'd, and care
> Sat on his faded cheek ; but under brows
> Of dauntless courage and considerate pride,
> Waiting revenge.

Milton.

XIII. FORMS OF POETRY.

As analytic definitions of poetry have never been satisfactory; as reason cannot explain imagination, nor science, poetry, — so adequate discriminations have rarely been made between lyric, epic, dramatic, and other forms of poetry. But the reader must feel and definitely manifest such differences through the natural languages, by realizing and expressing the imaginative and emotional activities of which these forms are the embodiment in words. Hence, a few suggestions may be given to assist or initiate the study of their essential nature.

A lyric is subjective and personal; it is the result of a vivid realization of some simple and specific situation. It is distinct from ballad poetry, which is narrative, and which produces its effect by a sequence of events. A lyric holds our interest by the pulsation of thought and feeling in the realization of this one idea or situation. Other pictures, situations, or events are brought up in contrast, or in some way are related to the one specific or governing event or idea. It may be the revelation of the love or tenderness of the human heart for some other soul, of the deepest experience face to face with great sorrow or great sin. It may be the expression of admiration for Nature, or of the worship of

God. Songs, hymns, and odes are forms of the lyric. They are nearly always short; and on account of their shortness, they are nearly always concentrated and intense.

There are an innumerable number of lyrics in the language; but, unfortunately, they are not often found in our school-readers. But a student can find large numbers of them in various collections; or, what is better, he can himself go to the great masters of poetry, where he will always find lyrics.

The Psalms are the most exalted examples of lyric expression. The reason is that they are the manifestation of an individual soul exalted or awakened by a thought of the Supreme Being. The nobility of the ideas, the simplicity and tenderness of the expression, the depth of insight, and the intensity of the passion have made these Psalms a medium of worship for the whole race.

Lyrics are the simplest of all forms of imaginative expression. They should, therefore, be first mastered by the student of vocal expression. When rightly practised, they have a wonderful effect upon the voice, tending to remove harshness, and developing sympathetic vibration and texture. The practice of a lyric tends to make the whole body, as well as the voice, responsive and flexible, and to bring them into sympathetic unity with the mind; such an exercise stimulates the breathing, and especially joyous lyrics furnish an exercise of untold value for health. Lyrics have been shown by the ablest authorities, such as Professor Norton, to be the most effective means of developing the imagination and the artistic nature. They develop insight; they secure the power to hold the mind in one simple specific situation; they secure control of feeling. They are short, and can be remembered and practised anywhere.

To read a lyric calls for such a vigorous exercise of the imagination as to awaken the reader's whole nature. The only way anything is made poetic is by intensity of realization. The reader must bring his imagination and whole nature to bear upon the specific situation until the thought and impulse are made personal and the expression spontaneous. All lyric art, especially poetry, must be the inevitable effect of the life and feeling caused by one situation.

Epic poetry is thought by many to be the most exalted form of poetry. It deals with a great era or epoch; it creates or portrays national types. It creates an Achilles as the representative or ideal of the Greeks, of their warlike spirit, their love of independence; it creates an Odysseus as the embodiment of that great people's conception of temperance, or " patience under trial by pleasure," long-suffering, and fortitude, or " patience under trial by pain, " — and so the Iliad and the Odyssey became a kind of Bible for the religion of a race. The epic is considered the most exalted form of poetry, because it unfolds not the ideal of an individual, but the ideal of a race. It portrays the subjective and objective combats of men; shows the individual and the nation their character and feeling, their struggles, failures, and successes.

The great epics are few, — such as the Iliad and the Odyssey, the Æneid, the Niebelungen Lied, the Divina Comedia, the Lusiad, Jerusalem Delivered, Paradise Lost; but narratives, tales, ballads, historical poems, and prose fiction are usually considered as belonging to lower forms of the epic. The highest epic work of the nineteenth century is possibly the " History of the French Revolution," by Carlisle.

The vocal rendering of the epic must be full of dignity. It must be ideal and noble; there must be simplicity and tenderness, deep emotions which are serious and noble, and which are felt by the whole race. Characters must be seen and felt as if alive; but they must also be typical. The whole nature of man must be awakened, and yet the expression must be extremely simple.

Dramatic poetry is objective. It is the human soul identifying itself with the point of view, the character, the feeling, the surroundings of another soul. It is the action or movement which is the expression of character; it is the conflict of soul with soul. It deals with the success or failure of life. Dramatic art deals with the motives and characteristics of men, and interprets the processes of developing or perverting character.

The lyric, the epic, and the dramatic are rarely separated completely from one another. In Homer's Iliad and Odyssey many of the dialogues are essentially dramatic. The finest parts of Milton's " Paradise Lost " are the lyrical outbursts of passion.

The Chorus was a lyric element which had a prominent place in the Greek drama. The lyrics in Shakespeare do not represent, as the Greek drama does, the audience, but are placed directly upon the stage as occasional songs. In Shakespeare's " Henry V.," where there are narrative links between the acts spoken by a so-called Chorus, there is an approach to the epic.

So akin are these forms of poetry that the reader must be able to render them all, in order to give any one form well. Dramatic without the lyric is apt to be imitative, and the lyric without the epic is apt to be too subjective. The true reader must, therefore, develop the mental and emotional action which causes these forms of poetry.

In speaking of the two forms of poetical impulse, — dramatic imagination and lyric or egoistic imagination, — Mr. Theodore Watts has made some valuable remarks which should be carefully weighed by the student of vocal expression: " The nature of this absolute vision, or true dramatic imagination, is easily seen if we compare the dramatic work of writers without absolute vision — such as Calderon, Goethe, Ben Jonson, Fletcher, and others — with the dramatic work of Æschylus and of Shakespeare. While of the former group it may be said that each poet skilfully works his imagination, of Æschylus and Shakespeare it must be said that each in his highest dramatic mood does not work, but is worked *by*, his imagination. Note, for instance, how the character of Clytæmnestra grows and glows under the hand of Æschylus. The poet of the Odyssey had distinctly said that Ægisthus, her paramour, had struck the blow; but the dramatist, having imagined the greatest tragic female in all poetry, finds it impossible to let a man like Ægisthus assist such a woman in a homicide so daring and so momentous. And when in that terrible speech of hers she justifies her crime (ostensibly to the outer world, but really to her own conscience), the way in which, by the sheer magnetism of irresistible personality, she draws our sympathy to herself and her crime is unrivalled out of Shakespeare, and not surpassed even there. In the great drama — in the Agamemnon, in Othello, in Hamlet, in Macbeth — there is an imagination at work whose laws are inexorable, are inevitable, as the laws by the operation of which the planets move round the sun." In another part of his essay, this high authority has said: "The artist's power of thought is properly shown not in the direct enunciation of ideas, but in mastery over motive." That is to say, the imagination is roused by the concentration of the mind of the writer upon the motive springs of character, and of his drama or story.

All this applies with double force to one who seeks to give expression to these sublime works. There must be a vision created by the dramatic imagination of the reader in epic or the higher dramatic forms of poetry, and a vivid scene so intensely realized and felt as to cause the inevitable modulations of the voice. The reader must not use or " skilfully work " his imagination; he must be moved *by* his imagination. The delicate textures, colors, and modulations of the voice, the supple actions of the face and of the body must be the direct result of poetic impulses.

As has been said, the full realization of the differences between the various forms of poetry cannot be attained by mere discussion. Poetry, like all art, must be felt and realized by each individual soul; for art is personal. It is " intrinsic, not extrinsic." It is only its surface that can be explained. The art faculties are too deep for complete rational analysis; their nature and energy must be felt in their exercise. Hence in the struggle to comprehend and to render any passage, the silent meditation over the masterpieces of poetry, followed by the effort to give them vocal interpretation, furnishes the best means of enabling any one to understand and to appreciate the essential nature of the sublimest forms of imaginative creation.

PROBLEM XVI. *Render passages from every form of poetry and literature, and note the peculiar action of the imagination in each case.*

SONG.

Ah ! my heart is pained with throbbing,
Throbbing for the May, —
Throbbing for the seaside billows,
Or the water-wooing willows,
Where in laughing and in sobbing
Glide the streams away.
Ah ! my heart, my heart is throbbing,
Throbbing for the May.

Waiting, sad, dejected, weary,
Waiting for the May,
Spring goes by with wasted warnings,
Moonlit evenings, sunbright mornings:
Summer comes, yet dark and dreary,
Life still ebbs away ;
Man is ever weary, weary,
Waiting for the May.

THE BROOKSIDE.

I WANDERED by the brookside, I wandered by the mill, —
I could not hear the brook flow, the noisy wheel was still ;
There was no burr of grasshopper, nor chirp of any bird,
But the beating of my own heart was all the sound I heard.

I sat beneath the elm-tree, I watched the long, long shade,
And as it grew still longer I did not feel afraid ;
For I listened for a footfall, I listened for a word, —
But the beating of my own heart was all the sound I heard.

He came not, — no, he came not : the night came on alone ;
The little stars sat one by one, each on his golden throne ;
The evening air passed by my cheek, the leaves above were stirred, —
But the beating of my own heart was all the sound I heard.

Fast silent tears were flowing, when something stood behind :
A hand was on my shoulder, — I knew its touch was kind :
It drew me nearer — nearer, — we did not speak one word,
For the beating of our own hearts was all the sound we heard.

Lord Houghton

How amiable are thy tabernacles,
O Lord of hosts !
My soul longeth, yea, even fainteth for the courts of the Lord ;
My heart and my flesh cry out unto the living God.
Yea, the sparrow hath found her an house,
And the swallow a nest for herself, where she may lay her young,
Even thine altars, O Lord of hosts,
My King, and my God.
Blessed are they that dwell in thy house :
They will be still praising thee [Selah.

Blessed is the man whose strength is in thee,
In whose heart are the high ways to Zion.
Passing through the valley of Weeping they make it a place of springs ;

Yea, the early rain covereth it with blessings.
They go from strength to strength,
Every one of them appeareth before God in **Zion.**
O Lord God of hosts, hear my prayer:
Give ear, O God of Jacob [Selah.

Behold, O God our shield,
And look upon the face of thine anointed.
For a day in thy courts is better than a thousand.
I had rather be a doorkeeper in the house of my **God**
Than to dwell in the tents of wickedness.
For the Lord God is a sun and a shield :.
The Lord will give grace and glory :
No good thing will he withhold from them that walk uprightly.
O Lord of hosts,
Blessed is the man that trusteth in thee.

Psalm lxxxiv

BUT up Achilles rose, the lov'd of Heaven ;
And Pallas on his mighty shoulders cast
The shield of Jove ; and round about his head
She put the glory of a golden mist,
From which there burnt a fiery-flaming light.
And as, when smoke goes heavenward from a town,
In some far island which its foes besiege,
Who all day long with dreadful martialness
Have poured from their own town ; soon as the sun
Has set, thick lifted fires are visible,
Which, rushing upward, make a light in the sky,
And let the neighbors know who may perhaps
Bring help across the sea, — so from the head
Of great Achilles went up an effulgence.
Upon the trench he stood, without the wall,
But mix'd not with the Greeks, for he rever'd
His mother's word : and so, thus standing there,
He shouted ; and Minerva, to his shout,
Added a dreadful cry ; and there arose
Among the Trojans an unspeakable tumult.
And as the clear voice of a trumpet, blown
Against a town by spirit-withering foes,
So sprang the clear voice of Æacides.
And when they heard the brazen cry, their hearts
All leap'd within them ; and the proud-maned horses
Ran with the chariots round, for they foresaw

> Calamity ; and the charioteers were smitten,
> When they beheld the ever-active fire
> Upon the dreadful head of the great-minded one
> Burning ; for bright-eyed Pallas made it burn.
> Thrice o'er the trench divine Achilles shouted ;
> And thrice the Trojans and their great allies
> Roll'd back ; and twelve of all their noblest men
> Then perish'd, crush'd by their own arms and chariots.

Iliad, book xviii. 203-231.   *Homer.*

————

He has witnessed overhead the infinite Deep, with greater and lesser lights, bright-rolling, silent-beaming, hurled forth by the hand of God ; around him and under his feet, the wonderfullest Earth, with her winter snow-storms and her summer spice-airs, and (unaccountablest of all) himself standing here. He stood in the lapse of Time ; he saw Eternity behind him and before him. The all-circling mysterious tide of Force, thousand-fold (for from force of thought to force of gravitation what an interval!) billowed shoreless on ; bore him along, — he too was part of it. From its bosom rose and vanished in perpetual change the lordliest Real-Phantasmagory (which was Being); and ever anew rose and vanished ; and ever that lordliest many-colored scene was full, another yet the same. Oak-trees fell, young acorns sprang : men too, new-sent from the Unknown, he met, of tiniest size, who waxed into stature, into strength of sinew, passionate fire and light : in other men the light was growing dim, the sinews all feeble ; they sank, motionless, into ashes, into invisibility; returned back to the Unknown, beckoning him their mute farewell. He wanders still by the parting spot ; cannot hear *them ;* they are far, how far! It was sight for angels and archangels ; for, indeed, God himself had made it wholly.

Carlyle.

————

LAST APPEARANCE OF LADY MACBETH.

Doctor. I have two nights watched with you, but can perceive no truth in your report. When was it she last walked ?

Gentlewoman. Since his Majesty went into the field, I have seen her rise from her bed, throw her night-gown upon her, unlock her closet, take forth paper, fold it, write upon it, read it, afterwards seal it, and again return to bed ; yet all this while in a most fast sleep.

Doc. A great perturbation in nature ! to receive at once the benefit of sleep, and do the effects of watching. In this slumbery agitation, besides her walking, and other actual performances, what, at any time, have you heard her say ?

Gen. That, sir, which I will not report after her.

Doc. You may, to me; and 't is most meet you should.

Gen. Neither to you, nor any one, — having no witness to confirm my speech. [*Enter Lady Macbeth, with a taper.*] Lo you, here she comes! This is her very guise; and, upon my life, fast asleep. Observe her; stand close.

Doc. How came she by that light?

Gen. Why, it stood by her: she has light by her continually; 't is her command.

Doc. You see, her eyes are open.

Gen. Ay, but their sense is shut.

Doc. What is it she does now? Look, how she rubs her hands.

Gen. It is an accustomed action with her, to seem thus washing her hands: I have known her continue in this a quarter of an hour.

Lady Macbeth. Yet, here 's a spot.

Doc. Hark! she speaks: I will set down what comes from her, to satisfy my remembrance the more strongly.

L. Macb. Out, damned spot! out, I say! — One; two: why, then 't is time to do 't. — Hell is murky! — Fie, my lord, fie! a soldier, and afeard? What need we fear who knows it, when none can call our power to account? — Yet who would have thought the old man to have had so much blood in him?

Doc. Do you mark that?

L. Macb. The thane of Fife had a wife: where is she now? — What, will these hands ne'er be clean? — No more o' that, my lord, no more o' that: you mar all with this starting.

Doc. Go to, go to! you have known what you should not.

Gen. She has spoke what she should not, I am sure of that: Heaven knows what she has known.

L. Macb. Here 's the smell of the blood still: all the perfumes of Arabia will not sweeten this little hand. Oh! Oh! Oh!

Doc. What a sigh is there! the heart is sorely charged.

Gen. I would not have such a heart in my bosom, for the dignity of the whole body.

Doc. Well, well, well, —

Gen. Pray God, it be, sir.

Doc. This disease is beyond my practice: yet I have known those which walked in their sleep, who have died holily in their beds.

L. Macb. Wash your hands, put on your night-gown; look not so pale: — I tell you yet again, Banquo 's buried; he cannot come out of his grave.

Doc. Even so?

L. Macb. To bed, to bed! there 's knocking at the gate. Come, come, come, come! give me your hand. What 's done cannot be undone: to bed, to bed, to bed! [*Exit Lady Macbeth.*

> *Doc.*   Will she go now to bed ?
> *Gen.*   Directly.
> *Doc.*   Foul whisperings are abroad.   Unnatural deeds
> Do breed unnatural troubles : infected minds
> To their deaf pillows will discharge their secrets.
> More needs she the divine than the physician. —
> God, God, forgive us all ! Look after her ;
> Remove from her the means of all annoyance,
> And still keep eyes upon her : — so, good-night.
> My mind she has mated, and amazed my sight :
> I think, but dare not speak.
>
> *Shakespeare.*

XIV. DEGREES OF IMAGINATION.

NOT only is imagination characteristic of all art and poetry, of all eloquence and beauty; not only is it the faculty which gives insight into the spiritual essence and loveliness of Nature and of all forms of human production, — but the degree of imagination is also the test of greatness in art.   The greater the activity of imagination embodied in a work of art, or awakened by its contemplation, the higher the rank of that work.

Art has been divided into the Beautiful, the Poetic, and the Sublime.   A painting, a poem, or a story may have the simplest subject for its theme.   A painting may represent a mere reflection of light upon a barn, and be beautiful.   A poem upon a daisy or a bluebird may be imaginative and pleasing.   The greatness of a work of art is not dependent upon its subject except in so far as this subject is a means of revealing insight.   When such an object as a pool of water or some aspect of light and shade is the motive of a painting, or a brook the subject of a poem, the imagination may be present and the work may be made beautiful; but it is not the highest exercise of the faculty.

But whenever the human soul is portrayed with an object, though it be a mere pool of water; whenever the object becomes a mirror of the heart of man, of his love of Nature, his gloom or his hope, his earnestness, his sincerity, and his realization of life and the universe, — art then becomes poetic.   Anything is poetic in proportion as the human soul becomes the central element.   Human loves, human interests, human suffering and aspiration, these are really the subjects of poetry. Outward objects are the mere means of expression

Art, however, can go further. It is sublime in proportion as the human element preponderates. In beautiful art the natural preponderates. In poetic art the human and the natural elements are in equipoise. In sublime art the human preponderates over the medium or the language, which is suggestive and in the background. In sublime art the idea is all absorbing; it must be so great as to overshadow the form; it must lift the soul above and beyond any external object or accident.

Science, it is said, is always impersonal. Art is always personal. Great art is dependent upon the ascendency of the personal element over the impersonal.

It is the imagination that makes the universe personal; that " conforms the outward show of things to the desires of the mind ; " that penetrates below mere facts to truth; that throws aside all superficial accidents. It is the imagination that enables the human mind to disengage itself from a prison of literal facts.

The whole struggle for expression is, after all, dependent upon the manifestations of the soul through the tones and modulations of the voice and the body. Whenever the imagination and the passions are united, and the voice and the body are made subordinate, or brought into such control that the action of imagination and feeling is at once seen through them, the first step in training has been taken.

Dobson's " Song of Four Seasons " is beautiful. There is, of course, some imagination required, but the action of the faculty is not very high. But in such a poem as Gosse's " Return of the Swallows, " while there is not the highest activity of the imagination, the mind is yet called upon to carry a more ideal conception. The same is true of Browning's " Apparitions " and " Love among the Ruins, " of Tennyson's " Bugle Song " and " Day Dream." But such poems as Shelley's " Ode to the West Wind, " " Prometheus Unbound, " Coleridge's " Ode to France, " Wordsworth's " Ode on Immortality, " some portions of Job, and the Prophecy of Isaiah, are rightly termed sublime.

PROBLEM XVII. — *Distinguish by vocal expression that which is simply beautiful from that which is more profound, that which is poetic from that which is more sublime.*

A SONG OF THE FOUR SEASONS.

WHEN Spring comes laughing by vale and hill,
By wind-flower walking and daffodil, —
Sing stars of morning, sing morning skies,
Sing blue of speedwell, — and my Love's eyes.

When comes the Summer full-leaved and strong,
And gay birds gossip the orchard long, —
Sing hid, sweet honey that no bee sips;
Sing red, red roses, — and my Love's lips.

When Autumn scatters the leaves again,
And piled sheaves bury the broad-wheeled wain, —
Sing flutes of harvest where men rejoice;
Sing rounds of reapers, — and my Love's voice.

But when comes Winter with hail and storm,
And red fire roaring and ingle warm, —
Sing first sad going of friends that part:
Then sing glad meeting, — and my Love's heart.

Austin Dobson.

THE RETURN OF THE SWALLOWS.

"OUT in the meadows the young grass springs,
  Shivering with sap," said the larks, "and we
Shoot into air with our strong young wings,
  Spirally up over level and lea;
Come, O Swallows, and fly with us,
Now that horizons are luminous!
    Evening and morning the world of light,
    Spreading and kindling, is infinite!"

Far away, by the sea in the south,
  The hills of olive and slopes of fern
Whiten and glow in the sun's long drouth,
  Under the heavens that beam and burn;
And all the swallows were gathered there
Flitting about in the fragrant air,
    And heard no sound from the larks, but flew
    Flashing under the blinding blue.

Out of the depths of their soft rich throats
  Languidly fluted the thrushes, and said :
" Musical thought in the mild air floats,
  Spring is coming and winter is dead !
Come, O Swallows, and stir the air,
For the buds are all bursting unaware,
  And the drooping eaves and the elm-trees long
  To hear the sound of your low sweet song.

Over the roofs of the white Algiers,
  Flashingly shadowing the bright bazaar,
Flitted the swallows, and not one hears
  The call of the thrushes from far, from far :
Sighed the thrushes ; then, all at once,
Broke out singing the old sweet tones, —
  Singing the bridal of sap and shoot,
  The tree's slow life between root and fruit.

But just when the dingles of April flowers
  Shine with the earliest daffodils,
When, before sunrise, the cold clear hours
  Gleam with a promise that noon fulfils, —
Deep in the leafage the cuckoo cried,
Perched on a spray by a rivulet-side,
  " Swallows, O Swallows, come back again
  To swoop and herald the April rain."

And something awoke in the slumbering heart
  Of the alien birds in their African air,
And they paused, and alighted, and twittered apart,
  And met in the broad white dreamy square ;
And the sad slave woman, who lifted up
From the fountain her broad-lipped earthen cup,
  Said to herself, with a weary sigh,
  " To-morrow the swallows will northward fly !"

Edmund William Gosse.

THOU deadly crater, moulded by my muse,
  Cast thou thy bronze into my bowed and wounded heart,
  And let my soul its vengeance to thy bronze impart.

On the cannon purchased by receipts from his public readings.   Victor Hugo.

THOU who passest by, say at Lacedaemon we lie here in obedience to her laws.

Inscription at Thermopile.   Simonides.

When, loved by poet and painter, the sunrise fills the sky ;
When night's gold urns grow fainter, and in depths of amber die ;
When the moon-breeze stirs the curtain, bearing an odorous freight, —
Then visions strange, uncertain, pour thick through the Ivory Gate.

Then the oars of Ithaca dip so silently into the sea,
That they wake not sad Calypso — and the Hero wanders free :
He breasts the ocean-furrows, at war with the winds of Fate ;
And the blue tide's low susurrus comes up to the Ivory Gate.

The Ivory Gate.   *Mortimer Collins.*

Sweet nurselings of the vernal skies,
   Bath'd in soft airs, and fed with dew,
What more than magic in you lies,
   To fill the heart's fond view ?
In childhood's sports, companions gay,
In sorrow, on Life's downward way,
How soothing ! in our last decay
   Memorials prompt and true.

Ye dwell beside our paths and homes, —
   Our paths of sin, our homes of sorrow ;
And guilty man, where'er he roams,
   Your innocent mirth may borrow.
The birds of air before us fleet,
They cannot brook our shame to meet —
But we may taste your solace sweet,
   And come again to-morrow.

Flowers.   *Keble.*

Where wast thou when I laid the foundations of the earth ?
Declare, if thou hast understanding.
Who determined the measures thereof, if thou knowest ?
Or who stretched the line upon it ?
Whereupon were the foundations thereof fastened ?
Or who laid the corner-stone thereof,
When the morning stars sang together,
And all the sons of God shouted for joy ?
Or who shut up the sea with doors,
When it brake forth, as if it had issued out of the womb, —
When I made the cloud the garment thereof,
And thick darkness a swaddling-band for it,
And prescribed for it my decree,
And set bars and doors,
And said, Hitherto shalt thou come, but no farther ;
And here shall thy proud waves be stayed ?

Book of Job.

ALAS ! they had been friends in youth ;
But whispering tongues can poison truth,
And constancy lives in realms above ;
And life is thorny, and youth is vain ;
And to be wroth with one we love
Doth work like madness in the brain.
And thus it chanced, as I divine,
With Roland and Sir Leoline.
Each spake words of high disdain
And insult to his heart's best brother:
They parted — ne'er to meet again !
But never either found another
To free the hollow heart from paining:
They stood aloof, the scars remaining,
Like cliffs which had been rent asunder ;
A dreary sea now flows between,
But neither heat nor frost nor thunder
Shall wholly do away, I ween,
The marks of that which once hath been.

Christabel.   *Coleridge.*

XV. USES OF IMAGINATION.

THE imagination is characteristic of every form of art and literature. There may be a poetic building or statue or painting, a poetic singer or reader, a poetic story in prose. Imagination is the faculty, poetry is the product. It is the faculty which sees through the actual to the ideal. It is the only power that can idealize the real, and realize the ideal. It is for this reason that imagination is so potent in the development of character.

The functions it discharges, the uses it serves, the forms it takes, are innumerable. One of the earliest objective forms is the myth. These show the early efforts of the race to interpret natural phenomena; the rising and the setting of the sun, the drifting clouds, the wandering and changing moon, embody the universal conceptions of the meaning of human life. The mythopœic instinct is an action of the imagination, and while many myths may have come down from barbarous ages and contain elements of cruelty, they are the products of this faculty. The myth is a struggle of the imagination to interpret life and to solve the riddle of the Sphinx.

The mythopœic faculty is supposed by many to be lost in modern civilization ; but the same power that created the myth of Apollo, or traced the meaning of Athene and the Dawn, is still active in man's mind. We still speak of the dawn of a new civilization. " Morning " has an imaginative and poetical as well as a literal meaning.

Again, folk-lore and fairy tales are the products of the imagination; and poets of our own day, consciously or unconsciously, often adopt the same form for the interpretation of the truth. Tennyson's " Day-Dream " is a part of his embodiment of the old fairy story of the Sleeping Beauty.

THE DEPARTURE.

AND on her lover's arm she leant,
   And round her waist she felt it fold,
And far across the hills they went
   In that new world which is the old :
Across the hills, and far away
   Beyond their utmost purple rim,
And deep into the dying day
   The happy princess follow'd him.

And o'er them many a sliding star,
   And many a merry wind was borne,
And, stream'd thro' many a golden bar,
   The twilight melted into morn. . . .
And o'er them many a flowing range
   Of vapor buoy'd the crescent bark,
And, rapt thro' many a rosy change,
   The twilight died into the dark.

" A hundred summers ! can it be ?
   And whither goest thou, tell me where ? "
" Oh, seek my father's court with me,
   For there are greater wonders there."
And o'er the hills, and far away
   Beyond their utmost purple rim,
Beyond the night, across the day,
   Thro' all the world she follow'd him.

The Day-Dream.   *Tennyson.*

Again, imagination is a faculty most important to oratory ; eloquence is one of its most immediate manifestations. The speaker needs imagination for the exaltation of his theme. He must give "a local habitation and a name" to mystic and abstract truths, must feel and make others feel the truth. The most abstract idea must be given concrete expression. The heart cannot be moved without a concrete or poetic embodiment of that which would otherwise be vaguely and dimly realized. The most important truth may be so given that its entire force is lost. Truth stated in mere abstract terms, or expressed in cold, hard tones by the voice, not only fails to kindle the heart, but it may awaken doubt, cool enthusiasm, and cause indifference. Unless the speaker gives an exalted vision, he will not awaken or elevate the conceptions of ordinary people. True oratory demands an active use of the imagination. The real office of oratory is to show truth as an object worthy to be sought. It aims not so much to teach or to give men new truth as to awaken a more vivid conception of a truth already known, and to stir deeper feeling, and to awaken a living motive for action. Oratory calls upon men to give their lives for their homes, for their country, or for the cause of truth. It aims to bring them to a more intense realization of their own ideals and convictions.

PROBLEM XVIII. *Study and read selections showing various uses of the imagination by the historian, the speaker, the story-teller, and the poet, and observe their peculiarities.*

THE Danube to the Severn gave
    The darken'd heart that beats no more ;
    They laid him by the pleasant shore,
And in the hearing of the wave.

There twice a day the Severn fills ;
    The salt sea-water passes by,
    And hushes half the babbling Wye,
And makes a silence in the hills.

In Memoriam.   *Tennyson.*

OUR fathers raised their flag against a power to which, for purposes of foreign conquest and subjugation, Rome in the height of her glory is not to be compared, — a power which has dotted the surface of the whole globe with her possessions and military posts ; whose morning drum-beat, following the sun in his course, and keeping pace with the hours, circles the earth with one continuous and unbroken strain of the martial airs of England.   *Webster.*

AGITATION means liberty. As health lies in labor, and there is no royal road to it but through toil, so there is no republican road to safety but in constant distrust. "In distrust," said Demosthenes, "are the nerves of the mind." Let us see to it that these sentinel nerves are ever on the alert. If the Alps, piled in cold and still sublimity, be the emblem of Despotism, the ever-restless ocean is ours, which, girt within the eternal laws of gravitation, is pure only because never still.

Wendell Phillips.

To those who live by faith, everything they see speaks of that future world; the very glories of Nature, the sun, moon, and stars, and the richness and the beauty of the earth, are as types and figures, witnessing and teaching the invisible things of God. All that we see is destined one day to burst forth into a heavenly bloom, and to be transfigured into immortal glory. Heaven at present is out of sight; but in due time, as snow melts and discovers what it lay upon, so will this visible creation fade away before those greater splendors which are behind it, and on which at present it depends. In that day shadows will retire, and the substance show itself. The sun will grow pale and be lost in the sky, but it will be before the radiance of Him whom it does but image, the Sun of Righteousness. . . . Our own mortal bodies will then be found in like manner to contain within them an inner man, which will then receive its due proportions, as the soul's harmonious organ, instead of the gross mass of flesh and blood which sight and touch are sensible of.

Newman.

WE are like southern plants, taken up to a northern climate and planted in a northern soil. They grow there, but they are always failing of their flowers. The poor exiled shrub dreams by a native longing of a splendid blossom which it has never seen, but is dimly conscious that it ought somehow to produce. It feels like the flower which it has not strength to make in the half-chilled but still genuine juices of its southern nature. That is the way in which the ideal life, the life of full completions, haunts us all. Nothing can really haunt us except what we have the beginning of, the native capacity for, however hindered, in ourselves. The highest angel does not tempt us because he is of another race from us; but God is our continual incitement because we are His children. So the ideal life is in our blood, and never will be still. We feel the thing we ought to be beating beneath the thing we are. Every time we see a man who has attained our human idea a little more fully than we have, it wakens our languid blood and fills us with new longings. When we see Christ, it is as if a new plant out of the southern soil were brought suddenly in among its poor stunted, transplanted brethren, and, blossoming in their sight, interpreted to each of them the restlessness and discontent which was in each of their poor hearts. When, led by Christ, we see God, it is as if the stunted, flowerless plants grew tall enough to stand up and look across all the miles that lie between, and see the glory of the perfect plant as it blooms in unhindered luxuriance in its southern home. And when we die and go to God, it is as if at last the poor shrub were plucked out of its exile and taken back and set where it belonged, in the rich soil, under the warm sun, where the patience which it had learned in its long waiting should make all the deeper and richer the flower into which its experience was set free to find its utterance.

The Withheld Completions of Life.   *Phillips Brooks.*

THEY gave their lives for their country, and gained for themselves a glory that can never fade, a tomb that shall stand as a mark forever. I do not mean that in which their bodies lie, but in which their renown lives after them, to be remembered forever on every occasion of speech or action which calls it to mind. For the whole earth is the grave and monument of heroes. It is not the mere graving upon marble in their native land which sets forth their deeds; but even in lands where they were strangers there lives an unwritten record in every heart — felt, though never embodied.

Funeral Oration.   *Pericles.*

XVI. FREEDOM OF THE IMAGINATION.

HE who, having no touch of the Muse's madness in his soul, comes to the door and thinks he will get into the temple by the help of Art, — he, I say, and his poetry, are not admitted.   *Plato.*

IMAGINATION is original; its action differs as widely as men do. Compare the imagination of Milton, for example, with that of any other author who has written in the English language. We find a peculiarity in him distinct from all others. He sees all objects in human form. His imagination acts in accordance with the mythopœic instinct of the Greeks. If he had been an artist, he would have been a sculptor. Take " L'Allegro," one of the simplest of his poems. Every little relation or effect of joy is here embodied in a plastic form. Quips, cranks, wiles, nods, laughter, and care are all transformed into living beings.

> HASTE thee, Nymph, and bring with thee
> Jest and youthful jollity,
> Quips and cranks and wanton wiles,
> Nods and becks, and wreathèd smiles
> Such as hang on Hebe's cheek,
> And love to live in dimple sleek ;
> Sport that wrinkled Care derides,
> And Laughter holding both his sides, —
> Come, and trip it as you go
> On the light fantastic toe ;
> And in thy right hand lead with thee
> The mountain nymph, sweet Liberty ;
> And if I give thee honour due
> Mirth, admit me of thy crew,
> To live with her, and live with thee
> In unreprovèd pleasures free.
>
> *Milton.*

Contrast this with Wordsworth, who if he had been an artist would probably have been a musician. So peculiar and distinct is the action of Wordsworth's imagination, that Coleridge said of certain lines that if he had met them in the wilds of Africa, he would have cried out " Wordsworth ! "

> I HEARD a stock-dove sing, or say,
> His homely tale this very day ;
> His voice was buried among trees,
> Yet to be come at by the breeze ;
> He did not cease, but cooed and cooed,
> And somewhat pensively he wooed :
> He sang of love with quiet blending,
> Slow to begin, and never ending ;
> Of serious faith and inward glee :
> That was the song — the song for me !
>
> *Wordsworth.*

How different is the imagination of Shelley! If he had been an artist, he would certainly have been a painter. No one but a painter's eye could have seen this beautiful picture : —

> WE paused beside the pools that lie under the forest bough ;
> Each seemed as 't were a little sky gulfed in a world below, —
> A firmament of purple.light, which in the dark earth lay,
> More boundless than the depth of night, and purer than the day ;
> In which the lovely forests grew, as in the upper air,
> More perfect both in shape and hue than any spreading there.

There lay the glade and neighbouring lawn, and through the dark green wood
The white sun twinkling like the dawn out of a speckled cloud.
Sweet views, which in our world above can never well be seen,
Were imaged by the water's love of that fair forest green.
And all was interfused beneath with an Elysian glow,
An atmosphere without a breath, a softer day below.
Like one beloved the scene had lent to the dark water's breast
Its every leaf and lineament with more than truth exprest,
Until an envious wind crept by, like an unwelcome thought,
Which from the mind's too faithful eye blots one dear image out.

THE WORLD'S WANDERERS.

TELL me, thou Star, whose wings of light
Speed thee in thy fiery flight,
In what cavern of the night
   Will thy pinions close now?

Tell me, Moon, thou pale and gray
Pilgrim of heaven's homeless way,
In what depth of night or day
   Seekest thou repose now?

Weary Wind, who wanderest
Like the world's rejected guest,
Hast thou still some secret nest
   On the tree or billow?

A Fragment.   *Shelley.*

Now, if the imagination acts differently in each author, it must act differently in each reader. A reader must be free to use his imagination in his own way; and true education will not interfere with his freedom, but will rather seek to develop differences and peculiarities.

Imagination is not limited to any set of subjects. It may deal with a simple description, or with a deep philosophic truth. It may serve to lift the most familiar and commonplace objects into right relations with the infinite and eternal; or it may touch the most profound truth, and bring it home to the heart.

Then, again, one author may lift his whole poem to an exalted height. In all his poems Tennyson "pitches the style at a high artistic level, from which he never once descends. Image follows image, picture succeeds picture,—each perfect, rich in color, clear in outline." Every line satisfies the most fastidious taste. Imagination envelops the whole. You do not pick out single lines as gems from Tennyson as you do from other authors. His imagination is concerned more in giving the whole an exaltation and coloring rather than in producing transcendent beauties in particular phrases or lines or passages.

ART AND SORROW.

On that last night before we went
 From out the doors where I was bred,
 I dreamed a vision of the dead,
Which left my after-morn content.

Methought I dwelt within a hall,
 And maidens with me : distant hills
 From hidden summits fed with rills
A river sliding by the wall.

The hall with harp and carol rang.
 They sang of what is wise and good
 And graceful.   In the centre stood
A statue veiled, to which they sang ;

And which, tho' veiled, was known to me, —
 The shape of him I loved, and love
 Forever : then flew in a dove
And brought a summons from the sea.

And when they learnt that I must go,
 They wept and wailed, but led the way
 To where a little shallop lay
At anchor in the flood below ;

And on by many a level mead,
 And shadowing bluff that makes the banks,
 We glided winding under ranks
Of iris, and the golden weed ;

And still as vaster grew the shore,
 And rolled the floods in grander space,
 The maidens gathered strength and grace
And presence, lordlier than before ;

And I myself, who sat apart
 And watched them, waxed in every limb :
 I felt the thews of Anakim,
The pulses of a Titan's heart :

As one would sing the death of war,
  And one would chant the history
  Of that great race which is to be,
And one the shaping of a star;

Until the forward-creeping tides
  Began to foam, and we to draw
  From deep to deep, to where we saw
A great ship lift her shining sides.

The man we loved was there on deck,
  But thrice as large a man he bent
  To greet us.   Up the side I went,
And fell in silence on his neck.

Whereat those maidens with one mind
  Bewailed their lot : I did them wrong.
  "We served thee here," they said, "so long,
And wilt thou leave us now behind?"

So rapt I was, they could not win
  An answer from my lips ; but he
  Replying, " Enter likewise ye
And go with us :" they entered in.

And while the wind began to sweep
  A music out of sheet and shroud,
  We steered her toward a crimson cloud
That land-like swept along the deep.

In Memoriam.   *Tennyson.*

How different it is with Wordsworth!   In his verse the most commonplace lines can be found; but occasionally the imagination has sudden flashes that seem to come from the very heart of Nature or the depth of the poet's soul.

Some one has said that Tennyson moves ever upon the mountain tops, but that Wordsworth quietly and simply descends to the smallest nooks and valleys.   His course is more uneven; he is concerned in a truly simple and natural way with the very least objects, while arising at times to the sublimest heights.

Note, for example, in the following extract, how quietly and simply he discusses a most ordinary event, and then toward the close how he suddenly passes with such imaginative force to the "central peace, subsisting at the heart of endless agitation."

I HAVE seen
A curious child, who dwelt upon a tract
Of inland ground, applying to his ear
The convolutions of a smooth-lipped shell ;
To which, in silence hushed, his very soul
Listened intensely ; and his countenance soon
Brightened with joy : for from within were heard
Murmurings, whereby the monitor expressed
Mysterious union with its native sea.
Even such a shell the universe itself
Is to the ear of Faith ; and there are times,
I doubt not, when to you it doth impart
Authentic tidings of invisible things, —
Of ebb and flow, and ever-during power ;
And *central peace, subsisting at the heart
Of endless agitation.*   Here you stand,
Adore, and worship, when you know it not ;
Pious beyond the intention of your thought ;
Devout above the meaning of your will.
Yes, you have felt, and may not cease to feel.

Wordswort.

Brougham has criticised Burke upon the passage here abridged, and upon his use of the figure of the gathering storm, and has compared it with the same figure in Demosthenes.

Professor Jebb says, however, that this is a failure to appreciate the different points of view. "Burke is a painter ; Demosthenes is a sculptor." That is to say, the imagination of the two men acted in a different way ; and it is very imperfect criticism that will compare the difference in the creative actions of their minds to the disparagement of either orator. The imagination in every human being is more or less peculiar and different. The imagination never copies or imitates. Whenever it is true it is original. It was impossible for Burke, with his modern training, to have portrayed his images like one educated beneath the Parthenon.

DESTRUCTION OF THE CARNATIC.

WHEN at length Hyder Ali found that he had to do with men who either would sign no convention, or whom no treaty and no signature could bind, and who were the determined enemies of human intercourse itself, he decreed to make the country possessed by these incorrigible and predestinated criminals a memorable example to mankind. He resolved, in the gloomy recesses of a mind capacious of such things, to leave the whole Carnatic an everlasting monument of vengeance, and to put perpetual desolation as a barrier between him and those against whom the faith which holds the moral elements of the world together was no protection.

. . . He drew from every quarter whatever a savage ferocity could add to his new rudiments in the art of destruction; and compounding all the materials of fury, havoc, and desolation into one black cloud, he hung for a while on the declivities of the mountains. Whilst the authors of all these evils were idly and stupidly gazing on this menacing meteor, which blackened all their horizon, it suddenly burst, and poured down the whole of its contents upon the plains of the Carnatic.

Then ensued a scene of woe, the like of which no eye had seen, no heart conceived, and of which no tongue can adequately tell. All the horrors of war before known or heard of were mercy to that new havoc. A storm of universal fire blasted every field, consumed every house, destroyed every temple. The miserable inhabitants, flying from their flaming villages, in part were slaughtered; others, without regard to sex, to age, to the respect of rank or sacredness of function, — fathers torn from children, husbands from wives, enveloped in a whirlwind of cavalry, and amidst the goading spears of drivers and the trampling of pursuing horses, — were swept into captivity in an unknown and hostile land. Those who were able to evade this tempest fled to the walled cities; but escaping from fire, sword, and exile, they fell into the jaws of famine. . . . So completely did these masters of their art — Hyder Ali and his more ferocious son — absolve themselves of their impious vow, that, when the British armies traversed, as they did, the Carnatic for hundreds of miles in all directions, through the whole line of their march they did not see one man, not one woman, not one child, not one four-footed beast of any description whatever. One dead, uniform silence reigned over the whole region. *Burke.*

THE people gave their voice, and the danger that hung upon our borders went by like a cloud. *Demosthenes.*

> WITH that I saw two swans of goodly hue
> Come softly swimming down along the lee :
> Two fairer birds I yet did never see ;
> The snow which doth the top of Pindus strow
> Did never whiter show ;
> Nor Jove himself, when he a swan would be
> For love of Leda, whiter did appear.

Yet Leda was (they say) as white as he,
Yet not so white as these, nor nothing near;
So purely white they were
That even the gentle stream, the which them bare,
Seem'd foul to them, and bade his billows spare
To wet their silken feathers, lest they might
Soil their fair plumes with water not so fair,
And mar their beauties bright
That shone as Heaven's light
Against their bridal day, which was not long.
    Sweet Thames! run softly, till I end my song.

From " Prothalamion."

ITYLUS.

Swallow, my sister, O sister swallow,
    How can thine heart be full of the spring?
        A thousand summers are over and dead.
What hast thou found in the spring to follow?
    What hast thou found in thy heart to sing?
        What wilt thou do when the summer is shed?

O swallow, sister, O fair swift swallow,
    Why wilt thou fly after spring to the south, —
        The soft south, whither thine heart is set?
Shall not the grief of the old time follow?
    Shall not the song thereof cleave to thy mouth?
        Hast thou forgotten ere I forget?

Sister, my sister, O fleet sweet swallow,
    Thy way is long to the sun and the south;
        But I, fulfilled of my heart's desire,
Shedding my song upon height, upon hollow,
    From tawny body and sweet small mouth
        Feed the heart of the night with fire.

I, the nightingale, all spring through,
    O swallow, sister, O changing swallow,
        All spring through, till the spring be done,
Clothed with the light of the night on the dew, —
    Sing, while the hours and the wild birds follow,
        Take flight and follow and find the sun.
        .   .   .   .

O sweet stray sister, O shifting swallow,
    The heart's division divideth us.
        Thy heart is light as a leaf of a tree,
But mine goes forth among sea-gulfs hollow,
    To the place of the slaying of Itylus,
        The feast of Daulis, the Thracian Sea.

O swallow, sister, O rapid swallow,
  I pray thee sing not a little space.
    Are not the roofs and the lintels wet ?
The woven web that was plain to follow,
  The small slain body, the flower-like face,
    Can I remember if thou forget?

O sister, sister, thy first-begotten !
  The hands that cling and the feet that follow,
    The voice of the child's blood crying yet,
" Who hath remembered me ? who hath forgotten ?"
  Thou hast forgotten, O summer swallow,
    But the world shall end when I forget.

Swinburne.

To me it is a most touching face ; perhaps of all the faces that I know, the most so. Blank there, painted on vacancy, with the simple laurel wound round it ; the deathless sorrow and pain, the known victory which is also deathless ; significant of the whole history of Dante! I think it is the mournfullest face that ever was painted from reality ; an altogether tragic, heart-affecting face. There is in it, as foundation of it, the softness, tenderness, gentle affection as of a child; but all this is as if congealed into sharp contradiction, into abnegation, isolation, proud, hopeless pain. A soft ethereal soul looking out so stern, implacable, grim-trenchant, as from imprisonment of thick-ribbed ice ! Withal it is a silent pain, too, — a silent, scornful one : the lip is curled in a kind of god-like disdain of the thing that is eating out his heart, — as if it .were, withal, a mean, insignificant thing; as if he whom it had power to torture and strangle were greater than it. The face of one wholly in protest, and life-long, unsurrendering battle, against the world, affection all converted into indignation, — an implacable indignation ; slow, equable, implacable, silent, like that of a god ! The eye, too, it looks out as in a kind of surprise, a kind of inquiry, Why was the world of such a sort ? This is Dante : so he looks, this " voice of ten silent centuries," and sings us his " mystic, unfathomable song."

The Face of Dante.   *Carlyle.*

WHAT needs my Shakespeare for his honoured bones
The labour of an age in pilèd stones,
Or that his hallowed reliques should be hid
Under a star-y pointing pyramid ?
Dear son of Memory, great heir of Fame,
What need'st thou such weak witness of thy name ?
Thou in our wonder and astonishment
Hast built thyself a livelong monument.

> For whilst to th' shame of slow-endeavouring Art
> Thy easy numbers flow, and that each heart
> Hath from the leaves of thy unvalued book
> Those Delphic lines with deep impression took, —
> Then thou our fancy of itself bereaving,
> Dost make us marble with too much conceiving;
> And so sepulchered, in such pomp dost lie,
> That kings for such a tomb would wish to die.
>
> *Milton.*

XVII. MISCONCEPTIONS AND ABUSES.

OF all the faculties the imagination is most frequently misconceived. To many it is simply the faculty of hallucination. Even some painters of the realistic type have declared imagination a hindrance to artistic work. These entirely overlook the fact that the greatest realist must give imaginative feeling to a simple touch of his brush, or he is not an artist.

Imagination does not deceive. Deceit is an abuse of the faculty. It does not cause delusion; it may create artistic illusion, but in this it looks through the external to the internal, through the body to the spirit. It uses facts to find truth. " It is, indeed, pre-eminently a truthful and truth-seeing power, perceiving subtle aspects of truth, hidden relations, far-reaching analogies, which find no entrance to us by any other inlet."

Again, imagination is not extravagant; fancy may exaggerate, but the imagination, never. Imagination is not a drunken, a flippant, or a trivial faculty. It does not dissipate noble emotion, but lies at the heart of our deepest experience.

Again, imagination is not a mere decorative faculty; it sees and creates beauty, but it does not adorn superficially. Its beauty is unfolded from the heart. It is not a faculty for fantastic or fictitious visions. Its highest characteristic is depth of insight. It must not be judged by its perversions and diseases, or by its lower functions, but by its highest and noblest characteristics. Its climax is not the literal fact, but truth. It never acts apart from truth. It is the faculty of all faculties that deals with the heart of things and the heart of man.

Again, imagination is not mere composition. Some one has said that man has the power to arrange and adjust his ideas, subordinate one and accentuate another; but this power he does not have over Nature. This arranging is, however, rather composition than imagination. When the arrangement is such as to manifest the ideal, when it is a spontaneous creation, it may be imaginative; but the imagination never acts mechanically. It does not construct and build; it gives life that unfolds itself in growth.

"Fancy," says Ruskin, "as she stays at the externals, can never feel. She is one of the hardest-hearted of the intellectual faculties, or rather one of the most purely and simply intellectual. She cannot be made serious, — no edge-tools but she will play with; whereas the imagination is in all things the reverse. She cannot be but serious; she sees too far, too darkly, too solemnly, too earnestly, ever to smile. There is something in the heart of everything, if we can reach it, that we shall not be inclined to laugh at."

The imagination is of all faculties most capable of abuse. It must be trained to use the material of real knowledge. There must be no sickly desire to run away from simple facts to that which is extravagant, unnatural, and untrue.

The imagination has much to do with moral life and character, and is kept from abuse by a perception of the true spirit of all things, by the moral and intellectual balance of the whole man; again, the imagination is kept normal by careful observation and thorough investigation. One of the worst abuses is calling upon it for facts as a substitute for hard work and earnest study to find the truth. "The gentleman calls upon his imagination for his facts and his memory for his tropes" was a witty reference to the perversion of each faculty. Lastly, man's creative powers are kept strong and true by constant study of the best poetry and art.

Some think that imagination must create some kind of ideal conception without materials for such a poem as Psalm xlvi. But true imagination finds the specific situation and the historical occasion as far as possible, and founds its creations upon truth. The situation is supposed by many of the best scholars to be after the destruction of the Assyrian hosts of Sennacherib.

The true reader will first study this great event, and his imagination out of the dry facts will create a living scene, and cause him to stand on the morning after that great relief and feel with those who poured forth their thanksgiving in such a noble ode.

THE GREAT DELIVERANCE.

God is our refuge and strength,
A very present help in trouble.
Therefore will we not fear though the earth be shaken ;
Though the mountains tremble on their bases in the heart of the seas.
Let the waters roar and foam !
Let the mountains shake before their waves !

There is a river whose streams make glad the city of God,
The holy place of the dwellings of the Most High !
God is in her midst ; she shall not be moved.
God shall help her, with the morning dawn.
The nations raged ; their kingdoms were moved against us ;
He uttered His voice, and the earth melted with fear !
The Lord of Hosts is with us ;
The God of Jacob is our refuge.

Come, behold the deeds of Jehovah,
What wondrous things He has done in the earth ;
He makes wars to cease to the end of the earth !
He breaks the bow; He snaps the spear asunder;
He burns the war chariot in the fire !

" Be still, and know that I am God ;
I will be exalted among the nations !
I will be exalted in the earth."
The Lord of Hosts is with us ;
The God of Jacob is our refuge.

Psalm xlvi.

The imagination is kept from abuse by contact with the grandest and noblest art. The artist must not only live in contact with masterpieces in his own special form of art, but he also needs to study the masterpieces in other forms of art. The true painter will study also good music, as the architect will study to appreciate sculpture, or the public reader or actor endeavor to appreciate painting.

The advice of Longfellow to Mary Anderson was: " Every day look upon some beautiful picture, read some beautiful poem, hear some beautiful piece of music." This not only develops the imagination, but keeps it active and normal, and prevents those diseases of the imagination some of which are the most fearful that afflict the human mind.

FROM THE DEFENCE OF POETRY.

POETRY lifts the veil from the hidden beauty of the world, and makes familiar objects be as if they were not familiar; it reproduces all that it represents, and the impersonations clothed in its Elysian light stand thenceforward, in the minds of those who have once contemplated them, as memorials of that gentle and exalted content which extends itself over all thought and actions with which it coexists. The great secret of morals is love; or a going out of our nature, and an identification of ourselves with the beautiful which exists in thought, action, or person, not our own. A man to be greatly good must imagine intensely and comprehensively; he must put himself in the place of another and of many others; the pains and pleasures of his species must become his own. The great instrument of moral good is the imagination; and poetry administers to the effect by acting upon the cause. Poetry enlarges the circumference of the imagination by replenishing it with thoughts of ever new delight, which have the power of attracting and assimilating to their own nature all other thoughts, and which form new intervals and interstices whose void forever craves fresh food. Poetry strengthens the faculty which is the organ of the moral nature of man, in the same manner as exercise strengthens a limb.

Poetry is indeed something divine. It is at once the centre and circumference of knowledge; it is that which comprehends all science, and that to which all science must be referred. It is at the same time the root and blossom of all other systems of thought; it is that from which all spring, and that which adorns all; and that which, if blighted, denies the fruit and the seed, and withholds from the barren world the nourishment and the succession of the scions of the tree of life. It is the perfect and consummate surface and bloom of all things; it is as the odour and the colour of the rose to the texture of the elements which compose it, as the form and splendour of unfaded beauty to the secrets of anatomy and corruption. What were virtue, love, patriotism, friendship; what were the scenery of this beautiful universe which we inhabit; what were our consolations on this side of the grave, and what were our aspirations beyond it, — if poetry did not ascend to bring light and fire from those eternal regions where the owl-winged faculty of calculation dare not ever soar?

Poetry is the record of the best and happiest moments of the happiest and best minds. We are aware of evanescent visitations of thought and feeling sometimes associated with place or person, sometimes regarding our own mind alone, and always arising unforeseen and departing unbidden, but elevating and delightful beyond all expression : so that even in the desire and the regret they leave, there cannot be but pleasure, participating as it does in the nature of its object. It is as it were the interpenetration of a diviner nature through our own; but its footsteps are like those of a wind over the sea, which the coming calm erases, and whose traces remain only as on the wrinkled sands which pave it. These and corresponding conditions of being are experienced principally by those of the most delicate sensibility and the most enlarged imagination ; and the state of mind produced by them is at war with every base desire. The enthusiasm of virtue, love, patriotism, and friendship is essentially linked with such emotions; and whilst they last, self appears as what it is, — an atom to a universe. Poets are not only subject to these experiences as spirits of the most refined organisation, but they can colour all that they combine with the evanescent hue of this ethereal world ; a word, a trait in the representation of a scene or a passion will touch the enchanted chord, and reanimate, in those who have ever experienced these emotions, the sleeping, the cold, the buried image of the past. Poetry thus makes immortal all that is best and most beautiful in the world ; it arrests the vanishing apparitions which haunt the interlunations of life, and veiling them, or in language or in form, sends them forth among mankind, bearing sweet news of kindred joy to those with whom their sisters abide, — abide, because there is no portal of expression from the caverns of the spirit which they inhabit into the universe of things. Poetry redeems from decay the visitations of the divinity in man.

Shelley.

IN THE STORM

A WILD rough night : and through the gloomy gray
One sees the blackness of the headland grow ;
One sees the whiteness of the upflung spray,
The whiteness of the breakers down below.

A wild wild night : and on the shingly rim
The furious sea-surge roars and frets and rives ;
And far away those black specks, growing dim,
Are tossing with their freights of human lives.

And all the while upon the silent height
The strong white star, beneath the starless sky,
Shines through the dimness of the troubled night,
Shines motionless while the vexed winds hoot by.

O steadfast light ! across dark miles of sea
How many straining eyes whence sleep is chased
Are watching through the midnight-storm for thee,
Large glimmering through the haze to the gray waste !

And in the night, fond mothers, scared awake,
And lonely wives, pushing the blind aside,
See thee, and bless thee for their sailor's sake,
And thank God thou art there, the dear ship's guide.

O strong calm star ! so watching night by night
And hour by hour, when storm-winds are astir,
They find thee changeless with thy patient light,
A beacon to the sea-tossed wanderer.

O strong and patient ! Once upon my life
Shone such a star ; and when the trouble wave
Reached me, and I grew faint with tempest strife,
Through all I saw that hope-star, and was brave.

O my lost star ! my star that was to me
Instead of sunlight that the happy know !
O weary way upon life's trackless sea !
And through the gloom there shines no beacon glow.

Augusta Webster.

XVIII. KNOWLEDGE AND EXPRESSION.

KNOWLEDGE has many degrees of definiteness. Many persons are content with vague ideas of the most common objects around them, as well as of all departments of science, literature, and art. Ask one of these whether he has a love for Shakespeare or not: " Why, of course! " yet he never gave it a thought. He loves poetry as a matter " of course," while he really has only a vague comprehension of what literature is, and no especial love for any author.

Literature is often studied historically, and no love is awakened for any one work. The spirit is not felt, the imagination is not awakened. Authors are but names, poems little more than words. Our understanding of a poem, oration, essay, or story should have the characteristics of perfect knowledge. For an appreciation of poetry or literature it is necessary to have a thorough understanding of the ideas beneath the words; for such an understanding is the basis of imaginative creation and sympathetic assimilation.

Such understanding is especially necessary to vocal expression. No man can express what he does not understand. He must not only understand the meaning of a phrase, — he must have in his mind a definite, ideal presence of which expression is simply the manifestation. The mere repetition of words is not expression. There must be distinct impression, and adequate and definite feeling, before there can be any truth or completeness of expression.

For more than a hundred years the basis of all studies on the relative perfection of knowledge has been an essay by Leibnitz. This essay is more or less obscure and difficult to understand. Professor Jevons has given an abridgment or illustration of it in his " Logic." So important is the subject to every student of vocal expression, that a few passages are selected for special study in relation to expression.

KNOWLEDGE is either obscure or clear ; either confused or distinct; either adequate or inadequate ; and lastly either symbolical or intuitive. Perfect knowledge must be clear, distinct, adequate, and intuitive ; if it fails in any one of these respects it is more or less *imperfect*. We may, therefore, classify knowledge as in the following scheme : —

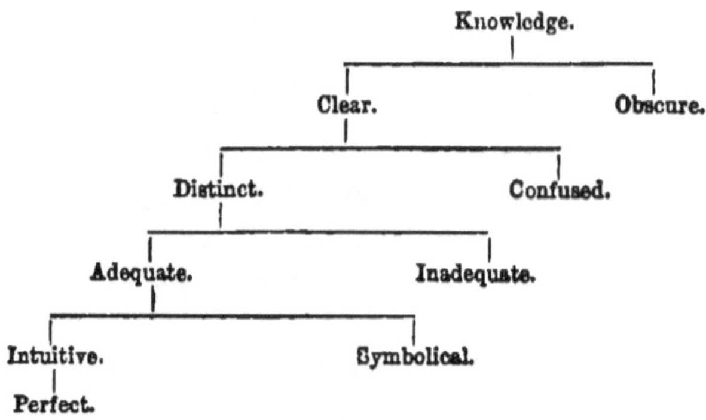

A notion, that is to say our knowledge of a thing, is *obscure* when it does not enable us to recognize the thing again and discriminate it from all other things. We have a clear notion of a rose and of most common flowers, because we can recognize them with certainty, and do not confuse them with each other. A shepherd acquires by practice a clear notion of each sheep of his flock, so as to enable him to single out any one separately.

Clear knowledge, again, is *confused* when we cannot distinguish the parts and qualities of the thing known, and can only recognize it as a whole. Though any one instantly knows a friend, and could discriminate him from all other persons, yet he would generally find it impossible to say how he knows him, or by what marks. He could not describe his figure or features but in the very roughest manner. A person unpractised in drawing, who attempts to delineate even such a familiar object as a horse or cow, soon finds that he has but a confused notion of its form, while an artist has a distinct idea of the form of every limb.

To have *adequate* knowledge of things, we must not only distinguish the parts which make up our notion of a thing, but the parts which make up those parts. To be completely adequate, our knowledge ought to admit of analysis after analysis *ad infinitum;* so that adequate knowledge would be impossible. But we may consider any knowledge adequate which carries the analysis sufficiently far for the purpose in view. A mechanist, for instance, has adequate knowledge of a machine if he not only know its several wheels and parts, but the purposes, materials, forms, and actions of those parts, — provided again that he knows all the mechanical properties of the materials, and the geometrical properties of the forms which may influence the working of the machine; but he is not expected to go on still further and explain why iron or wood of a particular quality is strong or brittle, why oil acts as a lubricator, or on what axioms the principles of mechanical forces are founded.

Lastly, we must notice the very important distinction of *symbolical* and *intuitive* knowledge. From the original meaning of the word, *intuitive* would denote that which we gain by seeing (Latin, *intueor*, to look at) ; and any knowledge which we have directly through the senses, or by immediate communication to the mind, is called *intuitive*. Thus we may learn intuitively what a square or a hexagon is, but hardly what a chiliagon, or figure of 1000 sides, is. We could not tell the difference by sight of a figure of 1000 sides and a figure of 1001 sides. Nor can we imagine any such figure completely before the mind. It is known to us only by name, or symbolically. All large numbers, — such as those which state the velocity of light (186,000 miles per second), the distance of the sun (91,000,000 miles), and the like, — are known to us only by symbols, and they are beyond our powers of imagination.

Whenever in common life we use words without having in mind at the moment their full and precise meaning, we possess symbolical knowledge only.

There is no worse habit for a student or reader to acquire than that of accepting words instead of a knowledge of things. It is perhaps worse than useless to read a work on natural history about Infusoria, Foraminifera, Rotifera, and the like, if these names do not convey clear images to the mind. Nor can a student who has not witnessed experiments, and examined the substances with his own eyes, derive any considerable advantage from works on chemistry and natural philosophy, where he will meet with hundreds of new terms which would be to him mere empty and confusing signs. On this account we should lose no opportunity of acquainting ourselves, by means of our senses, with the forms, properties, and changes of things, in order that the language we employ may, as far as possible, be employed *intuitively*, and we may be saved from the absurdities and fallacies into which we might otherwise fall.

The application of this to vocal expression is not difficult. A student in preparing for recitation learns his words, and thinks he is ready. There has been little or no meditation over the ideas; his knowledge, if he has any, is in a symbolic, not in an intuitive, state. He has a mere acquisition of terms; the ideas beneath are vague and inadequate, and of course expression must consequently be imperfect.

Effect follows adequate cause. The source of noble expression is thorough knowledge.

The application of these principles to imagination and feeling is of special importance in expression, because the depth and accuracy of knowledge results in adequate and definite feeling. True feeling is a response to knowledge, and true imaginative activity is founded upon accuracy of observation and knowledge. Men may, of course, have very definite knowledge, and discipline themselves to repress all imagination and emotion; but where there is a sympathetic study of a subject in relation to expression, not only is adequate knowledge secured, but vague emotions are intercepted and feeling grows definite. The imagination becomes dominated by the ideas, and changes with every change and point of view.

The distinction between symbolic and intuitive knowledge, and the superiority of the latter, are most important to expression. All imaginative action is intuitive. All true, intuitive conception in speaking is an incentive to right emotion.

No one should be called upon to read that which has not passed into the realm of intuitive knowledge. This principle applies in every case. Man can express only what he adequately understands. A student must be led gradually to secure perfect and intuitive knowledge of literature, and deeper and truer emotions and fuller expression.

On the other hand, the student must be given literature which demands intellectual effort for its comprehension. He must be encouraged to meditate upon great literature.

The necessity of adequate knowledge for truthful expression may be illustrated by Browning's monologue, "A Woman's Last Word." If one begins to read this without a clear conception of the whole, receiving ideas simply as they happen to come to the mind, expression will be vague. Here and there may be a clear idea, but there is no adequate expression of the whole. The poem requires a complete comprehension of the whole situation, before a single phrase can be realized imaginatively.

A woman is represented as talking to her husband, who has insisted upon her disclosing to him some event in her past life. She feels that she cannot make clear her love for another, and that to talk about it will create only misunderstanding. The poem is her speech, — a yielding, but with a request for postponement. With this knowledge gained, the conception of the poem grows clearer; then, and not till then, does the imaginative action of the poem begin. The reader can now secure an intuitive and imaginative point of view, and a conception of the poem adequate to expression.

A WOMAN'S LAST WORD.

Let 's contend no more, Love, strive nor weep:
All be as before, Love, — only sleep!
What so wild as words are? I and thou
In debate, as birds are, — hawk on bough!
See the creature stalking while we speak!
Hush and hide the talking, cheek on cheek!
What so false as truth is, false to thee?
Where the serpent's tooth is, shun the tree —
Where the apple reddens, never pry —
Lest we lose our Edens, Eve and I.
Be a god, and hold me with a charm!
Be a man, and fold me with thine arm!
Teach me, only teach, Love! As I ought
I will speak thy speech, Love, think thy thought —

> Meet, if thou require it, both demands,
> Laying flesh and spirit in thy hands.
> That shall be to-morrow, not to-night:
> I must bury sorrow out of sight, —
> Must a little weep, Love, (Foolish me !),
> And so fall asleep, Love, loved by thee.
>
> *Browning.*

PROBLEM XIX. *Read passages with different degrees of vividness and clearness of ideas, and note the fact that the imagination is more active and feeling more responsive in proportion to the mastery of the thought and definiteness of the understanding.*

IDENTITY.

> SOMEWHERE — in desolate wind-swept space —
> In Twilight land — in No-man's land —
> Two hungry Shapes met face to face,
> And bade each other stand.
>
> " And who are you ? " cried one, agape,
> Shuddering in the gloaming light.
> " I know not," said the second Shape,
> " I only died last night ! "
>
> *T. B. Aldrich.*

XIX. DEVELOPMENT OF IMAGINATION.

WHILE the imagination is a creative faculty, whose subtle processes defy analysis, still it must have material with which to act. There must exist in the mind an ample store of apperceptions, of ideal forms and beautiful images, as a basis for activity.

Such material the imagination cannot create for itself. It must come from experience, from a sympathetic and careful observation of Nature, art, and science.

Nature is one source whence it may be drawn. All poets, all artists, have a deep love for Nature. Admiration and wonder are born in each child; when wonder is lost, all teachableness, all receptivity, all hope and faith are lost. The first objects upon which the imagination is exercised is wondering admiration for trees and flowers, birds and brooks, skies and clouds. The imagination makes them live and move. Nature plays a part in

the education of man; she calls forth and complements his spirit.
A love of Nature is spontaneous. The child longs to be out of
doors. An education that warps this affection for Nature is
radically wrong.

Next in importance to the development of a genuine love for
Nature comes the study of painting, sculpture, and music. Art is
the interpretation of Nature; and it is only by a co-ordinate study
of art and Nature that we can awaken a true love of Nature on the
one hand, or of art on the other. Art has a specific language for
each of its forms or manifestations, and every human being must
be trained to read all these languages. Each art-work awakens
a peculiar action of the imagination in its creator, and also in the
one who simply appreciates and learns to love it. Every one
should endeavor to develop the power to think pictorially, so as to
appreciate painting; or to think plastically, so as to appreciate
sculpture. In short, every imagination should be trained to respond to a true painting, to a noble statue, to an artistic building,
and to every great art-work.

The one form of art which every person can carry with him is
literature; and primary dependence for the awakening of the imagination in most persons must be placed upon poetry and the works
of great authors.

Literature complemented by the other arts furnishes the highest
study and interpretation of Nature and humanity. With poetry,
the imagination of the race is forever intertwined. It is at once
the highest creation of the imagination and the most necessary
food for its development.

The one author who is especially helpful in the interpretation
of Nature, not only in youth but in old age, is Wordsworth. He
should be carefully studied by all students of vocal expression.
He brings imagination to little things; uses simple words; has no
sentimental sadness, no exaggerated and abnormal passion; and
gives little temptation to declamation.

Observe the simplicity of his insight, and the truthfulness and
beauty of his expression in this simple contemplation of two
mountain summits, yet how forcibly he holds our attention,
quickens our imagination, and stirs our feelings.

> "THOSE lusty twins," exclaimed our host, "if here
> It were your lot to dwell, would soon become
> Your prized companions.   Many are the notes
> Which, in his tuneful course, the wind draws forth
> From rocks, woods, caverns, heaths, and dashing shores ;
> And well those lofty brethren bear their part
> In the wild concert — chiefly when the storm
> Rides high ; then all the upper air they fill
> With roaring sound, that ceases not to flow,
> Like smoke, along the level of the blast,
> In mighty current ; theirs, too, is the song
> Of stream and headlong flood that seldom fails ;
> And, in the grim and breathless hour of noon,
> Methinks that I have heard them echo back
> The thunder's greeting.   Nor have Nature's laws
> Left them ungifted with a power to yield
> Music of finer tone ; a harmony,
> So do I call it, though it be the hand
> Of silence, though there be no voice : the clouds,
> The mist, the shadows, light of golden suns,
> Motions of moonlight, — all come thither, touch,
> And have an answer — thither come, and shape
> A language not unwelcome to sick hearts
> And idle spirits : there the sun himself,
> At the calm close of summer's longest day
> Rests his substantial orb ; between those heights
> And on the top of either pinnacle,
> More keenly than elsewhere in night's blue vault,
> Sparkle the stars, as of their station proud."

Wordsworth.

The one supreme author for the study of human nature is Shakespeare.   His works must be the chief text-book for all students of expression.

To repeat again the principle upon which these lessons are founded, *art must be studied as art and by means of art.* Hence, to develop the imagination, to secure a true appreciation of any literary work, there must be earnest study and practice to render the highest products of the artistic nature by the voice.   The most natural language, that of the voice, must be exercised to give expression to the noblest forms of poetry and literature.

Professor Shairp has some valuable suggestions to poets which apply with equal force to every kind of artist, and especially to the reader, the actor, or the speaker. " The imagination," he says, " must have a large store of material on which to work; this it cannot create for itself. From other regions it must be gathered, — from a wealth of mind in the poet himself; from large experience of life and intimate knowledge of Nature; from the exercise of his heart, his judgment, his reflection, indeed of his whole being, on all he has seen and felt. In fact, a great poet must be a man made wise by large experience, much feeling, and deep reflection: above all, he must have a hold of the great central truth of things. When these many conditions are present, then and then only can his imagination work widely, benignly, and for all time; then only can the poet become a

> " 'Serene creator of immortal things.'"

LITERATURE OF KNOWLEDGE AND OF POWER.

In that great social organ, which collectively we call literature, there may be distinguished two separate offices that may blend and often do so, but capable severally of a severe insulation, and naturally fitted for reciprocal repulsion. There is, first, the literature of *knowledge;* and, secondly, the literature of *power.* The function of the first is to *teach ;* the function of the second is to *move :* the first is a rudder, the second an oar or a sail. The first speaks to the mere discursive understanding; the second speaks ultimately, it may happen, to the higher understanding or reason, but always *through* affections of pleasure and sympathy. Remotely, it may travel towards an object seated in what Lord Bacon calls *dry* light; but proximately it does and must operate, else it ceases to be a literature of *power,* on and through that *humid* light which clothes itself in the mists and glittering *iris* of human passions, desires, and genial emotions. Men have so little reflected on the higher functions of literature, as to find it a paradox if one should describe it as a mean or subordinate purpose of books to give information. But this is a paradox only in the sense which makes it honourable to be paradoxical. Whenever we talk in ordinary language of seeking information or gaining knowledge, we understand the words as connected with something of absolute novelty. But it is the grandeur of all truth which *can* occupy a very high plane in human interests, that it is never absolutely novel to the meanest of minds : it exists externally by way of germ or latent principle in the lowest as in the highest, needing to be developed but never to be planted. To be capable of transplantation is the immediate criterion of a truth that ranges on a lower scale. Besides which, there is a rarer thing than truth; namely, *power* or deep sympathy with truth. What is the effect, for instance, upon society, of children? By the pity, by the tenderness, and by the peculiar modes of admiration which connect themselves with the helplessness, with the innocence, and with the simplicity of children, not only are the primal affections strengthened and continually renewed, but the qualities which are dearest in the sight of Heaven : the frailty, for instance, which appeals to forbearance, the innocence which symbolizes the heavenly, and the simplicity which is most alien from the worldly are kept up in perpetual remembrance, and their ideals are continually refreshed.

A purpose of the same nature is answered by the higher literature; namely, the literature of power. What do you learn from Paradise Lost? Nothing at all. What do you learn from a cookery-book? Something new, something that you did not know before, in every paragraph. But would you therefore put the wretched cookery-book on a higher level of estimation than the divine poem? What you owe to Milton is not any knowledge, of which a million separate items are still but a million of advancing steps on the same earthly level ; what you owe, is *power*, that is, exercise and expansion to your own latent capacity of sympathy with the infinite, where every pulse and each separate influx is a step upwards, — a step ascending as upon a Jacob's ladder from earth to mysterious altitudes above the earth. *All* the steps of knowledge, from first to last, carry you further on the same plane, but could never raise you one foot above your ancient level of earth ; whereas, the very *first* step in power is a flight, — is an ascending into another element, where earth is forgotten.

Were it not that human sensibilities are ventilated and continually called out into exercise by the great phenomena of infancy, or of real life as it moves through chance and change, or of literature as it re-combines these elements in the mimicries of poetry, romance, etc., it is certain that, like any animal power or muscular energy falling into disuse, all such sensibilities would gradually droop and dwindle. It is in relation to these great *moral* capacities of man that the literature of power, as contra-distinguished from that of knowledge, lives and has its field of action. . . . The commonest novel, by moving in alliance with human fears and hopes, with human instincts of wrong and right, sustains and quickens those affections. Calling them into action, it rescues them from torpor. And hence the pre-eminency over all authors that merely *teach*, of the meanest that *moves* ; or that teaches, if at all, indirectly *by* moving. The very highest work that has ever existed in the literature of knowledge is but a *provisional* work, — a book upon trial and sufferance. Let its teaching be even partially revised ; let it be but expanded, — nay even let its teaching be but placed in a better order, — and instantly it is superseded. Whereas the feeblest works in the literature of power, surviving at all, survive as finished and unalterable amongst men. For instance, the 'Principia' of Sir Isaac Newton was a book *militant* on earth from the first. In all stages of its progress it would have to fight for its existence, — first, as regards absolute truth ; secondly, when that combat is over, as regards its form or mode of presenting the truth. And as soon as a La Place, or anybody else, builds higher upon the foundations laid by this book, effectually he throws it out of the sunshine into decay and darkness ; by weapons won from this book he superannuates and destroys this book, so that soon the name of Newton remains as a mere *nominis umbra*, but his book, as a living power, has transmigrated into other forms. Now, on the contrary, the Iliad, the Prometheus of Æschylus, the Othello or King Lear, the Hamlet or Macbeth, and the Paradise Lost are not militant, but triumphant forever as long as the languages exist in which they speak or can be taught to speak. They never *can* transmigrate into new incarnations. To reproduce *these* in new forms or variations, even if in some things they should be improved, would be to plagiarize. A good steam-engine is properly superseded by a better ; but one lovely pastoral valley is not superseded by another, nor a statue of Praxiteles by a statue of Michael Angelo. These things are not separated by imparity, but by disparity; they are not thought of as unequal under the same standard, but as different in *kind*, and as equal under a different standard. Human works of immortal beauty and works of Nature in one respect stand on the same footing : they never absolutely repeat each other, never approach so near as not to differ ; and they differ not as better and worse, or simply by more and less, — they differ by undecipherable and incommunicable differences, that cannot be caught by mimicries, nor be reflected in the mirror of copies, nor become ponderable in the scales of vulgar comparison. . . . At this hour, five hundred years since their creation, the tales of Chaucer, never equalled on this earth for their tenderness and for life of picturesqueness, are read familiarly by many in the charming language of their natal day, and by others in the modernizations of Dryden, of Pope, and Wordsworth. At this hour, one thousand eight hundred years since their creation, the Pagan tales of Ovid, never equalled on this earth for the gayety of their movement and the capricious graces of their narrative, are read by all Christendom. This man's people and their monuments are dust ; but *he* is alive : he has survived them, as he told us that he had it in his commission to do, by a thousand years, — " and *shall* a thousand more."

All the literature of knowledge builds only ground-nests, that are swept away by floods or confounded by the plough ; but the literature of power builds nests in aërial altitudes of temples sacred from violation, or of forests inaccessible to fraud. *This* is a great prerogative of the *power* literature ; and it is a greater which lies in the mode of its influence. The *knowledge* literature, like the fashion of this world, passeth away. An Encyclopædia is its abstract ; and in this respect it may be taken for its speaking symbol, that, before one generation has passed, an Encyclopædia is superannuated ; for it speaks through the dead memory and unimpassioned understanding, which have not the *rest* of higher faculties, but are continually enlarging and varying their phylacteries. But all literature, properly so called — literature "κατ' ἐξοχήν," for the very same reason that it is so much more durable than the literature of knowledge — is (and by the very same proportion it is) more intense and electrically searching in its impressions. The directions in which the tragedy of this planet has trained our human feelings to play, and the combinations into which the poetry of this planet has thrown our human passions of love and hatred, or admiration and contempt, exercise a power bad or good over human life that cannot be contemplated, when stretching through many generations, without a sentiment allied to awe. And of this let every one be assured, — that he owes to the impassioned books which he has read many a thousand more of emotions than he can consciously trace back to them. Dim by their origination, these emotions yet arise in him, and mould him through life like the forgotten incidents of childhood.

De Quincey

BUT who is He, with modest looks,
And clad in homely russet brown ?
He murmurs near the running brooks'
A music sweeter than their own.

He is retired as noontide dew,
Or fountain in a noon-day grove ;
And you must love him, ere to you
He will seem worthy of your love.

The outward shows of sky and earth,
Of hill and valley, he has viewed ;
And impulses of deeper birth
Have come to him in solitude.

In common things that round us lie
Some random truths he can impart,—
The harvest of a quiet eye
That broods and sleeps on his own **heart.**

But he is weak ; both Man and Boy,
Hath been an idler in the land ;
Contented if he might enjoy
The things which others understand.

— Come thither in thy hour of strength ;
Come, weak as is a breaking wave !
Here stretch thy body at full length ;
Or build thy house upon his grave.

A Poet's Epitaph.   *Wordsworth.*

XX. VOCAL MANIFESTATIONS OF IMAGINATION: TOUCH

THE modulations of the voice are few and simple,— pause, inflection, change of pitch, touch, texture, and tone-color.

These may seem at first inadequate; but when we study the other arts, we find that the means of expression are always few and simple. There are but three colors; and these, with light and shade, and possibly the addition of line, are the painter's means of representing the infinite complexity of light and color, form and texture in Nature. Vocal expression, therefore, in having but a few simple elements, or means of expression, shares the character of all other arts.

The question arises, What are the peculiar effects of the imagination upon these vocal modulations?

All of these elements are used by the different powers of the man. But there are certain of these elements, such as inflection, which have a more immediate relationship to thinking and the intellect. Certain others, such as color and texture, have a more intimate relation with feeling. All these elements have a specific meaning and function; but they are used simultaneously, and for the revelation of the whole man.

What is the difference between the use of these elements in giving expression to ordinary thinking and in the expression of higher imaginative action and feeling?

Ordinary thinking accentuates them, enlarges them. Imagination tends to use them more delicately. Ordinary thinking expresses or emphasizes an idea by making a point salient, by making an inflection or a change of pitch longer, by giving a touch more force; but the imagination expresses itself more by a sympathetic modulation of the whole. As imagination relates ideas to each other, so it sympathetically relates and brings into unity very diverse vocal modulations. Ordinary thinking uses an inflection consciously, and with great deliberation; the imagination modulates the voice more spontaneously and unconsciously. Imagination makes all technique more transparent; brings the modulations nearer the soul, the execution nearer the feeling, so that all technical means are more concealed. Reason emphasizes more by isolation.

The imagination is the faculty that deals with relations. If a book and a hat be placed upon a sofa, and an unimaginative painter asked to paint them, he will make a study with each in more or less isolation,— simply presenting facts clearly and definitely. But the imaginative painter will look through the mere isolated facts concerning each object, and find a mystic kinship or connecting idea, and paint a picture full of expression.

The chief language of imagination is the refinement and harmonious co-operation of all the modulations of the voice.

There are, however, certain peculiar intimacies between the imagination and some modulations of the voice. One of these is *touch ;* as has been shown, the imagination excludes everything that is crude or exaggerated, and uses that which is more subtle and simple. Touch is especially liable to be perverted by mere mechanical or muscular use of the voice. Besides, touch is the most immediate and direct effect of force upon the voice; and as imagination is spontaneous and immediate in its action, its presence always gives delicacy, decision, and definiteness to the vocal touch. These qualities of touch also, when present, tend to awaken the imagination of the auditor.

While imagination renders the touch delicate, it must not be understood that there is consequently a lack of force. Notice the intensity and decision of the touch, in the following extract: —

> "Ah, once more," I cried, "ye stars, ye waters,
> On my heart your mighty charm renew ;
> Still, still let me, as I gaze upon you,
> Feel my soul becoming vast like you !"
>
> And with joy the stars perform their shining,
> And the sea its long moon-silver'd roll ;
> For self-poised they live, nor pine with noting
> All the fever of some differing soul.

Self-Dependence.   *Arnold.*

Thus it is not alone in the delicacy and decision of the touch that imagination reveals itself, but in the variety of the modulations of the touch which imagination causes.   Sometimes there is a very important representative element in the touch; for instance, notice the difference between the touch in these two illustrations:—

> Swift ran the searching tempest overhead ;
> And ever and anon some bright white shaft
> Burned thro' the pine-tree roof, here burned and there,
> As if God's messenger thro' the close wood screen
> Plunged and replunged his weapon at a venture,
> Feeling for guilty thee and me : then broke
> The thunder like a whole sea overhead.

Browning.

> Of a sudden the sun shone large and bright,
> As if he were staying away the night ;
> And the rain on the river fell as sweet
> As the pitying tread of an angel's feet.

Alice Cary.

PROBLEM XX.   *Give a decided but delicate touch with the voice which will be as suggestive as the brush-stroke of the greatest painter.*

CHRISTMAS HYMN.

> It was the calm and silent night !
>   Seven hundred years and fifty-three
> Had Rome been growing up to might,
>   And now was Queen of land and sea.
> No sound was heard of clashing wars ;
>   Peace brooded o'er the hushed domain ;
> Apollo, Pallas, Jove, and Mars,
>   Held undisturb'd their ancient reign,
>   In the solemn midnight
>   Centuries ago.

'T was in the calm and solemn night!
  The senator of haughty Rome
Impatient urged his chariot's flight,
  From lordly revel rolling home.
Triumphal arches gleaming swell
  His breast with thoughts of boundless sway;
What reck'd the Roman what befell
  A paltry province far away,
        In the solemn midnight
          Centuries ago.

Within that province far away
  Went plodding home a weary boor:
A streak of light before him lay,
  Fall'n through a half-shut stable door
Across his path.   He passed — for nought
  Told what was going on within;
How keen the stars! his only thought;
  The air how calm and cold and thin,
        In the solemn midnight
          Centuries ago.

O strange indifference! — low and high
  Drows'd over common joys and cares:
The earth was still — but knew not why;
  The world was listening — unawares.
How calm a moment may precede
  One that shall thrill the world forever!
To that still moment none would heed
  Man's doom was linked, no more to sever,
        In the solemn midnight
          Centuries ago.

It is the calm and solemn night!
  A thousand bells ring out, and throw
Their joyous peals abroad, and smite
  The darkness, charmed and holy now.
The night that erst no name had worn,
  To it a happy name is given;
 For in that stable lay new-born
  The peaceful Prince of Earth and Heaven,
        In the solemn midnight
          Centuries ago.

Domett

THE night has a thousand eyes, and the day but one;
Yet the light of the bright world dies with the dying sun.
The mind has a thousand eyes, and the heart but one;
Yet the light of a whole life dies when love is done.

Francis William Bourdillon

XXI. VOCAL MANIFESTATION OF IMAGINATION: PAUSE.

ANOTHER most dignified and important means of expression is pause. It shows the action of the mind as receiving an idea. It is the mind taking time to weigh and deeply realize the truth which it is to express. The absence of pauses denotes superficiality and lack of feeling. In proportion to the dignity and weight of the reading, the intensity and depth in the action of all the faculties of thought and feeling will be greater in number and length. Pause is one of the most dignified modes of expression.

Hence, as the imagination gives an exalted action of the mind, and is always associated with noble feeling and a living energy of all the faculties, there is a greater tendency to use pauses when there is action of the imagination than in the expression of ordinary thinking. The pauses are needed to give the mind time for depth of insight, and also to give both speaker and hearer time to create, appreciate, and feel the complex ideas and situations.

Moreover, imagination is contemplative; and contemplation requires time. Again, the imagination is reposeful; it does not didactically dominate, but sympathetically awakens attention. For these and many other reasons, actions of the imagination are especially associated with periods of silence.

I GO to prove my soul!
I see my way as birds their trackless way.
I shall arrive! What time, what circuit first,
I ask not: but unless God send His hail
Or blinding fireballs. sleet or stifling snow,
In some time, His good time, I shall arrive:
He guides me and the bird. In His good time.

Browning.

Thus, pause is a special means of manifesting the imaginative action. As silence is the most dignified form of revealing mental activity, and as the imagination is associated with every struggle to express the ideal or deep realization in thought, so, as the most ideal action of the mind, it requires the most ideal and simple as well as subtle methods of emphasis, and the most exalted and noble modes of expression.

I HAVE heard the long roar and surge of History, wave after wave, — as of the never-ending surf along the immense coast-line of West Africa.

I heard the world-old cry of the down-trodden and outcast: I saw them advancing always to victory.

I saw the red light from the guns of established order and precedent, — the lines of defence and the bodies of the besiegers rolling in dust and blood, yet more and ever more behind.

And high over the inmost citadel I saw magnificent, and beckoning ever to the besiegers, and the defenders ever inspiring, the cause of all that never-ending war,

The form of Freedom stand.

The Age-long War.   *Carpenter.*

WORLD-STRANGENESS.

STRANGE the world about me lies, never yet familiar grown, —
Still disturbs me with surprise, haunts me like a face half known.
In this house with starry dome, floored with gem-like plains and seas,
Shall I never feel at home, never wholly be at ease ?

On from room to room I stray, yet my Host can ne'er espy;
And I know not to this day whether guest or captive I.
So between the starry dome and the floor of plains and seas
I have never felt at home, never wholly been at ease.

William Watson.

IN my distress I called upon the Lord, and cried unto my God : he heard my voice out of his temple, and my cry before him came into his ears.   Then the earth shook and trembled, the foundations also of the mountains moved and were shaken, because he was wroth.   There went up a smoke out of his nostrils, and fire out of his mouth devoured: coals were kindled by it.   He bowed the heavens also, and came down ; and thick darkness was under his feet.   And he rode upon a cherub and did fly : yea, he flew swiftly upon the wings of the wind.   He made darkness his hiding-place, his pavilion round about him ; darkness of waters, thick clouds of the skies.   At the brightness before him his thick clouds passed, hailstones and coals of fire.   The Lord also thundered in the heavens, and the Most High uttered his voice; hailstones and coals of fire.   And he sent out his arrows, and scattered them ; yea, lightnings manifold, and discomfited them.   Then the channels of waters appeared, and the foundations of the earth were laid bare, at thy rebuke, O Lord, at the blast of the breath of thy nostrils. He sent from on high, he took me; he drew me out of many waters. He delivered me from my strong enemy, and from them that hated me; for they were too mighty for me. They came upon me in the day of my calamity: but the Lord was my stay.

From Psalm xviii.

XXII. VOCAL MANIFESTATION OF IMAGINATION: TONE-COLOR.

One of the chief means by which imagination manifests its activity through the voice is in the modulation of the texture and resonance of tone. The delicate modulation of pure tone by imagination and feeling may be named tone-color.

The color of the voice is wholly distinct from inflection. Inflection and changes of pitch are elements of form; but tone-color has respect to the modulation of the quality and resonance. Inflectional modulation for the most part, as has been shown, manifests the logical relation of ideas. Inflection shows the rational action of the mind; but tone-color manifests imaginative and emotional relations.

There is an important difference between quality and color of the voice. There are legitimate qualities, — such as purity, mellowness, resonance, and openness, — which are always present in good tone; and, on the other hand, there are illegitimate qualities of voice, such as nasality, throatiness, or flatness. These are faults, and should never be used in noble expression. Tone-color is the emotional modulation of good tone. Nasality is a quality but not a color of the voice. A nasal or throaty voice can hardly be colored by emotion. In fact, the voice must be made pure, free, open, resonant, and elastic by training before there can be any mastery or practice of tone-color in vocal expression.

This principle, which is a fundamental one in all vocal expression, has been violated by many "systems." The complete failure to recognize tone-color, and the perversion of inflection, the use of abnormal qualities and stresses to express emotion, have been the chief factors in degrading elocution, and in making it the slave of the lowest forms of literature. Until this fact is recognized, discussion of the nature and action of the imagination in relation to vocal expression is useless.

According to the mechanical system, only a few emotions can be expressed by pure tone; while according to the singer's, pure tone must be used in the expression of all noble emotion. There can be no doubt in the mind of any one that in all fine oratory and acting, the principles held by the leading teachers of song have been consciously or unconsciously obeyed. All noble emotions in any true vocal art manifest themselves through modulations of normal tone. It is only in the expression of secrecy of an abnormal type, and of the very lowest forms of anger, that an aspirate or throaty or nasal tone is used; and even in these cases it must only be suggested.

Every emotion has a distinct modulation of voice peculiar to itself. Joy has one color, love another, and patriotism still another. The elimination of abnormal qualities of voice as elements in vocal expression makes possible a greater, more delicate, and more natural variation of the voice, as well as truer expression.

Emotion modulates the color and texture of the voice, because it modifies or modulates the texture of the muscles of the body. It is the vibration of the muscles of the body which is chiefly concerned in producing the resonance of the voice. Any modulation of this muscular texture will therefore modulate the tone. In one emotion the muscular texture is firm; in another, soft and plastic. We see this in the face and in the hand. Instruments have been invented to measure the effect of the diffusion of emotion through the body. In this nervous diffusion and emotional vibration will be found the scientific explanation of the complex and beautiful modulations of tone in those whose imaginations and voices have been cultivated.

In a well-trained voice all parts of the body are brought into sympathy and co-ordination. The emotional activity centres in the diaphragm and the muscles controlling breath. Thus in a good voice the whole body is attuned like a vocal instrument, and emotion causes a sympathetic vibratory response.

Sound is vibration, and anything that interferes or changes the vibration modifies the sound. The kind of timber used in a piano or violin affects its tone. A tuner, after tuning a piano, may find one key where there is something wrong. He will examine the piano, and find that the cause is in some loose panel or screw, or in the presence of some foreign substance. If a mechanical instrument like a piano is so sensitive, how much more responsive must be an organic, living body, every part of which is in sympathetic relationship, and in fact a vital portion of a muscular and nervous system!

Tone-color is the pleasing and ideal element in vocal expression. It is the most poetic and imaginative. It reveals the highest and most delicate feeling. It discloses the mystic depth of the soul.

Resonance is often confounded with pitch. People desire low voices. Really, the desire is not for pitch, but for resonance. The sense of resonance and tone-color is rare, and must be developed.

The development of tone-color belongs rather to vocal training; but it is so important and so much neglected that it must receive some attention in this connection.

The most simple course is to read imaginative and emotional lyrics as simply as possible, beginning with joy and love, admiration of Nature, or some noble emotion. Noble emotion develops the nobler qualities of the voice. Husky tones and other imperfections may in a great measure be corrected by the right practice of joyous lyrics, such as Wordsworth's "Cuckoo."

Another method is to practise reading such short extracts as are found at the close of this lesson, in contrast with each other. Give joy in contrast with sorrow, and make the difference as delicate and as true as possible. The student must be able to define clearly twenty or thirty emotions without changing from the noble and normal qualities of his voice. At first, he will think it impossible to show so many differences; but after practice and right control over his voice, he will discover that he can discriminate a larger number, and that the human voice is capable of indicating every shade of feeling.

In such practice it is essential that constrictions, such as nasality and hardness, be removed from the voice. The tone must be round and smooth. The voice must be "placed."

In such practice, it is far better to use poetic and imaginative extracts, because tone-color is ideal and refined, and reveals the imaginative nature. Where there is no feeling, there can of course be no tone-color. Those who speak invariably in a cold and neutral manner, without imaginative response, or without allowing the imagination to dominate the feeling, have, of course, no tone-color. The voice itself may be naturally resonant, but tone-color be wholly lacking. Tone-color is the imaginative and emotional modulation of the resonance of the voice.

Work upon tone-color not only trains the power to distinguish subtleties, but it also tends to develop the imagination. Development of the imagination and of tone-color should go together.

PROBLEM XXI. *Arrange twenty to thirty short extracts or lines, each with different emotion, and render them truthfully by the voice.*

SING loud, O bird in the tree ! O bird, sing loud in the sky !
And honey-bees, blacken the clover seas ! there are none of you glad as I.

———

LIFE is no idle dream, but a solemn reality, based upon Eternity and encompassed by Eternity.   ———   *Carlyle.*

DAY is dying !   Float, O song, down the westward river !
Requiems chanting to the Day — Day, the mighty Giver.

———

OH, Brignall banks are wild and fair, and Greta woods are green,
And you may gather garlands there would grace a summer queen.

———

STILL, through our paltry stir and strife glows down the wished Ideal,
And Longing moulds in clay what Life carves in the marble Real.
          Lowell.

———

OH ! the bells of Shandon sound far more grand on
The pleasant waters of the river Lee.

———

HIGHER still and higher from the earth thou springest,
Like a cloud of fire the blue deep thou wingest,
And singing still dost soar, and soaring ever singest.

———

THE last link is broken that bound me to thee,
And the words thou hast spoken have rendered me free.

MERRILY, merrily goes the bark
  On a breeze from the northward free :
So shoots through the morning sky the lark,
  Or the swan through the summer sea.

Scott.

MARCH to the battle-field ! the foe is now before us;
Each heart is Freedom's shield, and heaven is shining o'er us.

O'Meara.

I HELD it truth, with him who sings
  To one clear harp in divers tones,
  That men may rise on stepping-stones
Of their dead selves to higher things.

AH ! that lady of the villa — and I loved her so —
Near the city of Sevilla — years and years ago.

Waller.

NEVER pay any attention to the understanding when it stands in opposition to any other faculty of the mind. The mere understanding, however useful and indispensable, is the meanest faculty in the human mind, and the most to be distrusted ; and yet the great majority of people trust to nothing else.

WHAT ho, my jovial mates ! come on ! we 'll frolic it
Like fairies frisking in the merry moonshine !

I COULD not love thee half so much, loved I not honour more.

THE mossy marbles rest on the lips that he has press'd in their bloom ; and the names he loved to hear have been carved for many a year on the tomb.

Holmes.

ONE morn I miss'd him on the custom'd hill,
Along the heath, and near his favourite tree :
Another came ; nor yet beside the rill,
Nor up the lawn, nor at the wood was he.

A SONG, oh a song for the merry May !
The cows in the meadow, the lambs at play,
A chorus of birds in the maple-tree,
And a world in blossom for you and me.

THE cloud-capped towers, the gorgeous palaces,
The solemn temples, the great globe itself,
Yea, all which it inherit, shall dissolve,
And, like this insubstantial pageant faded,
Leave not a rack behind.   We are such stuff
As dreams are made of, and our little life
Is rounded with a sleep.

AH, well! for us all some sweet hope lies
Deeply buried from human eyes;
And in the hereafter angels may
Roll the stone from its grave away!

Whittier.

UP! comrades, up! in Rokeby's halls
Ne'er be it said our courage falls.

BACK, ruffians! back! nor dare to tread
Too near the body of my dead.

No ray is dimmed, no atom worn,
  My oldest force is good as new;
And the fresh rose on yonder thorn
  Gives back the bending heavens in dew.

Emerson.

SHALL I, wasting in despair, die because a woman's fair?   Or my cheeks make pale with care 'cause another's rosy are?   Be she fairer than the day, or the flowery meads in May — if she be not so to me, what care I how fair she be?

George Wither.

HENCE! home, you idle creatures! get you home!

WE can show you where he lies, fleet of foot, and tall of size;
You shall see him brought to bay: waken, lords and ladies gay.

The Hunters. *Scott.*

AND so beside the Silent Sea I wait the muffled oar;
No harm from Him can come to me on ocean or on shore.
I know not where His islands lift their fronded palms in air;
I only know I cannot drift beyond His love and care.

MODEST and shy as a nun is she; one weak chirp is her only note:
Braggart and prince of braggarts is he, pouring boasts from his little throat.

— WAKE ! oh, wake ! and utter praise !
Who sank thy sunless pillars deep in earth ?
Who filled thy countenance with rosy light ?
Who made thee parent of perpetual streams ?

Mont Blanc. *Coleridge.*

———

OH, and proudly stood she up !   Her heart within her did not fail :
She looked into Lord Ronald's eyes, and told him all her nurse's tale.

———

THE silent organ loudest chants the master's requiem.

Emerson.

———

OUR birds of song are silent now ; few are the flowers blooming ;
Yet life is in the frozen bough, and Freedom's Spring is coming.

Massey.

PROBLEM XXII. *Select short extracts with subtle changes in the imaginative conception and feeling, and naturally reveal these by the color and texture of the voice.*

FIRM-PACED and slow, a horrid front they form, —
Still as the breeze, but dreadful as the storm !

———

WITH foreheads unruffled the conquerors come — but why have they muffled the lance and the drum ? . . . Ye saw him at morning how gallant and gay ! in bridal adorning the star of the day : now weep for the lover, — his triumph is sped ; his hope it is over ! the chieftain is dead ! But, oh for the maiden who mourns for that chief, . . . she sinks on the meadow, — in one morning-tide a wife and a widow, a maid and a bride !

———

CHANGE as ye list, ye winds ! my heart shall be
The faithful compass that still points to thee.

Black-eyed Susan. *Gay.*

———

I 'VE wandered east, I 've wandered west, through many a weary way ;
But never, never can forget the love of life's young day.

Motherwell.

———

I TOLD her how he pined : and ah ! the deep, the low, the pleading tone
With which I sang another's love, interpreted my own.

———

Too low they build who build below the stars.

Young.

———

So nigh is grandeur to our dust, so near is God to man,
When Duty whispers low, *Thou must,* the youth replies, *I can.*

Emerson.

The bee to the heather, the lark to the sky, the roe to the greenwood, and whither shall I ? Oh, Alice! ah, Alice! so sweet to the bee are the moorland and heather by Cannock and Leigh! Oh, Alice! ah, Alice! o'er Teddesley Park the sunny sky scatters the notes of the lark! Oh, Alice! ah, Alice! in Beaudesert glade the roes toss their antlers for joy of the shade! But Alice, dear Alice! glade, moorland, nor sky without you can content me, and whither shall I ?

Sir Henry Taylor.

GENEVIEVE.

Maid of my Love, sweet Genevieve !
In Beauty's light you glide along ;
Your eye is like the star of eve,
And sweet your Voice as Seraph's song.
Yet not your heavenly Beauty gives
This heart with passion soft to glow :
Within your soul a Voice there lives !
It bids you hear the tale of Woe.
When sinking low the Sufferer wan
Beholds no hand outstretch'd to save,
Fair, as the bosom of the Swan
That rises graceful o'er the wave,
I 've seen your breast with pity heave,
And therefore love I you, sweet Genevieve !

Coleridge.

SONG.

Blow, blow, thou winter wind, thou art not so unkind as man's ingratitude ; thy tooth is not so keen, because thou art not seen, although thy breath be rude.

Freeze, freeze, thou bitter sky, that dost not bite so nigh as benefits forgot : though thou the waters warp, thy sting is not so sharp, as friend remembered not.

Heigh, ho! sing, heigh, ho! unto the green holly : most friendship is feigning, most loving mere folly: then, heigh, ho! the holly! this life is most jolly.

Shakespeare.

THE LIGHT OF OTHER DAYS.

Oft in the stilly night ere slumber's chain has bound me, fond Memory brings the light of other days around me: the smiles, the tears of boyhood's years, the words of love then spoken ; the eyes that shone, now dimm'd and gone, the cheerful hearts now broken ! Thus in the stilly night ere slumber's chain has bound me, sad Memory brings the light of other days around me.

When I remember all the friends so link'd together I 've seen around me fall like leaves in wintry weather, I feel like one who treads alone some banquet-hall deserted, whose lights are fled, whose garlands dead, and all but he departed ! Thus in the stilly night ere slumber's chain has bound me, sad Memory brings the light of other days around me.

Moore.

———

WHERE sweeps round the mountains the cloud on the gale, and streams from their fountains leap into the vale, — like frighted deer leap when the storm with his pack rides over the steep in the wild torrent's track, — even there my free home is ; there watch I the flocks wander white as the foam is on stairways of rocks. Secure in the gorge there in freedom we sing, and laugh at King George, where the Eagle is king.

Wild Wagoner of the Alleghanies.   *Buchanan Read.*

———

XXIII. MANIFESTATION OF IMAGINATION : CHANGE OF PITCH.

CHANGE of pitch is one of the most fundamental of all modulations of the voice. It is a universal characteristic of naturalness; there is in fact a change of pitch between every word in conversation. Change of pitch is one of the first effects of thinking, over the voice.

There is, however, an unusual change of pitch which might be called change of key, that is very imaginative. It suggests a similar effect to that of light and shade.

Observe, for example, in the following extract, how the voice distinguishes between each of the pictures by both color and pitch, in proportion to the vividness and character of the picture of each successive object or scene. How widely different is the picture of the river from that of the brook, and of both from the ocean ! But when we come to the predication of all these pictures, there is a much greater change of pitch, with corresponding changes in the texture and color.

THE hills,
Rock-ribbed, and ancient as the sun ; the vales,
Stretching in pensive quietness between ;
The venerable woods ; rivers that move
In majesty, and the complaining brooks
That make the meadow green ; and, poured round all,
Old ocean's gray and melancholy waste, —
Are but the solemn decorations all
Of the great tomb of man.

Bryant.

Such changes as these are especially important in deep feeling; and while intense emotion calls for an increase of tone-color and texture, yet the change of pitch and the touch are especially important from the fact that they manifest volitional control over the emotion. Whenever there is a tendency to drift in feeling, the true imaginative touch, which is always radical, tends to drift into a meaningless swell, or a so-called medium stress; while the changes of pitch become merely passive drops of the voice, which tend, on being exaggerated, to sing-song.

There is one peculiarity about changes of pitch: they are not regular or rhythmic in natural expression.   Rhythm is the regulation or continuity of force, and is always normally manifested through touch; whenever there is a rhythmic modulation of inflection or changes of pitch, we have an elimination of thinking in all its forms and a sing-song melody.   Force is acting without being dominated by thinking; the feeling is acting without being stimulated by the mental pictures.   For this reason, there should be practice especially of change of pitch as directly expressive of the imaginative action of the mind.

LITTLE BOY BLUE.

THE little toy dog is covered with dust,
But sturdy and stanch he stands ;
And the little toy soldier is red with rust,
And his musket moulds in his hands.

Time was when the little toy dog was new,
And the soldier was passing fair ;
And that was the time when our Little Boy Blue
Kissed them and put them there.

"Now, don't you go till I come," he said ;
"And don't you make any noise !"
So toddling off to his trundle-bed
He dreamt of the pretty toys.

And as he was dreaming, an angel song
Awakened our Little Boy Blue, —
Oh, the years are many, the years are long,
But the little toy friends are true !

> Aye faithful to Little Boy Blue they stand,
> Each in the same old place, —
> Awaiting the touch of a little hand,
> The smile of a little face.
>
> And they wonder, as waiting these long years through
> In the dust of that little chair,
> What has become of our Little Boy Blue
> Since he kissed them and put them there.
>
> *Eugene Field.*

XXIV. INTENSITY AND REPOSE.

ARE there any general qualities or characteristics which show the presence of the imagination, or any peculiarities which show its absence in different forms of art, but especially in vocal expression?

When there is absence of imagination, there is a tendency merely to reproduce facts. Imagination breathes the life of personality into art; it unites the feeling and the fact. Absence of imagination is denoted by labor, by stiltedness, by loudness, by any crude modulation of the voice, by sudden and violent changes, by extravagant surprises of any kind; the presence of imagination is noted by directness and simplicity, by unity in the midst of the most complex elements, by great variation and naturalness in the modulations of the voice, by a sense of hidden life and mystery, by a sympathetic response and co-operation of the powers of the whole man. Absence of imagination is indicated by the use of only one modulation of the voice at the expense of the others; by the use of volitional, deliberative, or conscious force; by self-consciousness, and by a lack of natural vocabulary. Imagination brings a large vocabulary of the modulations of the voice, freedom from self-consciousness, with ease and naturalness.

Among the many qualities of expression which are characteristic of imagination may be mentioned intensity.

Intensity is in proportion to the activity at the centre. It proceeds from control without destruction, the retention or the reserve of the excitement which any emotion arouses without repressing it. Steam is intense in proportion to its compression or confinement, and so with emotion.   If there is no control over emotion, if the reader passively surrenders himself to the first impulse, passion causes mere noise or outward motions, and runs to waste.

A normal human being is one whose thought and emotion are balanced by will.   Thought without will or emotion is not natural, and nor is will or emotion without thought.   In the strong man there is co-ordinate action of the three elemental powers of his being.

Hence, emotion naturally implies control.   When emotion is controlled, its activity is diffused through the whole body.   Emotion must especially affect the breathing, or the muscles regulating the breathing, so as to cause activity in the middle of the body. When the breath is elastically and naturally retained in connection with emotion, the least touch of the voice will have character and power.   This is the primary characteristic of the right use of the voice, and of a modulation of the texture and color of the tone. With such a retention of breath, every modulation suggests situation, feeling, and imaginative action.

Weakness is the result of a want of intensity in the expression of emotion.

There are noble and ignoble elements in nearly every emotion. Sorrow, for example, may degenerate into a passive whine; but controlled, retained, and suggested, it awakens sympathy, and is noble and heroic.   There are always two emotions which seem very much alike, but which are far apart.   One is weak, and the other is strong.   Brass may be so polished as to look like gold. Who can tell the difference between melted lead and melted silver? But the difference is brought out by time.   Anger and indignation, sympathy and pity, excitement and hurry, intensity and nervousness, are only a few of the emotions too often confused with one another.

The chief difference between emotions so closely akin is in the element of imaginative, stimulous, and volitional control.   Sorrow, for example, implies a struggle for control over a certain emotion, while sadness is a passive indulgence of possibly the same feeling. The difference in these emotions consists more or less in the attitude of the man. In fact, expression does not always directly manifest the feeling, but rather displays the attitude of the man towards it, his victory over it, or his yielding to it. Hence, control of breath is the most fundamental agent in the control of passion, and the chief element in the expression of emotion. This is especially true of sorrow. It is the struggle to control sorrow that indicates the strong man. It is only a weak man who yields, and exhibits his tears and other effects of feeling. The strong man treasures his tears; he struggles with his breath until his voice is clear. Sorrow is thus an emotion which demands intensity and suggestiveness.

All emotion represents either a stage of cumulation and progression, or of retrogression and prostration. An emotion in its retrogressive or prostrate stage is indicative of weakness. Repose demands that emotion be expressed in a stage of accumulation and control. The steam that runs a locomotive is not merely the small amount that escapes in the piston. Steam has no power except from the energy of an accumulated and restrained mass behind that which is used.

Emotion in the speaker or reader awakens sympathy and a corresponding condition in the hearer, in proportion as its cause is suggested. No one can *give* an emotion to another: feeling can only be awakened; for the roused imagination of each hearer is the cause of his own emotion. It is for this reason that suggestion of the accumulation of emotion indicates strength, while an advertisement of exhaustion indicates weakness. In the expression of any emotion, the control or the retention of the condition, the sustaining of the cause, is most important.

There can be no laughter without control of breath. The activity given by the emotion to the respiratory muscles causes the laugh. An artistic or voluntary laugh is most difficult: few can laugh naturally before an audience. Few of the best actors have a good laugh. One explanation for this is the lack of control over breath, or the lack of the response of the vocal mechanism to imaginative feeling.

One who tells a comical story must have control over himself in order to have any effect upon others. There is a comical picture called " A Good Story." One monk, with his hat on and an umbrella in his hand, sits erect with a smile on his face; the other monk lies back in his chair convulsed with laughter. It is easy to perceive which told the story. The emotion of the teller is one of joyous surprise at its effect upon the other. He has controlled his own feeling so as to dominate the emotion of his listener.

Intensity and repose, therefore, relate chiefly to the attitude of the man toward feeling and expression; to the control of, or the power to reserve and accumulate, emotion. They are secured when the man is able to sustain his intellectual or imaginative activity in such relation to his sensibility as to accumulate and yet direct feeling.

> DARK, deep, and cold the current flows
> Unto the sea where no wind blows,
> Seeking the land which no one knows.
> O'er its sad gloom still comes and goes
> The mingled wail of friends and foes,
> Borne to the land which no one knows.
> Alone with God, where no wind blows,
> And Death, his shadow — doomed, he goes :
> That God is there the shadow shows.
> O shoreless Deep, where no wind blows !
> And, thou, O Land which no one knows !
> That God is All, His shadow shows.

Plaint.   *Elliott.*

Again, all emotion is expressed as ideally as possible. Of course, truthfulness or naturalness is a great law; but one may be weak and another strong. What is natural to a strong man may not be so to the weak one. Of course, art will choose what is natural to the strong rather than what is characteristic of the weak. A strong man, after losing his mother, does not go about whining and pouring out his tears and revealing his sorrow. He reserves it. His voice is more subdued ; he speaks a little slower; he shows effort in controlling his breath. Natural dignity requires this. There is a fundamental impulse in sorrow to cause tears, and to agitate the breath and voice; but there is also an effort in the strong man to control it.

There is thus in the expression of all the emotions a conflict of tendencies. In heroic, patriotic, or sublime emotion, the natural impulse is toward extravagance and declamation; but at the same time there is an inclination to reserve. There is spontaneous effort everywhere in humanity to sustain conditions, and expression must regard this.

Thus we find from our study of emotion that the first or wildest impulse need not be the dominant one. There is co-ordination of impulses in all true abandon. Contrary tendencies toward excitement and reserve must be properly balanced in order to gain the repose and intensity which characterize all noble expression.

THE OLD GRENADIER'S STORY.

'T was the day beside the Pyramids, — it seems but an hour ago, —
That Kleber's Foot stood firm in squares, returning blow for blow.
The Mamelukes were tossing their standards to the sky,
When I heard a child's voice say, " My men, *teach me the way to die !* "

' T was a little drummer, with his side torn terribly with shot ;
But still he feebly beat his drum, as though the wound were not.
And when the Mamelukes' wild horse burst with a scream and cry,
He said, " O men of the Forty-third, *teach me the way to die !*

" My mother has got other sons, with stouter hearts than mine,
But none more ready blood for France to pour out free as wine.
Yet still life 's sweet," the brave lad moaned, " fair are this earth and sky ;
Then, comrades of the Forty-third, *teach me the way to die !* "

Oh, never saw I sight like that ! The sergeant flung down flag,
Even the fifer bound his brow with a wet and bloody rag,
Then looked at locks and fixed their steel, but never made reply,
Until he sobbed out once again, " *Teach me the way to die !* "

Then, with a shout that flew to God, they strode into the fray ;
I saw their red plumes join and wave, but slowly melt away.
The last who went — a wounded man — bade the poor boy good-bye,
And said, " We men of the Forty-third *teach you the way to die !* "

Then, with a musket for a crutch, he leaped into the fight ;
I, with a bullet in my hip, had neither strength nor might.
But, proudly beating on his drum, a fever in his eye,
I heard him moan, " The Forty-third *taught me the way to die !* "

They found him on the morrow, stretched on a heap of dead ;
His hand was in the grenadier's who at his bidding bled.
They hung a medal round his neck, and closed his dauntless eye ;
On the stone they cut, " The Forty-third *taught him the way to die !* "

'T is forty years from then till now, the grave gapes at my feet;
Yet when I think of such a boy I feel my old heart beat.
And from my sleep I sometimes wake, hearing a feeble cry,
And a voice that says, "Now, Forty-third, *teach me the way to die!*"

Thornbury.

XXV. SUGGESTION.

"THERE are," said Professor Monroe, "three great words in expression, — imagination, sympathy, and suggestion." The last of these is vitally connected with the other two.

Suggestion implies that all expression is only a hint, that truth and passion cannot be given adequately. Thought and feeling are subtle and spiritual, transcending all symbols. A word is but a conventional symbol, and all expression only an intimation. If we have seen an object, and have associated a word with it in common with others, the name will call up the object, and a more or less adequate conception of it will be formed. Other things being equal, however, all names are inadequate, and simply stand for ideas and objects familiar to ordinary minds. Hence such higher actions of the mind, as imagination and feeling, can be suggested only to corresponding faculties in other men.

To understand this more fully, some study of the nature of expression will be helpful. We are apt to consider that thought and emotion can be given to our fellow-men. But, as we have said, this cannot be done. We cannot impart an emotion or thought to any being whose nature is unlike our own. All expression implies simply communion. It is the union of mind with mind. All that one man can do is to awaken in another mind the same faculties which are active in his own. A word evokes only ideas previously associated with it. A combination of words and ideas, however, may suggest new conceptions and truths, and arouse another mind to apprehend them. By an appeal to the imagination and to sympathy, one mind can be awakened by another to higher creative activity.

Vocal expression uses a great many languages simultaneously. Inflection, however, and tone-color are not languages which furnish symbols or signs of ideas; they merely hint in a natural way the degree of sympathy, the point of view, the purpose and feeling of the speaker. Words also are mere suggestions; yet they far more adequately represent ideas than do inflection or tone-color in the voice.

In the expression of feeling, it is necessary to suggest the cause. A man crying on the street may awaken in the beholder either pity or ridicule, but the emotion he feels himself is not awakened in another until he conveys the cause. Thus some forms of expression are necessarily associated with others. True expression of feeling must be associated with the expression of thought.

Thus all expression must be complete; any isolated language will be a very imperfect medium. True expression is a complex combination of suggestions through various languages. Not only so, but where expression is made too definite and representative in the use of any one language, it is rendered more inadequate and superficial. The common-place expressions or statements of literal facts are never suggestive. The higher the subject and the deeper the feeling, the more expression is dependent upon intimation.

Again, the subjects of the highest expression are not objects of sense. The great literatures of the world, the greatest subjects of human thought, have not been seen by ourselves: they belong to history, or are in the soul of man. Even with our eyes we see but the outside of things. The closest observer is one who not only uses his eyes, but his imagination.

Poetry calls upon us to express ideas of eternity. We must conceive the transcendent ideals of the human mind. We must struggle even for an imperfect conception of God.

We must express, in short, things which cannot be adequately conceived. How can we do this? Take, for example, an extract such as this, —

> Roll on, thou deep and dark blue ocean, roll !
> Ten thousand fleets sweep over thee in vain.
>
> *Byron.*

No mind can adequately conceive the ocean. But to try to express the ocean itself is wholly to misconceive expression. Expression, especially vocal expression, is subjective; it reveals the attitude of the mind. It manifests the activity of the mind rather than the concept of the mind. It reveals the act of comprehending rather than comprehension itself. Hence, what can be done in such a situation is to awaken another mind with ours, to stretch out for a comprehension of the sea. We cannot conceive adequately the whole ocean, but we can show others how far our mind can reach; and as other minds are like our own, we can inspire them also to reach with us. The great speaker must have such a trained imagination that he can show greater activity of the mind in comprehending such things, and stimulate other minds to a greater stretch, and to act beyond their customary limits.

The same is true of our efforts to express our conception of a mountain, or any unusual or sublime idea.

> Mont Blanc yet gleams on high: the power is there,
> The still and solemn power of many sights
> And many sounds, and much of life and death.
> In the calm darkness of the moonless nights,
> In the lone glare of day, the snows descend
> Upon that Mountain; none beholds them there,
> Nor when the flakes burn in the sinking sun,
> Or the star-beams dart through them. — Winds contend
> Silently there, and heap the snow with breath
> Rapid and strong, but silently! Its home
> The voiceless lightning in these solitudes
> Keeps innocently, and like vapour broods
> Over the snow. The secret strength of things
> Which governs thought, and to the infinite dome
> Of heaven is as a law, inhabits thee!
> And what were thou, and earth and stars and sea,
> If to the human mind's imaginings
> Silence and solitude were vacancy?

Mont Blanc.   *Shelley.*

Here the mind must struggle to comprehend Mont Blanc, or a certain part of it. The reader may awaken the memory of one who has seen the mountain; but no two persons have seen exactly the same things in a mountain, and if his expression is perfect, or in proportion as it is perfect, he will awaken in another mind a point of view different from his own. He will stimulate imagination more than memory.

Thus we can express the inexpressible. Man may awaken a higher conception of deity in the soul of his fellow-man. His own conception of deity may be very inadequate, but he does not express this; he simply awakens another soul to a sympathetic effort, to a higher struggle toward adequate conception.

The highest expression shows the attitude of the man and of his awakened powers. It gives to another a point of view; it reveals the soul's effort and struggle. It shows the mind's sympathetic relations or bearings toward truth, indicates and draws another mind into sympathetic and corresponding activity.

The chief agent of the human soul in manifesting its activity is the human voice. A word is a symbol of an idea; it represents an idea. The modulations of the voice, its inflections, pitches, textures, and color, cannot do this. But they can discharge as high a mission. They can show the active exertion of the soul; they can discover its sympathetic attitude; they intimate the powers of the soul which are active. Hence, of all forms of expression, vocal expression is the most suggestive and the most intimately associated with the imagination and sympathy. It can be degraded to the lowest depth, but it can also rise to the loftiest height, and manifest the greatest activity of the human soul.

The noblest speech is not that which is greatest in itself, but that which most quickly arouses imagination and feeling.

The true function of vocal expression is to suggest what cannot be adequately represented, to manifest and suggest what words cannot give. Delivery is a present active thing; it shows a living active mind.

The highest activity of the soul is imagination, and its supremest law of manifestation is suggestion. If the voice is to be modulated to manifest the deepest feelings and intuitions, the sublimest flights of the soul; if we are to feel that "The peak is high, and the stars are high, and the thought of a man is higher;" if we are ever to realize that there is "A deep below the deep, and a height beyond the height; [that] our hearing is not hearing, and our seeing is not sight," — then no mechanical rules can be laid down. The imagination and the higher faculties must be stimulated; the whole nature must be broadened, — in short, the mind must be brought to the highest possible conception and appreciation of poetic and artistic activity.

THE VOICE AND THE PEAK.

THE voice and the Peak far over summit and lawn,
The lone glow and long roar green-rushing from the rosy thrones of dawn !
All night have I heard the voice rave over the rocky bar,
But thou wert silent in heaven; above thee glided the star.

Hast thou no voice, O Peak, that standest high above all ?
" I am the voice of the Peak; I roar and rave, for I fall.
A thousand voices go to North, South, East, and West ;
They leave the heights and are troubled, and moan and sink to their rest.

" The fields are fair beside them, the chestnut towers in his bloom ;
But they — they feel the desire of the deep — fall, and follow their doom.
The deep has power on the height, and the height has power on the deep ;
They are raised forever and ever, and sink again into sleep."

Not raised forever and ever ; but when their cycle is o'er,
The valley, the voice, the peak, the star pass, and are found no more.
The Peak is high, and flush'd at his highest with sunrise fire ;
The Peak is high, and the stars are high, and the thought of a man is higher.

A deep below the deep, and a height beyond the height !
Our hearing is not hearing, and our seeing is not sight.
The voice and the Peak far into heaven withdrawn,
The lone glow and long roar green-rushing from the rosy thrones of dawn !

Tennyson.

AND all day long a bird sings there,
　　And a stray sheep drinks at the pond at times ;
The place is silent and aware ;
　　It has had its scenes, its joys, and crimes,
But that is its own affair.

By the Fireside.   Browning

SONG.

I DREAMED that I woke from a dream, and the house was full of light ;
At the window two angel Sorrows held back the curtains of night.
The door was wide, and the house was full of the morning wind ;
At the door two armèd warders stood silent, with faces blind.

I ran to the open door, for the wind of the world was sweet ;
The warders with crossing weapons turned back my issuing feet.
I ran to the shining windows — there the winged Sorrows stood ;
Silent they held the curtains, and the light fell through in a flood.

I clomb to the highest window — Ah ! there with shadowed brow
Stood one lonely radiant Sorrow: and that, my love, was thou.
I bowed my head before her, and stood trembling in the light ;
She dropped the heavy curtain, and the house was full of night.
From "Wilfrid Cumbermede."   *George Macdonald.*

WE are spirits in a prison, able only to make signals to each other,
but with a world of things to think and say which our signals cannot
describe at all.   *Carlyle.*

THE lark above our heads doth know a heaven we see not here below ;
She sees it, and for joy she sings ; then falls with ineffectual wings.
Ah, soaring soul ! faint not nor tire !   Each heaven attained reveals a higher.
Thy thought is of thy failure ; we list raptured, and thank God for thee.
  A Violinist.   *Bourdillon.*

YOUTH AND AGE.

VERSE, a breeze 'mid blossoms straying,
Where Hope clung feeding, like a bee, —
Both were mine !   Life went a-maying
        With Nature, Hope, and Poesy,
            When I was young !
When I was young ?   Ah, woful when !
Ah ! for the change 'twixt Now and Then !
This breathing house not built with hands,
This body that does me grievous wrong,
O'er aery cliffs and glittering sands
How lightly then it flash'd along —
Like those trim skiffs, unknown of yore,
On winding lakes and rivers wide,
That ask no aid of sail or oar,
That fear no spite of wind or tide !
Nought cared this body for wind or weather
When Youth and I lived in 't together.

    Flowers are lovely; Love is flower-like ;
Friendship is a sheltering tree ;
Oh ! the joys, that came down shower-like,
Of Friendship, Love, and Liberty,
            Ere I was old !

    Ere I was old ?   Ah, woful Ere,
Which tells me Youth 's no longer here !
O Youth ! for years so many and sweet
'T is known that Thou and I were one,
I 'll think it but a fond conceit —

It cannot be that Thou art gone !
Thy vesper-bell hath not yet toll'd —
And thou wert aye a masker bold !
What strange disguise hast now put on
To make believe that thou art gone ?
I see these locks in silvery slips,
This drooping gait, this alter'd size:
But Springtide blossoms on thy lips,
And tears take sunshine from thine eyes !
Life is but Thought : so think I will
That Youth and I are housemates still.

Dew-drops are the gems of morning,
But the tears of mournful eve !
Where no hope is, life 's a warning
That only serves to make us grieve
    When we are old:
That only serves to make us grieve
With oft and tedious taking-leave,
Like some poor nigh-related guest
That may not be dismist,
Yet hath out-stay'd his welcome while,
And tells the jest without the smile.

Coleridge.

ABT VOGLER.

[After he has been extemporizing upon the musical instrument of his invention.]

WOULD that the structure brave, the manifold music I build,
  Bidding my organ obey, calling its keys to their work,
Claiming each slave of the sound, at a touch, as when Solomon willed
  Armies of angels that soar, legions of demons that lurk,
Man, brute, reptile, fly, — alien of end and of aim,
  Adverse, each from the other heaven-high, hell-deep removed, —
Should rush into sight at once as he named the ineffable Name,
  And pile him a palace straight, to pleasure the princess he loved !

Would it might tarry like his, the beautiful building of mine,
  This which my keys in a crowd pressed and importuned to raise !
Ah, one and all, how they helped, would dispart now and now combine,
  Zealous to hasten the work, heighten their master his praise !
And one would bury his brow with a blind plunge down to hell,
  Burrow awhile and build, broad on the roots of things,
Then up again swim into sight, having based me my palace well,
  Founded it, fearless of flame, flat on the nether springs.

And another would mount and march, like the excellent minion he was,
   Ay, another and yet another, one crowd but with many a crest,
Raising my rampired walls of gold as transparent as glass,
   Eager to do and die, yield each his place to the rest:
For higher still and higher (as a runner tips with fire,
   When a great illumination surprises a festal night —
Outlining round and round Rome's dome from space to spire)
   Up, the pinnacled glory reached, and the pride of my soul was in sight.

In sight? Not half! for it seemed, it was certain, to match man's birth;
   Nature in turn conceived, obeying an impulse as I ;
And the emulous heaven yearned down, made effort to reach the earth,
   As the earth had done her best, in my passion, to scale the sky :
Novel splendours burst forth, grew familiar and dwelt with mine,
   Not a point nor peak but found and fixed its wandering star ;
Meteor-moons, balls of blaze : and they did not pale nor pine,
   For earth had attained to heaven, there was no more near nor far.

Nay, more: for there wanted not who walked in the glare and glow,
   Presences plain in the place ; or, fresh from the Protoplast,
Furnished for ages to come, when a kindlier wind should blow,
   Lured now to begin and live, in a house to their liking at last ;
Or else the wonderful Dead who have passed through the body and gone,
   But were back once more to breathe in an old world worth their new :
What never had been, was now ; what was, as it shall be anon ;
   And what is — shall I say, matched both ? for I was made perfect too.

All through my keys that gave their sounds to a wish of my soul,
   All through my soul that praised as its wish flowed visibly forth,
All through music and me ! For think, had I painted the whole,
   Why, there it had stood, to see, nor the process so wonder-worth :
Had I written the same, made verse, — still, effect proceeds from cause ;
   Ye know why the forms are fair, ye hear how the tale is told ;
It is all triumphant art, but art in obedience to laws,
   Painter and poet are proud in the artist-list enrolled : —

But here is the finger of God, a flash of the will that can,
   Existent behind all laws, that made them, and lo, they are !
And I know not if, save in this, such gift be allowed to man,
   That out of three sounds he frame, not a fourth sound, but a star.
Consider it well : each tone of our scale in itself is nought ;
   It is everywhere in the world — loud, soft, and all is said :
Give it to me to use ! I mix it with two in my thought :
   And, there ! Ye have heard and seen : consider and bow the head !

Well, it is gone at last, the palace of music I reared;
 Gone ! and the good tears start, the praises that come too slow;
For one is assured at first, one scarce can say that he feared,
 That he even gave it a thought, the gone thing was to go.
Never to be again !   But many more of the kind
 As good, nay, better perchance : is this your comfort to me ?
To me, who must be saved because I cling with my mind
 To the same, same self, same love, same God : ay, what was, shall be.

Therefore to whom turn I but to thee, the ineffable Name ?
 Builder and maker, thou, of houses not made with hands !
What, have fear of change from thee who art ever the same ?
 Doubt that thy power can fill the heart that thy power expands ?
There shall never be one lost good !   What was, shall live as before ;
 The evil is null, is nought, is silence implying sound ;
What was good shall be good, with, for evil, so much good more :
 On earth the broken arcs ; in the heaven, a perfect round.

All we have willed or hoped or dreamed of good shall exist, —
 Not its semblance, but itself ; no beauty, nor good, nor power
Whose voice has gone forth, but each survives for the melodist
 When eternity affirms the conception of an hour.
The high that proved too high, the heroic for earth too hard,
 The passion that left the ground to lose itself in the sky,
Are music sent up to God by the lover and the bard ;
 Enough that he heard it once : we shall hear it by-and-by.

And what is our failure here but a triumph's evidence
 For the fulness of the days ?   Have we withered or agonized ?
Why else was the pause prolonged but that singing might issue thence ?
 Why rushed the discords in but that harmony should be prized ?
Sorrow is hard to bear, and doubt is slow to clear ;
 Each sufferer says his say, his scheme of the weal and woe :
But God has a few of us whom he whispers in the ear ;
 The rest may reason and welcome : 't is we musicians know.

Well, it is earth with me ; silence resumes her reign :
 I will be patient and proud, and soberly acquiesce.
Give me the keys.   I feel for the common chord again,
 Sliding by semitones, till I sink to the minor, — yes,
And I blunt it into a ninth, and I stand on alien ground,
 Surveying awhile the heights I rolled from into the deep ;
Which, hark ! I have dared and done, for my resting-place is found,
 The C Major of this life : so, now I will try to sleep.

Robert Browning

II.

ASSIMILATION, OR DRAMATIC RELATIONS.

XXVI. IDEAS AND EXPERIENCE.

ADEQUATE expression implies the presentation of ideas, thought, relations, and experience; words are the symbols which form the medium of communication, and if they are not understood, there can be little communication of thought. But ideas must be represented, and a correspondence brought about between the conceptions in the mind of the speaker and those in the mind of the hearer. Conceptions alone, however vivid, do not result in perfect expression: they must be presented in such a way as to form a natural and logical sequence. Expression, however, may still be imperfect, as thought may be cold, abstract, and formal, and awaken little or no response. True expression must not only communicate thought, but awaken dispositions favorable or unfavorable to its reception. Thus, the ideal relations of conceptions must be given as well as their logical relations. Each conception must be presented as part of a situation, and each thought with a background. Something more than mere thinking is needed: the imagination and the artistic nature must be awakened.

Even this is not all. Expression must manifest the man himself. It must not only clearly convey his ideas and thoughts; it must show his feelings, his earnest convictions, his interest in relation to the thoughts he utters. Every thought, according to some psychologists, has a co-ordinate response in feeling, which is an essential part of it, and which must not be separated from it in true expression. Where thought is separated from emotion, the voice will be cold and hard, and the expression neutral.

The utterance of words forms the mechanical part of vocal expression. It will be discussed under vocal training.

Conceptions in relation to vocal expression have already been considered; also the logical relations of ideas, and the imagination, or the ideal relations of ideas.

The next step in our discussion is the study of the various degrees and modes of assimilation, and the response to thought, or the effect of thinking upon feeling, the conditions of experience, and its relations to expression, — in other words, the dramatic relations of ideas.

> NEXT morning, waking with the day's first beam,
> He said within himself, "It was a dream!"
> But the straw rustled as he turned his head,
> There were the cap and bells beside his bed,
> Around him rose the bare, discolored walls,
> Close by, the steeds were champing in their stalls,
> And in the corner, a revolting shape,
> Shivering and chattering sat the wretched ape.
> It was no dream; the world he loved so much
> Had turned to dust and ashes at his touch!

Robert of Sicily.   *Longfellow.*

In these lines of Longfellow we find not only successive ideas in a logical sequence, not merely imaginative conceptions of the whole situation, and of every object or scene in succession, — elements which have been explained, but something more. The reader, thoroughly imbued with the imaginative situation, identifies himself with each mental act. Each event occurs in natural order; the reader shares King Robert's bewilderment on waking up, his vague understanding of what has happened, his gradual realization of the truth. He hears the "straw rustle," discovers the "cap and bells," the "bare discolored walls," "the steeds;" feels dismay as he observes in the corner "the wretched ape." Then follows the full realization of all, — "it was no dream."

The words, the pictures, the thought, the situations, or the feelings alone are inadequate; it is their harmonious union that produces perfect expression. Words are only symbols of ideas, and when given as mere objects of attention in themselves are not a means of expression. A single conception may be so isolated as to hinder thought; for thought is a comparison of ideas, and requires continuity. With the revelation of ideas in sequence, expression really begins, because a corresponding current of ideas can be thus awakened in another mind. But this is not all that is required for complete expression. Expression, to tell the whole truth, must show the sympathy of the thinking mind; must reveal the relation of the speaker to truth, his belief in it, or antagonism to it,—in short, his point of view, his mental attitude, and the degree and character of his assimilation.

To give a thought as such merely for the sake of thought may not only destroy interest in it, but neutralize and even pervert the truth it contains. Experience is a part of truth; or, at the very least, a realization of it.

A wide difference exists between fact and truth. Truth is found only in the relationship and unity of facts, or in the union of fact with experience. The real truth in a poem, essay, or speech consists not in mere facts, but in feeling and sympathy. What is the real truth of the Twenty-third Psalm? A mere neutral statement of its facts, however clear, cannot give its spirit.

If nothing is perceived but abstract ideas, the result is commonplace prose; the real spirit and soul are lost.

Experience gives definiteness of character; it implies the wisdom of an expert. The word etymologically implies going through and coming out of something. Accordingly, experience is the result of passing through and coming out of certain situations. Thus, experience in life develops character; the lack of the development of character is almost synonymous with lack of experience. Experience places a definite mark upon personality. The word "character" comes from the Greek, and means mark. In its highest sense it is applied only to a human being; but it may be taken in an objective sense, and applied to everything. In Nature, every pebble, every stone, every tree, every leaf, has its character. Each has passed through a specific and definite experience, and received a peculiar mark. There is no monotony except in death. A machine may make a million buttons or pins alike, but whatever is a part of Nature has a distinct and definite character.

All this applies especially to vocal expression. Each idea, each situation, each picture or thought, when properly conceived and assimilated, gives a specific and definite mark to every phrase, every word, every tone used in expressing it. Thus, a phrase, to have character, must have a manifestation, not of the thought only, but of the experience of the soul that thinks it. Expression has character in proportion to the union of thought with its associated experience.

Monotony is the death of all true feeling and discrimination, and since all thinking starts in discrimination, if there is no difference suggested, there will be little thought awakened in speaker or hearer.

The cause of monotony is not invariably, however, a lack of thought. It is frequently due to a lack of sympathy with the thought. Many persons are taught to conceal feeling, to render everything upon a neutral plane, or without any sympathetic relationship. Enthusiasm is not desirable in society; conventionality tends to repress experience; so men give thought merely for thought, without assimilation of its spirit. Many seem to think it egotistic to give conceptions and experience at the same time. There is a certain form of self-styled culture, which consists in an assumed indifference to everything in life, pretending to occupy a plane too high and exalted to be concerned with the ordinary events of existence. But this is not natural, and it is death to all artistic power.

Every child utters not only its thoughts but its experience in a perfectly frank way. Neutrality is unnatural, and is the result of false education, of repression and conventionality. There is a natural instinct in the human heart to identify itself with the truth.

We come, therefore, to an important step in expression,—the presentation of the truth by manifesting the whole personality: the development of the natural power to identify himself with the situation about which he speaks; to reveal in expression his point of view, and his relations to the truth; to bring into harmony the natural witnesses to the truth, so that all expression may be the telling of the truth, the whole truth, and nothing but the truth; and to secure that assimilation which is the fundamental requisite of all effective oratory, which is not only the soul of histrionic expression and reading, but of speaking, — the manifesting of the whole nature, the interpretation of truth by human character.

PROBLEM XXIII. *In a simple sequence of conceptions reproduce all the actions of the mind and feeling which would result if we had ourselves been a participant in the events and scenes which are recorded in words.*

THE LAUREL-SEED.

A DESPOT gazed on sunset clouds, then sank to sleep amidst the gleam ; —
Forthwith, a myriad starving slaves must realize his lofty dream.
Year upon year, all night and day, they toiled, they died — and were replaced ;
At length, a marble fabric rose, with cloud-like domes and turrets graced.

No anguish of those herds of slaves e'er shook one dome or wall asunder,
Nor wars of other mighty Kings, nor lustrous javelins of the thunder.
One sunny morn a lonely bird passed o'er, and dropt a laurel-seed ;
The plant sprang up amidst the walls, whose chinks were full of moss and weed.

The laurel-tree grew large and strong, its roots went searching deeply down ;
It split the marble walls of Wrong, and blossomed o'er the Despot's crown.
And in its boughs a nightingale sings to those world-forgotten graves ;
And o'er its head a skylark's voice consoles the spirits of the slaves.

Horne.

THE ELDER BROTHER.

A GENTLEMAN of England had two sons, the eldest of whom, eager for adventure, and weary of the restraints of home, obtained his father's permission to go abroad. Ten years later, a traveller, prematurely old, covered with rags and dust, stopped at an inn near the paternal estate. Nobody knew him, although, by his conversation, he appeared to have had some previous acquaintance with the neighborhood. Among other questions, he asked concerning the father of the two sons. "Oh, he's dead," said the landlord, — "been dead these five years, poor old man !—dead and forgotten long ago!"

"And his sons?" said the traveller, after a pause; " I believe he had two." "Yes, he had, Thomas and James. Tom was the heir, but he was unsteady, — had a roving disposition, gave his father no end of trouble. Poor old man! poor old man !" And the landlord, shaking his head sorrowfully, drained a good tankard of his own ale, by way of solace to his melancholy reflections.

The traveller passed a trembling hand over his own pale brow and rough beard, and said again : " But James, the second son, — he is — alive ?" " You would think so, " said the landlord, smacking his lips. " Things have happened well for him : the old man dead; his brother dead too — " " His brother dead?" said the traveller, with a start.

"Dead, or as good as dead. He went off on his travels ten years ago, and has never been heard of since. So James has come into the estate,—and a brave estate it is ; and a gay gentleman is James. What! going, sir?" "I beg your pardon," said the traveller, rising, " I — I have business with this James."

He proceeded at once to the house of the younger brother, whom he found just mounting his horse at the door of the paternal mansion. James, taking him for a common beggar, repulsed him rudely, when the traveller cried out, in deep agitation :   "James! my brother James! Don't you know me? I am your long-lost brother Thomas !" "Thomas ! Zounds, Tom !" said James, in utter astonishment. "Where in the name of wonder did you come from ?"   "The ship in which I sailed fell into the hands of pirates. I was sold as a slave in Algiers. I have but lately made my escape, and begged my way home. O James ! " sobbed forth the wretched man, quite overcome by his emotions. "Bless my heart ! Is it possible! " said James, by this time recovering from his surprise, and beginning to think that for him to regain a brother was to lose an estate. "I heard you were dead. I have the best evidence that you are dead!—I mean, that my brother Thomas is dead. I don't know you, sir! You must be an impostor, sir ! — Dick, send this beggar away ! "   And without giving the amazed Thomas a chance to remonstrate, or prove the truth of his story, James leaped upon his horse and galloped off.

The elder brother, driven from the house to which he was himself the rightful heir, penniless, and a stranger in his own country, returned to the village, where he endeavored in vain to enlist some old friends of his father in his behalf. His changed appearance justified them in refusing to recognize him; and his brother had now grown to be a man of influence whom they feared to offend. At last, however, he found an honest attorney to credit his story and undertake his cause. " If I win it for you," said he, " you shall give me a thousand pounds. If I fail, I shall expect nothing, as you will have nothing to give. And failure is very likely; for your brother will be exceedingly liberal with your money, and it will be hard to find a judge or jury or witness that he will not be able to bribe. But I will do what I can; and in the mean time I will advance you what money you need to live upon."

Fully satisfied of Thomas's integrity, and moved by his expressions of gratitude to make still greater exertions in his behalf, the attorney resolved to go up to London, and lay the case before Sir Matthew Hale, the Lord Chief Justice of the King's bench,—a man no less conspicuous for his abilities than for his upright and impartial character. Sir

Matthew listened with patience to the story, and also to the attorney's suspicions as to the means that would be used to deprive the elder brother of his right. "Go on with the regular process of the law," said he; "and notify me when the trial is to take place." The attorney did so, but heard nothing from Sir Matthew in reply.

The day of trial came; and the elder brother's prospects looked dark in the extreme. That morning a coach drove up to the house of a miller in the neighboring town. A gentleman alighted and went in. After saluting the miller, he told him he had a request to make, which was that he would exchange clothes with him, and allow his coachman to remain there with the carriage until the following day. The miller at first thought the stranger was joking; and on being convinced to the contrary, would fain have fetched his best suit; but no, — the stranger would have none but the dusty clothes he had on. The exchange was soon effected, and the stranger, transformed to a white-coated honest-faced old miller, proceeded on foot to the village where the court was sitting.

The yard of the court-hall was crowded with people waiting for the celebrated case to be called. Among them a sturdy miller — who must have come from a distance, since nobody knew him — was seen elbowing his way. The elder brother was there, looking pale and anxious. "Well, my friend," said the miller, accosting him, " how is your case likely to get on?" "I don't know," replied Thomas; "badly, I fear; since I have reason to suppose that both judge and jury are heavily bribed, while I have to depend solely upon the justice of my cause." Finding a sympathetic listener, he went on to relate all the circumstances of his case in a simple and sincere manner, which carried conviction with it.

"Cheer up, my friend!" said the miller, grasping his hand. "I have had some experience in these cases, and perhaps I can help you a little. If you will follow my advice, it can do no harm, and it may be of use to you." The elder brother willingly caught at anything that might give the least prospect of success. "Well, then," said the miller, " when the names of the jury are called over, object to one of them, no matter which. The judge will perhaps ask what your reasons are: then say, 'I object to him by the rights of an Englishman, without giving my reasons why.' Then if asked what person you would prefer in his place, you can look carelessly round and mention me. I think I may be of some use to you, though I can't promise."

Something in the honest old fellow's manner inspired confidence, and the elder brother gladly agreed to follow his directions. Soon the trial began. As the names of the jury were called, Thomas rose and objected to one of them. "And pray," said the judge, sternly, "why do you object to that gentleman as juryman?" "I object to him, my lord, by the rights of an Englishman, without giving my reasons why." "And whom do you wish to have in his place?" "An honest man, my lord, if I can get one!" cried Thomas, looking round. "Yon miller—I don't know his name—I'd like him." "Very well," says his lordship, "let the miller be sworn."

Accordingly the miller was called down from the gallery, and impanelled with the rest of the jury. He had not been long in the box, when he observed, going about among the jurymen, a bustling, obsequious little man, who presently came to him, and smilingly slipped five guineas into his hand, intimating that they were a present from the younger brother. "Yonder is a very polite man!" said the miller, to his next neighbor in the box. "I may well say so," said the delighted juryman, "since he has given me ten guineas to drink our friend James's health." And, on further inquiry, the miller discovered that each man had received double the sum presented to himself.

He now turned his whole attention to the trial, which appeared to lean decidedly in favor of the younger brother; for while a few witnesses timidly testified to the plaintiff's striking resemblance to the elder brother, others swore positively that the elder brother was dead and buried. When his lordship came to deliver his charge to the jury, he took no notice whatever of several palpable contradictions in the testimony of these false witnesses, but proceeded to expatiate upon the evidence as if it had been overwhelmingly in James's favor.

When he had concluded, the usual question was put to the jury: were they all agreed? The foreman rose, with his ten guineas jingling in his pocket, and was about to reply, supposing all to have been equally convinced with himself, by the same golden arguments; when the miller stepped forward, calling out: "No, my lord, we are not all agreed!" "And pray," said his lordship, frowning with contempt and impatience, "what objections have you?" "I have many objections, my lord! In the first place, all these gentlemen of the jury have received ten broad pieces of gold from the younger brother, while I have received but five!" Having made this simple announcement, to the consternation of the court, and to the amusement of the spectators, the supposed miller proceeded to point out the contradictory evidence which had been adduced, in such a strain of eloquence that all present—especially the elder brother and the attorney—were filled with amazement. At length the judge, unable to contain himself, called out with vehemence:

"Who are you? Where do you come from? What is your name?"
To which the miller calmly replied: "I come from Westminster Hall;
my name is Matthew Hale; I am Lord Chief Justice of the King's
Bench ; and convinced as I am of your entire unfitness to hold so high
a judicial position, from having observed your iniquitous and partial
proceedings this day, I command you to come down from that tribunal
which you have so disgraced. I will try this case myself." Sir Matthew
then ascended the bench in his miller's coat and wig, ordered a new
jury to be impanelled, re-examined the witnesses, and drew out confes-
sions of bribery from those who had sworn to the elder brother's death.
He then summed up the case anew, and it was unhesitatingly decided
in the elder brother's favor.   *Anon.*

XXVII. IDENTIFICATION.

THEN the Master, with a gesture of command, waved his hand ; and at the
word, loud and sudden, there was heard, all around them and below, the
sound of hammers, blow on blow, knocking away the shores and spurs. And
see ! she stirs ! she starts, she moves, she seems to feel the thrill of life
along her keel ; and, spurning with her foot the ground, with one exulting,
joyous bound, she leaps into the ocean's arms. And lo ! from the assembled
crowd there rose a shout, prolonged and loud, that to the ocean seemed to
say, "Take her, O bridegroom, old and gray ; take her to thy protecting
arms, with all her youth and all her charms."

The Building of the Ship.   *Longfellow.*

IF we read over the foregoing extract indifferently, or without
re-living the situations, the expression of the voice is consequently
negative and neutral; but if the mind really sees each scene, and
feels the movement of the events or situations, voice and body
are freely and naturally modulated.

Thus the real cause of genuine experience in oratorical delivery
or dramatic expression, is the identification of the speaker or reader
with the thought or situation. This is true whether we objectively represent the characteristics or actions of an object, or
whether we manifest our own feeling for the scene or object of
attention. In either case, unless the expression is meant to be
cold and mechanical, or mere imitation, sympathetic identification
of the reader with the scene must cause the experience.

The soul of all true expression is sympathy. The imagination conceives the scenes and situations, reproduces them in a nat-

ural order, and thus awakens sympathy, and creates an emotional response.

The true secret of assimilation and of truthfulness of experience is the identification with acts or events. This we do by holding the scenes and situations definitely before our minds. The ideas live and the events move; " ideal presence " dominates experience and determines the expression.

THE THREE FISHERS.

THREE fishers went sailing out into the West —
    Out into the West as the sun went down ;
Each thought of the woman who loved him the best,
    And the children stood watching them out of the town :
For men must work, and women must weep ;
And there 's little to earn, and many to keep,
    Though the harbor bar be moaning.

Three wives sat up in the light-house tower
    And trimmed the lamps as the sun went down ;
And they looked at the squall, and they looked at the shower,
    And the rack it came rolling up, ragged and brown.
But men must work, and women must weep,
Though storms be sudden and waters deep,
    And the harbor bar be moaning.

Three corpses lay out on the shining sands
    In the morning gleam as the tide went down,
And the women are watching and wringing their hands
    For those who will never come back to the town :
For men must work, and women must weep —
And the sooner it 's over, the sooner to sleep —
    And good-bye to the bar and its moaning.

Charles Kingsley.

Possibly the simplest illustration of man's identification of himself with an ideal scene, or with what has been called " ideal presence," may be found in a familiar story, such as " Paul Revere's Ride." The word " good-night " may be spoken in a hundred different ways, according to the conception of the mind, or the experience felt in the heart. The truthful rendering in this particular instance depends upon the conception of night, the danger, the patriotic endeavor, the resolution, and the pledge of the two men to each other which initiated a revolution. We then, with these elements in mind, observe the muffled oar, and each centre of attention in succession. The intense feeling awakened makes the "Somerset" seem a phantom ship and its masts and spars the bars of a prison.

In the same way we wander with Revere's friend Newman, sharing his anxiety and discovering the "muster of men," "the sound of arms," and "the tread of the grenadier." We do not think consciously perhaps of what kind of a man he was, or imitate his conceivable actions; but we put ourselves in his place.

An imaginative atmosphere surrounds us in climbing the ladder. At one point fancy may so realize the churchyard and the whole scene below, that we are led to an objective representation of the wind's whisper "all is well." In this, however, there is danger of losing the central grasp of the situation, and passing to an identification with a mere accident. The movements of the central events and of passion must dominate the reader through successive steps.

So of Paul Revere on the other shore: the reader may be an external observer of his acts until the events begin to move, and then, if he has genuine assimilation, becomes so identified with the movement of imaginary events that he participates in the scene.

PAUL REVERE'S RIDE.

LISTEN, my children, and you shall hear of the midnight ride of Paul Revere, on the eighteenth of April, in Seventy-Five: hardly a man is now alive who remembers that famous day and year.

He said to his friend: "If the British march by land or sea from the town to-night, hang a lantern aloft in the belfry-arch of the North-Church tower, as a signal-light, — one if by land, and two if by sea; and I on the opposite shore will be, ready to ride and spread the alarm through every Middlesex village and farm, for the country folk to be up and to arm." Then he said good-night, and with muffled oar silently row'd to the Charlestown shore, just as the moon rose over the bay, where swinging wide at her moorings lay the Somerset, British man-of-war: a phantom ship, with each mast and spar across the moon, like a prison-bar, and a huge, black hulk, that was magnified by its own reflection in the tide.

Meanwhile his friend, through alley and street, wanders and watches with eager ears, till in the silence around him he hears the muster of men at the barrack-door, the sound of arms, and the tramp of feet, and the measured tread of the grenadiers marching down to their boats on the shore. Then he climb'd to the tower of the church, up the wooden stairs, with stealthy tread, to the belfry-chamber overhead, and startled the pigeons from their perch on the sombre rafters, that round him made masses and moving shapes of shade ; up the trembling ladder, steep and tall, to the highest window in the wall, where he paused to listen and look down a moment on the roofs of the quiet town, and the moonlight flowing over all.

Beneath, in the churchyard, lay the dead in their night-encampment on the hill, wrapp'd in silence so deep and still, that he could hear, like a sentinel's tread, the watchful night-wind as it went creeping along from tent to tent, and seeming to whisper, "All is well !" A moment only he feels the spell of the place and the hour, the secret dread of the lonely belfry and the dead ; for suddenly all his thoughts are bent on a shadowy something far away, where the river widens to meet the bay, — a line of black, that bends and floats on the rising tide, like a bridge of boats.

Meanwhile, impatient to mount and ride, booted and spurr'd, with a heavy stride on the opposite shore walk'd Paul Revere. Now he patted his horse's side, now gazed on the landscape far and near, then impetuous stamp'd the earth, and turn'd and tighten'd his saddle-girth ; but mostly he watch'd with eager search the belfry-tower of the old North Church, as it rose above the graves on the hill, lonely and spectral, and sombre and still. And, lo ! as he looks, on the belfry's height, a glimmer, and then a gleam of light ! He springs to the saddle, the bridle he turns, but lingers and gazes, till full on his sight, a second lamp in the belfry burns !

A hurry of hoofs in a village street, a shape in the moonlight, a bulk in the dark, and beneath from the pebbles, in passing, a spark struck out by a steed that flies fearless and fleet : that was all ! and yet, through the gloom . and the light, the fate of a nation was riding that night ; and the spark struck out by that steed, in his flight, kindled the land into flame with its heat.

It was twelve by the village clock when he cross'd the bridge into Medford town ; he heard the crowing of the cock, and the barking of the farmer's dog, and felt the damp of the river-fog, that rises when the sun goes down. It was one by the village clock when he rode into Lexington. He saw the gilded weathercock swim in the moonlight as he pass'd, and the meeting-house windows, blank and bare, gaze at him with a spectral glare, as if they already stood aghast at the bloody work they would look upon. It was two by the village clock when he came to the bridge in Concord town. He heard the bleating of the flock, and the twitter of birds among the trees, and felt the breath of the morning breeze blowing over the meadows brown. And one was safe and asleep in his bed who at the bridge would be first to fall, who that day would be lying dead, pierced by a British musket-ball.

You know the rest. In the books you have read how the British regulars fired and fled ; how the farmers gave them ball for ball, from behind each fence and farmyard-wall, chasing the red-coats down the lane, then crossing the fields to emerge again under the trees at the turn of the road, and only pausing to fire and load.

So through the night rode Paul Revere ; and so through the night went his cry of alarm to every Middlesex village and farm, — a cry of defiance, and not of fear ; a voice in the darkness, a knock at the door, and a word that shall echo forevermore ! For, borne on the night wind of the Past, through all our history, to the last, in the hour of darkness and peril and need, the people will waken and listen to hear the hurrying hoof-beat of that steed, and the midnight message of Paul Revere.

Longfellow.

THE PIPER.

PIPING down the valleys wild, piping songs of pleasant glee,
On a cloud I saw a child ; and he, laughing, said to me,
"Pipe a song about a lamb !"   So I piped with merry cheer.
" Piper, pipe that song again !"   So I piped ; he wept to hear.
"Drop thy pipe, thy happy pipe ; sing thy songs of happy cheer !"
So I sang the same again, while he wept with joy to hear.
" Piper, sit thou down and write in a book, that all may read !"
So he vanished from my sight, and I plucked a hollow reed,
And I made a rural pen, and I stained the water clear ;
And I wrote my happy songs every child may joy to hear.

Blake.

XXVIII. CHANGES IN FEELING.

IN all thinking there is a series of continual changes, the mind by progressive transition passing from idea to idea.   As each idea causes an emotional response, how do changes of feeling compare with changes of ideas?   Emotion has a more vital and immediate relation to the voice and body than thinking.   Thought is revealed more by symbols, feeling rather by natural signs and languages. Hence, transitions of emotion are more definitely shown through the action of voice and body than transitions in thinking.   Emotion is a response to thought, a movement of the whole man, caused by ideas; hence, transitions of emotion are slower than transitions of thought.   Thinking may be excited quickly, but passion is gradually aroused.   Emotion flows like a stream, and admits only of direction and guidance.   As the waves of the ocean slowly respond to the wind, and do not immediately subside when the wind has ceased to blow, so passion may not immediately respond; but when once aroused, it tends to increase, or it may react rhythmically.   The domination of passion thus requires vivid realization of ideas, and frequently sudden and extreme changes of situation, which must during a pause completely change expression.

Thought is manifested through melody and form, passion through rhythm and tone-color. Rhythm in expression manifests the pulsation of passion. Rhythm does not change so quickly or frequently as form, which is a perpetual change; but its changes are very important, as they show the transitions in the weight of ideas, their importance, and the degree of excitement they awaken in the man,— his earnestness, his intensity, or his control.

Transitions of experience are very important, because often they can be expressed only by an indication of change. Some of the deeper and more intense passions can be only delicately suggested. Some passions can be indicated only by contrast, or by a sudden reaction. Monotony of feeling causes sameness of movement. Passion has a strong tendency to drift into monotony. Naturalness and power, therefore, depend upon the development of versatility, or readiness of response to every variation of thought and feeling. Development of control is dependent upon the union of the movement of passion with thought. Each change in situation must cause a change in feeling and expression.

PROBLEM XXIV. *Read passages with changes of situation, giving such strong attention to each one successively as to cause a distinct feeling and expression.*

THY braes were bonny, Yarrow stream,
When first on them I met my lover;
Thy braes how dreary, Yarrow stream,
When now thy waves his body cover!

Logan.

ONE cruel blow had fallen on him, when Nicholas Nickleby cried, "Stop!" "Who cried 'Stop!'" "I did. This must not go on." "Must not go on!" "No! Must not! Shall not! I will prevent it! You have disregarded all my quiet interference in this miserable lad's behalf; you have returned no answer to the letter in which I begged forgiveness for him, and offered to be responsible that he would remain quietly here. Don't blame me for this public interference. You have brought it upon yourself, not I." "Sit down, beggar!" "Wretch, touch him again at your peril! I will not stand by and see it done.

My blood is up, and I have the strength of ten such men as you. I have a series of personal insults to avenge, and my indignation is aggravated by the cruelties practised in this cruel den. Have a care, or the consequences will fall heavily upon your head!"

Dickens.

WARSAW's last champion from her height surveyed,
Wide o'er the fields, a waste of ruin laid;
O Heaven! he cried, my bleeding country save!
Is there no hand on high to shield the brave?
Yet, though destruction sweep these lovely plains,
Rise, fellow-men! our country yet remains!
By that dread name, we wave the sword on high,
And swear for her to live, with her to die!

Fall of Poland. *Campbell.*

THE heavens are veined with fire! And the thunder, how it rolls! In the lullings of the storm the solemn church-bell tolls for lost souls; but no sexton sounds the knell. In that belfry, old and high, unseen fingers sway the bell, as the wind goes tearing by! How it tolls for the souls of the sailors on the sea! God pity them! God pity them! wherever they may be.

Aldrich.

SIR HARCOURT fallen desperately in love with me? With me! That is delicious! Ah!—ha! ha! ha! I see my cue. I'll cross his scent — I'll draw him after me. Ho! ho! won't I make love to him? Ha!— Here they come to dinner. I'll commence my operations on the governor immediately. Ha! ha! ha! how I will enjoy it!

London Assurance. *Boucicault.*

I ONLY wish I'd got him safe in these two motherly arms, and would n't I hug him and kiss him! Lawk! I never knew what a precious he was — but a child don't not feel like a child till you miss him. Why, there he is! Punch and Judy hunting, the young wretch, it's that Billy as sartin as sin! But let me get him home, with a good grip of his hair, and I'm blest if he shall have a whole bone in his skin!

Thomas Hood.

Lady Teazle. For my part, I should think you would like to have your wife thought a woman of taste.

Sir Peter Teazle. Ay; there again — taste. Zounds! madam, you had no taste when you married me!

Lady T. That's very true, indeed, Sir Peter; and after having married you, I should never pretend to taste again, I allow.

Sheridan.

> THEY are here !   They rush on !   We are broken !   We are gone !
> Our left is borne before them like stubble on the blast.
> O Lord, put forth thy might !   O Lord, defend the right !
> Stand back to back, in God's name, and fight it to the last !

As experience gives character, what peculiar experiences give character to the lines in " Marmion," called Lochinvar ? It belongs to the age of chivalry; it has a heroic element; it is a spirited story; it has the atmosphere of high comedy, with a rapid movement of events. Lochinvar must be introduced to the audience as an object of admiration. If the reader has no admiration for him, he can awaken none in his listeners. Admiration lies at the base of all noble feeling. A sympathetic relationship toward a subject alone makes experience possible. This admiration permeates the first six lines. The changes in passing from Lochinvar to his horse, to his sword, are not very important. At the beginning of the second stanza we come to changes in situation. In the first two lines we see Lochinvar dashing across the country, and our admiration leads us to sympathetic identification of ourselves with his excitement and speed. In the second and third lines we even fly to Netherby before him, and realize what is about to happen there. Our sympathy for him passes into indignation at his enemies, and regret at the course of events. All hurry subsides, the rhythm completely changes. In the last two lines, at the sight of the supplanter, indignation gives way to contempt. All these changes of experience must be so felt as to change the expression. As Lochinvar arrives, his coolness restores our confidence. In the second line we keep our admiration centred upon him as we experience contempt for the cowardly bridesmen and brothers. As the father steps forward every word vibrates with his spirit. " His hand on his sword " must be given with his spirit of antagonism. It must not be a meaningless accident. The way in which small phrases like this are given tests the real artist. This clause shows the gradual identification of the reader with the father, which has a climax in the quotation.

Such changes continue throughout the poem. In the first line of the fifth stanza a subtle change in expression is caused by our admiration for the hero Lochinvar, and then for Ellen. We do

not admire them in the same way. In the next line the feeling
for them both causes another difference in the voice. In the third
line the mother does not "fret" as the father "fumes." The
difference, however, rests not upon these special words, but upon
the whole clauses. Words only give a hint of a situation. The
imaginative reader manifests his feeling and conception through
the whole clause. Lines containing such definite conceptions and
transitions of feeling should be practised as definite problems by
all who wish to secure control over emotion, and to develop imaginative and dramatic versatility.

LOCHINVAR.

O YOUNG Lochinvar is come out of the West, —
Through all the wide Border his steed was the best !
And, save his good broadsword, he weapon had none, —
He rode all unarmed, and he rode all alone.
So faithful in love, and so dauntless in war,
There never was knight like the young Lochinvar.

He stayed not for brake, and he stopped not for stone,
He swam the Eske River where ford there was none ;
But, ere he alighted at Netherby gate,
The bride had consented, the gallant came late :
For a laggard in love, and a dastard in war,
Was to wed the fair Ellen of brave Lochinvar.

So boldly he entered the Netherby hall,
'Mong bridesmen and kinsmen, and brothers, and all.
Then spoke the bride's father, his hand on his sword
(For the poor craven bridegroom said never a word),
" O, come ye in peace here, or come ye in war,
Or to dance at our bridal, young Lord Lochinvar ? "

" I long wooed your daughter, — my suit you denied ; —
Love swells like the Solway, but ebbs like its tide ;
And now am I come, with this lost love of mine
To lead but one measure, drink one cup of wine.
There are maidens in Scotland, more lovely by far,
That would gladly be bride to the young Lochinvar."

The bride kissed the goblet ; the knight took it up,
He quaffed off the wine, and he threw down the cup.
She looked down to blush, and she looked up to sigh,
With a smile on her lip and a tear in her eye.
He took her soft hand, ere her mother could bar —
" Now tread we a measure ! " said young Lochinvar.

So stately his form, and so lovely her face,
That never a hall such a galliard did grace ;
While her mother did fret, and her father did fume,
And the bridegroom stood dangling his bonnet and plume ;
And the bride-maidens whispered, " 'T were better by far
To have matched our fair cousin with young Lochinvar."

One touch to her hand, and one word in her ear,
When they reached the hall-door, and the charger stood near ;
So light to the croup the fair lady he swung,
So light to the saddle before her he sprung.
" She is won ! we are gone ! over bank, bush, and scar ;
They 'll have fleet steeds that follow," quoth young Lochinvar.

There was mounting 'mong Græmes of the Netherby clan ;
Forsters, Fenwicks, and Musgraves, they rode and they ran ;
There was racing and chasing on Cannobie Lee,
But the lost bride of Netherby ne'er did they see.
So daring in love, and so dauntless in war,
Have ye e'er heard of gallant like young Lochinvar ?

Sir Walter Scott.

KEENAN'S CHARGE.

THE sun had set ; the leaves with dew were wet ; down fell a bloody dusk on the woods that second of May, where Stonewall's corps, like a beast of prey, tore through with angry tusk. "They have trapped us, boys !" rose from our flank a voice. With a rush of steel and smoke, on came the thousands straight, eager as love and wild as hate ; and our line reeled and broke, — broke and fled; no one stayed — but the dead ! With curses, shrieks, and cries, horses, wagons, and men tumbled back through the shuddering glen, and above us the fading skies.

There 's one hope still, — those batteries parked on the hill ! "Battery wheel ['mid the roar] ! Pass pieces ; fix prolonge to fire retiring. Trot !" In the panic dire a bugle rings "Trot !" — and no more. The horses plunged, the cannon lurched and lunged, to join the hopeless rout. But suddenly rode a form calmly in front of the human storm, with a stern, commanding shout, "Align those guns" [We knew it was Pleasonton's] ! The cannoneers bent to obey, and worked with a will, at his word ; and the black guns moved as if they had heard. But, ah, the dread delay ! "To wait is crime ; O God, for ten minutes' time !" The general looked around ; there Keenan sat, like a stone, with his three hundred horse alone, — less shaken than the ground. "Major, your men ?" — "Are soldiers, General." "Then, charge, Major ! Do your best ; hold the enemy back at all cost, till my guns are placed, — else the army is lost. You die to save the rest !"

By the shrouded gleam of the Western skies brave Keenan looked in Pleasonton's eyes for an instant, — clear, and calm, and still ; then, with a smile, he said, "I will. — Cavalry, charge !" Not a man of them shrank. Their sharp full cheer, from rank on rank, rose joyously, with a willing breath, — rose like a greeting hail to death. Then forward they sprang, and spurred and clashed ; shouted the officers crimson-sash'd ; rode well the men, each brave as his fellow, in their faded coats of the blue and yellow; and above in the air, with an instinct true, like a bird of war their pennon flew. With clank of scabbards and thunder of steeds, and blades that shine like sun-lit reeds, and strong brown faces bravely pale, for fear their proud attempt shall fail, three hundred Pennsylvanians close on twice ten thousand foes.

Line after line the troopers came to the edge of the wood, that was ring'd with flame, — rode in and sabred and shot and fell ; nor came one back his wounds to tell. And full in the midst rose Keenan, tall in the gloom, like a martyr awaiting his fall, while the circle stroke of his sabre, swung 'round his head, like a halo there luminous hung. Line after line ; ay, whole platoons, struck dead in their saddles, of brave dragoons by the maddened horses were onward borne and into the vortex flung, trampled and torn. As Keenan fought with his men side by side, so they rode, till there were no more to ride. But over them, lying there shattered and mute, what deep echo rolls ? — 'T is a death salute from the cannon in place ; for, heroes, you braved your fate not in vain : the army was saved !

Over them now — year following year — over their graves the pine cones fall, and the whip-poor-will chants his spectre call ; but they stir not again, they raise no cheer, they have ceased. But their glory shall never cease, nor their light be quenched in the light of peace ; for the rush of that charge is resounding still that saved the army at Chancellorsville.

George Parsons Lathrop.

XXIX. CONTRAST.

CHANGES of feeling may arise in two ways: by contrast and gradation, or by natural progression or retrogression. Contrast is the more salient of these, for deep feeling often changes naturally to its opposite, and there are certain emotions so deep that they can be touched only momentarily, or suggested by opposition.

> THEY sought him east, they sought him west,
> They sought him all the forest thorough ;
> They only saw the cloud of night,
> They only heard the roar of Yarrow.

Logan.

In the first two of these lines, the whole search is recounted with anxiety and dread, and in the last two the sad result, despair and anguish, are brought into opposition.

MODEST and shy as a nun is she, one weak chirp is her only note ; braggart and prince of braggarts is he, pouring boasts from his little throat : " Bob-o-link, bob-o-link, spink, spank, spink ; never was I afraid of man ; catch me, cowardly knaves, if you can.   Chee, chee, chee."
Robert of Lincoln.   *Bryant.*

Descriptive contrasts are often found.   In these lines the two birds are delicately and harmoniously contrasted.   We sympathize with her modesty and her poor chirp, and feel his pride and exultation.   Her modesty and his sportive boastfulness are suggested and emphasized by contrast.

WHERE shall the lover rest, whom the fates sever, from his true maiden's breast parted forever ?   Where, through groves deep and high, sounds the far billow, where early violets die, under the willow.   There, through the summer day, cool streams are laving ; there, while the tempests sway, scarce are boughs waving ; there, thy rest shalt thou take, parted forever, never again to wake, never, O never !

Where shall the traitor rest, he, the deceiver, who could win maiden's breast, ruin, and leave her ?   In the lost battle, borne down by the flying, where mingles war's rattle with groans of the dying.   Her wing shall the eagle flap o'er the false-hearted ; his warm blood the wolf shall lap ere life be parted.   Shame and dishonour sit by his grave ever, blessing shall hallow it never, O never !   *Scott.*

As certain shades of color can be distinguished only by opposition with others, so in this beautiful song the character of the false lover is shown by contrast with the sympathy of Nature for the true and faithful.   With whatever definiteness of feeling the second part of the poem may be given, it will have little effect by itself.   It is only by its opposition to the first that its real intensity is felt and expressed.   Such contrasts should be thoroughly studied and harmoniously rendered by the voice.   Practice like this develops not only that beauty of tone-color which is the highest charm of vocal expression, but genuine simplicity of feeling and resonance of the voice as well.

The contrast must be very subtle and true.   It must be a genuine opposition, and not a discord or mere change.   As harmony in color demands great care in using the right shades, so in vocal expression great care must be taken that the right elements are brought into opposition.

A FEVER in these pages burns beneath the calm they feign ;
A wounded human spirit turns, here, on its bed of pain.
Yes, though the virgin mountain-air fresh through these pages blows ;
Though to these leaves the glaciers spare the soul of their mute snows ;
Though here a mountain-murmur swells of many a dark-bough'd pine ;
Though, as you read, you hear the bells of the high-pasturing kine —
Yet, through the hum of torrent lone, and brooding mountain-bee,
There sobs I know not what ground-tone of human agony.

*Obermann.**Matthew Arnold.*

At times there is a subtle imaginative contrast where two elements or points of view are blended, the change from one to another occurring freely and alternately throughout the poem, as is the case in Matthew Arnold's Obermann. Here the roaring of the mountain stream, the mute snows, and the murmuring pines are used as a means of showing deep feeling. Without the contrast our sympathy and imagination could hardly be touched; and unless this contrast is shown in the vocal expression the spirit of the poem is not rendered.

THE one with yawning made reply :
" What have we seen ? — Not much have I !
Trees, meadows, mountains, groves, and streams,
Blue sky and clouds, and sunny gleams."
The other, smiling, said the same,
But with face transfigured and eye of flame :
" Trees, meadows, mountains, groves, and streams !
Blue sky and clouds, and sunny gleams."

Brooks.

Contrasts cannot be rendered mechanically; they can be manifested in vocal expression only by means of sympathetic assimilation. At first thought the above lines are simply a contrast of indifference to interest; but when we try to express them we find, paradoxical as it may seem, that indifference cannot be expressed indifferently. A mere imitation of yawning and indifference awakens no interest. We must have a positive emotional attitude toward the indifferent man. We must in a sense enjoy him, and interpret his attitude with a certain earnestness which is our own. We do not express his indifference, but our own estimate of it; we can express only our own feeling. " No man can give anything to his fellowman but himself." If style in writing is the man himself, this is much more true of vocal expression. So of the second man, while

our sympathy is more positive, his smiling and eye of flame cannot be literally reproduced, — they can only be suggested by manifesting our appreciation, our admiration for his enjoyment of the
real beauty of nature.

This positive personal relationship, however, does not limit
expression, — it exalts it, and gives it greater variety than the
mechanical imitation that would summon up two men and imitate
their supposed actions. Moreover, there is greater possibility of
variety and truthfulness of interpretation by the sympathetic
method. The reader, for example, may show contempt for the
first man, or feel a humorous enjoyment of his inability to appreciate the beauty of his surroundings, and either might serve as a
truthful contrast.

Contrasts are often so delicate that they are entirely overlooked
by an unimaginative reader.

> O MIGHT we live together in a lofty palace hall
> Where joyful music rises, and where scarlet curtains fall.
> O might we live together in a cottage mean and small,
> With sods of grass the only roof, and mud the only wall !

Lovely Mary Donnelly.   *William Allingham.*

> YON deep bark goes where traffic blows
> From lands of sun to lands of snows;—
> This happier one, its course is run
> From lands of snow to lands of sun.
>
> O happy ship, to rise and dip,
> With the blue crystal at your lip !
> O happy crew, my heart with you
> Sails, and sails, and sings anew ! ”

                                                          Read.

Browning's monologue, “ Up at the Villa and Down in the
City,” shows how feelings or prejudices color objects in antagonism
to the ordinary view, and for this reason the contrast should be
exaggerated. The speaker has contempt for everything at the
villa; even what others consider beautiful, “ the hill o’ergrown
with olive trees,” “ the cypress,” “ the ploughed land,” “ the wild
tulip,”— are all ugly to him; and all that a normal mind dislikes
in the city are to him objects of the greatest admiration.

There is not only a contrast between the city and the villa, but
in the attitude of the character towards what is usually felt in the

contemplation of such objects. In fact, we enjoy this piece all the more because our feelings are directly opposed to his. There is a contrast thus felt and suggested between the reader and the character he is portraying. He is interpreting the very opposite of the feeling he would naturally have, and exaggerates and enjoys it all the more for this very reason. The emotion is dramatic, but is perfectly natural. Dramatic emotion in lower comedy and farce has often this character of opposition. The feeling of this " Italian person of quality" is given with great zest, but in such a way as to show the peculiarities of his character, and if not to awaken ridicule, certainly in such a way as to strengthen the very opposite feeling in the hearer toward these objects.

UP AT A VILLA—DOWN IN THE CITY.

[As distinguished by an Italian Person of Quality.]

HAD I but plenty of money, money enough and to spare,
The house for me, no doubt, were a house in the city-square ;
Ah, such a life, such a life, as one leads at the window there !

Something to see, by Bacchus, something to hear, at least !
There, the whole day long, one's life is a perfect feast ;
While up at a villa one lives, I maintain it, no more than a beast.

Well now, look at our villa ! stuck like the horn of a bull
Just on a mountain's edge as bare as the creature's skull,
Save a mere shag of a bush with hardly a leaf to pull !
— I scratch my own, sometimes, to see if the hair's turned wool.

But the city, oh the city — the square with the houses ! Why ?
They are stone-faced, white as a curd, there's something to take the eye !
Houses in four straight lines, not a single front awry !
You watch who crosses and gossips, who saunters, who hurries by :
Green blinds, as a matter of course, to draw when the sun gets high ;
And the shops with fanciful signs which are painted properly.

What of a villa ? Though winter be over in March by rights,
'T is May perhaps ere the snow shall have withered well off the heights :
You 've the brown ploughed land before, where the oxen steam and wheeze,
And the hills over-smoked behind by the faint gray olive trees.

Is it better in May, I ask you ? you 've summer all at once ;
In a day he leaps complete with a few strong April suns !
'Mid the sharp short emerald wheat, scarce risen three fingers well,
The wild tulip, at end of its tube, blows out its great red bell,
Like a thin clear bubble of blood, for the children to pick and sell.

Is it ever hot in the square? There's a fountain to spout and splash!
In the shade it sings and springs; in the shine such foam-bows flash
On the horses with curling fish-tails, that prance and paddle and pash
Round the lady atop in the conch — fifty gazers do not abash,
Though all that she wears is some weeds round her waist in a sort of sash!

All the year long at the villa, nothing's to see though you linger,
Except yon cypress that points like Death's lean lifted forefinger.
Some think fireflies pretty, when they mix in the corn and mingle,
Or thrid the stinking hemp till the stalks of it seem a-tingle.
Late August or early September, the stunning cicala is shrill,
And the bees keep their tiresome whine round the resinous firs on the hill.
Enough of the seasons, — I spare you the months of the fever and chill.

Ere opening your eyes in the city, the blessed church-bells begin :
No sooner the bells leave off, than the diligence rattles in :
You get the pick of the news, and it costs you never a pin.
By and by there's the travelling doctor gives pills, lets blood, draws teeth ;
Or the Pulcinello-trumpet breaks up the market beneath.
At the post-office such a scene-picture — the new play, piping hot!
And a notice how, only this moruing, three liberal thieves were shot.
Above it, behold the archbishop's most fatherly of rebukes,
And beneath, with his crown and his lion, some little new law of the Duke's!
Or a sonnet with flowery marge, to the Reverend Don So-and-so
Who is Dante, Boccaccio, Petrarca, Saint Jerome, and Cicero,
"And moreover," (the sonnet goes rhyming,) "the skirts of Saint Paul
    has reached,
Having preached us those six Lent-lectures more unctuous than ever he
    preached."
Noon strikes, — here sweeps the procession! our Lady borne smiling and
    smart
With a pink gauze gown all spangles, and seven swords stuck in her heart !
Bang, whang, whang, goes the drum, *tootle-te-tootle* the fife ;
No keeping one's haunches still : it's the greatest pleasure in life.

But bless you, it's dear — it's dear ! fowls, wine, at double the rate.
They have clapped a new tax upon salt, and what oil pays passiug the gate
It's a horror to think of.   And so, the villa for me, not the city !
Beggars can scarcely be choosers — but still — ah, the pity, the pity !
Look, two and two go the priests, then the monks with cowls and sandals,
And the penitents dressed in white shirts, a-holding the yellow candles.
One, he carries a flag up straight, and another a cross with handles,
And the Duke's guard brings up the rear, for the better prevention of
    scandals.
Bang, whang, whang, goes the drum, *tootle-te-tootle* the fife.
Oh, a day in the city-square, there is no such pleasure in life!

Browning.

"Two hands upon the breast, and labor's done;
Two pale feet crossed in rest — the race is won;
Two eyes with coiu-weights shut, and all tears cease;
Two lips where grief is mute, anger at peace;" —
So pray we oftentimes, mourning our lot:
God in his kindness answereth not.

"Two hands to work addrest aye for his praise;
Two feet that never rest walking his ways;
Two eyes that look above through all their tears;
Two lips still breathing love, not wrath nor fears;" —
So pray we afterwards, low on our knees;
Pardon those erring prayers! Father, hear these!

Now and Afterwards.   *Dinah Maria Mulock Craik.*

PAIN IN A PLEASURE BOAT.

Boatman. Shove off there! — ship the rudder, Bill — cast off! she's under
    way!

Mrs. F. She's under what? — I hope she's not! good gracious, what a spray!

B. Run out the jib, and rig the boom! keep clear of those two brigs!

M. I hope they don't intend some joke by running of their rigs!

B. Bill, shift them bags of ballast aft — she's rather out of trim!

M. Great bags of stones! they're pretty things to help a boat to swim!

B. The wind is fresh — if she don't scud, it's not the breeze's fault!

M. Wind fresh, indeed! I never felt the air so full of salt!

B. That schooner, Bill, harn't left the roads, with oranges and nuts.

M. If seas have roads, they're very rough — I never felt such ruts!

B. It's neap, ye see, she's heavy lade, and could n't pass the bar.

M. The bar! what, roads with turnpikes too? I wonder where they are!

B. Ho! Brig ahoy! hard up! hard up! that lubber cannot steer!

M. Yes, yes — hard up upon a rock! I know some danger's near!
    Lord, there's a wave! it's coming in! and roaring like a bull!

B. Nothing, ma'am, but a little slop! Go large, Bill! keep her full!

M. What, keep her full! what daring work! when full, she must go down!

B. Why, Bill, it lulls! ease off a bit — it's coming off the town!
    Steady your helm! we'll clear the *Pint!* lay right for yonder pink!

M. Be steady — well, I hope they can! but they've got a pint of drink!

B. Bill, give that sheet another haul — she'll fetch it up this reach.

M. I'm getting rather pale, I know, and they know it by that speech!
    I wonder what it is, now, but — I never felt so queer!

B. Bill, mind your luff — why, Bill, I say, she's yawing — keep her near!

M. Keep near! we're going farther off; the land's behind our backs.

B. Be easy, ma'am, it's all correct, that's only 'cause we tacks;
    We shall have to beat about a bit — Bill, keep her out to sea.

M. Beat who about? keep who at sea? — how black they look at me!

B. It 's veering round — I knew it would ! off with her head ! stand by !
M. Off with her head ! whose ? where ? what with ? — an axe I seem to spy !
B. She can't keep her own, you see ; we shall have to pull her in !
M. They 'll drown me, and take all I have ! my life 's not worth a pin !
B. Look out, you know, be ready, Bill — just when she takes the sand !
M. The sand — O Lord ! to stop my mouth ! how everything is planned !
B. The handspike, Bill — quick, bear a hand ! now, ma'am, just step ashore !
M. What ! ain't I going to be killed — and weltered in my gore ?
    Well, Heaven be praised ! but I 'll not go a-sailing any more !

Hood.

XXX. GRADATION.

CONTRAST in transition of feeling occurs occasionally, and is of
importance; but gradation or progression of emotion is continually
taking place, even in connection with contrast, and is still more
important. The power to grade, accumulate, control, or to show
retrogressive truthfulness of feeling, is the especial mark of a true
vocal artist. As in painting the subtle variety of one tone shows
the artist in color, as in music the delicate crescendo or diminu-
endo reveals the power of the musician, so the ability to indicate
the accumulation or progressive transition of emotion shows the
greatest power in vocal expression.

> YE living flowers that skirt the eternal frost !
> Ye wild goats sporting round the eagle's nest !
> Ye eagles, playmates of the mountain storm !
> Ye lightnings, the dread arrows of the clouds !
> Ye signs and wonders of the elements !
> Utter forth "God !" and fill the hills with praise !

In these lines there is a climax in the objects presented, and
a gradual progression and increase of the feeling of sublimity.
Starting with the living flowers, the mind climbs to the eagles
and the lightnings. This gradual progression of feeling is not
only necessary, but very effective. There must be reserve and
delicacy in the first in order to give possibility of gradation.

> FLOWER in the crannied wall,
>   I pluck you out of the crannies ; —
> Hold you here, root and all, in my hand,
> Little flower ; — but if I could understand
> What you are, root and all, and all in all,
>   I should know what God and man is.

There is here a gradual transition from objective observation to the deepest subjective contemplation. The flower is admired, first, as an object of attention in the wall. Then it is brought nearer, in the hand; then still nearer, in sympathy and admiration, it becomes a window through which the soul looks out into the eternal mystery.

Contrast and gradation are rarely separated. The secret of them both is the sympathetic identification of the reader's mind with the situations or events, or with a process of thought in another mind.

Hardly any practice can be arranged which will more effectively develop truthfulness of feeling and responsive co-ordination of the whole nature of man than the practice of various forms of transition. Contrast and gradation include only two forms of changes in feeling. There are subtle transitions in every great work from the objective to the subjective, from the didactic to the spiritual; in the person addressed, or in the situation, which the speaker or reader or actor must interpret, or the result will be monotonous and mechanical. Monotony is not only the worst of faults,— it is associated with many faults; for it results from a failure to think genuinely each idea, and to feel truly each specific situation,— the soul of all naturalness and power in expression.

Transitions occur in the most dignified poetry and literature, and nowhere more frequently than in the Scriptures. Note, for example, the rendering of any of the parables, or an account of the miracles in the gospels. How sudden are the changes of situation and experience in the prophets ! What subtle transitions of experience in the parallelisms of Hebrew poetry ! What abrupt transitions in the Psalms from talking to man to a direct address to God ! Yet these sudden changes are perfectly natural to any one whose imaginative nature has been trained, or who has preserved the dramatic naturalness of the child.

In the deepest and most exalted lyric feeling, the gradations are very delicate. In " Nathan Hale," for example, one strong situation is held vividly before the mind from first to last. There are many changes and references, but the brave hero led forth to die is the conception which dominates our emotion. The marked changes of transition do not greatly affect the flow of this intense stream. The same is true, also, of the "Three Fishers," by Kingsley.

NATHAN HALE.

To drum-beat and heart-beat, a soldier marches by:
There is color in his cheek, there is courage in his eye,
Yet to drum-beat and heart-beat in a moment he must die.
By starlight and moonlight, he seeks the Briton's camp;
He hears the rustling flag, and the armèd sentry's tramp;
And the starlight and moonlight his silent wanderings lamp.

With slow tread and still tread he scans the tented line,
And he counts the battery guns by the gaunt and shadowy pine;
And his slow tread and still tread gives no warning sign.
The dark wave, the plumed wave, it meets his eager glance;
And it sparkles 'neath the stars, like the glimmer of a lance, —
A dark wave, a plumed wave, on an emerald expanse.

A sharp clang, a steel clang, and terror in the sound !
For the sentry, falcon-eyed, in the camp a spy hath found;
With a sharp clang, a steel clang, the patriot is bound.
With calm brow, steady brow, he listens to his doom ;
In his look there is no fear, nor a shadow-trace of gloom ;
But with calm brow, steady brow, he robes him for the tomb.

In the long night, the still night, he kneels upon the sod ;
And the brutal guards withhold e'en the solemn Word of God !
In the long night, the still night, he walks where Christ hath trod.
'Neath the blue morn, the sunny morn, he dies upon the tree ;
And he mourns that he can lose but one life for Liberty ;
And in the blue morn, the sunny morn, his spirit-wings are free.

But his last words, his message-words, they burn, lest friendly eye
Should read how proud and calm a patriot could die,
With his last words, his dying words, a soldier's battle-cry.
From Fame-leaf and Angel-leaf, from monument and urn,
The sad of earth, the glad of heaven his tragic fate shall learn ;
And on Fame-leaf and Angel-leaf the name of *Hale* shall burn !

Francis M. Finch.

AND the men turned from thence, and went toward Sodom : but Abraham stood yet before the Lord.

And Abraham drew near, and said, Wilt thou destroy the righteous with the wicked ? Peradventure there be fifty righteous within the city : wilt thou destroy, and not spare the place for the fifty righteous that are therein ? That be far from thee to do after this manner, to slay the righteous with the wicked, and that the righteous should be as the wicked ; that be far from thee : shall not the Judge of all the earth do right ? And the Lord said, If I find in Sodom fifty righteous, within the city, then I will spare all the place for their sakes.

And Abraham answered, and said, Behold now, I have taken upon me to speak unto the Lord, which am but dust and ashes : Peradventure there shall lack five of the fifty righteous : wilt thou destroy all the city for lack of five ? And he said, I will not destroy it if I find there forty and five. And he spake unto him yet again, and said, Peradventure there shall be forty found there. And he said, I will not do it for the forty's sake.

And he said unto him, Oh let not the Lord be angry, and I will speak : Peradventure there shall thirty be found there. And he said, I will not do it, if I find thirty there. And he said, Behold now, I have taken upon me to speak unto the Lord : Peradventure there shall be twenty found there. And he said, I will not destroy it for the twenty's sake. And he said, Oh let not the Lord be angry, and I will speak yet but this once: Peradventure ten shall be found there. And he said, I will not destroy it for the ten's sake. And the Lord went his way, as soon as he had left communing with Abraham : and Abraham returned unto his place.

______

THE HAPPY HEART.

ART thou poor, yet hast thou golden slumbers !
  O sweet content !
Art thou rich, yet is thy mind perplexèd ?
  O punishment !
Dost thou laugh to see how fools are vexèd
To add to golden numbers, golden numbers ?
O sweet content ! O sweet O sweet content !
 Work apace, apace, apace, apace ;
 Honest labour bears a lovely face ;
Then hey nonny nonny, hey nonny nonny !

Canst drink the waters of the crispèd spring ?
  O sweet content !
Swimm'st thou in wealth, yet sink'st in thine own tears ?
  O punishment !
Then he that patiently want's burden bears
No burden bears, but is a king, a king !
O sweet content ! O sweet O sweet content !
 Work apace, apace, apace, apace ;
 Honest labour bears a lovely face ;
Then hey nonny nonny, hey nonny nonny !   *Dekker.*

WITH cautious step, and ear awake,
He climbs the crag and threads the brake ;
And not the summer solstice, there,
Temper'd the midnight mountain air,
But every breeze, that swept the wold,
Benumb'd his drenchèd limbs with cold.
In dread, in danger, and alone,
Famish'd and chill'd, through ways unknown,
Tangled and steep, he journey'd on ;
Till, as a rock's huge point he turn'd,
A watch-fire close before him burn'd.

Beside its embers red and clear,
Bask'd, in his plaid, a mountaineer ;
And up he sprung with sword in hand, —
"Thy name and purpose ! Saxon, stand !" —
"A stranger." — " What dost thou require ?" —
"Rest and a guide, and food and fire.
My life 's beset, my path is lost,
The gale has chill'd my limbs with frost." —
"Art thou a friend to Roderick ?" — "No." —
"Thou darest not call thyself a foe ?" —
"I dare ! to him and all the band
He brings to aid his murderous hand."

Lady of the Lake.   *Scott.*

XXXI. IMITATION AND ASSIMILATION.

SOFT is the strain when Zephyr gently blows,
And the smooth stream in smoother numbers flows ;
But when loud surges lash the sounding shore,
The hoarse rough verse should like the torrent roar.

THE method usually adopted in rendering these lines is to imitate the breeze in the expression of the first and the second lines, and then to imitate the lashing of the waves in the last two lines. In this way, it is argued, there is given variety in objective representation.

We find, however, that there is a different method of giving expression to the different ideas. We can create imaginatively the two images or illustrations, and instead of putting ourselves into an attitude of mind to objectively represent or imitate them, we can manifest the feeling they awaken.

The first of these methods may be called imitation; the second may be here named Assimilation. Which of the two is the right one? No more important question can be asked for the higher development of vocal expression.

Ideas, of course, are not words. The word "imitation" is used in many senses by different writers. Coleridge says the word "copying" should be used for the lower form of objective representation, and that the word "imitation" should be reserved for its higher aspect. Ruskin, on the contrary, uses imitation as synonymous with the lowest form of copying, and as antagonistic to all true artistic representation. Most writers use the word in the sense of Ruskin.

To Aristotle, art was the imitation of Nature; but Nature to the Greeks was a process, not a product. The imitation of a process, especially that of Nature, is totally different from the imitation of a product, an expression, objective sound, or character.

In one sense of the word imitation, all education starts with it. The little child learns to speak, some think, by imitation; but there is a spontaneous impulse to utterance before it is able to imitate a word. This spontaneous impulse from within is the chief cause of language. Imitation must be adopted occasionally in the teaching of vocal training, and to some extent in vocal expression; but it is an expedient used only for stimulation of the psychic processes, or to bring them into relation with other minds. Those who prefer the terms "Mechanical Imitation" and "Sympathetic Imitation," in place of the words used here, — Imitation and Assimilation, — would, of course, make the same distinction. However they may be named, there are two essentially different processes or methods in expression. One method endeavors by mechanical expedients to re-produce certain external facts; the other centres in the man and manifests the impressions made upon him, — gives his feeling for the object, rather than attempts to represent the object itself. The one expresses external differences; the other reveals the subjective differences in the impression produced upon the man.

If vocal expression is taught by imitation, the originality and the special power of each individual are destroyed, and sameness is sure to result.   The lowest literature or art has much imitation; the highest has little, or none at all.

CHAMOUNI AT SUNRISE.[1]

FROM the deep shadow of the still fir-groves
Trembling I look to thee, eternal height !
Thou dazzling summit, from whose top my soul
Floats, with dimmed vision, to the infinite !

Who sank in earth's firm lap the pillars deep
Which hold through ages thy vast pile in place ?
Who reared on high, in the clear ether's vault,
Lofty and strong, thy ever-radiant face ?

Who poured you forth, ye mountain torrents wild,
Down thundering from eternal winter's breast ?
And who commanded, with almighty voice,
"Here let the stiffening billows find their rest " ?

Who points to yonder morning-star his path,
Borders with wreaths of flowers the eternal frost ?
To whom, in awful music, cries the stream,
O wild Arveiron ! in fierce tumult tossed ?

Jehovah ! God ! bursts from the crashing ice ;
The avalanche thunders down the steeps the call :
Jehovah ! rustle soft the bright tree-tops,
Whisper the silver brooks that murmuring fall.

Translated by Dwight.   *Fredrike Brün.*

To illustrate further so as to discriminate the imitative from the assimilative point of view, take this poem on " Chamouni," which probably suggested to Coleridge his Hymn to Mont Blanc.   The former method endeavors to imitate the crushing ice of an avalanche, in repeating " Jehovah God ; " and so in the third line the word " Jehovah " must be spoken in imitation of the breeze among the trees, or the brooks.

But he who reads from assimilation adopts the point of view of a sympathetic spectator.   He imaginatively creates and hears even more than the imitator, — the crushing ice and the thunder of the avalanche ; but instead of imitating the external noise, he feels the meaning of the sounds, and expresses the reverent feeling which is awakened in his heart.   There is a certain representation,

[1] See Coleridge's Hymn, p. 40.

but it is an accident, and in the background. There is a difference, that is to say, between the first two and the second two lines of the last stanza. Sympathetic observation of the ice and the avalanche causes lines one and two to vibrate more or less with a sense of power, and the last two lines to express the softness of the breeze among the trees and the tenderness of the murmuring brook; but this is not imitation, — it is a sympathetic identification with the scene. The reader manifests his feeling, and does not represent external sounds. The effect is similar, but the process totally different, and the process in this case is everything.

There are, however, differences in the effect. Imitation is mechanical, and is applied most frequently to individual words. Assimilation is suggestive, imaginative, reveals the character of the man, and differs with every one who reads the passage. It does not deal with single words, but gives atmosphere to the whole sentence. Moreover, the voice cannot represent the sound of the avalanche, and the effort is ridiculous. In the highest literature the great artist manifests what he feels of the scene in the simplest way.

Looking at these two methods, therefore, it can be seen that assimilation causes expression to come from the mental identification of one's self with the scene. It manifests the effect of sympathetic observation. It is a spontaneous and natural mode, from within out, characteristic of all life. Imitation, on the other hand, is more or less an external thing. It acts from without, copying objective sounds and facts. Its highest success depends upon vocal dexterity. Assimilation comes from within. It enters into participation with the heart of things. Imitation reproduces external characteristics, assimilation expresses an identification of internal processes. It deals with a cause, with the heart. Imitation begins with effects, and ends by calling attention to the execution. The other makes expression an outgrowth as natural as the song of the bird or the blooming of the flower. The imagination penetrates to the soul of things, and awakens a deep response from the human heart. Imitation is antagonistic to imagination; it centres in mechanical expertness.

Note, again, the effect of each method upon the auditor. The one appeals to the mind, the other chiefly to the eye or the ear. One appeals to the creative instinct, the deeper feelings and sympathies of the soul; the other calls for admiration of skill. Imitation dulls the sensibilities to noble passion, and the auditor becomes a mere spectator of performance. One is dramatic, the other spectacular.

The method by imitation is usually regarded as an essential element in dramatic art. Whatever is dramatic or histrionic is often considered as primarily imitative. But imitation belongs to farce, and the lowest forms of expression. Here is one acting the part of an old man. He places his legs near together and stiffens them; he cramps his voice; and tries to imitate a few of the accidents of age; but assimilation penetrates to the heart, and identifies the actor with the conception of the personality. The whole body, if trained to be responsive, co-operates naturally with the expression. Imitation aggregates; it is always one-sided; it only uses certain parts or agents of the body. Imitation can never produce the unity and spontaneity which are the universal qualities of nature. It is only by assimilation that one soul can identify itself with another, which is the fundamental element of the dramatic. A character portrayed by assimilation seems to live and move. Every part is consistent with every other part. It is not imitative patch-work, but the sympathetic manifestation of a personality. Thus imitation is not dramatic, because it can only give accidents and oddities, while the essence of the dramatic is the interpretation of character, the manifestation of the response in experience to ideas.

There is no loss so great as the loss of originality. Every soul to be alive must act in its own way, in accordance with its own impressions, its own instincts. Vocal expression is the freest art, because it lies closest to nature. God has given the soul of man an inborn instinct which awakens and thrills him; the artist looks into the face of nature and feels mysteries to which he gives voice. We are not to bow down to wood or stone, for He is the Life; He is the vine, we the branches.

In the lower forms of literature much imitative modulation is possible; but in Wordsworth's great " Ode on Immortality," Keats' " Hymn to Intellectual Beauty," or Shelley's " Ode to the

West Wind," note how little imitation is found. There is much in " Midsummer's Night's Dream," or the " Comedy of Errors," but little in " Hamlet " and " Macbeth." Imitation cannot interpret great poetry; its use in delivery has often degraded great poems to the level of farce.

The aim of all expression is to bring a soul into right relationship with truth. The highest thing one soul can do for another is to give it a point of view. Imitation establishes a superficial relationship, a mechanical, unsympathetic point of view. Imagination and sympathetic insight suggest the right point of view in expressing the idea. The true reader appeals to the mind, not to sense, awakens thought, presents a new aspect, appeals to imagination and to sympathy. His character lives. He does not please the fancy, but awakens imagination and passion. His art is not the product of a machine, not an aggregation of parts, but an organism with a heart and soul.

IDEAS OF IMITATION.

Whenever anything looks like what it is not, the resemblance being so great as *nearly* to deceive, we feel a kind of pleasurable surprise, an agreeable excitement of mind, exactly the same in its nature as that which we receive from juggling. Whenever we perceive this in something produced by art, that is to say, whenever the work is seen to resemble something which we know it is not, we receive what I call an idea of imitation. . . . Now two things are requisite to our complete and more pleasurable perception of this: first, that the resemblance be so perfect as to amount to a deception ; secondly, that there be some means of proving at the same moment that it *is* a deception. The most perfect ideas and pleasures of imitation are, therefore, when one sense is contradicted by another, both bearing as positive evidence on the subject as each is capable of alone ; as when the eye says a thing is round, and the finger says it is flat ; they are, therefore, never felt in so high a degree as in painting, where appearance of projection, roughness, hair, velvet, etc., are given with a smooth surface, or in wax-work, where the first evidence of the senses is perpetually contradicted by their experience ; but the moment we come to marble, our definition checks us, for a marble figure does not look like what it is not: it looks like marble, and like the form of a man, but it *is* marble, and it *is* the form of a man. It does not look like a man, which it is not, but like the form of a man, which it is. Form is form, whether in marble or in flesh —

not an imitation or resemblance of form, but real form. The chalk outline of the bough of a tree on paper, is not an imitation; it looks like chalk and paper — not like wood, and that which it suggests to the mind is not properly said to be *like* the form of a bough, it *is* the form of a bough. Now, then, we see the limits of an idea of imitation; it extends only to the sensation of trickery and deception occasioned by a thing's intentionally seeming different from what it is ; and the degree of the pleasure depends on the degree of difference and the perfection of the resemblance, not on the nature of the thing resembled. . . . These ideas and pleasures are the most contemptible which can be received from art; first, because it is necessary to their enjoyment that the mind should reject the impression and address of the thing represented, and fix itself only upon the reflection that it is not what it seems to be. All high or noble emotion or thought are thus rendered physically impossible, while the mind exults in what is very like a strictly sensual pleasure. . . .

Ideas of imitation are contemptible in the second place, because not only do they preclude the spectator from enjoying inherent beauty in the subject, but they can only be received from mean and paltry subjects, because it is impossible to imitate anything really great. We can "paint a cat or a fiddle, so that they look as if we could take them up;" but we cannot imitate the ocean, or the Alps. We can imitate fruit, but not a tree; flowers, but not a pasture; cut-glass, but not the rainbow. All pictures in which deceptive powers of imitation are displayed are therefore either of contemptible subjects, or have the imitation shown in contemptible parts of them, bits of dress, jewels, furniture, etc.

Thirdly, these ideas are contemptible, because no ideas of power are associated with them ; to the ignorant, imitation, indeed, seems difficult, and its success praiseworthy, but even they can by no possibility see more in the artist than they do in a juggler, who arrives at a strange end by means with which they are unacquainted.

Ruskin.

WHEN Ajax strives some rock's vast weight to throw,
The line, too, labors, and the words move slow ;
Not so, when swift Camilla scours the plain,
Flies o'er the unbending corn and skims along the main.

Pope.

WORDS are instruments of music : an ignorant man uses them for jargon ; but when a master touches them they have unexpected life and soul. Some words sound out like drums ; some breathe memories sweet as flutes; some call like a clarionet ; some shout a charge like trumpets; some are sweet as children's talk; others rich as a mother's answering back.

"Come, if you dare!" our trumpets sound ;
"Come, if you dare !" the foes rebound ;
  "We come, we come !"
Says the double beat of the thund'ring drum :
  Now they charge on amain,
  Now they rally again.
The gods from above the mad labour behold,
And pity mankind that will perish for gold.

Buz, quoth the blue fly, hum, quoth the bee ;
Buz and hum they cry, and so do we,
In his ear, in his nose, thus, do you see ?
He ate the dormouse ; else it was he.   *Ben Jonson.*

DOVER BEACH.

The sea is calm to-night ; the tide is full ; the moon lies fair upon the Straits ; on the French coast the light gleams, and is gone ; the cliffs of England stand, glimmering and vast, out in the tranquil bay. Come to the window : sweet is the night-air ! only from the long line of spray where the ebb meets the moon-blanched sand, listen ! you hear the grating roar of pebbles which the waves suck back, and fling, at their return, up the high strand, begin and cease, and then again begin, with tremulous cadence slow, and bring the eternal note of sadness in.

Sophocles long ago heard it on the Ægean, and it brought into his mind the turbid ebb and flow of human misery : we find also in the sound a thought, hearing it by this distant northern sea. . . .   *Matthew Arnold.*

THE KITCHEN CLOCK.

Knitting is the maid o' the kitchen, Milly ; doing nothing sits the chore boy, Billy : "Seconds reckoned, seconds reckoned, every minute, sixty in it. Milly, Billy, Billy, Milly, tick-tock, tock-tick, nick-knock, knock-nick, knockety-nick, nockety-knock " — goes the kitchen clock.

Closer to the fire is rosy Milly, every whit as close and cosy, Billy : "Time's a-flying, worth your trying ; pretty Milly — kiss her, Billy ! Milly, Billy, Billy, Milly, tick-tock, tock-tick, now — now — quick — quick ! knockety-nick, nickety-knock " — goes the kitchen clock.

Something 's happened, very red is Milly, Billy boy is looking very silly ; " Pretty misses, plenty kisses ; make it twenty, take a plenty. Billy, Milly, Milly, Billy, right — left, left — right, that 's right, all right, knockety-nick, nickety-knock " — goes the kitchen clock.

Weeks gone, still they 're sitting, Milly, Billy ; oh, the winter winds are wondrous chilly ! "Winter weather, close together ; would n't tarry, better marry, Milly, Billy, Billy, Milly, two — one, one — two, don't wait, 't won't do, knockety-knick, nickety-knock " — goes the kitchen clock.

Winters two have gone, and where is Milly? Spring has come again, and where is Billy? "Give me credit, for I did it ; treat me kindly, mind you wind me. Mister Billy, mistress Milly, my — O, O — my, by-by, by-by, nickety-knock, cradle rock" — goes the kitchen clock.

Cheney.

XXXII. MANIFESTATION AND REPRESENTATION.

IT has been shown that imitation belongs to the lowest forms of art, if, in fact, it be not characteristic of entire absence of proper artistic imagination and feeling. True artistic expression has been shown to be due to assimilation, — not to external manipulation, but to a sympathetic realization of imaginative situations which will create such an inner life as will cause a modulation of voice and body.

There are, however, two modes of expressing assimilation which need to be carefully discriminated. They are not inconsistent with each other, may exist simultaneously, and are really two co-ordinate and necessary modes of expressing imaginative and sympathetic action ; but their processes are distinct, and they give rise to different artistic effects. They have been called in the "Province of Expression," Representation and Manifestation.

Manifestation is a revelation of man's own thought and feeling in his own way. It is subjective, personal, sympathetic, revealing as directly as possible the character and feeling of the man himself. It is direct and immediate, lyric rather than dramatic.

Representation results from a sympathetic identification of the speaker with a situation intense enough to reproduce the process of thought and feeling in a definite, objective body. It results from such identification that leads to a conscious or unconscious presentation of objective actions or effects. It may reveal the thought and feeling in the form in which a distinct type of character would give it.

Manifestation is more subjective, representation is more objective. Manifestation shows the man himself, the feelings that awaken in his breast; representation realizes the object so vividly that it desires to present its own form. Both of them are natural and the result of genuine thinking and feeling, of sympathetic identification, or assimilation.

To illustrate these two modes of assimilation, take "The Cavalier's Escape," by Thornbury. The poem refers to a simple situation. It is essentially a lyric, and in reading most of the lines, we manifest directly the simple emotions and responses to the ideas; but there are certain lines where we identify ourselves so fully with the Cavalier, and so vividly imagine the scene, that the words become the objective body of ideas. Though "pad, pad" in the first lines directly represent the light, quick step of his chestnut, they are not imitative. Their expression depends upon the reader's dramatic assimilation of the Cavalier's exultant admiration for his horse and of her movement.

"Trample, trample," "trap, trap," express the heavy tread and labored movement of the horses of his enemies. His contempt inspires his imagination to conceive these definitely, and his voice to represent them.

THE CAVALIER'S ESCAPE.

TRAMPLE! trample! went the roan, trap! trap! went the gray;
But pad! *pad!* PAD! like a thing that was mad, my chestnut broke away.
It was just five miles from Salisbury town, and but one hour to day.

Thud! *thud!* came on the heavy roan, rap! *rap!* the mettled gray;
But my chestnut mare was of blood so rare, that she showed them all the way.
Spur on! spur on! I doffed my hat, and wished them all good-day.

They splashed through miry rut and pool, splintered through fence and rail;
But chestnut Kate switched over the gate — I saw them droop and fail.
To Salisbury town — but a mile of down, once over this brook and rail.

Trap! trap! I heard their echoing hoofs past the walls of mossy stone;
The roan flew on at a staggering pace, but blood is better than bone.
I patted old Kate, and gave her the spur, for I knew it was all my own.

But trample! trample! came their steeds, and I saw their wolf's eyes burn;
I felt like a royal hart at bay, and made me ready to turn.
I looked where highest grew the may, and deepest arched the fern.

I flew at the first knave's sallow throat, — one blow, and he was down.
The second rogue fired twice, and missed; I sliced the villain's crown.
Clove through the rest, and flogged brave Kate, *fast, fast to Salisbury town!*

Pad! pad! they came on the level sward, thud! thud! upon the sand;
With a gleam of swords, and a burning match, and a shaking of flag and band;
But one long bound, and I passed the gate, safe from the canting band.

George Walter Thornbury.

Now, if a reader imagines the scene, conceives the Cavalier's character, and assimilates his feeling, the expression is true, natural representation; but if he tries to embody mechanically in his voice these effects as effects, then he has imitation, not assimilation.

This poem is peculiarly and necessarily representative; but mechanical imitation degrades it, because it carries the mind away from the central passion. Besides, only a few words are representative. The second time he refers to his own horse he has no representative words. This shows that representation is only occasional and accidental; that it is even then due to assimilation, not to imitation.

Thus, representation is not identical with imitation. Imitation copies effects, and acts from without inward. Representation, on the contrary, is the objective embodiment of the subjective assimilation of a living process. It proceeds from within outward. It is a revelation, simple and natural, of genuine thought and feeling. It springs from a desire for objective form, to make the external body present the life within. It is due to the fact that all expression is a revelation to sense of what is mystic and subjective. Each objective form results from a process of identification, not from external imitation of accidents.

There are thus really three modes of expression. The lowest mode is imitation, or an external mechanical manipulation by man of his voice and body, so as to convey an impression. The second is a representation due to dramatic realization of actions, and to vivid, imaginative conceptions. It is spontaneous and natural, and due wholly to sympathetic identification or assimilation. The third method is a manifestation of the feeling of the man. It is due to sympathy, and appeals to sympathy. It conveys an impression, not by representing the thought, or object, or action, but by revealing the feeling it awakens.

So common is the confusion of imitation with representation, that it may be well to illustrate further the differences:—

O HOW our organ can speak with its many and wonderful voices!—
Play on the soft lute of love, blow the loud trumpet of war,
Sing with the high sesquialtro, or, drawing its full diapason,
Shake all the air with the grand storm of its pedals and stops.

Take these four lines from Storey's poem on Language, given in all the books as the best illustration of what is called "imitative modulation." According to the method by imitation, the first line is simple narrative, and is given without any definite character; then there follows imitation of "the lute," of "the trumpet," of the high stop of the organ, and last of the full diapason. Contrast with this the method of assimilation. The first line gets its character from the general thought, from the feeling of admiration for power of expression. The comparison with the organ is not made literally. The mind holds the imaginative and central idea as the source of the feeling, and all the rest is but illustration. In the first line, therefore, the feeling of admiration gives the words definite character; the feeling is expressed which really causes all the following figures. Then when the lute is used as a means of expressing the power of words or of the voice to manifest tenderness, there is not the imitation of the lute, but the expression of the tenderness itself of which the lute is a mere example. The symbol, in other words, is not followed mechanically, but the heart feels the central idea which caused the figure. Vocal expression is a direct language. It is a subjective means of manifesting feeling. To imitate the lute would make vocal expression mechanical, artificial, and superficial.

The same is true of the trumpet of war. Realization and admiration of the power of voice or of words to express force, are felt, and the war trumpet is used as a suggestive illustration of this fact. An intelligent reader feels the point of view of the writer, and does not merely reproduce his figures by mechanical imitation, but goes through the imaginative process that chose the figures and expresses the feeling that rises in response to ideas.

Assimilation thus acts from within outward; and while it sometimes results in an objective representation, such representation is a direct revelation of feeling, and is not a mechanical process. Thus representation implies subjective assimilation and life as its cause. It is objective form resulting from within outward, not from an external imitation of accidents.

Is the dramatic rendering of a character by the process of imitation or the process of representation? Low farce, or mere caricature, may proceed by imitation, but any noble form of dramatic expression must proceed by sympathetic representation.

Booth and Salvini never changed their voices so that they were not recognized. Their art was suggestive. It is only a mechanical elocutionist or manipulator of his voice who tries to change it so that it will not be recognized. In the highest tragedy, there is representation but little imitation.

In the impersonation of Barbara Frietchie in Whittier's poem, imitation or the mechanical method of dramatic representation says "she is ninety years old; such a person would have a very broken voice and trembling limbs." Hence the reader gives the words she is supposed to speak, with a mechanical imitation of a quivering voice and with shaking hands. But this is foreign to the spirit of the poem. We should be far more concerned with the emotion of patriotism and courage that dominated her than with her age. The suggestion of great age is secondary and accidental, but her patriotism, her courage are primary and fundamental to the poem; they are its theme.

True dramatic art is the revelation of the heart and motive, not an imitation of mere accidents; it is the subjective assimilation of another's character; it feels another's point of view. Imitation is its greatest counterfeit and enemy.

BARBARA FRIETCHIE.

UP from the meadows rich with corn, clear in the cool September morn, the clustered spires of Frederick stand green-walled by the hills of Maryland. Round about them orchards sweep, apple and peach tree fruited deep, fair as the garden of the Lord to the eyes of the famished rebel horde, on that pleasant morn of the early fall when Lee marched over the mountain-wall, — over the mountain winding down, horse and foot, into Frederick town.

Forty flags with their silver stars, forty flags with their crimson bars, flapped in the morning wind : the sun of noon looked down, and saw not one. Up rose old Barbara Frietchie then, bowed with her fourscore years and ten ; bravest of all in Frederick town, she took up the flag the men hauled down ; in her attic window the staff she set, to show that one heart was loyal yet.

Up the street came the rebel tread, Stonewall Jackson riding ahead. Under his slouched hat left and right he glanced : the old flag met his sight. "Halt!" — the dust-brown ranks stood fast. "Fire!" — out blazed the rifle-blast. It shivered the window, pane and sash ; it rent the banner with seam and gash.   Quick, as it fell, from its broken staff dame Barbara snatched the silken scarf.   She leaned far out on the window-sill and shook it forth with a royal will.   "Shoot, if you must, this old gray head, but spare your country's flag," she said.   A shade of sadness, a blush of shame, over the face of the leader came ; the nobler nature within him stirred to life at that woman's deed and word.   "Who touches a hair of yon gray head dies like a dog !   March on !" he said.

All day long through Frederick street sounded the tread of marching feet ; all day long that free flag tost over the heads of the rebel host.   Ever its torn folds rose and fell on the loyal winds that loved it well ; and through the hill-gaps sunset light shone over it with a warm good-night.   Barbara Frietchie's work is o'er, and the Rebel rides on his raids no more.   Honor to her ! and let a tear fall, for her sake, on Stonewall's bier.   Over Barbara Frietchie's grave, flag of Freedom and Union, wave ! peace and order and beauty draw round thy symbol of light and law ; and ever the stars above look down on thy stars below in Frederick town !

Whittier.

HOTSPUR'S DEFENCE.

My liege, I did deny no prisoners,
But, I remember, when the fight was done,
When I was dry with rage, and extreme toil,
Breathless and faint, leaning upon my sword,
Came there a certain lord, neat, trimly dress'd,
Fresh as a bridegroom ; and his chin new reap'd,
Show'd like a stubble-land at harvest-home ;
He was perfumèd like a milliner;
And 'twixt his finger and thumb he held
A pouncet-box which ever and anon
He gave his nose, and took 't away again ; —
Who, therewith angry, when it next came there,
Took it in snuff ; — and still he smil'd and talk'd ;
And, as the soldiers bore dead bodies by,
He called them — untaught knaves, unmannerly,
To bring a slovenly unhandsome corse
Betwixt the wind and his nobility.
With many holyday and lady terms
He question'd me ; among the rest demanded
My prisoners, in your majesty's behalf.
I then, all smarting, with my wounds being cold,
To be so pester'd with a popinjay,
Out of my grief and my impatience,
Answer'd neglectingly, I know not what ;
He should, or he should not ; — for he made me mad

To see him shine so brisk, and smell so sweet,
And talk so like a waiting gentlewoman,
Of guns, and drums, and wounds (God save the mark !),
And telling me, the sovereign'st thing on earth
Was parmaceti for an inward bruise ;
And that it was great pity, so it was,
That villanous saltpetre should be digg'd
Out of the bowels of the harmless earth,
Which many a good tall fellow had destroyed
So cowardly ; and but for these vile guns,
He would himself have been a soldier.
This bald, disjointed chat of his, my lord,
I answer'd indirectly, as I said ;
And I beseech you, let not his report
Come current for an accusation,
Betwixt my love and your high majesty.

Henry IV. Part I.   *Shakespeare*

XXXIII. ELEMENTS OF DRAMATIC INSTINCT.

THE word "dramatic" comes from a Greek word meaning to act.
Hence, whatever is dramatic refers in some sense to action.
Action implies a motive or a cause, and a conscious result or effect.
Dramatic action as usually understood refers to the interpretation
of character by the manifestation of human feelings, motives, and
aims. It implies that the writer, reader, or speaker is an active
participant, not one sitting at a distance reflecting and moralizing
over facts or events. The word " dramatic," directly or indirectly,
immediately or figuratively, has some reference to the revelation of
the life and movement of passion and character through the voice
and body.

Action is the highest and most direct revelation of character,
and dramatic action is the means adopted by which one human
being interprets the character of another, or manifests the character
imaginatively in some specific situation. It is on account of the
intimacy of dramatic action with character, its great power of
interpretation, that the drama, as an art, has been most potent for
good or evil in all ages.

The term "dramatic," however, is not merely applied to the expression of character; it applies also to the expression of ideas and

feelings. The word "dramatic " is broader than the word "drama." Drama signifies a form of literature which deals with the dramatic, but anything is dramatic that reveals the relation of experience to thought, or gives ideas or events in such a way as to move or act as in nature. Hence, the term "dramatic" is often applied to the expression of simple phases of thought and experience. Any phase is given dramatically when it is given with a distinct character caused by definite feeling of a specific situation. Even an idea or thought, when embodied in a definite situation so as to cause definite emotion, or shown as the peculiar product of a definite character, is dramatic. Thus Thucydides, it has been said, was dramatic because he " presented facts or events themselves, and not reflections upon them." He gave events in such a relation to each other that they interpreted themselves.

So much for the word "dramatic." What is meant by the word "instinct"? Instinct has been called "unconscious reason." It refers to a spontaneous action of the mind; hence dramatic instinct means the spontaneous realization of ideas in living relations, and of the motive and manifestations of character. It is innate in the human heart, — in some form common to every nation and individual. It is the little child's first means of getting outside itself.

There are usually considered to be two elements in dramatic instinct, — imagination and sympathy. Imagination gives insight into another's point of view, creates situations, penetrates to the aim and motive-springs of character, while sympathy enables us to identify ourselves with these.

The nature of dramatic instinct will be seen more clearly from illustrations than from abstract explanations. Take, for example, the character of Shylock. A reader may analyze his character; he may decide upon his age, he may deliberately bend his back and assume an artificial throaty voice; but such conscious acts have nothing whatever to do with dramatic instinct. True dramatic instinct penetrates to the heart of the Jew, sees his point of view, feels his hate, and realizes something of the results of ages of persecution, of which Shylock is the outcome. There are changes of voice, of melody, of body, of walk, but there is no patchwork. The very texture of the muscles of the body are modulated; the personality of the speaker, in short, has entered into an instinctive assimilation of the character. The isolated execution of specific external acts is most antagonistic to the true spirit of dramatic instinct.

BASSANIO AND SHYLOCK.

Shylock. Three thousand ducats, — well.

Bassanio. Ay, sir, for three months.

Shy. For three months, — well.

Bass. For the which, as I told you, Antonio shall be bound.

Shy. Antonio shall be bound, — well.

Bass. May you stead me ? Will you pleasure me ? Shall I know your answer ?

Shy. Three thousand ducats for three months, and Antonio bound.

Bass. Your answer to that.

Shy. Antonio is a good man.

Bass. Have you heard any imputation to the contrary ?

Shy. Ho ! no, no, no, no ; — my meaning, in saying he is a good man, is to have you understand me that he is sufficient. Yet his means are in supposition ; he hath an argosy bound to Tripolis, another to the Indies ; I understand moreover upon the Rialto, he hath a third at Mexico, a fourth for England ; and other ventures he hath, squandered abroad. But ships are but boards, sailors but men ; there be land-rats and water-rats, land-thieves and water-thieves, — I mean, pirates : and then there is the peril of waters, winds, rocks. The man is, notwithstanding, sufficient. Three thousand ducats ; — I think I may take his bond.

Bass. Be assured you may.

Shy. I will be assured I may ; and, that I may be assured, I will bethink me. May I speak with Antonio ?

Bass. If it please you to dine with us.

Shy. Yes, to smell pork ; to eat of the habitation which your prophet the Nazarite conjured the Devil into. I will buy with you, sell with you, talk with you, walk with you and so following ; but I will not eat with you, drink with you, nor pray with you. What news on the Rialto ? — Who is he comes here ?   [*Enter* ANTONIO.

Bass. This is Signior Antonio.

Shy. [*Aside.*] How like a fawning publican he looks !

> I hate him for he is a Christian ;
> But more, for that in low simplicity
> He lends out money gratis, and brings down
> The rate of usance here with us in Venice.
> If I can catch him once upon the hip,
> I will feed fat the ancient grudge I bear him.
> He hates our sacred nation; and he rails,

> Even there where merchants most do congregate,
> On me, my bargains, and my well-won thrift,
> Which he calls interest: Cursed be my tribe,
> If I forgive him !
>
> *Bass.* Shylock, do you hear ?
> *Shy.* I am debating of my present store ;
> And, by the near guess of my memory, I cannot instantly raise up
>   the gross
> Of full three thousand ducats : What of that ?
> Tubal, a wealthy Hebrew of my tribe,
> Will furnish me. But, soft ; how many months
> Do you desire ? — [*To* ANT.] Rest you fair, good Signior ;
> Your worship was the last man in our mouths.

Merchant of Venice.   *Shakespeare.*

Another means of realizing the nature of dramatic instinct and of developing its power is to take the most familiar word, such as "Yes" or "No," and give it with a dozen different imaginative situations, or characters. It may be given with reluctance, with command, with timidity, with fear, with tenderness, with anger. It may also be given as spoken under various circumstances by different characters. It may be given by a boy confessing his fault, or by the joyful eager response when asked if he wishes to go fishing.

WELL. Yes. No. What. Where. Why. There. Indeed. I saw him. There it is. The sun went down. He is gone. He fell. It sank. He rose. I was there. Come in. Come here. Sit down. There is the door. Here it is. He sat down.

A short sentence or phrase may also be given with specific situations; for example, the words, " He fell," can be spoken with a ludicrous situation in mind, some one falling on the ice or from a bicycle; it may refer to a little child who is hurt, or who is not hurt; it may be spoken so as to show anxiety; it may refer to the downfall of some great man ; it may be used literally or figuratively. The possible situations and characters are practically innumerable, and in each case where the situation is definitely conceived by the imagination and the assimilative instinct, and causes genuine identification and feeling, the expression will have a distinct character.

YOUR father is coming across the square. I saw your brother on the street to-day. Your father was on the train this morning. Your mother came from Chicago last night. Your room-mate took the prize yesterday. I shall go down the bay by boat this evening.

It may further aid in realizing what is dramatic to take a sentence, such as " I saw your father in the street," change the logica relation of the thought and ideas from simple and vague information to the assertion of the fact that you saw him, and state the fact in opposition to some one else's father, or where you saw him in opposition to some other place, and you will find that such antitheses and logical relations of ideas are shown by inflection and other modes of emphasis. Take the same sentence, and speak it with different dramatic situations, such as running in with joyful surprise, or with disturbed surprise, or sorrow, or triumph, or to give warning, and you will find that such situations cause not only inflections, but tone-color and modulations of the texture of the voice with pantomine. These are the special means that reveal imaginative situations, or the dramatic identification of the reader or speaker with scenes, events, or characters.

According to Professor A. W. Ward, possibly the highest English-speaking authority on the subject of the drama, " The art of acting is an indispensable adjunct of the dramatic arts." The dramatic and the histrionic arts are to him " really inseparable from one another. Properly speaking, no drama is such until it is acted." Accordingly, in rendering dramatic passages, not only the vocal expression, but also the face and body, are modulated and dominated by the successive situations; for pantomimic expression is more dramatic than even vocal expression. Hence, the expressive modulation of the body is called dramatic action. The methodic or logical instinct reveals itself more by inflectional modulations. The imaginative or creative instinct manifests its conceptions of ideal relations and situations by means of tone-color and texture, while dramatic instinct reveals itself more by action. Vocal and pantomimic expression, however, in all their forms are always intertwined. Words and action can be isolated even more than vocal expression. Vocal expression, in some of its subtlest forms, depends upon the modulation of the body; but in true expression they are rarely found separate from each other. They form a unity. Whenever a man is natural, he uses them all.

By dramatic action, however, is not meant gesticulation. True expressive actions in nature are very subtle. The twinkle of the eye, the expansion of the chest, the elevation of the whole body, the lifting of the head, or the expansion of the hand, — these are the natural expression of dramatic instinct. The extravagant gesticulation which has come from perverted study, that has been in vogue for a hundred years in English elocution, is utterly foreign to all imaginative conception or dramatic instinct and feeling.

The natural languages taken together are the true means of revealing dramatic assimilation. In fact, some of the most subtle dramatic elements in any poem can be revealed only by these languages. For example, in the " Merchant of Venice," one of the most important points in the play is where old Shylock conceives his scheme about the pound of flesh. Did it come upon him suddenly or gradually? At what point was it first suggested to his mind? Shakespeare gives no hint of this in Shylock's words, nor can he do so. It must come from the histrionic instinct of the actor. He must judge of this by the whole situation; in fact, it must be revealed by Shylock when Antonio or Bassanio is speaking, and can only be revealed by dramatic action. Was it conceived by old Shylock during the contemptuous speech made by Antonio? Again, in " Hamlet," at what point in the play did he suspect that his uncle had killed his father? Did he suspect it before the ghost told him? " Oh, my prophetic soul, my uncle!" shows that it was earlier. How and where should this prophetic action of Hamlet's mind be revealed by the artist who renders the part? For my part, I think it is indicated in the previous scene, where Horatio, Bernardo, and Marcellus came to tell him of the ghost. I think it appeared at one point in the words " Very like," which to my mind should be given subjectively and aside, with a deep feeling of premonition. Whether it is right or not, the true interpretation of a play demands such intimations, — vaguely, it may be, but still natural and dramatic suggestions of the spirit of thoughts and feelings which are too subtle to be put into words. Tones and actions manifest the deepest and subtlest feelings and intuitions, and hence form the soul of dramatic expression.

The elements of dramatic instinct are best found and developed apart from stage representation. Students should arrange and dramatize scenes from stories, and give them as dialogues, but nearly always without "make-up" or scenery. These must only be used after the dramatic intuitions have been awakened, or an amateurish trust in mere "business" is acquired. Besides, some of the most dramatic passages in literature are incapable of stage representation. How dramatic is the following passage, and what a fine dialogue students can arrange from it, — leaving the coach and the situation wholly to the imagination; but to represent it on the stage, all reference as to the coach would have to be omitted.

PETER POUNCE AND THE PARSON.

PETER POUNCE, being desirous of having some one to whom he might communicate his grandeur, told the parson he would convey him home in his chariot. This favor was, by Adams, with many bows and acknowledgments, accepted, though he afterward said he ascended the chariot rather that he might not offend than from any desire of riding in it, for that in his heart he preferred the pedestrian even to the vehicular expedition. The chariot had not proceeded far, before Mr. Adams observed it was a very fine day. "Ay, and a very fine country, too," answered Pounce.

"I should think so more," returned Adams, "if I had not lately travelled over the Downs, which I take to exceed this, and all other prospects in the universe." "A fig for prospects," answered Pounce; "one acre here is worth ten there: for my part, I have no delight in the prospect of any land but my own."

"Then," said Adams, "you can indulge yourself in many fine prospects of that kind." "I thank God I have a little," replied the other, "with which I am content, and envy no man. I have a little, Mr. Adams, with which I do as much good as I can."

Adams answered "that riches, without charity, were nothing worth; for that they were a blessing only to him who made them a blessing to others." "You and I," said Peter, "have different notions of charity. I own, as it is generally used, I do not like the word, nor do I think it becomes one of us gentlemen; it is a mean, parson-like quality; though I would not infer that many parsons have it neither."

"Sir," said Adams, "my definition of charity is, a generous disposition to relieve the distressed." "There is something in that definition," answered Peter, "which I like well enough ; it is, as you say, a disposition — and does not so much consist in the act as in the disposition to do it : but, alas! Mr. Adams, who are meant by the distressed ? believe me, the distresses of mankind are mostly imaginary, and it would be rather folly than goodness to relieve them."

" Sure, sir," replied Adams, " hunger and thirst, cold and nakedness, and other distresses which attend the poor, can never be said to be imaginary evils." "How can any man complain of hunger," said Pounce, " in a country where such excellent salads are to be gathered in almost every field ? — or of thirst, where every stream and river produce such delicious potations ? — and as for cold and nakedness, they are evils introduced by luxury and custom. A man naturally wants clothes no more than a horse or any other animal ; and there are whole nations who go without them. But these are things, perhaps, which you, who do not know the world — "

" You will pardon me, sir," returned Adams ; "I have read of the *Gymnosophists.*" "A plague of your Jehosophats," cried Peter ; " the greatest fault in our constitution is the provision made for the poor, except that perhaps made for some others. Sir, I have not an estate which doth not contribute almost as much again to the poor as to the landtax ; and I do assure you I expect myself to come to the parish in the end."

To which Adams giving a dissenting smile, Peter thus proceeded : " I fancy, Mr. Adams, you are one of those who imagine I am a lump of money ; for there are many who I fancy believe that not only my pockets, but my whole clothes are lined with bank bills ; but, I assure you, you are all mistaken : I am not the man the world esteems me. If I can hold my head above water, it is all I can. I have injured myself by purchasing ; I have been too liberal of my money. Indeed, I fear my heir will find my affairs in a worse situation than they are reputed to be. Ah! he will have reason to wish I had loved money more and land less. Pray, my good neighbor, where should I have that quantity of money the world is so liberal to bestow on me ? Where could I possibly, without I had stole it, acquire such a treasure ?"

" Why, truly," said Adams, "I have been always of your opinion ; I have wondered, as well as yourself, with what confidence they could report such things of you, which have to me appeared as mere impossibilities ; for you know, sir, and I have often heard you say it, that your wealth is of your own acquisition ; and can it be credible that in your short time you should have amassed such a heap of treasure as these people will have you are worth ? Indeed, had you inherited an estate like Sir Thomas Booby, which had descended in your family through many generations, they might have had a color for their assertions." "Why, what do they say I am worth?" cries Peter, with a malicious sneer.

"Sir," answered Adams, "I have heard some aver you are not worth less than twenty thousand pounds." At which Peter frowned. "Nay, sir," said Adams, " you ask me only the opinion of others ; for my own part, I have always denied it, nor did I ever believe you could possibly be worth half that sum."

"However, Mr. Adams," said he, squeezing him by the hand, " I would not sell them all I am worth for double that sum; and as to what you believe, or they believe, I care not a fig. I am not poor, because you think me so, nor because you attempt to undervalue me in the country. I know the envy of mankind very well ; but I thank heaven I am above them. It is true, my wealth is of my own acquisition. I have not an estate like Sir Thomas Booby, that hath descended in my family through many generations; but I know heirs of such estates, who are forced to travel about the country, like some people in torn cassocks, and might be glad to accept of a pitiful curacy, for what I know ; yes, sir, as shabby fellows as yourself, whom no man of my figure, without that vice of good-nature about him, would suffer to ride in a chariot with him."

"Sir," said Adams, " I value not your chariot of a rush; and if I had known you had intended to affront me, I would have walked to the world's end on foot, ere I would have accepted a place in it. However, sir, I will soon rid you of that inconvenience!" And so saying, he opened the chariot door, without calling to the coachman, and leaped out into the highway, forgetting to take his hat along with him; which, however, Mr. Pounce threw after him with great violence.

Henry Fielding.

CONFESSIONS.

WHAT is he buzzing in my ears? "now that I come to die,
Do I view the world as a vale of tears?" ah, reverend sir, not I !
What I viewed there once, what I view again where the physic bottles stand
On the table's edge, — is a suburb lane, with a wall to my bedside hand.
That lane sloped, much as the bottles do, from a house you could descry
O'er the garden wall : is the curtain blue or green to a healthy eye ?
To mine it serves for the old June weather blue above lane and wall ;
And that farthest bottle labelled " Ether" is the house o'ertopping all.
At a terrace, somewhere near the stopper, there watched for me one June,
A girl : I know, sir, it 's improper, my poor mind is out of tune.

Only there was a way . . . you crept close by the side, to dodge
Eyes in the house, two eyes except : they styled their house "The Lodge."
What right had a lounger up their lane ? but, by creeping very close,
With the good wall's help, — their eyes might strain and stretch themselves
    to Oes,
Yet never catch her and me together, as she left the attic, there,
By the rim of the bottle labelled "Ether," and stole from stair to stair,
And stood by the rose-wreathed gate. Alas, we loved, sir — used to meet :
How sad and bad and mad it was — but then, how it was sweet !

Browning.

XXXIV. POINT OF VIEW.

WHATEVER is seen by man is perceived from some one point of view. Power to change points of view, to appreciate or to understand the attitude of other men, lies at the foundation of all appreciation of art, or even of truth. An isolated fact has little significance. It is the union of facts, the sympathetic relation of facts to the mind and heart, that gives that co-ordination of the objective with the subjective necessary to the realization of truth.

A fruitful source of narrowness in character and of monotony and artificiality in expression is one-sidedness or limitation of point of view. To understand the simplest object requires that it shall be seen from different directions and in varied relations. All genuineness or truthfulness of feeling depends upon point of view, for it is chiefly this that stimulates any sympathetic response.

Now Harry he had long suspected this trespass of old Goody Blake, and vowed that she should be detected, and he on her would vengeance take. And oft from his warm fire he 'd go, and to the fields his road would take, and there, at night, in frost and snow, he watched to seize old Goody Blake. And once behind a rick of barley, thus looking out did Harry stand ; the moon was full and shining clearly, and crisp with frost the stubble land. He hears a noise — he 's all awake ; again ! — on tiptoe down the hill he softly creeps. 'T is Goody Blake ! she 's at the hedge of Harry Gill. Right glad was he when he beheld her ; stick after stick did Goody pull : he stood behind a bush of elder, till she had filled her apron full. When with her load she turned about, the by-road back again to take, he started forward with a shout, and sprang upon poor Goody Blake. .

And fiercely by the arm he took her, and by the arm he held her fast, and fiercely by the arm he shook her, and cried, " I 've caught you then at last ! "

Then Goody, who had nothing said, her bundle from her lap let fall; and kneeling on the sticks, she prayed to God that is the judge of all. She prayed, her withered hand uprearing, while Harry held her by the arm, "God! who art never out of hearing, O may he never more be warm!" The cold, cold moon above her head, thus on her knees did Goody pray: young Harry heard what she had said, and icy cold he turned away.

Point of view can be better illustrated than defined. In the preceding passage what emotion or expression should be given to the clauses referring to the moon and the frost?   Our own point of view might lead to admiration of them, but they cause an antagonistic exultation in Harry, since the one will enable him to see, and the other to hear, Goody Blake.   In reading the lines, however, we might express our regret for his revengeful spirit.   Again, we may identify ourselves with him as "he hears a noise," and its repetition, with his stealthy approach, his discovery that it is Goody ; or we may look on and express our contempt for his action; or again we may identify ourselves with him till her name is spoken, then change our point of view and express "She is at the hedge" with regret.   So the next clause "right glad," etc., may be given with his cruel delight, or with our feeling against him; or we can give this clause with his feeling, and express our own in the next.   In the sentence "When with her load" etc., we may start with regret and pity for her, then give his point of view, and represent his spirit and feeling with underlying antagonism to him, then after the word "and" we may return to our own feeling of pity for her.

These possible ways of rendering the passage illustrate the fact that consciously, or unconsciously, the reader adopts some point of view for each phrase, and so determines his feeling and expression. It is a definite point of view, which makes expression dramatic. The ability to vary the point of view, and the instinct to conceive the right one in any specific case, is a most important element of all forms of vocal expression.   The instinct that conceives a point of view is one of the most important in the human mind.   It is as important for success in life as for attainment in reading and speaking.   Each must be able to see things as others see them, or he cannot come into contact with his race or be able to mould them in any way.   A lack of power to vary points of view or to appreciate that of other ages, other nations, other beliefs, or other feelings than our own is the characteristic of a narrow and bigoted soul.

Point of view is an important element in the effectiveness of any art. Ordinary writing can give us thought, but it cannot give point of view. It takes poetry, the drama, or the novel to do this. Every man can look at nature, but a painting can show how superficial has been his observation, and give a point of view by which he is brought face to face with the real beauty of nature. Every great art work gives men a new point of view. Art lifts us into sympathy with each other, to a plane from which we can see with each other's eyes.

The proper apprehension of truth depends upon the ability to appreciate various points of view. As a case in court is weak where there is but one witness; as the life of Christ would have been more effectively assailed had there been but one gospel; as the Master's words would have been local and temporary without the parable; as many witnesses are required to establish a truth, — so the individual soul must ever be led to see with other eyes, to understand really the meaning of the smallest event. A man who never studies art, never reads poetry or fiction, never hears any music, public reading, or dramatic representation, loses his grasp over his fellow-men. He has overlooked one of the fundamental necessities of human nature.

There is no place where point of view has such importance as in vocal expression. Here is found the very soul of all dramatic expression, of all true oratory, and of all effective interpretation, of literature through the voice. Vocal expression, more than any other form of art, can give varieties of points of view. It can reveal and interpret a greater number of mental and emotional attitudes toward truth than painting or poetry.

One of the sublimest illustrations of point of view is the parable misnamed "The Prodigal Son." The aim of this parable is to give an individual soul a right point of view from which to appreciate the character of God, and his relation to men, as well as man's two leading modes of going astray, and of losing sympathy with the Father of all. To give this truth to mankind even Christ was compelled to employ art, for art is a necessity of human nature. Without it there can be no adequate appreciation of truth. The parable was the art of our Master. "Because of the hardness of the heart," parables were given so as to embody a truth for all ages, which would not be explicit but implicit, which would "Do the thing that breeds the thought," or evoke the divine spirit in man to realize what could not be given by explanation, but only by implication.

Without entering into analysis, let us take a few subordinate clauses as illustrations of the necessity of right point of view to true vocal expression, and of the power of vocal expression to interpret points of view. Take the answer of the servant to the elder brother; what was the servant's feeling? Verbal exegesis will not help us. The exegesis must be dramatic. What was his point of view? To give it as neutral is to violate the fundamental principle of human nature, and to introduce a discord into the story. From the general nature of servants, there would be joy at the killing of the calf, and the giving of this speech joyously emphasizes the cold bearing of the elder brother by contrast. He is thus isolated, and his selfishness made salient. The point of view, therefore, of the servant must be in sympathy with the younger brother, and his words must be given with joy.

As another illustration, take the clause, "He was angry." The typical and self-styled dramatic reader gives all such subordinate clauses as merely explanatory and narrative. It is only when he finds a quotation that he gives it any feeling or character. But there are subordinate clauses which give the different points of view of the narrator, and which are, if possible, more dramatic than any direct quotation. This clause will be most naturally given from the point of view of the reader himself, who stands in the place of a sympathetic spectator. He may be astonished, or disappointed, or indignant. The feeling of astonishment coloring these words possibly best interprets the spirit of the parable. The next clause, "and would not go in," may be given with regret or noble indignation; the next, with admiration for the noble tenderness and love of the father. When we do finally come to the direct words of the elder brother, the change in point of view to the representation of his feeling makes still more emphatic his character and place in the parable.

PARABLE OF THE FATHER.

A CERTAIN man had two sons : and the younger of them said to his father, Father, give me the portion of thy substance that falleth to me. And he divided unto them his living. And not many days after the younger son gathered all together, and took his journey into a far country; and there he wasted his substance with riotous living. And when he had spent all, there arose a mighty famine in that country; and he began to be in want. And he went and joined himself to one of the citizens of that country; and he sent him into his fields to feed swine. And he would fain have been filled with the husks that the swine did eat : and no man gave unto him. But when he came to himself he said, How many hired servants of my father's have bread enough and to spare, and I perish here with hunger! I will arise and go to my father, and I will say unto him, Father, I have sinned against heaven, and in thy sight : I am no more worthy to be called thy son : make me as one of thy hired servants. And he arose, and came to his father. But while he was yet afar off, his father saw him, and was moved with compassion, and ran, and fell on his neck, and kissed him. And the son said unto him, Father, I have sinned against heaven, and in thy sight : I am no more worthy to be called thy son. But the father said to his servants, Bring forth quickly the best robe, and put it on him ; and put a ring on his hand, and shoes on his feet : and bring the fatted calf, and kill it, and let us eat, and make merry : for this my son was dead, and is alive again; he was lost, and is found. And they began to be merry.

Now his elder son was in the field : and as he came and drew nigh to the house, he heard music and dancing. And he called to him one of the servants, and enquired what these things might be. And he said unto him, Thy brother is come; and thy father hath killed the fatted calf, because he hath received him safe and sound. But he was angry and would not go in; and his father came out and entreated him. But he answered and said to his father, Lo, these many years do I serve thee, and I never transgressed a commandment of thine: and yet thou never gavest me a kid, that I might make merry with my friends : but when this thy son came, which hath devoured thy living with harlots, thou killedst for him the fatted calf. And he said unto him, Son, thou art ever with me, and all that is mine is thine. But it was meet to make merry and be glad : for this thy brother was dead, and is alive again ; and was lost, and is found.

. . . Once in the old Colonial days,
    Two hundred years ago and more,
A boat sail'd down through the winding ways
    Of Hampton River to that low shore,
Full of a goodly company
Sailing out on the summer sea,
Veering to catch the land-breeze light,
With the Boar to left and the Rocks to right.

In Hampton meadows, where mowers laid
    Their scythes to the swaths of salted grass,
" Ah, well-a-day ! our hay must be made ! "
    A young man sigh'd who saw them pass.
Loud laugh'd his fellows to see him stand
Whetting his scythe with a listless hand,
Hearing a voice in a far-off song,
Watching a white hand beckoning long.

" Fie on the witch ! " cried a merry girl,
    As they rounded the point where Goody Cole
Sat by her door with her wheel atwirl,
    A bent and blear-eyed poor old soul.
" Oho ! " she mutter'd, " ye 're brave to-day !
But I hear the little waves laugh and say,
' The broth will be cold that waits at home ;
For it 's one to go, but another to come ! ' "

" She 's cursed," said the skipper ; " speak her fair :
    I 'm scary always to see her shake
Her wicked head, with its wild gray hair,
    And nose like a hawk, and eyes like a snake."
But merrily still, with laugh and shout,
From Hampton River the boat sail'd out,
Till the huts and the flakes on the Star seem'd nigh,
And they lost the scent of the pines of Rye.

They dropp'd their lines in the lazy tide,
    Drawing up haddock and mottled cod ;
They saw not the shadow that walk'd beside,
    They heard not the feet with silence shod :
But thicker and thicker a hot mist grew,
Shot by the lightnings through and through ;
And muffled growls, like the growl of a beast,
Ran along the sky from west to east.

Then the skipper look'd from the darkening sea
  Up to the dimm'd and wading Sun ;
But he spake like a brave man cheerily,
  " Yet there is time for our homeward run."
Veering and tacking, they backward wore ;
And, just as a breath from the woods ashore
Blew out to whisper of danger past,
The wrath of the storm came down at last !

The skipper haul'd at the heavy sail :
  " God be our help," he only cried,
As the roaring gale, like the stroke of a flail,
  Smote the boat on its starboard side.
The shoalsmen look'd, but saw alone
Dark films of rain-cloud slantwise blown,
Wild rocks lit up by the lightning's glare,
The strife and torment of sea and air.

Goody Cole look'd out from her door :
  The Isles of Shoals were drown'd and gone,
Scarcely she saw the Head of the Boar
  Toss the foam from tusks of stone.
She clasp'd her hands with a grip of pain,
The tear on her cheek was not of rain :
" They are lost," she mutter'd, " boat and crew !
Lord, forgive me ! my words were true ! "

Suddenly seaward swept the squall :
  The low Sun smote through cloudy rack ;
The shoals stood clear in the light, and all
  The trend of the coast lay hard and black :
But, far and wide as eye could reach,
No life was seen upon wave or beach ;
The boat that went out at morning never
Sail'd back again into Hampton River.

From Rivermouth Rocks.   ————   *Whittier.*

TO A SKYLARK.

ETHEREAL minstrel ! pilgrim of the sky !
Dost thou despise the earth where cares abound ?
Or, while the wings aspire, are heart and eye
Both with thy nest upon the dewy ground ? —
Thy nest which thou canst drop into at will,
Those quivering wings composed, that music still !

> To the last point of vision, and beyond,
> Mount, daring warbler ! that love-prompted strain
> (Twixt thee and thine a never-failing bond)
> Thrills not the less the bosom of the plain :
> Yet might'st thou seem, proud privilege ! to sing
> All independent of the leafy spring.
>
> Leave to the nightingale her shady wood ;
> A privacy of glorious light is thine,
> Whence thou dost pour upon the world a flood
> Of harmony, with rapture more divine, —
> Type of the wise who soar, but never roam,
> True to the kindred points of heaven and home !
>
> *Wordsworth.*

XXXV. ATTITUDE OF THE MAN.

> But, soft ; behold ! lo, where it comes again !
> I'll cross it, though it blast me. — Stay, illusion !

Hamlet.   *Shakespeare.*

How different is Hamlet's manner when he speaks to his companions and when he addresses the ghost?   Such a change may possibly
be considered by some as identical with point of view, but it is
essentially different, and at any rate a specific application of the
principle already explained.

> Give me another horse ! — bind up my wounds! —
> Have mercy, Jesu ! — Soft ! I did but dream. —
> O coward conscience, how dost thou afflict me ! —

Richard III.   *Shakespeare.*

Note the changes in Richard's exclamation on awaking from his
dream.   The first two clauses are parts of his dream, the third is a
prayer, in the fourth he wakes to a realization that it was all a
dream, and in the last line he condemns himself.   The greater the
definiteness with which the process of the mind in passing from
idea to idea can be revealed, the more effective will be the expression ; but the attitude of the man is just as important.   It sometimes reveals more salient changes of feeling than the idea itself.

> "Oh ! may we all for death prepare !
> What has he left ? and who 's his heir ?"

Verses on his own death.   *Swift.*

This change of mental attitude, or direction, is very common and very important in some forms of comedy. Dean Swift used it with most telling effect in his poem on his own death. What sharp contrasts he portrays in the mental attitudes of his card-playing female friends: —

> My female friends, whose tender hearts
> Have better learned to act their parts,
> Receive the news in doleful dumps :
> "The Dean is dead (pray, what is trumps ?)."
> Then, "Lord have mercy on his soul !
> (Ladies, I 'll venture for the vole).
> Six deans, they say, must bear the pall
> (I wish I knew what king to call).
> Madam, your husband will attend
> The funeral of so good a friend ?"
> "No, madam, 't is a shocking sight ;
> And he 's engaged to-morrow night ;
> My Lady Club will take it ill
> If he should fail her at quadrille.
> He loved the Dean — (I lead a heart) ;
> But dearest friends, they say, must part.
> His time is come ; he ran his race ;
> We hope he 's in a better place."

Verses on his own death.   *Swift.*

Hood has two poems which afford very ludicrous contrasts. In the "Ode to my Infant Son" (see Classics page 415), he gives the differences between a professional attitude, such as the writer of poetry assumes, and which can be easily applied to the delivery of the preacher, the lawyer, the lecturer, or the actor when he has a general or vague relation to truth, and when he has a definite attitude to each specific idea in its turn. In one is shown vague general emotion, which, of course, tends to make the voice monotonous, and in the other emotion is created by the successive specific conceptions. So in "Domestic Asides" we have the conventional society attitude of mind, while in the parentheses we have the genuine attitude, which is usually concealed. The proper practice of these two poems will be helpful in breaking up mannerisms. The "ministerial tone," as it is called, results chiefly from the effect of a professional attitude of mind; so of staginess. Mannerisms arise from the want of specific ideas and a definite attitude toward each successive conception.

DOMESTIC ASIDES.

I REALLY take it very kind — this visit, Mrs. Skinner —
I have not seen you such an age — (the wretch has come to dinner !)
Your daughters, too — what loves of girls !   what heads for painters' easels !
Come here, and kiss the infant, dears — (and give it, p'rhaps, the measles !)

Your charming boys I see are home from Reverend Mr. Russell's —
'T was very kind to bring them both — (what boots for my new Brussels !)
What ! little Clara left at home ? well, now, I call that shabby !
I should have loved to kiss her so — (a flabby, dabby babby !)

And Mr. S., I hope he 's well ? but, though he lives so handy,
He never once drops in to sup — (the better for our brandy !)
Come, take a seat — I long to hear about Matilda's marriage ;
You 've come, of course, to spend the day (thank Heaven ! I hear the carriage !)

What ! must you go ? — next time I hope you 'll give me longer measure.
Nay, I shall see you down the stairs — (with most uncommon pleasure !)
Good bye ! good bye ! Remember, all, next time you 'll take your dinners —
(Now, David — mind, I 'm not at home, in future, to the Skinners.)

Hood.

One of the best illustrations of point of view and attitude of the reader's mind is Scott's account of the battle of Flodden Field in " Marmion." The poet so arranges his narrative as to give us a definite point of view from which our imagination can create and observe the battle. We stand on a little hill at the rear of the English right wing. He has made Marmion a participant in the battle, but he has done more; he brings Lady Clare, a delicate and tender maiden, in whose fate he has already enlisted a deep interest, to this same hill, and in direct contact with the fierceness of war. Thus he gives us not only a point of view, but an attitude of imaginative sympathy and interest. To heighten the effect she is finally left entirely alone amidst the noise and confusion of the fight.

According to history, the whole battle turns upon the fact that the English reserve was brought up to aid the wing of the English army, which was at first defeated. Who sent the word or gave the key to this situation is unknown; but Scott, with that consummate

art which enabled him to unite fiction and history, makes this deed
the last act in the life of his imaginary Marmion. He brings us
thus into a sympathetic attitude with the turning-point of the
battle. By these means events which in other hands would
have been a dry record of facts, are given a living and dramatic
sequence.

These, however, are general points. Take the last stanza of
the description, in which Marmion dies. The reader must identify himself now with the attitude and bearing of Clare, now with
that of Marmion, then with that of the Monk, and must con-
stantly return to his own as a living spectator of the whole scene.
He must be dominated by the whole situation and by the attitude
of each character, and his imagination and emotion must respond
to the spirit of every event.

When Marmion begins to revive he is first bewildered, looks
around for his squires, discovers them, shows antagonism, realizes
the inevitable; then suddenly comprehends the crisis of the
battle, sends Blount and Fitz Eustace on their errands, and sinks
down in despair with his last few words. With all these, the
reader must successively identify himself.

In the last stanza, in speaking of the acts of Clare, the reader's
feeling is unconsciously hers; in speaking of the Monk it changes
to his; and then to that of Marmion. The indirect quotation,
the description of his actions, must be just as dramatic as the
direct personations or quotations. When we come to the words
of the Monk, we find a change in the very midst of the words of
the speaker. He first addresses the Fiend, then tenderly addresses the sinner, then turns aside and speaks to himself. How
different are his expressions in these three attitudes of his mind!
The reader must not only feel the character and point of view of
the priest in general, but must think and feel with him specifically
these transitions in the attitude of his mind. Suddenly the attention changes to the battle, Marmion thrills with a realization that
the victory will be gained. Then the reader must change suddenly from dramatic identification with Marmion to his own lyric
feeling, and give with the greatest intensity, but with the utmost
simplicity, the six simple words which suggest his death.

With that, straight up the hill there rode two horsemen drenched with gore, and in their arms, a helpless load, a wounded knight they bore. His hand still strained the broken brand ; his arms were smeared with blood and sand. Dragged from among the horses' feet, with dinted shield, and helmet beat, the falcon-crest and plumage gone, can that be haughty Marmion ! . . . Young Blount his armor did unlace, and, gazing on his ghastly face, said, "By Saint George, he 's gone ! that spear-wound has our master sped, — and see the deep cut on his head ! good-night to Marmion." — " Unnurtured Blount ! thy brawling cease ; he opes his eyes," said Eustace ; " peace ! "

When, doffed his casque, he felt free air, around 'gan Marmion wildly stare : " Where 's Harry Blount ? Fitz-Eustace where ? linger ye here, ye hearts of hare ! redeem my pennon, — charge again ! cry — ' Marmion to the rescue ! ' — Vain ! last of my race — on battle-plain that shout shall ne'er be heard again ! — yet my last thought is England's — fly, to Dacre bear my signet ring : tell him his squadrons up to bring. Fitz-Eustace, to Lord Surrey hie ; Tunstall lies dead upon the field, his life-blood stains the spotless shield : Edmund is down : — my life is reft ; the admiral alone is left. Let Stanley charge with spur of fire, — with Chester charge, and Lancashire, full upon Scotland's central host, or victory and England 's lost. Must I bid twice ? — hence, varlets! fly ! leave Marmion here alone — to die." They parted, and alone he lay ; Clare drew her from the sight away, till pain wrung forth a lowly moan, and half he murmured, " Is there none, of all my halls have nurst, page, squire, or groom, one cup to bring of blessed water from the spring, to slake my dying thirst ? "

O woman ! in our hours of ease, uncertain, coy, and hard to please, and variable as the shade by the light, quivering aspen made ; when pain and anguish wring the brow, a ministering angel thou ! — Scarce were the piteous accents said, when, with the baron's casque, the maid to the nigh streamlet ran : forgot were hatred, wrongs, and fears ; the plaintive voice alone she hears, sees but the dying man. She stooped her by the runnel's side, but in abhorrence backward drew ; for, oozing from the mountain's side, where raged the war, a dark red tide was curdling in the streamlet blue. Where shall she turn ! — behold her mark a little fountain cell, where water, clear as diamond-spark, in a stone basin fell. Above, some half-worn letters say, Drink, weary pilgrim, drink and pray, for the kind soul of Sybil Gray, who built this cross and well. She filled the helm, and back she hied, and with surprise and joy espied a monk supporting Marmion's head ; a pious man, whom duty brought to dubious verge of battle fought, to shrive the dying, bless the dead.

Deep drank Lord Marmion of the wave, and, as she stooped his brow to lave, — " Is it the hand of Clare," he said, " or injured Constance, bathes my head ? " then as remembrance rose, — " Speak not to me of shrift or prayer ! I must redress her woes. Short space, few words, are mine to spare ; forgive and listen, gentle Clare ! " " Alas ! " she said, " the while, — O, think of your immortal weal! in vain for Constance is your zeal; she died at Holy Isle." Lord Marmion started from the ground, as light as if he felt no wound: though in the action burst the tide, in torrents, from his wounded side. "Then it was truth," he said : "I knew that the dark presage must be true. I would the Fiend, to whom belongs the vengeance due to all her wrongs, would spare me but a day! for wasting fire, and dying groan, and priests slain on the altar stone, might bribe him for delay. It may not be! — this dizzy trance — curse on yon base marauder's lance, and doubly cursed my failing brand! a sinful heart makes feeble hand." Then, fainting, down on earth he sunk, supported by the trembling monk.

With fruitless labor, Clara bound, and strove to stanch the gushing wound : the monk, with unavailing cares, exhausted all the Church's prayers. Ever, he said, that, close and near, a lady's voice was in his ear, and that the priest he could not hear; for that she ever sung, "*In the lost battle, borne down by the flying, where mingles war's rattle with groans of the dying!*" so the notes rung. "Avoid thee, Fiend! with cruel hand shake not the dying sinner's sand! O, look, my son, upon yon sign of the Redeemer's grace divine ; O, think on faith and bliss! — By many a death-bed I have been, and many a sinner's parting seen, but never aught like this." The war, that for a space did fail, now trebly thundering swelled the gale, and — Stanley! was the cry, — a light on Marmion's visage spread, and fired his glazing eye : with dying hand, above his head, he shook the fragment of his blade, and shouted, "Victory!— Charge, Chester, charge! on, Stanley, on!" were the last words of Marmion. *Scott.*

The reader must be true to the point of view he has chosen and the character he is representing. In explanatory clauses he has more freedom in changing his attitude than in representing the words of a character; but such narrative phrases are none the less dramatic. In all cases he must have that versatility which is characteristic of every sympathetic and genuine man. Every explanatory clause of this poem must be given specific, dramatic character.

The actor is confined chiefly to the attitude of a personator, but the reader or dramatic speaker has a greater number of attitudes and points of view. Hence, public reading and speaking demand thorough study of the principles involved in this aspect of assimilation. Every change in point of view and in the attitude of the man must be suggested. This cannot be given by objective scenery, as on the stage. There must be an appeal to imagination; hence, there must be a greater grasp of situations. He must suggest more points of view than the most difficult part in any drama. An actor may get along without dramatic instinct, but it is absolutely essential to the reader.

The higher the literature the more subtle and frequent are the transitions. The reading of the Scriptures demands continual changes in point of view and attitude of the reader. In the sublime lyrics called the Psalms there are sudden changes in attention and sympathy in the very midst of a clause; and the right rendering of the spirit of such passages depends upon a manifestation of these changes.

For we know in part, and we prophecy in part: but when that which is perfect is come, that which is in part shall be done away. When I was a child, I spake as a child, I felt as a child, I thought as a child : now that I am become a man, I have put away childish things. For now we see in a mirror, darkly; but then face to face : now I know in part ; but then shall I know even as also I have been known.

Notice in the above extract the attitude of the mind toward that which is perfectly familiar; no one doubts " For we know in part." But the end of the sentence contains something remarkable, and the rhythm and expression change. So in the last sentence the first clause is something familiar and understood. The true reader gives this with the attitude of familiarity; but he gives with the attitude of wonder the words " But then face to face." " Now I know in part " calls for an attitude of familiarity, but the last requires the attitude of wonder and sublime faith. Where all are read with one attitude of mind, the force, spirit, and even true meaning of the passage is lost.

ELIJAH AT CARMEL.

And it came to pass after many days, that the word of the Lord came to Elijah, in the third year, saying, Go, shew thyself unto Ahab ; and I will send rain upon the earth. And Elijah went to shew himself unto Ahab. And the famine was sore in Samaria. And Ahab called Obadiah, which was over the household. (Now Obadiah feared the Lord greatly: for it was so, when Jezebel cut off the prophets of the Lord, that Obadiah took an hundred prophets, and hid them by fifty in a cave, and fed them with bread and water.) And Ahab said unto Obadiah, Go through the land, unto all the fountains of water, and unto all the brooks : peradventure we may find grass and save the horses and mules alive, that we lose not all the beasts. So they divided the land between them to pass throughout it : Ahab went one way by himself, and Obadiah went another way by himself. And as Obadiah was in the way, behold, Elijah met him : and he knew him, and fell on his face, and said, Is it thou, my lord Elijah? And he answered him, It is I : go, tell thy lord, Behold, Elijah is here. And he said, Wherein have I sinned, that thou wouldest deliver thy servant into the hand of Ahab, to slay me? As the Lord thy God liveth, there is no nation or kingdom, whither my lord hath not sent to seek thee : and when they said, He is not here, he took an oath of the kingdom and nation, that they found thee not. And now thou sayest, Go, tell thy lord, Behold, Elijah is here. And it shall come to pass, as soon as I am gone from thee, that the spirit of the Lord shall carry thee whither I know not ; and so when I come and tell Ahab, and he cannot find thee, he shall slay me : but I thy servant fear the Lord from my youth. Was it not told my lord what I did when Jezebel slew the prophets of the Lord, how I hid an hundred men of the Lord's prophets by fifty in a cave, and fed them with bread and water? And now thou sayest, Go, tell thy lord, Behold, Elijah is here : and he shall slay me. And Elijah said, As the Lord of hosts liveth, before whom I stand, I will surely shew myself unto him to-day. So Obadiah went to meet Ahab, and told him : and Ahab went to meet Elijah. And it came to pass, when Ahab saw Elijah, that Ahab said unto him, Is it thou, thou troubler of Israel? And he answered, I have not troubled Israel ; but thou, and thy father's house, in that ye have forsaken the commandments of the Lord, and thou hast followed the Baalim. Now therefore send, and gather to me all Israel unto Mount Carmel, and the prophets of Baal four hundred and fifty, and the prophets of the Asherah four hundred, which eat at Jezebel's table. So Ahab sent unto all the children of Israel, and gathered the prophets together unto Mount Carmel. And Elijah came near unto all the people, and said, How long halt ye between two opinions? If the Lord be God, follow him : but if Baal, then follow him. And the people answered him not a word. Then said Elijah unto the people, I, even I only, am left a prophet of the Lord ; but Baal's prophets are four hundred and fifty men. Let them therefore give us two bullocks ; and let them choose one bullock for themselves, and cut it in pieces, and lay it on the wood, and put no fire under : and I will dress the other bullock, and lay it on the wood, and put no fire under. And call ye on the name of your god, and I will call on the name of the Lord : and the God that answereth by fire, let him be God. And all the people answered and said, It is well spoken. And Elijah said unto the prophets of Baal, Choose you one bullock for yourselves, and dress it first; for ye are many; and call on the name of your god, but put no fire under. And they took the bullock which was given them, and they dressed it, and called on the name of Baal from morning even until noon, saying, O Baal, hear us. But there was no voice, nor any that answered. And they leaped about the altar which was made. And it came to pass at noon, that Elijah mocked them, and said, Cry aloud: for he is a god; either he is musing, or he has gone aside, or he is in a journey, or peradventure he sleepeth, and must be awaked. And they cried aloud, and cut themselves after their manner with knives and lances, till the blood gushed out upon them. And it was so, when midday was past, that they prophesied until the time of the offering of the evening oblation; but there was neither voice, nor any to answer, nor any that regarded. And Elijah said unto all the people, Come near unto me; and all the people came near unto him. And he repaired the altar of the Lord that was thrown down. And Elijah took twelve stones, according to the number of the tribes of the sons of Jacob, unto whom the word of the Lord came, saying, Israel shall be thy name. And with the stones he built an altar in the name of the Lord; and he made a trench about the altar, as great as would contain two measures of seed. And he put the wood in order, and cut the bullock in pieces, and laid it on the wood. And he said, Fill four barrels with water, and pour it on the burnt offering, and on the wood. And he said, Do it the second time; and they did it the second time. And he said, Do it the third time; and they did it the third time. And the water ran round about the altar; and he filled the trench also with water. And it came to pass at the time of the offering of the evening oblation, that Elijah the prophet came near, and said, O Lord, the God of Abraham, of Isaac, and of Israel, let it be known this day that thou art God in Israel, and that I am thy servant, and that I have done all these things at thy word. Hear me, O Lord, hear me, that this people may know that thou, Lord, art God, and that thou hast turned their heart back again. Then the fire of the Lord fell, and consumed the burnt offering, and the wood, and the stones, and the dust, and licked up the water that was in the trench. And when all the people saw it, they fell on their faces: and they said, The Lord, he is God; the Lord, he is God. And Elijah said unto them, Take the prophets of Baal; let not one of them escape. And they took them: and Elijah brought them down to the brook Kishon, and slew them there. And Elijah said unto Ahab, Get thee up, eat and drink; for there is the sound of abundance of rain. So Ahab went up to eat and to drink. And Elijah went up to the top of Carmel; and he bowed himself down upon the earth, and put his face between his knees. And he said to his servant, Go up now, look toward the sea. And he went up, and looked, and said, There is nothing. And he said, Go again seven times. And it came to pass at the seventh time, that he said, Behold, there ariseth a cloud out of the sea, as small as a man's' hand. And he said, Go up, say unto Ahab, Make ready thy chariot, and get thee down, that the rain stop thee not. And it came to pass in a little while, that the heaven grew black with clouds and wind, and there was a great rain. And Ahab rode, and went to Jezreel. And the hand of the Lord was on Elijah; and he girded up his loins, and ran before Ahab to the entrance of Jezreel.

1 Kings 18.

THE LADIES OF ST. JAMES'S.

A PROPER NEW BALLAD OF THE COUNTRY AND THE TOWN.

THE ladies of St. James's go swinging to the play;
   Their footmen run before them, with a " Stand by ! Clear the way ! "
But Phyllida, my Phyllida ! she takes her buckled shoou,
   When we go out a-courting beneath the harvest moon.

The ladies of St. James's wear satin on their backs;
   They sit all night at *Ombre*, with candles all of wax:
But Phyllida, my Phyllida! she dons her russet gown,
   And runs to gather May dew before the world is down.

The ladies of St. James's ! they are so fine and fair,
   You 'd think a box of essences was broken in the air :
But Phyllida, my Phyllida ! the breath of heath and furze,
   When breezes blow at morning, is not so fresh as hers.

The ladies of St. James's ! they 're painted to the eyes;
   Their white it stays for ever, their red it never dies :
But Phyllida, my Phyllida ! her color comes and goes;
   It trembles to a lily, — it wavers to a rose.

The ladies of St. James's ! You scarce can understand
   The half of all their speeches, their phrases are so grand :
But Phyllida, my Phyllida ! her shy and simple words
   Are clear as after rain-drops the music of the birds.

The ladies of St. James's ! they have their fits and freaks;
   They smile on you — for seconds, they frown on you — for weeks :
But Phyllida, my Phyllida ! come either storm or shine,
   From Shrove-tide unto Shrove-tide, is always true — and mine.

> My Phyllida ! my Phyllida ! I care not though they heap
>   The hearts of all St. James's, and give me all to keep ;
> I care not whose the bea ties of all the world may be,
>   For Phyllida — for Phyllida is all the world to me !
>
> *Austin Dobson.*

XXXVI. PERSONATION AND PARTICIPATION.

> " HALT ! " — the dust-browned ranks stood fast ;
> " Fire ! " — out blazed the rifle-blast.
>
> *Whittier.*

IN reading these two lines, the quoted words are given in one way, and the rest in another. The two words quoted are given so .s to suggest the spirit of a commander at the head of an army; they are given objectively, according to our conception of a distinct character in a specific situation. If both lines are read naturally, with intense realization of the situation, the subordinate clauses have also a distinct and definite character. They are made to manifest the feeling which awakens in our own heart in contemplation of the events. We consciously or unconsciously become sympathetic spectators of the scene. As we hear the command, we begin to feel anxious for the flag and for Barbara Fritchie; and as the command to fire is given, the intense suspense increases.

The mind's attitude in speaking the quoted words may be called Personation, and that in speaking the subordinate clauses may be called Participation. In the first, we dramatically represent or suggest a character. In the second, the reader's own feelings and sympathies in relation to the events are expressed; he becomes a sympathetic participant in the scene. At first, the speaker tries to represent the feeling, bearing, or character of a man; his own feeling is subordinated to his identification with the feeling of another; but in the subordinate clauses his own emotions assert themselves, and he himself becomes in imagination a part of the scene.

These two attitudes, or forms of manifesting dramatic sympathy, are universally present in all forms of literature, are found in the conversation of daily life, and constitute two modes of dramatic expression which are very important. They ever act in co-operation; and one must never be subordinated or used to the entire exclusion of the other. One is more objective, the other more subjective; one represents, the other manifests; one is occasional, the other almost continuous. One reveals our conception of a character, and our identification with the processes of his mind and his modes of expression; the other shows our own feeling, our sympathetic or dramatic participation in the scene, our response not only to the character or characters, but to every event and situation.

Which of these modes is superior? Both are natural and necessary; but our public readers, and even our speakers, at the present time incline to exaggerate dramatic personation, and to forget entirely that there is such a thing as dramatic participation. The reader must be himself before he can be any one else. Even an actor must himself have a great personality if he is to reflect or represent a great personality. He must be a well educated man, with all his powers harmoniously trained, if he is to identify himself sympathetically with the highest characteristics.

Participation as a form of dramatic assimilation is very apt to be overlooked. There are certain points in which its importance is clearly shown. Personation is used only occasionally; it occurs only in direct quotation; but participation is continuous, and applies to every form of expression. Personation belongs only to a few forms of literature, participation to all. Participation belongs to subordinate clauses, and leads to a great variety of points of view; personation, on the contrary, must present a definite conception of a character.

Again, dramatic participation in ordinary reading and narration must lead up to personation, must be its justification. Mere mechanical personation is mockery. It may occur in inferior literature for mere entertainment; but in the highest forms, in tragedy, and in all sublime histrionic expression, sympathetic participation is the foundation and background of all personation.

In the following extract from Longfellow's "Robert of Sicily," there are many clauses where participation leads to personation, and where true expression flows naturally from one into the other.

For example, the words " Half choked with rage " are given with the direct realization of Robert's character and mood, which only breaks out in his direct words, " Open; 't is I, the King ! " If the explanatory clause is given tamely, and a sudden endeavor be made to represent Robert in the quotation, we have an illustration of the most vicious form of public reading, which is, alas ! too common, — an imitative manipulation of the voice in certain words or clauses, without any imaginative or dramatic assimilation of the spirit of the poem.

WHEN he awoke, it was already night; the church was empty, and there was no light, save where the lamps, that glimmered few and faint, lighted a little space before some saint. He started from his seat and gazed around, but saw no living thing, and heard no sound. He groped towards the door, but it was locked ; he cried aloud, and listened, and then knocked, and uttered awful threatenings and complaints and imprecations upon men and saints. The sounds re-echoed from the roof and walls as if dead priests were laughing in their stalls.

At length the sexton, hearing from without the tumult of the knocking and the shout, and thinking thieves were in the house of prayer, came with his lantern, asking, "Who is there ?" Half choked with rage, King Robert fiercely said, "Open; 't is I, the King ! Art thou afraid ?" The frightened sexton, muttering, with a curse, "This is some drunken vagabond, or worse!" turned the great key and flung the portal wide. A man rushed by him at a single stride, haggard, half-naked, without hat or cloak, who neither turned, nor looked at him, nor spoke, but leaped into the blackness of the night, and vanished like a spectre from his sight.

Robert of Sicily, brother of Pope Urbane, and Valmond, Emperor of Allemaine, despoiled of his magnificent attire, bareheaded, breathless, and besprent with mire, with sense of wrong and outrage desperate, strode on and thundered at the palace gate ; rushed through the courtyard, thrusting in his rage to right and left each seneschal and page, and hurried up the broad and sounding stair, his white face ghastly in the torches' glare. From hall to hall he passed with breathless speed ; voices and cries he heard, but did not heed, until at last he reached the banquet-room, blazing with light, and breathing with perfume.

There on the dais sat another king, wearing his robes, his crown, his signet-ring, King Robert's self in features, form, and height, but all transfigured with angelic light ! It was an angel; and his presence there with a divine effulgence filled the air, — an exaltation piercing the disguise, though none the hidden angel recognize.

A moment speechless, motionless, amazed, the throneless monarch on the angel gazed, who met his look of anger and surprise with the divine compas-

sion of his eyes; then said, "Who art thou? and why com'st thou here?"
To which King Robert answered, with a sneer, "I am the King, and come to
claim my own from an impostor, who usurps my throne!" And suddenly, at
these audacious words, up sprang the angry guests, and drew their swords.
The angel answered, with unruffled brow, "Nay, not the King, but the King's
jester; thou henceforth shalt wear the bells and scalloped cape, and for thy
counsellor shall lead an ape; thou shalt obey my servants when they call, and
wait upon my henchmen in the hall."

Deaf to King Robert's threats and cries and prayers, they thrust him from
the hall and down the stairs. A group of tittering pages ran before, and as
they opened wide the folding-door, his heart failed, for he heard with strange
alarms the boisterous laughter of the men at arms, and all the vaulted chamber roar and ring with the mock plaudits of "Long live the King!"

In the following poem, the writer adopts the point of view of a
sympathetic spectator as the predominant one. The first lines must
be given with great imaginative realization of the situation and
the scene. The darkness must be felt by the reader, the silent
woods, the subtle sense of danger and duty. As a sympathetic
spectator he must even speculate as to what the soldier is thinking. In "Hush! hark!" he stops and listens with his hero, and
in the next line becomes reassured. Then the reader's or author's
own words express the thoughts, and then describe "the wrench-
ing of the gun." He is led gradually to the personation of the
enemy, and also to the objective rendering of the hero's cry of
alarm.

THE FALL OF D'ASSAS.

ALONE, through gloomy forest shades, a soldier went by night;
No moonbeam pierced the dusky glades, no star shed guiding light;
Yet, on his vigil's midnight round, the youth all cheerly passed,
Unchecked by aught of boding sound that muttered in the blast.

Where were his thoughts that lonely hour? In his far home; perchance
His father's hall, his mother's bower, 'midst the gay vines of France.
Hush! hark! did stealing steps go by? Came not faint whispers near?
No! The wild wind hath many a sigh, amid the foliage sere.

Hark! yet again!—and from his hand what grasp hath wrenched the blade?
O, single 'midst a hostile band, young soldier, thou 'rt betrayed!
"Silence!" in undertones they cry; "no whisper—not a breath!
The sound that warns thy comrades nigh shall sentence thee to death."

Still at the bayonet's point he stood, and strong to meet the blow ;
And shouted, 'midst his rushing blood, "Arm ! arm ! Auvergne ! the foe !"
The stir, the tramp, the bugle-call, he heard their tumults grow ;
And sent his dying voice through all, — "Auvergne ! Auvergne ! the foe !"

Mrs. Hemans.

The importance of dramatic participation is especially seen in the reading of the Scriptures. We can personate only what is on a level with us, or is below us. We cannot personate God. But while we cannot dramatically represent what is above us, by dramatic participation we can reverently and truthfully suggest the most exalted idea and experience possible for the human soul. We can even suggest that which transcends human understanding. Participation can show the imaginative and emotional realization of that which is only an object of faith, and not an object of sense.

In the reading of the Scriptures, therefore, where God is supposed to speak, though we cannot dramatically personate, we can disclose the impression produced upon us, or the effect of His words. We do not give His words as we suppose them to have been spoken; we manifest the reverence and awe which they would cause in ourselves if we heard him. This manifestation of subjective impression is the noblest power of vocal expression.

In the following sublime passage how weak would be the effort to imitate or personate the "still, small voice;" but how tremendously effective it is to manifest, in pronouncing these words, the feeling which they awakened! The same is true of the words spoken directly to Elijah.

AND Ahab told Jezebel all that Elijah had done, and withal how he had slain all the prophets with the sword. Then Jezebel sent a messenger unto Elijah, saying, So let the gods do to me, and more also, if I make not thy life as the life of one of them by to-morrow about this time. And when he saw that, he arose, and went for his life, and came to Beer-Sheba, which belongeth to Judah, and left his servant there. But he himself went a day's journey into the wilderness, and came and sat down under a juniper tree: and he requested for himself that he might die ; and said, It is enough ; now, O Lord, take away my life ; for I am not better than my fathers. And he lay down and slept under a juniper tree ; and, behold, an angel touched him, and said unto him, Arise and eat. And he looked, and, behold, there was at his head a cake baken on the coals, and a cruse of water. And he did eat and drink, and laid him down again. And the angel of the Lord came again the second time, and touched him, and said, Arise and eat; because the journey is too great for thee. And he arose, and did eat and drink, and went in the strength of that meat forty days and forty nights unto Horeb the mount of God. And he came thither unto a cave, and lodged there; and, behold, the word of the Lord came to him, and he said unto him, What doest thou here, Elijah? And he said, I have been very jealous for the Lord, the God of hosts; for the children of Israel have forsaken thy covenant, thrown down thine altars, and slain thy prophets with the sword: and I, even I only, am left; and they seek my life, to take it away. And he said, Go forth, and stand upon the mount before the Lord. And, behold, the Lord passed by, and a great and strong wind rent the mountains, and break in pieces the rocks before the Lord; but the Lord was not in the wind: and after the wind an earthquake; but the Lord was not in the earthquake: and after the earthquake a fire; but the Lord was not in the fire: and after the fire a still small voice. And it was so, when Elijah heard it, that he wrapped his face in his mantle, and went out, and stood in the entering in of the cave. And, behold, there came a voice unto him, and said, What doest thou here, Elijah? And he said, I have been very jealous for the Lord, the God of hosts; for the children of Israel have forsaken thy covenant, thrown down thine altars, and slain thy prophets with the sword; and I, even I only, am left; and they seek my life, to take it away. And the Lord said unto him, Go, return on thy way to the wilderness of Damascus: and when thou comest, thou shalt anoint Hazael to be king over Syria: and Jehu the son of Nimshi shalt thou anoint to be king over Israel: and Elisha the son of Shaphat of Abel-meholah shalt thou anoint to be prophet in thy room. And it shall come to pass, that him that escapeth from the sword of Hazael shall Jehu slay: and him that escapeth from the sword of Jehu shall Elisha slay. Yet will I leave me seven thousand in Israel, all the knees which have not bowed unto Baal, and every mouth which hath not kissed him. So he departed thence, and found Elisha the son of Shaphat, who was plowing, with twelve yoke of oxen before him, and he with the twelve: and Elijah passed over unto him, and cast his mantle upon him. And he left the oxen, and ran after Elijah, and said, Let me, I pray thee, kiss my father and my mother, and then I will follow thee. And he said unto him, Go back again; for what have I done to thee? And he returned from following him, and took the yoke of oxen, and slew them, and boiled their flesh with the instruments of the oxen, and gave unto the people, and they did eat. Then he arose, and went after Elijah, and ministered unto him.

1 *Kings* 19.

Actors have more personation than participation; they primarily aim to represent everything objectively. In orators, however, dramatic participation transcends personation. It is only occasionally, and in more playful moods, or in the subordinate parts, that personation is found in the highest forms of oratory. The public reader should have thorough command of both modes. This is another matter which goes to show, that if public readers were thoroughly educated, and imbued with the spirit of art and the various forms of literature, and had right conceptions of the character and various forms of poetic expression, they could discharge a higher function in public entertainment than is possible on the stage.

The true actor, however, must have participation. If his art is merely representative, it tends to become merely imitative and mechanical, and is usually confined to the lower forms of dramatic representation. Even in him sympathetic participation must underlie, cause, and continually transcend all personation.

Assimilation thus acts in these two ways. They are both natural, and in the highest dramatic art complement each other. The true reader must show his own feeling and point of view, the sympathetic attitude of his mind, and manifest his own participation in the smallest event. As the stage requires many subordinate characters, each of whom must show his own interest in the moving scene in order to create illusion, so the speaker or reader must show sympathetic identification of himself with every subordinate clause and phrase. Nothing must be neutral, negative, or indifferent. Everything must be positive, and bear a sympathetic relationship with the great centre of interest, and must reflect as in a mirror the central spirit of the situation.

O MY husband, brave and gentle ! O my Bernal, look once more
On the blessèd cross before thee ! Mercy ! mercy ! all is o'er."
Dry thy tears, my poor Ximena; lay thy dear one down to rest ;
Let his hands be meekly folded, lay the cross upon his breast. . . . .

Close beside her, faintly moaning, fair and young, a soldier lay,
Torn with shot and pierced with lances, bleeding slow his life away ;
But, as tenderly before him the lorn Ximena knelt,
She saw the Northern eagle shining on his pistol belt.

With a stifled cry of horror straight she turn'd away her head ;
With a sad and bitter feeling look'd she back upon her dead ;
But she heard the youth's low moaning, and his struggling breath of pain,
And she raised the cooling water to his parching lips again.

Whisper'd low the dying soldier, press'd her hand, and faintly smiled :
Was that pitying face his mother's ? did she watch beside her child ?
All his stranger words with meaning her woman's heart supplied ;
With her kiss upon his forehead, " Mother ! " murmur'd he, and died.

" A bitter curse upon them, poor boy, who led thee forth
From some gentle, sad-eyed mother, weeping, lonely, in the North ! "
Spake the mournful Mexic woman, as she laid him with her dead,
And turn'd to soothe the living still, and bind the wounds which bled.

Angels of Buena Vista.   ——————   *Whittier.*

I ONCE saw a poor fellow, keen and clever,
Witty and wise :— he paid a man a visit,
And no one noticed him, and no one ever
Gave him a welcome.   " Strange ! " cried I, " whence is it ? "
  He walked on this side, then on that,
  He tried to introduce a social chat ;
Now here, now there, in vain he tried ;
Some formally and freezingly replied,
           And some
Said by their silence — " Better stay at home."

  A rich man burst the door ;
  As Crœsus rich, I 'm sure
He could not pride himself upon his wit,
And as for wisdom, he had none of it ;
He had what 's better ; he had wealth.
  What a confusion ! — all stand up erect —
These crowd around to ask him of his health ;
  These bow in *honest* duty and respect ;
And these arrange a sofa or a chair,
And these conduct him there.
" Allow me, sir, the honor ; " — Then a bow
Down to the earth — Is 't possible to show
Meet gratitude for such kind condescension ?

> The poor man hung his head,
> And to himself he said,
> " This is indeed beyond my comprehension : "
> Then looking round,
> One friendly face he found,
> And said, " Pray tell me why is wealth preferred
> To wisdom ? " — " That 's a silly question, friend ! "
> Replied the other — " have you never heard,
> A man may lend his store
> Of gold or silver ore,
> But wisdom none can borrow, none can lend ? "
>
> *Khemnitzer.*

XXXVII. ASSIMILATION AND QUOTATION.

> WHATEVER I do, and whatever I say,
> Aunt Tabitha tells me that is n't the way ;
> When she was a girl (forty summers ago),
> Aunt Tabitha tells me they never did so.

IN these lines, by Dr. Holmes, there are no quotation marks; but whenever a statement is made by a character similar to the one supposed to be speaking in the poem, an objective coloring will be given to such phrases as " that is n't the way " and " they never did so." These two clauses are only indirect quotations, if they can be regarded as quotations at all. But one with a vigorous imagination and a strong dramatic instinct, especially in excitable moods, will involuntarily quote and personate the one whose sentiments he is supposed to represent. This is especially true of such emotions as sarcasm and antagonism; there is a greater tendency to caricature and exaggeration in these emotions, but the principle holds true. There is a universal desire for definite representation. The fables which have lived from age to age, the myths of the race, the historical legends, arose from this demand of the imagination. The dramatic instinct has many forms, and is universal. It is often very imaginative and suggestive.

Making the tomb and the rose directly speak in the following poem awakens deep feeling in our hearts, but the representation is very delicate and subjective.

THE Tomb said to the Rose, " Tell me, with all the tears Morn sheds o'er thee, what dost thou do, fair garden pride ? "

"With all that drops, day after day, into thy yawning depths, oh, say!
what dost thou do?"

The Rose replied, "Sad Tomb! into a subtle scent of ambergris and
honey, blent, do I convert those dew-drops bright!"

"And I create, O Rosebud fair, from ev'ry soul which enters here, an
angel-form, with wings of light!"

The Tomb and the Rose.   *Victor Hugo.*

In the vocal rendering of such passages, the dramatic representation must be delicately suggested. If made too literal, the spirit
of the poetry is spoiled. The tomb and the rose are ideal conceptions, and there is dramatic participation rather than dramatic
personation. This sympathetic assimilation is subjective, and has
very little objective representation. The imaginative conception
of the truth has become so vivid as to take dramatic form, but the
feeling is fully as lyric as it is dramatic; or, perhaps, it should be
said that the highest dramatic expression is as fully subjective as
it is objective.

The distinction between lyric and dramatic often exists only in
name. All great dramatic art implies the lyric, and all lyric art
contains a dramatic element. Just as subjective and objective are
two aspects of the same thing, so dramatic and lyric are different
points of view, different modes by which the human soul realizes
truth. In all great poetry and art, and in all rendering, there is
the union and co-ordination of antithetic elements.

If we take up now a common dialogue in which ignoble emotions chiefly predominate, the difference will be more saliently
shown in expression. Here the quotations are made literal, the
objective element is far more pronounced, and even the types of
character more definitely rendered.

MY SPOUSE NANCY.

Husband, husband, cease your strife, nor longer idly rave, sir;
Though I am your wedded wife, yet I am not your slave, sir.
"One of two must still obey, Nancy, Nancy;
Is it man, or woman, say, my spouse Nancy?"
If 't is still the lordly word, service and obedience,
I'll desert my sovereign lord, and so good bye, allegiance!
"Sad will I be, so bereft, Nancy, Nancy,
Yet I'll try to make a shift, my spouse Nancy."

> My poor heart then break it must, my last hour — I 'm near it :
> When you lay me in the dust, think, think how you will bear it.
> "I will hope and trust in Heaven, Nancy, Nancy ;
> Strength to bear it will be given, my spouse Nancy."
> Well, sir, from the silent dead still I 'll try to daunt you ;
> Ever round your midnight bed horrid sprites shall haunt you.
> "I 'll wed another like my dear Nancy, Nancy ;
> Then all ghosts will fly for fear — my spouse Nancy."

Quotation marks are mechanical, and can show no degrees; but vocal expression must quote, and be able to suggest various degrees of representation. The voice must show delicate and indirect references and indications as well as the most direct quotations. There must be sympathetic assimilation of the spirit of the passage, and among the complex elements the most important are the persons who spoke the words. Truthful rendering must at all times show the direct participation of the reader in the thought and feeling of the original speaker; and at times his participation is so intense that indirect quotations become more important than direct ones, and even a clause which shows the effect of the direct quotation upon the reader or speaker becomes more important than either. In some poems or stories, where the sympathetic feeling is more or less lyric, the mind may be so intensely concerned with the universal truth, or the deep passion, that even direct quotations are placed in the background. No rule can be laid down; it is a matter of dramatic instinct, and different poems will be read differently on different occasions, and by different persons.

There is among our public readers an almost universal tendency to exaggerate quotations unduly. These are given great importance and emphasis, while clauses which are not quoted are rendered by the voice as something negative and neutral, without any definite coloring or character. But especially in the higher forms of vocal expression, such as the reading of the Scriptures, the epic, or the ballad, the result of this neutralizing of all but quotations is an artificial effect. In comedy and farce, the method tends to confine readers to the lower forms of literature.

Occasionally, explanatory clauses are intended by the author to be subordinate, as in Browning's "Ben Karshook's Wisdom."

This poem is essentially dramatic. The whole thought of the poem is centred in the speakers and the sentiments they utter, not in any event or in the effect of their words upon the listener. Such forms of literature, however, are unusual.

BEN KARSHOOK'S WISDOM.

I.

"Would a man 'scape the rod?" — Rabbi Ben Karshook saith,
"See that he turns to God the day before his death."
"Ay, could a man inquire when it shall come!" I say.
The Rabbi's eye shoots fire — "Then let him turn to-day!"

II.

Quoth a young Sadducee, — "Reader of many rolls,
Is it so certain we have, as they tell us, souls?" —
"Son, there is no reply!" the Rabbi bit his beard:
"Certain, a soul have *I* — *We* may have none," he sneered.
Thus Karshook, the Hiram's-Hammer, the Right-Hand Temple column,
Taught babes their grace in grammar, and struck the simple, solemn.

Browning.

WHEN.

Sun comes, moon comes, time slips away.
Sun sets, moon sets, love, fix a day.
"A year hence, a year hence," "we shall both be gray."
"A month hence, a month hence."   "Far, far away."
"A week hence, a week hence."   "Ah, the long delay."
"Wait a little, wait a little, you shall fix a day."
"To-morrow, love, to-morrow, and that 's an age away."
Blaze upon her window, sun, and honour all the day.

Tennyson.

To-day my lord of Amiens and myself
Did steal behind him, as he lay along
Under an oak, whose antique root peeps out
Upon the brook that brawls along this wood;
To the which place a poor sequestered stag,
That from the hunters' aim had ta'en a hurt,
Did come to languish; . . . thus the hairy fool,
Much markèd of the melancholy Jaques,
Stood on the extremest verge of the swift brook,
"*Poor deer*," quoth he, "*thou mak'st a testament
As worldings do, giving thy sum of more
To that which had too much;*" then, being there alone,

Left and abandoned of his velvet friends :
"'*T is right,*" quoth hè, "*thus misery doth part*
The flux of company ; " anon, a careless herd,
Full of the pasture, jumps along by him,
And never stays to greet him : "*Ay,*" quoth Jaques,
" *Sweep on, you fat and greasy citizens ;*
'*T is just the fashion : wherefore do you look*
Upon that poor and broken bankrupt there ? "
Thus most invectively he pierceth through
The body of the country, city, court,
Yea, and of this our life ; swearing that we
Are mere usurpers, tyrants, and what's worse,
To fright the animals, and to kill them up,
In their assigned and native dwelling-place.

Shakespeare.

THE WRECK OF THE HESPERUS.

It was the schooner Hesperus that sail'd the wintry sea ;
And the skipper had taken his little daughter to bear him company.
Blue were her eyes as the fairy-flax, her cheeks like the dawn of day,
And her bosom white as the hawthorn buds that ope in the mouth of May.

The skipper he stood beside the helm, his pipe was in his mouth,
And he watch'd how the veering flaw did blow the smoke now west, now south.
Then up and spake an old sailor, — had sail'd the Spanish main, —
" I pray thee, put into yonder port, for I fear a hurricane.

" Last night the Moon had a golden ring, and to-night no Moon we see ! "
The skipper, he blew a whiff from his pipe, and a scornful laugh laugh'd he.
Colder and louder blew the wind, a gale from the north-east :
The snow fell hissing in the brine, and the billows froth'd like yeast.

Down came the storm, and smote amain the vessel in its strength ;
She shudder'd and paused, like a frighten'd steed, then leap'd her cable's
    length.
" Come hither ! come hither ! my little daughter, and do not tremble so ;
For I can weather the roughest gale, that ever wind did blow."

He wrapp'd her warm in his seaman's coat against the stinging blast ;
He cut a rope from a broken spar, and bound her to the mast.
" O father ! I hear the church-bells ring, O say, what may it be ? "
"'T is a fog-bell on a rock-bound coast ! " and he steer'd for the open sea.

" O father ! I hear the sound of guns, O say, what may it be ? "
" Some ship in distress, that cannot live in such an angry sea ! "
" O father ! I see a gleaming light, O say, what may it be ? "
But the father answer'd never a word, a frozen corpse was he.

Lash'd to the helm, all stiff and stark, with his face turn'd to the skies,
The lantern gleam'd through the gleaming snow on his fix'd and glassy eyes.
Then the maiden clasp'd her hands and pray'd, that saved she might be ;
And she thought of Christ, who still'd the wave on the Lake of Galilee.

And fast thro' the midnight dark and drear, thro' the whistling sleet and snow,
Like a sheeted ghost, the vessel swept towards the reef of Norman's Woe.
And ever, the fitful gusts between, a sound came from the land ;
It was the sound of the trampling surf on the rocks and the hard sea-sand.

The breakers were right beneath her bows, she drifted a dreary wreck,
And a whooping billow swept the crew like icicles from her deck.
She struck where the white and fleecy waves look'd soft as carded wool,
But the cruel rocks, they gored her side like the horns of an angry bull.

Her rattling shrouds, all sheath'd in ice, with the masts went by the board ;
Like a vessel of glass, she stove and sank.   Ho ! ho ! the breakers roar'd !
At daybreak, on the bleak sea-beach, a fisherman stood aghast,
To see the form of a maiden fair lash'd close to a drifting mast.

The salt sea was frozen on her breast, the salt tears in her eyes ;
And he saw her hair, like the brown sea-weed, on the billows fall and rise.
Such was the wreck of the Hesperus, in the midnight and the snow !
Christ save us all from a death like this, on the reef of Norman's Woe !

Longfellow.

XXXVIII. ASSIMILATION AND DIALECT.

VERY close to quotation or personation is dialect.   How far shall
a reader or an actor, in giving the speech of others, present the
peculiarities of utterance or dialect?   It is suggestive that dialect
readings are considered as belonging to the lower class of literature.   There is a tendency to the merely imitative, as dialectic
tendencies are accidental, and have little vital connection with the
processes of thought and feeling.   There is a connection, however,
in some forms of humor and pathos, or in grotesque expression;
note its expressive power, for example, in Irish or Scotch.

Dialect does not consist in the pronunciation of elements, or
even of individual words; hence, mere change of vowels or conso-
nants will not make the dialect expressive or natural.   There is a
certain melody or rhythm which is peculiar to every nation.   This
is very important as a means of expression, because it shows their
peculiarity of character, their modes of thought and feeling.

In fact, dialectic changes, though at first they seem to be superficial, and merely a subject for imitation, are expressive of life. They are not adopted for their own sake, but heighten the impression of truthfulness.

Hence, dialect when used is a part of the process of assimilation. They must result from sympathetic identification of the reader with his character. He must so reproduce in himself the processes of thinking and feeling that dialect is made a necessity.

Imitation, therefore, is apt to mislead. Even in matters of dialect, it tends to reproduce the literal rather than the essential. Where the whole energy is taken up with the literal mispronunciations, the real process of thinking, peculiarities of feeling, the oddities of the character, — in other words, the psychic elements, — are entirely lost.

It should be carefully noted by all public readers that dialectic peculiarities can be only suggested. To give Scotch or Irish dialect in an extreme form renders the words unintelligible. All expression must be clear and easily understood.

> . . . An' the judge took a big pinch iv snuff, and he says,
> "Are you guilty or not, Jim O'Brien, av you plaze?"

> An' all held their breath in the silence of dhread,
> An' Shamus O'Brien made answer and said :
> "My lord, if you ask me, if in my life-time
> I thought any treason, or did any crime
> That should call to my cheek, as I stand alone here,
> The hot blush of shame, or the coldness of fear,
> Though I stood by the grave to receive my death-blow,
> Before God and the world I would answer you, no !
> But if you would ask me, as I think it like,
> If in the rebellion I carried a pike,
> An' fought for ould Ireland from the first to the close,
> An' shed the heart's blood of her bitterest foes,
> I answer you, yes ; and I tell you again,
> Though I stand here to perish, it's my glory that then
> In her cause I was willing my veins should run dhry,
> An' that now for her sake I am ready to die."

> Then the silence was great, and the jury smiled bright,
> An' the judge was n't sorry the job was made light ;

By my sowl, it 's himself was the crabbed ould chap !
In a twinklin' he pulled on his ugly black cap.
Then Shamus's mother in the crowd standin' by,
Called out to the judge with a pitiful cry:
"O judge ! darlin', don't, Oh, don't say the word !
The crathur is young, have mercy, my lord ;
He was foolish ; he did n't know what he was doin'.
You don't know him, my lord, — Oh, don't give him to ruin !
He 's the kindliest crathur, the tendherest hearted ;
Don't part us forever, we that 's so long parted.
Judge, mavourneen, forgive him, forgive him, my lord,
An' God will forgive you — Oh, don't say the word ! "

That was the first minute that O'Brien was shaken,
When he saw that he was not quite forgot or forsaken ;
An' down his pale cheeks, at the word of his mother,
The big tears wor runnin' fast, one afther th' other ;
An' two or three times he endeavored to spake,
But the sthrong, manly voice used to falther and break ;
But at last, by the strength of his high-mounting pride,
He conquered and masthered his grief's swelling tide,
"An'," says he, "mother, darlin', don't break your poor heart.
For, sooner or later, the dearest must part."

CUDDLE DOON.

THE bairnies cuddle doon at nicht wi' muckle faucht an' din.
" O, try and sleep, ye waukrife rogues ; your father 's comin' in."
They never heed a word I speak : I try to gie a froon ;
But aye I hap them up, an' cry, " O, bairnies, cuddle doon ! "

Wee Jamie wi' the curley heid — he aye sleeps next the wa' —
Bangs up au' cries, " I want a piece " — the rascal starts them a'.
I rin an' fetch them pieces, drinks, — they stop a wee the soun', —
Then draw the blankets up, and cry, " Noo, weanies, cuddle doon ! "

But, ere five minutes gang, wee Rab cries oot, frae 'neath the claes,
" Mither, mak' Tam gie ower at ance ; he 's kittlin' wi' his taes."
The mischief 's in that Tam for tricks: he 'd bother half the toon ;
But aye I hap them up, and cry, " O, bairnies, cuddle doon ! "

At length they hear their father's fit ; an', as he steeks the door,
They turn their faces to the wa', while Tam pretends to snore.
" Hae a' the weans been gude ? " he asks, as he pits aff his shoon.
" The bairnies, John, are in their beds, an' lang since cuddled doon."

An', just afore we bed oorsels, wo look at oor wee lambs :
Tam has his airm roun' wee Rab's neck, an' Rab his airn roun' Tam's.
I lift wee Jamie up the bed, an', as I straik each croon,
I whisper, till my heart fills up, " O, bairnies, cuddle doon 1 "

The bairnies cuddle doon at nicht wi' mirth that 's dear to me ;
But soon the big warl's cark an' care will quaten doon their glee :
Yet, come what will to ilka ane, may He who sits aboon
Aye whisper, though their pows be bauld, " O, bairnies, cuddle doon ! "

Anderson.

XXXIX. PURPOSES IN EXPRESSION.

THE opinion is held by many that art aims simply to entertain or
to amuse ; that it exists entirely for its own sake, and if consistent
with itself, no more is required of it.   It thus has nothing to do
with morals or the ethical nature of man, and is hence without
purpose.   Oratory, on the other hand, such men consider, aims to
instruct or to persuade, and hence striving for something beyond
itself, has an ethical element which separates it from such an art
as painting, or the drama.

All expression, however, aims directly or indirectly to produce
an effect upon another mind.   Hence, consciously or unconsciously,
every form of art has some kind of purpose.   The chief difference
between an artistic purpose and the oratorical purpose is the fact
that in art the purpose is hidden, indirect or more or less unconscious, while in teaching or speaking, the purpose is manifest,
direct, and consciously dominates the artist's method of procedure, if it is not frankly stated by him and understood by his
audience.

This distinction is not wholly true.   A purely conscious or direct
presentation of the aim is only a command, and is not only inartistic,
but does not even appeal to the rational nature.   A mere command
requires unquestioning, unthinking obedience, and this, under no
consideration, could be dignified by the name of Oratory.

Thus the common distinction is not adequate ; but if we seek
deeper, we find a common ground upon which a noble speech and
a noble painting alike depend.   Expression of every form in

poetry, painting, sculpture, architecture, the drama, and oratory, aims to awaken the same faculties in another mind which are active in the mind of the artist.

All expression is founded upon communion of different minds. The painter tries to convey to another the impression a landscape makes upon him. If he merely mechanically reproduces the form and colors of the scene, he belongs on a very low plane. Only in proportion as he manifests his own faculties or feeling in realizing the scene, will he rise into the realm of poetry, or the sublime in art. Thus the fundamental test of nobility of expression depends upon the degree to which the artist manifests the activity of his faculties and awakens the imagination and feeling of the minds he addresses.

Thus, every form of art endeavors to influence the human mind. Purpose is implied even in that literature or work which aims simply to amuse.

The element which underlies all purposes in expression might possibly be best named by the word " influence." " Macbeth" is not a sermon, or a didactic lesson upon the nature of the human conscience; but it influences men by making them realize the nature of conscience and the results of disobeying it. A great painting has profound movement. The Cologne Cathedral may influence men to worship. Its soaring arches may soften the hardest heart that enters, and cause the most irreverent to remove his hat.

Accordingly, in proportion as a speaker unconsciously influences men without dictation, will his effect be the greater.

The conscious or the oratoric purposes are, according to Delsarte, to instruct, to move, and to persuade.

These three purposes are simply the outgrowth of the three natures of man. Instruction is an endeavor to make a man think. To move men is simply to awaken them. Persuasion aims not only to make a man think and to awaken him to the realization of certain facts, but it goes even farther, and endeavors to arouse his will.

These three do not include, of course, all purposes; they simply name three of the most important conscious purposes. The speaker may convince, inspire, arouse, rebuke, reprove, exhort, entreat, reject, condemn, judge, and the like, but the character of all of these depends upon the part of the nature of the speaker which is awake, and the part of his auditors to which he appeals.

There is no worse fault nor more common one in speaking than monotony of purpose. A man who does nothing but teach will affect only a small part of the nature of his auditors, and will become a pedant. He who seeks only to interest or to move is apt to appeal more and more to the lower nature of his audience, and become a demagogue or a sensationalist. He who exhorts and tries to persuade men continually without making them think or without making their vital natures live, also becomes abnormal.

These purposes vary continually. One is dependent upon another; they continually intermingle, and any true speaker makes constant transitions from one to another. He only is a great orator who is able to pass readily from any one purpose to another. The speaker must appeal to the whole nature of his audience, and be able to move any part of the nature of man at will. Hence, exercise in a great variety of purposes embodied in very short, sharply contrasted extracts is very important for all.

There are three professions named on account of these purposes; but while the teacher more especially teaches, and the popular orator simply moves, and the preacher persuades, still these three purposes are combined in all noble expression.

There are many passages of literature in which the definite aim regarding another mind is not manifest. There are many other passages which may be used with any one of the purposes. Students should arrange a great many purposes, such as to teach, to warn, to encourage, to apologize, to reprove, to rebuke, to inspire, to arouse, to allay excitement; select passages for their illustration, and practise them in contrast.

These may be given also under different situations. For example, to arouse to joy, to arouse to battle, to arouse courage, to arouse hope, to arouse faith. The variations are innumerable.

Purposes should not be confounded with emotion. It is good practice to keep the purpose the same, but vary the feeling or the person against whom the feeling is directed.

PROBLEM XXV. *Contrast several extracts with varied purposes, and conceive and assimilate carefully the difference of aim.*

HURRAH ! hurrah ! the west wind comes freshening down the bay !
The rising sails are filling, give way, my lads, give way.

Whittier.

THE aids to noble life are all within.

Cordelia.   O thou good Kent, how shall I live and work,
To match thy goodness ?   My life will be too short,
And every measure fail me.

" FORWARD, the light brigade !   Charge for the guns ! " he said.

Tennyson.

WHEN all thy mercies, O my God, my rising soul surveys,
Transported with the view, I 'm lost in wonder, love, and praise.

BEAR with me, good boy, I am much forgetful.
Canst thou hold up thy heavy eyes awhile,
And touch thy instrument a strain or two ?

WE have not wings, we cannot soar ;
    But we have feet to scale and climb
By slow degrees, by more and more,
    The cloudy summits of our time.

Longfellow.

WHICH is the real hereditary sin of humanity ? Do you imagine that I shall say pride, or luxury, or ambition ?   No! I shall say indolence. He who conquers that can conquer all.

PROBLEM XXVI. *Vividly conceive the ideas and situation of some animated extract, and read it so as to move another.*

YE sons of Freedom, wake to glory !
    Hark ! hark ! what myriads bid ye rise !
Your children, wives, and grandsires hoary,
    Behold their tears and hear their cries.

FLING broad the sail, dip deep the oar :
To sea ! to sea ! the calm is o'er.

HEW down the bridge, Sir Consul, with all the speed ye may ;
I, with two more to help me, will hold the foe in play.
In yon straight path a thousand may well be stopped by three ;
Now who will stand on either hand and keep the bridge with me ?

Macaulay.

COME, brothers ! let me name a spell shall rouse your souls again,
And send the old blood bounding free through pulse, and heart, and vein !
Call back the days of bygone years — be young and strong once more ;
Think yonder stream, so stark and red, is one we 've crossed before. . . .
Stayed we behind, that glorious day, for roaring flood or linn ?
The soul of Græme is with us still — now, brothers ! will ye in !

Aytoun.

PROBLEM XXVII. *Appeal to men's spiritual nature, and endeavor to awaken nobler thoughts, feeling, or choice ideals.*

BE patient ! oh, be patient ! though yet our hopes are green,
The harvest-fields of freedom shall be crowned with sunny sheen.

Linton.

BE noble ! and the nobleness that lies
In other men, sleeping, but never dead,
Will rise in majesty to meet thine own.

Lowell.

To thine own self be true, and keep thy mind from sloth, thy heart from soil ;
Press on ! and thou shalt surely reap a heavenly harvest for thy toil.

Park Benjamin.

FIGHT on, thou brave true heart, and falter not, through dark fortune and through bright. The cause thou fightest for, so far as it is true, no further, yet precisely so far, is very sure of victory. The falsehood alone of it will be conquered, will be abolished, as it ought to be : but the truth of it is part of Nature's own laws, co-operates with the World's eternal tendencies, and cannot be conquered.

Carlyle.

PROBLEM XXVIII. *Take the same extract, and give it in many ways, so as to make men think, to move them, to awaken spiritual feeling, to please, reprove, or warn.*

NOT only around our infancy
Doth heaven with all its splendors lie ;
Daily, with souls that cringe and plot,
We Sinais climb, and know it not.

Lowell.

THE quality of mercy is not strain'd ;
It droppeth as the gentle rain from heaven
Upon the place beneath ; it is twice bless'd ;
It blesseth him that gives, and him that takes :
'T is mightiest in the mightiest ; it becomes
The thronèd monarch better than his crown :
His sceptre shows the force of temporal power,

The attribute to awe and majesty,
Wherein doth sit the dread and fear of kings:
But mercy is above this sceptred sway;
It is enthronèd in the hearts of kings:
It is an attribute of God himself:
And earthly power doth then show likest God's,
When mercy seasons justice. Therefore, Jew,
Though justice be thy plea, consider this, —
That in the course of justice, none of us
Should see salvation; we do pray for mercy;
And that same prayer doth teach us all to render
The deeds of mercy.

Merchant of Venice.

PROBLEM XXIX. *Read some passage with transitions of purpose, so as to suggest the variation.*

MOOR, moor the barge, ye gallant crew; and, gentle lady, deign to stay:
Rest thee in Castle Ravensheuch, nor tempt the stormy firth to-day.

———

GENERALLY speaking, an author's style is a faithful copy of his mind. If you would write a lucid style, let there first be light in your own mind; and if you would write a grand style, you ought to have a grand character.

———

Kent. Fare thee well, king: sith thus thou wilt appear,
Freedom lives hence, and banishment is here.
[*To Cordelia.*] The gods to their dear shelter take thee, maid,
That justly think'st, and hast most rightly said!
[*To the Sisters.*] And your large speeches may your deeds approve,
That good effects may spring from words of love.
Thus Kent, O princes, bids you all adieu;
He 'll shape his old course in a country new.

Shakespeare.

———

ADAM AND ORLANDO.

Orlando. Who 's there?
Adam. What, my young master? — O my gentle master!
O my sweet master! O you memory
Of old Sir Rowland! why, what make you here?
Why are you virtuous? Why do people love you?
And wherefore are you gentle, strong, and valiant?
Why would you be so fond to overcome
The bony priser of the humorous duke?
Your praise is come too swiftly home before you.
Know you not, master, to some kind of men
Their graces serve them but as enemies?
No more do yours: your virtues, gentle master,

Are sanctified and holy traitors to you.
Oh, what a world is this, when what is comely
Envenoms him that bears it !
  Orl. Why, what 's the matter ?
  Adam.   O unhappy youth,
Come not within these doors ; within this roof
The enemy of all your graces lives.
Your brother — (no, no brother ; yet the son —
Yet not the son — I will not call him son
Of him I was about to call his father), —
Hath heard your praises ; and this night he means
To burn the lodging where you used to lie,
And you within it : if he fail of that,
He will have other means to cut you off :
I overheard him, and his practices.
This is no place ; this house is but a butchery :
Abhor it, fear it, do not enter it.
  Orl. Why, whither, Adam, wouldst thou have me go ?
  Adam. No matter whither, so you come not here.
  Orl. What ! wouldst thou have me go and beg my food ?
Or with a base and boist'rous sword enforce
A thievish living on the common road ? ;
This I must do, or know not what to do :
Yet this I will not do, do how I can ;
I rather will subject me to the malice
Of a diverted blood, and bloody brother.
  Adam. But do not so. I have five hundred crowns,
The thrifty hire I saved under your father,
Which I did store, to be my foster-nurse
When service should in my old limbs lie lame,
And unregarded age in corners thrown :
Take that ; and He that doth the ravens feed,
Yea, providently caters for the sparrow,
Be comfort to my age ! Here is the gold ;
All this I give you. Let me be your servant :
Though I look old, yet I am strong and lusty ;
For in my youth I never did apply
Hot and rebellious liquors in my blood,
Nor did not with unbashful forehead woo
The means of weakness and debility ;
Therefore my age is as a lusty winter,
Frosty, but kindly : let me go with you ;
I 'll do the service of a younger man
In all your business and necessities.

    Orl. O good old man, how well in thee appears
The constant service of the antique world,
When service sweat for duty, not for meed !
Thou art not for the fashion of these times,
Where none will sweat but for promotion ;
And having that, do choke their service up
Even with the having : it is not so with thee.
But, poor old man, thou prun'st a rotten tree,
That cannot so much as a blossom yield,
In lieu of all thy pains and husbaudry.
But come thy ways ; we 'll go along together ;
And ere we have thy youthful wages spent,
We 'll light upon some settled low content.
    Adam. Master, go on, and I will follow thee,
To the last gasp, with truth and loyalty. —
From seventeen years, till now almost fourscore,
Here lived I, but now live here no more.
At seventeen years many their fortunes seek ;
But at fourscore it is too late a week ;
Yet fortune cannot recompense me better
Than to die well, aud not my master's debtor.

Shakespeare.

XL. FORMS OF THE DRAMATIC.

IT has been shown that whatever is concerned with the revelation
of character or the interpretation of the motives of men, or the
manifestation of the life of the movement of thought and passion,
is dramatic. The nature of the dramatic will be made still clearer
by the study of some of its forms as embodied in literature.

The highest form of dramatic art deals with the loftiest emotions,
situations, and motives of the human soul. The highest form of
the drama deals with the destiny of man, and the problem of suffering. That suffering is one of the chief means of education in the
school of life cannot be doubted. Whether it is the result of a man's
own sin, or of the mistakes of others, the chief means for the
development and refining of the human soul is by means of pain.
According to the common theory of religion, the race is to be
redeemed and saved by the Divine sharing in man's pain.

Tragedy, the highest form of the drama, is the artistic representation of suffering. In tragedy, human endeavor attains its aims

through death. Seemingly, it is the drama of failure, but there is something of victory at the heart; it is ever the overcoming of suffering by the heroism of the human soul.

The struggle to explain tragedy has exercised great minds from the time of the Greeks. That in its noblest form it has added to the refining influences was first proved by Aristotle in his theory called the "catharsis of emotion." The chief difference between comedy and tragedy is that the noblest tragedy achieves its victory through death, while comedy secures it by endeavor or by a fortuitous concurrence of circumstances. Comedy is victory in time; tragedy shows us the struggle, but conceals the victory as part of the sublime mystery of existence; thus our conceptions of tragedy will depend upon our theory of life, our opinion as to the destiny of the race, or the individual. Some of the tragedies of the Greeks seem to have no element of victory, except in the heroic conquest of the fear of death.

Tragedy is always dignified and noble. It is serious, though humorous elements may be woven into it by a Shakespeare. This is done for contrast, to heighten the sublime effect. The chief characteristics of tragedy are depth, intense simplicity, and dignity; poise, balance, and temperance; freedom from extravagance and exaggeration. The element of exhibition is absent; the whole appeal is to the mind.

Next to tragedy the highest form of dramatic art is comedy. In our country the word is loosely used, and anything ludicrous is called comedy. Comedy sees human experiences in their hopeful aspect. From the first note in tragedy, we feel the impossibility of avoiding the catastrophe; but in comedy from the outset there is a feeling of hope and expectation. We feel that there is not so much sin as misunderstanding and mistake, and that time will make everything clear. It is more playful and free, lacking something of the sublime movement of tragedy.

One of the greatest comedies ever written is Goldsmith's "She Stoops to Conquer." The timid young man, fearful of society, in awe of the lady to whom he comes to pay his court, in dread of entering the house of her father, is directed to it as to an inn where he meets his proposed and dreaded father-in-law, and takes him for an inn-keeper, and the maiden of whom he is so fearful for a bar-maid. The audience and all the characters upon the stage are in the secret, and we expect every moment that his eyes will be opened.

A more serious form of comedy represents sin which is thwarted, as in "Much Ado about Nothing." In Shakespeare if any character is killed the play is a tragedy, otherwise it is a comedy. "Cymbeline" is full of comic elements, but since Cloten is killed, though everybody wants to see him die, it is reckoned a tragedy; yet it is essentially a comedy, because all sins and mistakes are rectified, and the end of the play causes joy and exaltation, while the depth of sympathy and feeling of reverent awe as to the great mysteries of life are kept in the background.

Is the "Merchant of Venice" a comedy or a tragedy? No one is killed, so this easy method of classification ranks it as a comedy, yet the feeling at the exit of old Shylock is intensely tragic. In fact, it is impossible to draw the line rigidly between comedy and tragedy. Both elements are found in the "Merchant of Venice;" and in all comedies, especially in Shakespeare's best, there is a touch of tragic emotion. Somewhere we feel something of the deep mystery of human failure and human suffering, and in most of them there is some character which arouses the deepest sympathy with suffering.

A lower form of the dramatic is farce. In comedy the outcome of joy depends mainly upon character. Circumstances and situation have something to do with it, but the centre of our interest is in the working of the mind. In farce, the characters are secondary to the situations. Everything is exaggerated and extravagant in farce. The subject of farce is generally the lower aspects of life; the characters are undignified and abnormal. Tragedy deals with human character, its sins and sufferings; comedy with character in relation to mistakes and errors, which will be corrected by time. We study the peculiarities of men, but we feel continually the bright side of life, that all things are working together for good. In farce we deal with people's foibles and weaknesses, but the mistakes are chiefly due to circumstances and not to peculiarities of character. In tragedy the rhythm is dignified, every movement simple, every tone of the voice chastened by the mystery of death. In comedy, everything reveals character; the appeal is still to the imagination, to the mind. In farce the appeal is often to the eye; no deep thought is required; no imagination nor sympathy is awakened. In comedy we laugh *with* men, in farce we laugh *at* them.

Farces are nearly always short. Their subject is but the odd moments of life. Comedy and tragedy unfold deep plots, and give us the two sides of the great struggle of the human soul in time; they are the histrionic expression of History, " whose home is the bosom of God, and whose voice is the harmony of the world." In comedy we find the superiority of nature to human conventionalities, but in farce we move freely and easily amid the constrictions of worldly conventionalities without being made free from them. Comedy deals with the probable, farce with the improbable. Comedy never steps beyond the bounds of possibilities; farce is a law to itself, and its extravagant exaggerations and impossibilities are often its chief elements.

The lowest form of the drama is the burlesque. Burlesque may be high or low. Sometimes, very often in fact, it ranks above farce, but it is a lower form of art. Burlesque deals with caricature. It shows men their weaknesses, reveals to them those things of which they are unconscious. In a theatre in London in the old days, an actress appeared in a hat of rather an unusual size. In another theatre a burlesque actress brings forth the same hat, but as big as a wagon wheel. The audience recognized the caricature, recognized the weakness of which it was an exaggeration, and this was the source of the pleasure.

The motive of burlesque is sometimes higher than farce. It deals with mistakes and evils, and may have a wholesome effect. Frequently it fulfils Shakespeare's conception of the drama, inasmuch as it "holds a mirror up to nature;" and while it may not as comedy show virtue her own feature, it does frequently show "scorn her own image." Hence, it has its use, though it may not rise to the dignity of comedy and tragedy, which can show "the very age and body of the time, its form and presence."

Burlesque is often directed against forms of expression, and becomes the means in the realm of dramatic art of discovering the un-ideal, and indirectly of awakening a conception of the ideal. It is concerned with the abnormal, but its higher forms do not deal with the abnormal merely for its own sake: they bring the abnormal into direct contrast and opposition with the normal.

In comedy or tragedy all abnormal characters are in opposition to normal ones. This is not true in farce or burlesque, unless indirectly. Burlesque is a negative form of dramatic art, superficial, flippant, and capable of abuse, and occupies a low place, because it lacks seriousness.

In all high comedy or tragedy there is direct reference to the ideal. Wherever abnormal characters are introduced in Shakespeare, they are introduced for a specific purpose in relation to the ideal characters in the play. At first thought, Sir Toby, Sir Andrew Aguecheek, Maria, the Fool, and Malvolio in "Twelfth Night" are farcical characters, and if alone they certainly would be; but they are not alone. They reflect the weakness and follies of their superiors; they illustrate the same theme in a lower strata of society. Malvolio's self-love, his egotistical unconsciousness of his weakness, is an exaggerated and extravagant embodiment of the same fault in the Duke.

A failure on the part of many public readers to realize the difference between the high and the low in art has worked great harm. Many think that because they deal with death they are concerned with tragedy. Even "Hamlet" can be so rendered as to appear to be a melodrama, or even a farce. Many amateur performances of tragedy would be ludicrous if it were not for a feeling of sorrow at the unconscious degradation of art.

Public readers in their abridgment of plays for public presentation are apt to eliminate too much the normal characters. While people do not laugh at the normal characters, yet their presence makes the abnormal characters more pleasing because of their opposition to the normal.

In the arrangement of a program there should be variety. Professor Monroe used to say that when he had been sent for by some committee to read, they would beg him to give only comic selections; but he would ask them, for his own sake, to allow him to give something from Shakespeare, and he invariably received more commendation from an ordinary audience for that than for anything else. The managers of a performance hardly realize what is going on; they think if the audience are shouting with laughter that they are being pleased. But the deepest pleasure in life does not call for extravagant laughter. Deep and noble joy, to use a paradox, is serious. Joy may cause tears as well as sorrow; at any rate, the law of rhythm must always be obeyed. Shakespeare is himself the highest example of obedience to this great law.

In some sense it is impossible to define the difference between the high and the low in dramatic art. It is a question of taste, and taste is something which results from direct exercise and contemplation. The best method, therefore, for the student is to exercise himself directly in the different forms of the dramatic for the development of his own taste, for the awakening of imagination and sympathy and the higher elements of true dramatic instinct.

All forms of the drama have their place. Students who are stiff and constrained need farce and burlesque for the development of abandon. Even the person who is highest in the ability to control tragic emotion must work in the realm of comedy, lest he lose the nearness of the sublime to the ridiculous. The great writers of comedy have nearly always been masters of pathos, possibly because without a sense of the humorous, pathos becomes bathos.

A few simple suggestions should be remembered. The higher the dramatic art, the more will assimilation predominate; the lower it is, the greater the amount of imitation. The high calls for imagination, sympathy, and suggestion; the low, for sensation and exhibition. The high demands intensity, depth of feeling, and self-control; the low, extravagance and exaggeration. The high requires delicacy, subtlety, and refinement; the low, caricature and extravagance.

It is good practice for every student to take some simple poem, and read it with different degrees of dignity. "The Low Backed Car," for example, I have heard rendered as a noble and ideal lyric, though with a grotesque element; and I have also heard it made farcical and coarse. High art is not wholly dependent upon the subject. A great theme may be degraded by bad art, and a very simple theme elevated by noble rendering. "Sally in our Alley" and "Black-eyed Susan" deal with low forms of character; but their simplicity, imagination, and sympathetic suggestiveness make them worthy to be included in the most refined collection of lyrics.

Is "'Twixt Axe and Crown" part of a melodrama or a tragedy?

PROBLEM XXX. *Select from Shakespeare, or other dramatic authors, soliloquies and dialogues to illustrate farce, comedy, and tragedy; also selections of various kinds, and render them in contrast according to their artistic character.*

"OH, yes! Oh, yes! Oh, yes! ding-dong!" The bellman's voice is loud and strong; so is his bell: "Oh, yes! ding-dong!" He wears a coat with golden lace; see how the people of the place come running to hear what the bellman says! "Oh, yes! Sir Nicholas Hildebrand has just returned from the Holy Land, and freely offers his heart and hand — Oh, yes! Oh, yes! Oh, yes! ding-dong!" All the women hurry along, maids and widows, a clattering throng. "Oh, sir, you are hard to understand! To whom does he offer his heart and hand? Explain your meaning, we do command!" "Oh, yes! ding-dong! you shall understand! Oh, yes! Sir Nicholas Hildebrand invites the ladies of this land to feast with him, in his castle strong, this very day at three. Ding-dong! Oh, yes! Oh, yes! Oh, yes, ding-dong!" Then all the women went off to dress, Mary, Margaret, Bridget, Bess, Patty, and more than I can guess. They powdered their hair with golden dust, and bought new ribbons — they said they must — but none of them painted, we will trust. Long before the time arrives, all the women that could be wives are dressed within an inch of their lives.   *Cicely and The Bears.*

"I SPEAK not to implore your grace, well know I for one minute's space successless might I sue: nor do I speak your prayers to gain; for if a death of lingering pain, to cleanse my sins, be penance vain, vain are your masses too. — I listen'd to a traitor's tale, I left the convent and the veil; for three long years I bow'd my pride, a horse-boy in his train to ride; and well my folly's meed he gave, who forfeited, to be his slave, all here, and all beyond the grave. — He saw young Clara's face more fair, he knew her of broad lands the heir, forgot his vows, his faith foreswore, and Constance was belov'd no more. — 'Tis an old tale, and often told; but did my fate and wish agree, ne'er had been read, in story old, of maiden true betray'd for gold, that loved, or was avenged, like me ! . . . Now, men of death, work forth your will, for I can suffer, and be still ; and come he slow, or come he fast, it is but Death who comes at last." Fix'd was her look, and stern her air : back from her shoulders streamed her hair ; the locks, that wont her brow to shade, stared up erectly from her head. . . .

"Sister, let thy sorrows cease ; sinful brother, part in peace !" From that dire dungeon, place of doom, of execution too, and tomb, paced forth the judges three ; sorrow it were, and shame, to tell the butcher-work that there befell, when they had glided from the cell of sin and misery. An hundred winding steps convey that conclave to the upper day ; but, ere they breathed the fresher air, they heard the shriekings of despair, and many a stifled groan : with speed their upward way they take, (such speed as age and fear can make,) and cross'd themselves for terror's sake, and hurried, tottering on.

Marmion. *Scott.*

Falstaff. I call thee coward ! I'll see thee hanged ere I call thee coward ; but I would give a thousand pound I could run as fast as thou canst. You are straight enough in the shoulders ; you care not who sees your back. Call you that backing of your friends ? A plague upon such backing !

Henry IV. *Shakespeare.*

'TWIXT AXE AND CROWN.

Elizabeth. Methinks I see my England, like the eagle,
Pruning her unchained wing for freer flight,
Fuller in focus of the glorious sun
Than e'er she flew till now. Great deeds, great words,
That make great deeds still greater ! Poesy
Fired with new life ; her soldiers conquering,
Her sailors braving unknown seas, to plant
The germ of a new England in the West —
Acorn, it may be, of a daughter oak,
Broader and stronger than the parent tree !
But I speak wildly, yet speak what I think,
As friend may speak to friend, and not be chidden.
　Paget. Ashes of age are gray upon my head.
Methought they had smothered my heart's fires as well :
But something glows beneath them, hearing you.
May Heaven speed the good time, and guard you, madam,
To make our England great and glorious
In man's deeds, as your words. For what 't is now
I lay most charge upon the Spanish match.
Pray Heaven your Highness lend no ear to those
That work on you to wed a foreign prince.
　Eliz. Elizabeth mates not — or she mates in England.
I have a vow for that.

Paget.   Heaven grant you keep it,
And me to bless your mating, when it come.
And now, farewell, sweet lady.   I will take
Much comfort to our friends from this good news
Of your fair health and firm fix'd resolution.

        [*He bows, kisses her hand, and exit.*
 Eliz.   Fare you well !
Ah, Courtenay, he dreams not that 't is love's vow
I hold, not policy's ! Oh, my true lord,
How heavy drags the time, waiting for thee !
Three whole months, and no tidings !   I am sick
Of longing for his letter — but this audience
Of Master Renard.   I see in his coming
Ill omen to my peace ; but I am armed,
I think, against him, and all enemies,
With love and loyalty for talisman. [*Enter* RENARD *and three of his suite.*
 Renard. [*Kneeling.*] Most gracious lady ! —. . .
There 's nothing stands between the crown and you
But a few sad hours of a sick Queen's life —
Which, let 's pray, may be mercifully shortened !
It is that crown Philip would help you bear
With strength of policy and stay of love.
 Eliz. [*With bitter irony.*] Even such love as he has showed my sister,
Turning from her untended bed of death
With this unnatural tender of his hand ! [*With contempt, rising to wrath.*
Say, did you take me for a fool or beast ?
A monster without brains or without heart ?
To come to me — you, and your worthy master,
With offers so accursed, and gifts so vile !
Out of my sight, lest I forget my sex
And strike thee !
 Ren.   Have a care, my passionate madam.
The Queen still lives, and a Queen's dying arm
Can strike, when others guide.   Even now a warrant
Of treason hangs suspended o'er your head.
 Eliz.   Treason !
 Ren. Aye, treason.   Courtenay is in England —
Has raised all Suffolk, in your name and his.
His treason is your treason ; the first stroke
That Courtenay strikes finds echo in the fall
Of your head on the scaffold !
 Eliz.   So be it !
When Courtenay strikes that blow, let my head fall.
My life upon his loyalty !

Ren.   You have staked
And lost !   Without there !   [*One of his suite advances.*
                    This to Lord Chandos !   [*Gives warrant.*] . . . [*Enter* Sussex.
Eliz.   My Lord of Sussex !   [Sussex *kneels.*
Rise, my good lord !   Your face of gloom but tells
What we have heard already — the Queen 's dead.
  Sussex. The Queen ne'er dies, and so long live the Queen !
  Eliz. You come in time ; an hour, and you had met us,
Escorted to the tower.
  Sussex.   The Tower ?
  Eliz.   For treason —
In aiding and abetting Edward Courtenay,
Who, Master Renard late declared, has landed
And risen in arms in Suffolk.
  Sussex.   So 't was bruited.
  Eliz. But 't is not true ?
  Sussex.   No. 'T was one Thomas Cleobury,
Who took my Lord of Devonshire's arms and title.
His levies are dispersed, and himself ta'en.
  Eliz. Ha ! said I not ?   Courtenay was not in England !
See a post straight dispatched to him at Padua.
We would he first had news of our accession.
  Sussex. My liege, no post can reach him now !
  Eliz. What mean you ?
  Sussex.   He is dead.
  Eliz.   Dead ! Nay, my Lord,
Here 's too much death : one death that crowns a queen,
And one that robs a woman's heart of more
Than crowns can give.   Dead ! When ? Where ? tell me all.
  Sussex. He died at Padua.   His servants brought
The tidings to the court just as I left.
  Eliz. Dead ! Was there naught — no word for me — no token ?
  Sussex. Pardon, madam.
                    This ring and letter —   [*Holds them out.*
  Eliz. [*Passionately grasping them.*]   And thou keep'st them from me,
And let 'st me prate and pule when I might hold
Something he has touched, and breathed upon,
And warmed with his last breath of dying love !   [*Looking at the letter.*
True friend ! lost lord ! sole love ! 't is thy dear hand ;
And these blurred spots are tears methinks — or kisses.
Thus let me put my tears and kisses to them.   [*Kisses letter.*
Thus only are we fated to be joined.
[*Reads.*] Dear love and lady, — When thou read'st these lines
The hand that scarce can trace them will be cold.

My last breath went to pray all blessings on thee:
For thee my heart beat, till it beat no more.
They that severed hands have wedded souls:
We are one now and forever — aye, one now —
And ever — and no separation more !   [*Sinks into chair.   Burst of trumpets.*
                              What 's that ?   [*Enter Harrington.*
     Harrington.   The Lords of the Council and the great ones
Of the City come to hail their gracious Queen Elizabeth.
     Eliz.   [Sadly.] — What love is left to me now
But their love ? What to live for but to make
Them happier than their Queen can ever be.   [*Trumpets.   Enter procession.*
     Omnes [Kneeling].   Long live Elizabeth !   Long live the Queen !
Eiz.   [Rising with great emotion — lays her hand upon the crown.]
Great King of Kings ! 't is thou hast willed it me.
Guide me that I may wear it, by thy will.   [*Trumpets and cheering.*
                                                           Taylor.

XLI. MONOLOGUES.

AMONG the many forms of the dramatic in literature, one of the
latest to be developed is the monologue, a kind of subjective drama.
Only one character speaks, but he must so express his ideas as to
reveal not only his own character, but that of the person to whom
he is speaking, and sometimes the character of which he is speaking, as well as to convey clearly his meaning.

The person who renders the monologue must speak " in character," or give it with a definite conception of the character that
speaks.   The monologue is just as dramatic as the play, and calls
for just as definite conception of character.   The monologue, however, differs from the play; it is more subjective; there is no
scenery ; — the situation must be created by the imagination, and
the imagination, of course, must penetrate to the deepest motives.

It is an important form of the dramatic for study, because it calls
for definite thinking, great activity of the imagination, and deep
insight into character.

In order to understand the monologue, let us compare it with
soliloquy.   Soliloquy is simply thinking aloud.   A man does not
exactly talk to himself, which in some of its forms might become a
monologue.   In soliloquy the man simply reveals by words the
current of the thought that dominates him.   Shakespeare is the

only master of this form of writing.   In the hands of others it is apt to degenerate into mere chaotic wandering, or rise into a kind of personal monologue or declamation.

Monologue is not oratory nor a speech spoken to an audience; it is nearly always spoken to one individual.   It is an artistic study of the relation of two minds, of the influence of the one over the other.

A monologue requires careful and thorough study.   It cannot be read like a narrative, which explains itself as it proceeds.   The one who renders a monologue must read it over to get a general conception of it.   In fact, before one can render a monologue, he must settle first who speaks, and form an adequate conception of the peculiarities of the character.   He must also form a picture of the situation by which the character is surrounded.   Next, he must understand to whom the character speaks; sometimes he must understand of whom he speaks; last of all, he must understand thoroughly the thought that is to be conveyed.   All these must be brought into harmonious co-ordination before there can be any true rendering of the monologue.

Usually one of these elements predominates; in some cases the character to whom the man speaks is the most important; in others, there is no hint of the person to whom he speaks; while the person of whom he speaks is as important as the speaker in Browning's " My Last Duchess " or his " Spanish Cloister."

The monologue has become an important form of art, on account of the tendency of men in our day to conceal their emotions.   We no longer see upon the street such dramatic scenes as Shakespeare saw.   The real struggle of human life, the real battle, has been made in the depths of each man's soul.   Hence, dramatic art or the interpretation of human character must in some way interpret this struggle.

There is an objection to monologues on account of the fact that they are obscure, but by following the suggestions made, when the reader can first satisfactorily answer the questions, *who, where, to whom,* or *of whom, and what,* many of the most difficult monologues, such as those by Browning, become clear and simple.   Their difficulty, in short, is chiefly on account of their dramatic character.

There are points in which the monologue is superior to the drama. It can touch upon certain aspects and problems of human life which are not possible in the play.   Again, too much of the modern stage is simply concerned with make-ups and various exhibitions and spectacular representations which are totally antagonistic to all true dramatic art.   This is more or less impossible in the monologue.

Students should arrange and abridge monologues and short stories from many sources, and dramatize and present scenes from novels, as well as recite and act scenes from tragedies, comedies, farces, and burlesques, so as to be able to understand clearly the distinction between every form and degree of dramatic expression.

A TALE.

What a pretty tale you told me once upon a time—
Said you found it somewhere (scold me !) was it prose or was it rhyme,
Greek or Latin ?   Greek, you said, while your shoulder propped my head.
Anyhow there 's no forgetting this much if no more,
That a poet (pray, no petting !) yes, a bard, sir, famed of yore,
Went where suchlike used to go, singing for a prize, you know.
Well, he had to sing, nor merely sing but play the lyre ;
Playing was important clearly quite as singing : I desire,
Sir, you keep the fact in mind for a purpose that 's behind.
There stood he, while deep attention held the judges round,
— Judges able, I should mention, to detect the slightest sound
Sung or played amiss : such ears had old judges, it appears !
None the less, he sang out boldly, played in time and tune,
Till the judges, weighing coldly each note's worth, seemed, late or soon,
Sure to smile " In vain one tries picking faults out : take the prize ! "
When, a mischief !   Were they seven strings the lyre possessed ?
Oh, and afterwards eleven, thank you ! Well, sir, — who had guessed
Such ill-luck in store ? — it happed one of those same seven strings snapped.

All was lost, then ! No ! a cricket (what " cicada " ?   Pooh !)
— Some mad thing that left its thicket for mere love of music — flew
With its little heart on fire, lighted on the crippled lyre.
So that when (Ah joy !) our singer for his truant string
Feels with disconcerted finger, what does cricket else but fling
Fiery heart forth, sound the note wanted by the throbbing throat ?
Ay and, ever to the ending, cricket chirps at need,
Executes the hand's intending, promptly, perfectly, — indeed
Saves the singer from defeat with her chirrup low and sweet.
Till, at ending, all the judges cry with one assent
" Take the prize — a prize who grudges such a voice and instrument ?
Why, we took your lyre for harp, so it shrilled us forth F sharp ! "

Did the conqueror spurn the creature, once its service done ?
That 's no such uncommon feature in the case when Music's son
Finds his Lotte's power too spent for aiding soul-development.
No ! This other, on returning homeward, prize in hand,
Satisfied his bosom's yearning : (sir, I hope you understand !)
— Said, " Some record there must be of this cricket's help to me ! "
So, he made himself a statue : marble stood, life-size ;
On the lyre, he pointed at you, perched his partner in the prize ;
Never more apart you found her, he throned, from him, she crowned.

That 's the tale : its application ? Somebody I know
Hopes one day for reputation through his poetry that 's — Oh,
All so learned and so wise, and deserving of a prize !
If he gains one, will some ticket, when his statue 's built,
Tell the gazer, " 'T was a cricket helped my crippled lyre, whose lilt
Sweet and low, when strength usurped softness' place i' the scale, she chirped ?
For as victory was nighest, while I sang and played, —
With my lyre at lowest, highest, right alike, — one string that made
' Love ' sound soft was snapt in twain, never to be heard again, —
Had not a kind cricket fluttered, perched upon the place
Vacant left, and duly uttered ' Love, Love, Love,' whene'er the bass
Asked the treble to atone for its somewhat sombre drone."
But you don't know music ! Wherefore keep on casting pearls
To a — poet ! All I care for is — to tell him that a girl's
" Love" comes aptly in when gruff grows his singing. (There, enough !)

Browning.

INCIDENT OF THE FRENCH CAMP.

You know, we French stormed Ratisbon : a mile or so away
On a little mound, Napoleon stood on our storming-day ;
With neck out-thrust, you fancy how, legs wide, arms locked behind,
As if to balance the prone brow oppressive with its mind.

Just as perhaps he mused, " My plans that soar, to earth may fall,
Let once my army-leader Lannes waver at yonder wall — "
Out 'twixt the battery-smokes there flew a rider, bound on bound
Full-galloping : nor bridle drew until he reached the mound.

Then off there flung in smiling joy, and held himself erect
By just his horse's mane, a boy : you hardly could suspect —
(So tight he kept his lips compressed, scarce any blood came through)
You looked twice ere you saw his breast was all but shot in two.

" Well," cried he, " Emperor, by God's grace we 've got you Ratisbon !
The Marshal 's in the market-place, and you 'll be there anon
To see your flag-bird flap his vans where I, to heart's desire,
Perched him ! " The chief's eye flashed ; his plans soared up again like fire.

The chief's eye flashed ; but presently softened itself, as sheathes
A film the mother-eagle's eye when her bruised eaglet breathes;
" You 're wounded ! "—" Nay," the soldier's pride touched to the quick, he
    said :
" I 'm killed, Sire ! " And his chief beside, smiling the boy fell dead.

Browning.

XLII. MEANS OF REVEALING TRANSITIONS.

How should the voice reveal changes in situation, relation, mental attitude, purpose, or feeling? In general, any such change will call for some change in voice or body, and whenever any change in voice or body is the direct result of a change in thought or feeling, we have expression. Only in proportion to the eradication of meaningless changes, or changes which are merely physical or nervous, will expression be noble.

When we seek for the nature and number of the modulations of voice which express the dramatic changes in thought and feeling, conceptions of character, and sympathetic relationship, they seem as inadequate as was the case with imagination. We have only pause, change of pitch, change of inflection, change in the color or texture of the voice, change of rhythmic movement, and the like. But though these changes are few in number and slight in character, we find them sufficient. Not only this, but we find also that the more subtle the changes of voice, the more beautiful and exalted will be the expression. In fact, the means adopted in any art seem totally inadequate to accomplish the effect. Take, for example, painting. How few are the colors in the noblest painting, and yet what depth of color is suggested! A painter who uses a great number of colors loses all power to suggest color, as a leading English painter once said: "One color is gold; two, silver; three, lead." We stand close to one of the portraits of Stuart, and there seems to be nothing but a very thin meaningless layer of pigment; move farther away, and the very subtlest expression of the eye lives with absolute fidelity.

In vocal expression, especially, there is great danger of exaggeration. The words convey the story; the changes of voice and body simply give the subtle feeling and relationship of the speaker.   Feeling cannot be conveyed.   Only a hint of the imagination of another that will awaken the same faculties is needed, and the more delicately given the better.   Exaggerated changes in voice and body call the attention of the auditor to the vocal actions themselves, and fail to reveal the mental changes in the continuity of thought and emotion.   Where all attention is directed to the manner, expression is destroyed and not aided. All transitions should be such as will simply stimulate the mind to think and feel in a natural sequence.   Hence, imitation or mechanical exaggeration may interrupt and break this continuity, while the simplest change or transition may stimulate it.   In the practice of transitions, therefore, changes should be as subtle and definite as possible, and the variety of these changes simple and genuine as in nature.

One temptation is to adopt changes which can be executed by mechanical manipulation of the voice.   This arises from a lack of faith in the power of the imagination and feeling to cause expression, or in the flexibility of the voice to respond to them. As the worst of all faults is felt to be monotony, and as every speaker, reader, or actor fears tameness, there is a natural disposition to exaggerate variations at first and adopt mechanical and imitative expedients.   The chief cause of monotony, however, is a neutral habit of mind, which reveals itself in an inability to group situations, or in merely abstract thinking.   Hence, the remedy is to think genuinely each idea, to conceive individually each situation, and to realize each point of view, and to manifest each mental and emotional change as simply and naturally as possible.

Inflection shows the relationship of ideas, and the processes of thinking them.   Inflections are present in proportion to the rethinking of the ideas by the reader or speaker at the time he speaks.   The other modes of revealing transitions are more imaginative or emotional.   Among these, pause is very essential, because a pause indicates that the mind is undergoing a change and must have sufficient time to create the new situation or idea and to give up to it.   So there can hardly be a transition of any kind without pause.

Changes of pitch always go with pauses. A pause without change of pitch is a hesitation. The change of pitch is the most natural hint of the fact that the mind has a new idea or situation, or has adopted a new point of view. When extreme, it shows that a great deal has happened. If we keep on the same pitch and make no pause in reading these lines, we fail to realize the significance of the words, at least, till after they are spoken; but an extreme change of pitch with a pause, change of texture and tone-color shows a realization of what has happened.

> Charge ! Chester, charge ! On ! Stanley, on !
> Were the last words of Marmion.

Changes in the color of the voice are extremely subtle, and reveal the nature of the feeling itself. Every emotion has a distinct effect upon the resonance of the voice, and a distinct texture or color; tone-color, or the emotional modulation of resonance, is one of the most important of all means for the manifestation of transitions of delicate feeling. The modulation of texture has a distinct importance in dramatic expression. It has the same relation to tone-color that a bearing has to an attitude. It expresses deeper, more permanent conditions; it gives the character or attitudes of the character, while tone-color manifests more the changes in feeling in response to successive ideas. For example, a reader with a proper conception of each character will have different textures for Antonio and for Shylock; but this is not mechanical manipulation, but a natural expression; hence, each emotion felt by either character has a specific color. Texture is simply a deeper modulation, which, when natural, does not interfere with the modulation of tone-color. It is just here that assimilative methods show their infinite superiority to imitative methods.

> *Shylock.* Jailer, look to him ; — tell not me of mercy : —
> This is the fool that lent out money gratis : —
> Jailer, look to him.
> *Antonio.* Hear me yet, good Shylock.
> *Shylock.* I 'll have my bond ; I will not hear thee speak :
> I 'll have my bond ; and therefore speak no more.
> I 'll not be made a soft and dull-eyed fool,
> To shake the head, relent, and sigh, and yield

> To Christian intercessors. Follow not ;
> I 'll have no speaking ; I will have my bond.

Merchant of Venice.   *Shakespeare.*

All modes are consistent with each other and exist simultaneously, for each has a distinct meaning of its own. It is by their harmonious combination that vocal expression gains its power to reveal successive changes.

While modes of revealing transitions depend upon harmonious relation to the spirit of the speech, poem, story, part, or play, still it is very important for the student to make isolated studies of special parts where various kinds of changes occur. All great painters make studies of every limb and leaf, of every rock, of the transient effect of light upon the water, of the vibration and texture of the surface of a human limb, and of every shade of color; so the student of vocal expression must exercise himself upon the rendering of specific lines and transitions, and as a painter's study is a more literal reproduction, is more exaggerated than his picture, so the rendering of these special extracts should be an accentuation of a specific truth to give the mind a firm grasp of the means of expression. These should be blended later into a harmonious rendering of a whole poem, story, oration, or representation as the painter uses his studies. It is only by accenting essential elements that power can be secured in any form of art.

> " Make way for Liberty," he cried :
> Made way for Liberty, and died !

> O LARKS ! sing out to the thrushes, and thrushes, sing as you soar !
> I think when another spring blushes I can tell you a great deal more.

> I COULD not love thee, dear, so much, loved I not honour more.

> O BEAUTEOUS birds ! methinks ye measure
> Your movements to some heavenly tune !
> O beauteous birds ! 't is such a pleasure
> To see you move above the moon.

> So stately her bearing, so proud her array,
> The main she will traverse for ever and aye.
> Many ports will exult at the gleam of her mast !
> — Hush ! hush ! thou vain dreamer, this hour is her last !

O'ER the deep !   O'er the deep !
Where the whale, and the shark, and the sword-fish sleep,
Outflying the blast and the driving rain,
The Petrel telleth her tale — in vain ;
For the mariner curseth the warning bird
Who bringeth him news of the storm unheard !
Ah ! thus does the prophet, of good or ill,
Meet hate from the creatures he serveth still :
Yet he ne'er falters : — So, Petrel, spring
Once more o'er the waves on thy stormy wing !

Up the dale and down the bourne, o'er the meadows swift we fly ;
Now we sing, and now we mourn, now we whistle, now we sigh.

Summer Wind.   *Darley.*

THERE groups of merry children played ;
There youths and maidens, dreaming, strayed.
O precious hours !   O golden prime,
And affluence of love and time !
Even as a miser counts his gold,
Those hours the ancient time-piece told :
    " Forever — never ! never — forever ! "

Longfellow.

No, I will weep no more.   In such a night
To shut me out ! Pour on ; I will endure.
In such a night as this !   O Regan, Goneril !
Your old kind father, whose frank heart gave all, —
O, that way madness lies ; let me shun that ;
No more of that.

HARK ! distant voices, that lightly ripple the silence deep !
No ; the swans that, circling nightly, through the silver waters sweep.
See I not, there, a white shimmer ? Something with pale silken shrine '
No ; it is the column's glimmer, 'gainst the gloomy hedge of pine.

FROM that chamber, clothed in white,
The bride came forth on her wedding night;
There, in that silent room below,
The dead lay, in his shroud of snow ;
And, in the hush that followed the prayer,
Was heard the old clock on the stair, —
    " Forever — never ! never — forever ! "

"Ho ! why dost thou shiver and shake, Gaffer Gray ?
And why does thy nose look so blue ?"
"'T is the weather that 's cold, 't is I 'm grown very old,
And my doublet is not very new, — well-a-day !"

Halcroft.

"LOOK, Katie ! look, Katie ! when Lettice came here to be wed
She stood where that sunbeam drops down, and all white was her gown ;
And she stepped upon flowers they strewed for her."   Then quoth small Seven,
"Shall I wear a white gown, and have flowers to walk upon ever ?"
All doubtful : "It takes a long time to grow up," quoth Eleven ;
"You 're so little, you know, and the church is so old, it can never
Last on till you 're tall."

THE MAID OF ISLA.

OH, Maid of Isla, from the cliff that looks on troubled wave and sky,
Dost thou not see yon little skiff contend with ocean gallantly ?
Now beating 'gainst the breeze and surge, and steep'd her leeward deck in foam,
Why does she war unequal urge ? — Oh, Isla's maid, she seeks her home.

Oh, Isla's maid, yon sea-bird mark, her white wing gleams thro' mist and spray,
Against the storm-cloud, lowering dark, as to the rock she wheels away ; —
Where clouds are dark and billows rave, why to the shelter should she come
Of cliff, exposed to wind and wave ? — Oh, Maid of Isla, 't is her home !

As breeze and tide to yonder skiff, thou 'rt adverse to the suit I bring,
And cold as is yon wintry cliff, where sea-birds close their wearied wing.
Yet cold as rock, unkind as wave, still, Isla's maid, to thee I come ;
For in thy love, or in his grave, must Allan Vourich find his home.

Scott.

THE CHURCHYARD STILE.

I LEFT thee young and gay, Mary, when last the thorn was white ;
I went upon my way, Mary, and all the world seemed bright ;
For though my love had ne'er been told, yet, yet I saw thy form
Beside me, in the midnight watch ; above me, in the storm.
And many a blissful dream I had, that brought thy gentle smile,
Just as it came when last we leaned upon the Churchyard Stile.

I 'm here to seek thee now, Mary, as all I love the best ;
To fondly tell thee how, Mary, I 've hid thee in my breast.
I came to yield thee up my heart, with hope, and truth, and joy,
And crown with Manhood's honest faith the feelings of the Boy.
I breathed thy name, but every pulse grew still and cold the while,
For I was told thou wert asleep just by the Churchyard Stile.

My messmates deemed me brave, Mary, upon the sinking ship ;
But flowers o'er thy grave, Mary, have power to blanch my lip.
I felt no throb of quailing fear amid the wrecking surf ;
But pale and weak I tremble here, upon the osiered turf.
I came to meet thy happy face, and woo thy gleesome smile,
And only find thy resting-place close by the Churchyard Stile.

Oh ! years may pass away, Mary, and sorrow lose its sting ;
For Time is kind, they say, Mary, and flies with healing wing ;
The world may make me old and wise, and Hope may have new birth ;
And other joys and other ties may link me to the earth ;
But Memory, living to the last, shall treasure up thy smile,
That called me back to find thy grave close to the Churchyard Stile.

Eliza Cook.

ONE WAY OF LOVE.

ALL June I bound the rose in sheaves.
Now, rose by rose, I strip the leaves
And strow them where Pauline may pass.
She will not turn aside ?   Alas !
Let them lie.   Suppose they die ?
The chance was they might take her eye.

How many a month I strove to suit
These stubborn fingers to the lute !
To-day I venture all I know.
She will not hear my music ?   So !
Break the string ; fold the music's wing :
Suppose Pauline had bade me sing !

My whole life long I learn'd to love.
This hour my utmost art I prove
And speak my passion — heaven or hell ?
She will not give me heaven ?   'T is well !
Lose who may — I still can say,
Those who win heaven, bless'd are they !

Browning.

DAYBREAK.

A WIND came up out of the sea,
And said, " O mists, make room for me ! "
It hailed the ships, and cried, " Sail on,
Ye mariners, the night is gone ! "
And hurried landward far away,
Crying, " Awake ! it is the day ! "
It said unto the forest, " Shout !
Hang all your leafy banners out ! "

> It touched the wood-bird's folded wing,
> And said, "O bird, awake and sing!"
> And o'er the farms, "O chanticleer,
> Your clarion blow! the day is near!"
> It whispered to the fields of corn,
> "Bow down, and hail the coming morn!"
> It shouted through the belfry-tower,
> "Awake, O bell! proclaim the hour!"
> It crossed the church-yard with a sigh,
> And said, "NOT YET! IN QUIET LIE!"
>
> *Longfellow.*

XLIII. MOVEMENT.

FORCE in Nature acts rhythmically; it acts and reacts. It does not move in a uniform stream, but by alternate pulsations and relaxations.

Rhythm has been defined as "proportion in time." This is its artistic use in music. Rhythm in Nature is the pulsation due to harmonious action between a force and that which resists it. Wherever there is a unity of forces acting upon a unity of resistances, rhythm will be the result. Where a confusion of forces acts upon a chaos of resistances, rhythm is destroyed.

The only place where a violation of rhythm occurs is in man. The reason is that he can do things mechanically as well as naturally; that is, he can directly apply his will in such a way as to interfere with the spontaneous propulsion of the natural forces of his nature.

Rhythm always results from free manifestation of force. Storms move rhythmically; so do the waves of the sea and the waters of Niagara. The mysterious co-ordination of forces everywhere in Nature is thus revealed. The earth and all the planets move in rhythmic orbits; and the smallest vine circles rhythmically to find the support by which it can climb. Nothing in Nature moves without rhythmic alternation.

Again, rhythm is a characteristic of life. The heart beats rhythmically. The acts of respiration and digestion are performed rhythmically.

The mind acts rhythmically in all its processes. There can be

no thinking without rhythmic pulsation. It would seem, therefore, that rhythm should be one of the most important characteristics of vocal expression.

There are, however, two forms of rhythm; or possibly we
should say that it is important to distinguish between natural
rhythm and its mechanical expression or use in art.

Metre is not the same as rhythm; it is an artificial expression
of rhythm. Rhythm is its soul. The reader of poetry must
preserve the metre at all hazards; but the rhythm of vocal expression is something deeper and freer than this verbal expression
of rhythm.

Again, rhythm is the fundamental element of music; music
starts with rhythm. The beating of the drum, " the tongs and the
bones," and the dance, are nothing but rhythm and its modulations.
Transitions in movement form one of its most important elements.
The time must be kept, or harmony and the polyphonous union
of many instruments will be impossible. But rhythm in music
has a mechanical regularity which is rarely if ever found in
speech or Nature. Rhythm which is deeper than time, or at
least the measure of time, is in music made primarily a matter
of time. It is not free except in a solo, and then only in a partial
degree.

But rhythm in speech is free. The pulsation does not necessarily take place at any instant of time. The proportion is between the impression and the expression; between the taking and
the giving of an idea. There is no mechanical regularity in the
pulsations for the *sake* of regularity. Each pulsation is in direct
proportion to the mental energy and cumulation of feeling.

Thus there is an artificial rhythm, which is a regulation of the
action of force, making it regular, and giving " proportion in time
as symmetry is proportion in space; " but deeper than this, there
is the rhythmic pulsation of Nature herself, which is also regular,
but which can be made to obey the free movement of thought.
Passion tends to move with the regular pulsation of the beating of
the heart; but the mind, changing its situation, or the object of
its attention, makes transitions in feeling, and thus continually
varies the rhythm according to the processes of thought.

Hence rhythm can be made part of a mechanical structure, as in poetry, or it may be simply a response to the processes of thought, as in conversation.

Vocal expression must at all times directly manifest the rhythmic process of the mind. In the reading of poetry, however, it not only does this, but is simultaneously true to the rhythmic structure of the metre. The reader can preserve both, because rhythm is deeper than metre, and in obeying the law of rhythm, the metre is also preserved.

All vocal expression is *in time*. Man measures time by rhythm, by sequence of pulsations. Hence changes in rhythm are the most important expression of changes in thought and passion.

The modulation of rhythm by emotion and thought is called "movement," a term which has a meaning in every art. For example, it has been said that Barye showed the movement of an animal in his statues. The first line of his first sketch showed the essential action or character of the animal portrayed.

The term is also used in painting, and has a special force in music; but these uses of the word are figurative. The primary meaning of the word is dramatic. It is in the drama and in vocal expression that its direct and primary significance is found.

The nature of movement may be more or less understood from a study of the law of velocity. Vocal or pantomimic expression moves slowly in proportion to the dignity, weight, or importance which the reader attaches to his ideas, or in proportion to the degree of control, the depth or intensity of passion; while, on the other hand, that which is considered superficial, trite, or unimportant, is given more rapidly.

Movement, however, is not a mere matter of slowness or rapidity. A passage may be read slowly, and yet not be lifted out of the commonplace. It may, in fact, be made superficial and tedious; while, on the other hand, a passage of great weight does not lose by a certain kind of speed. It is the rhythmic pulsation that is suggested, not the absolute amount of time that is taken in the reading that gives the expression. For example, if the first of the following passages be read with its ordinary movement, and with long pauses introduced, it is merely made tedious.

Then if the second be read with the movement natural to the first, it is turned into commonplace superficiality; nor can pauses redeem it until the rhythmic pulsation is changed.

> So light to the croup the fair lady he swung,
> So light to the saddle before her he sprung.
>
> *Scott.*

> O THOU Eternal One ! whose presence bright
>   All space doth occupy, all motion guide ;
> Unchanged through time's all-devastating flight ;
>   Thou only God !   There is no God beside.

The two great faults in movement are tediousness and hurry, each of which indicates a disproportion between time and rhythmic pulsation.   Tediousness is a short pendulum in a long period of time; and hurry is the forcing of one's rate.

Movement can only be suggested, and after being suggested, continues during the pause.   The way a few words are spoken gives the rhythm to the thought and feeling, and this continues during the silence.

Changes in movement, indicating as they do transitions in these elements, are of great importance, and occur continually in all vocal expression.   Where the changes of rhythm are artificial, or the movement monotonous, there is no true assimilation.

A story is primarily dependent upon the movement of events. Hence, whenever something happens, especially if unexpected, there is a transition in movement, though it may be only momentary.   Notice for example in the following extract how the reader changes his movement in sympathy with Lartius and Herminius.

But meanwhile axe and lever have manfully been plied, and now the bridge hangs tottering above the boiling tide. "Come back, come back, Horatius !" loud cried the fathers all.   "Back, Lartius ! back, Herminius ! back, ere the ruin fall !"   Back darted Spurius Lartius ; Herminius darted back : and as they passed, beneath their feet they felt the timbers crack.   But when they turned their faces, and on the farther shore saw brave Horatius stand alone, they would have crossed once more.   But with a crash like thunder fell every loosened beam, and, like a dam, the mighty wreck lay right athwart the stream: and a long shout of triumph rose from the walls of Rome, as to the highest turret-tops was splashed the yellow foam.

Every passion has a movement peculiar to itself. Take any illustration where there are changes in feeling, and note the fact that unless there be a change of movement, there can hardly be a change in feeling, or even any change of the other modulations of the voice.

Notice the fine transitions of movement in the last stanza of Paul Revere (p. 202). The events are first literally referred to, and then their historical significance.

The higher the literature or the greater the dignity of vocal expression, the more will transitions of movement be necessary. Thus, in the reading of the Scriptures, change of movement is one of the most effective means of interpreting the thought, weight, dignity, or feeling of the message. In the Beatitudes notice the difference between the announcement of the principal clause and the reason assigned. Observe also in the following illustrations while all is solemn, yet the clauses " few there be that find it " and " many there be that go in thereat " are spoken with regret. A delicate change of tone-color, with slower movement, implies an appreciation of the situation.

Enter ye in at the strait gate, for wide is the gate, and broad is the way that leadeth to destruction, and many there be which go in thereat: because strait is the gate, and narrow is the way which leadeth unto life, and few there be that find it.

In the climax of the Sermon on the Mount, the words " and it fell " are given as if the reader were himself taking warning, hence the movement is slower than the preceding words. Notice also the last verse of the chapter, which is not a part of the address but a description of its effect; when this is given simply and colloquially, it accentuates the weight of movement in the sermon itself.

Every one therefore which heareth these words of mine, and doeth them, shall be likened unto a wise man, which built his house upon the rock : and the rain descended, and the floods came, and the winds blew, and beat upon that house ; and it fell not: for it was founded upon the rock. And every one that heareth these words of mine, and doeth them not, shall be likened unto a foolish man, which built his house upon the sand: and the rain descended, and the floods came, and the winds blew, and smote upon that house; and it fell : and great was the fall thereof.

And it came to pass, when Jesus ended these words, that the multitudes were astonished at his teaching : for he taught them as one having authority, and not as their scribes. *Matt.* vii. 24-29.

THE HUNT.

In the bright October morning Savoy's duke had left his bride.
From the castle, past the drawbridge, flow'd the hunters' merry tide.
Steeds are neighing, gallants glittering, gay her smiling lord to greet,
From her mullion'd chamber-casement smiles the Duchess Marguerite.
From Vienna, by the Danube, here she came, a bride, in spring,
Now the autumn crisps the forest ; hunters gather, bugles ring.
Hounds are pulling, prickers swearing, horses fret, and boar-spears glance.
Off, — they sweep the marshy forests, westward on the side of France.
Hark ! the game's on foot ; they scatter, — down the forest-ridings lone,
Furious, single horsemen gallop.   Hark ! a shout, — a crash, — a groan.
Pale and breathless came the hunters — on the turf dead lies the boar.
Ah ! the duke lies stretched beside him senseless, weltering in his gore.

In the dull October evening, down the leaf-strewn forest-road,
To the castle, past the drawbridge, came the hunters with their load.
In the hall, with sconces blazing, ladies waiting round her seat,
Clothed in smiles, beneath the dais sate the Duchess Marguerite.
Hark ! below the gates unbarring, tramp of men, and quick commands.
" 'T is my lord come back from hunting," — and the duchess claps her hands.
Slow and tired came the hunters ; stopp'd in darkness in the court.
" Ho ! this way, ye laggard hunters. To the hall. What sport ! what sport ! "
Slow they entered with their master ; in the hall they laid him down.
On his coat were leaves and blood-stains, on his brow an angry frown.
Dead her princely youthful husband lay before his youthful wife,
Bloody 'neath the flaring sconces : and the sight froze all her life.
In Vienna, by the Danube, kings hold revel, gallants meet.
Gay of old amid the gayest was the Duchess Marguerite.
In Vienna, by the Danube, feast and dance her youth beguiled :
Till that hour she never sorrow'd, but from then she never smiled.

The Church of Brou.   *Matthew Arnold.*

In this extract we nave first the joy of the duchess, the initiation and the excitement of the hunt, and then the death of the duke.   This death, however, is not chosen as the climax of sympathy, but its revelation to the wife.   The poet brings us slowly and sorrowfully toward the castle, bearing the heavy load.   Then the movement of her great joy, unconscious of the coming agony, brings by rhythmic reaction the climax of intensity.

Professor Bain has called the description of Mont Blanc by Coleridge (p. 40) "still-life description at its utmost sublimity," and has compared it with "the greater impressiveness of action," as illustrated in Byron's "Thunderstorm."

The sky is changed ! and such a change ! O Night, and Storm, and Darkness, ye are wondrous strong, yet lovely in your strength, as the light of a dark eye in woman ! Far along, from peak to peak, the rattling crags among, leaps the live thunder ! — not from one lone cloud, but every mountain now hath found a tongue ; and Jura answers, through her misty shroud, back to the joyous Alps, who call to her aloud ! and this is in the night. — Most glorious night ! *Thou* wert not sent for slumber ! let me be a sharer in thy fierce and far delight, — a portion of the tempest and of thee ! How the lit lake shines, — a phosphoric sea, — and the big rain comes dancing to the earth ! and now again 't is black — and now, the glee of the loud hills shakes with its mountain mirth, as if they did rejoice o'er a young earthquake's birth.

One difference between this and Coleridge's hymn is a difference in movement. The lines or words referring to "a dark eye in woman," have been sometimes regarded as a Byronic blemish, but does not even this phrase aid in giving life and movement to the storm ? Often what we have considered as blemishes, are found after deeper study to be qualities.

Away ! away to the rocky glen, where the deer are wildly bounding !
And the hills shall echo in gladness again, to the hunter's bugle sounding.

————

Lord, Thou hast been our dwelling-place in all generations. Before the mountains were brought forth, or ever Thou hadst formed the earth and the world, even from everlasting to everlasting, thou art God.

Problem XXXI. — *Read light and exultant lines in contrast with those full of weight. Also, practise various transitions in degrees of excitement or control, dignity or weight of ideas, and changes from exultation to regret, and from one point of view or emotion to another.*

With that he cried and beat his breast ; for, lo ! along the river's bed a mighty eagre reared his crest, and uppe the Lindis raging sped. It swept with thunderous noises loud ; shaped like a curling snow-white cloud, or like a demon in a shroud. . . . So farre, so fast the eagre drave, the heart had hardly time to beat, before a shallow seething wave sobbed in the grasses at oure feet ; the feet had hardly time to flee before it brake against the knee, and all the world was in the sea.   Upon the roofe we sate that night ; the noise of bells went sweeping by, I marked the lofty beacon light stream from the church tower, red and high, — a lurid mark and dread to see ; and awsome bells they were to mee, that in the dark rang " Enderby."   They rang the sailor lads to guide from roofe to roofe who fearless rowed ; and I — my sonne was at my side, and yet the ruddy beacon glowed ; and yet he moaned beneath his breath, " O come in life, or come in death ! O lost ! my love, Elizabeth."   And didst thou visit him no more ? thou didst, thou didst, my daughter deare ; the waters laid thee at his doore, ere yet the early dawn was clear.   Thy pretty bairns in fast embrace, the lifted sun shone on thy face, downe drifted to thy dwelling-place.

Out — out into the darkness — faster, and still more fast;
The smooth grass flies behind her, the chestnut wood is passed;
She looks up ; the clouds are heavy : why is her steed so slow ? —
Scarcely the wind beside them can pass them as they go.
" Faster ! " she cries, " oh, faster ! "   Eleven the church bells chime ;
" O God," she cries, " help Bregenz, and bring me there in time ! "
But louder than bells ringing, or lowing of the kine,
Grows nearer in the midnight the rushing of the Rhine.
Shall not the roaring waters their headlong gallop check ?
The steed draws back in terror, she leans upon his neck
To watch the flowing darkness ; the bank is high and steep ;
One pause — he staggers forward, and plunges in the deep.
She strives to pierce the darkness, and looser throws the rein ;
Her steed must breast the waters that dash above his mane.
How gallantly, how nobly, he struggles through the foam,
And see — in the far distance, shine out the lights of home !

From Legend of Bregenz.   *Adelaide Procter.*

Hurrah ! hurrah ! a single field hath turned the chance of war.
Hurrah ! hurrah ! for Ivry and King Henry of Navarre !
Oh, how our hearts were beating, when, at the dawn of day,
We saw the army of the League drawn out in long array ;
With all its priest-led citizens, and all its rebel peers,
And Appenzel's stout infantry, and Egmont's Flemish spears !
There rode the brood of false Lorraine, the curses of our land !
And dark Mayenne was in the midst, a truncheon in his hand ;
And, as we looked on them, we thought of Seine's empurpled flood,
And good Coligni's hoary hair all dabbled with his blood ;
And we cried unto the living God, who rules the fate of war,
To fight for His own holy Name, and Henry of Navarre.

> The King has come to marshal us, in all his armor drest,
> And he has bound a snow-white plume upon his gallant crest.
> He looked upon his people, and a tear was in his eye ;
> He looked upon the traitors, and his glance was stern and high.
> Right graciously, he smiled on us, as rolled from wing to wing,
> Down all our line, in deafening shout, "God save our lord the King !"
> "And if my standard-bearer fall, — as fall full well he may,
> For never saw I promise yet of such a bloody fray, —
> Press where ye see my white plume shine, amid the ranks of war,
> And be your oriflamme, to-day, the helmet of Navarre."

GLORIOUSLY, Max! gloriously! There were sixty horses in the field, all mettle to the bone; the start was a picture. Away we went in a cloud, pell-mell, helter-skelter, — the fools first, as usual, using themselves up. We soon passed them, — first your Kitty, then my Blueskin, and Craven's colt last. Then came the tug — Kitty skimmed the walls — Blueskin flew over the fences — the colt neck-and-neck, and half a mile to run — at last the colt baulked a leap and went wild. Kitty and I had it all to ourselves — she was three lengths ahead as we breasted the last wall, six feet, if an inch, and a ditch on the other side. Now, for the first time, I gave Blueskin his head — ha! ha! Away he flew like a thunderbolt — over went the filly — I over the same spot, leaving Kitty in the ditch — walked the steeple, eight miles in thirty minutes, and scarcely turned a hair.

XLIV. THE DEVELOPMENT OF ASSIMILATION.

THUS far some of the sympathetic actions or relations of the mind have been discussed, and exercises presented to develop them. Of the importance of this, little need be said. The variety and force, as well as the charm of vocal expression, depend upon assimilation and its revelation. Without assimilation there can be no truthfulness of emotion, which is just as important as truthfulness of thought, for truthfulness of expression depends equally upon both. The best method of securing assimilation is the development of the imagination and dramatic instinct. There are, however, many difficulties in the practice of assimilation. In the first place, men do not realize their lack of it; do not perceive that truth may be merely in the memory, and bear no relation to their experience or character. There is thus great need of a teacher who has great insight to show the student wherein he fails to have the right attitude towards truth. Many speakers seem to have no power to change their point of view or relation to truth or to auditor. Many clergymen teach didactically not only in delivering every idea of the sermon, but in reading the Bible, and even in prayer.

The whole work of studying literature should be so systematized as to centre in assimilation and the development of the imagination and dramatic instinct of the student. This is one of the special reasons why vocal expression should be the chief aid in the study of literature.

The beginning and the procedure must vary more or less with each particular case. The student should begin with something he likes and can comprehend; but he should be led as soon as possible to something more difficult. The study of literature must not be undertaken as a pure matter of enjoyment, but as a study, though not a mechanical one; there should always be something of delight in it, as the chief aim of literature is to give pleasure.

It is best usually to begin with lyrics and narratives. The lyric develops emotion, causes intense realization of simple situations, and trains the mind to hold a situation until feeling dominates the voice. It is the first means of disciplining imaginative attention. In proportion to the depth of its feeling, a lyric is most easily assimilated, and has the most immediate effect upon the imagination and also upon dramatic instinct; in fact, dramatic action without the lyric element is apt to be mechanical-and imitative.

Simultaneously with the lyric — or before it with children — should come study of the story or narrative poem. It is important that the story shall be poetic. This has a different effect from that of the lyric. The story or ballad will develop the sequence of ideas. It will lead the mind to associate picture with picture, and develop that progressive imaginative conception which is the soul of dramatic movement.

This method of dealing with the individual follows the order of race development. As the song and the ballad are among the earliest forms of literature, so they should be the earliest in education. The epic is more or less of an extended ballad, and should be studied usually before the dramatic form.

The various forms of literature should be practised with a careful realization of the spirit of each. An epic we may read in contrast with a lyric; a short story or a dramatic composition may be compared with an oration.

Famous orations should also be studied. There has been great imperfection, however, in the method of such work. The student often separates oratory from any dramatic and assimilative action; he has an extravagant idea of speaking, and so declaims with loud tones, and thus totally perverts the true action of the mind in reading and in speaking.

Again, the student should be tested, not only in the study of literature, but in every practical form of speaking. He should read, recite, impersonate, speak extemporaneously, conduct a conversation, tell a story, debate, and exercise himself, in short, in every phase of vocal expression, and compare these with each other to find his faults and needs.

But again, the student must not disdain work upon the most elemental exercises; he should read in direct contrast diverse emotions. For example, he should take a line of joy and read it in direct contrast with a line of sorrow, and ascertain if he has mannerisms which prevent his making definite contrast. Such exercises quicken the consciousness of the student for form. Many able scholars are unable to recognize that they give such lines exactly alike. Such an exercise is most important to the speaker; it makes him definite in his thought in imaginative action and assimilation, and produces truthfulness of emotion. Such an exercise tends to make him realize his lack of versatility and responsiveness, of power to create and assimilate a situation.

A comparison of modes of expression is an important aid in testing assimilation as well as for its development. A speaker can test his relation to thought by rendering a monologue. It furnishes a mirror to his consciousness of himself. Again, one who always speaks in one way may occasionally adopt a different method, and so find another point of view from which to study himself.

Nor should the student underestimate exercises in transition, such as have been unfolded in the preceding lessons.   He should practise poems full of sudden contrasts, or gradations, or changes in point of view and feeling.

Any great poem, which may at first seem to be monotonous, will be found to be full of such changes.   The student should not practise that alone which he can do best, but also what he feels less able to express.   He should meditate over the greatest poetry, and struggle to reveal the deepest and most delicate variations of the imagination.   His first aim is the development of his nature, and not the mere rendering of a special selection.

A few methods for the development of assimilation will now be discussed separately on account of their importance, to secure a broader and deeper understanding of the nature of assimilation, and also to correct the common misconceptions regarding them.

XLV. THE EDUCATIONAL VALUE OF DIALOGUES.

SINCE dramatic instinct is so important, the question naturally arises respecting the use of dialogues for its education.   There are those who think that all histrionic art is useless; that it is even deleterious to character to assume a part.

The best answer to this is the study of the little child.   The very first means a child adopts to get out of itself, or to realize the great world about it, is by dramatic action and instinct.   No child was ever born with any mind at all, that had not some of this instinct; and the more promising the child, the more is it dramatic and imaginative.   Dramatic instinct is universal.   It is the secret of all success; it is the instinct by which man sees things from different points of view, by which he realizes the ideal in character in contrast to that which is not ideal.

Philosophers have shown that education begins in a kind of imitation.   Many do not like the word "imitation," and perhaps "dramatic assimilation" would be better.   But by whatever name it may be called, it is the instinctive identification of ourselves with the situation or point of view, the life or the feeling of another. The imaginative creation, the sympathetic identification of the child or the human being with the great world, and the exuberance of life expressed in dramatic play, is a most essential part of the development of a human being.

Professor Monroe was once asked by a clergyman for private lessons. He told him that was impossible. " Well," said the minister, " what can I do then ?" " Go home and read Shakespeare dramatically." Why was such advice given? Because the struggle to read Shakespeare would get the minister out of himself. The struggle to realize how men of different types of character would speak certain things, would make him conscious whether he, himself, spoke naturally. He would, in short, become aware of his mannerisms, of his narrow gamut of emotions, his sameness of point of view; he would be brought into direct contact with the process of his own mind in thinking.

It is important and helpful to induce one with a mannerism to use some form of speaking unusual to him, a new kind of theme, a different situation or purpose. Such an exercise is afforded to the speaker by the right study of a dialogue. The struggle to realize the dramatic creations of Shakespeare is a great help in widening a man's conception or realization of his race. For the same reason readers or actors may be made to speak.

The educational value of play has been proved by Froebel, and is too well recognized to need discussion. The most important things of life are learned unconsciously. When we are too conscious of our growth there is apt to be something wrong. Growth is spontaneous, unconscious, involuntary. Let the teacher of delivery train the speaker to speak only or the actor to act only, and his student is apt to become stilted, labored, and unconscious of his needs; but let the same student face another in a simple dialogue, and the teacher can put his finger upon the labor and can make the pupil realize it.

The dialogue develops self-control; it teaches command of thought, of imagination, and passion. It makes us realize the nature of expression, its subjective processes, and its direct relationship to other minds. That there is danger in histrionic expression all will admit. But there is danger in everything. The most effective things in the world are the most capable of perversion; but possibility of perversion only proves the power of such an exercise for good when rightly used.

Take the vast accumulation of dry, vague criticisms which have been heaped upon Shakespeare. Hundreds of books, for example, have been written upon the one play of " Hamlet." To understand " Hamlet," shall we read these books? That is the best way to lose our imaginative insight into such a masterpiece. Study the play itself; try to render certain of its dialogues and soliloquies. While we may not be able to discover all there is in it by such a method, we shall at least have a higher appreciation of its greatness. Someone has said that we can always explain what we do not understand, but never explain what we thoroughly appreciate. This paradox is true in the study of art and literature. Art appeals to the heart, and not to the head; to imagination and feeling, and not to reason. The process of reasoning about a picture is necessarily analytic and not synthetic, and from the heart of the picture; and this is true also of " Hamlet." The merely theoretic study of the drama is as bad as the merely theoretic study of painting, which is condemned by all artists. Books about art and about literature are rarely good, and of value only so far as they cause a better appreciation of the right point of view and lead to artistic endeavor of some kind. Explanation is often an interpolation and alteration.

The present condition of dramatic art is deplorable. Men go to the theatre merely for amusement, and not for education. It is chiefly in Germany that there is any educational use of the drama. We have no spontaneous expressions of disapproval at the theatre. In some quarters, there is approval of everything, in others, approval of nothing. There is a failure to appreciate the real character of dramatic art. Dramatic art has in all ages been the most popular. It is dear to the popular heart because it is most closely connected with the idea of play. As all art is play reduced to the principle of order, we can see the effect of dramatic art upon other arts.

In all ages of the world dramatic art has been the most potent for good or evil. There is great need for the educational use of the noblest drama, to develop public taste, and to drive from the boards those things which tend to degrade. The true principle is, please people above the plane of the actual along the line of their ideals and you elevate them; while if they are pleased on a plane below their everyday thought and feeling, they are degraded.

There are great dangers in amateur performances. They are often artificial and extravagant, because amateurs study without any principle, but only by imitation. Dramatic expression needs careful direction, with a broad study and appreciation of art.

The special safeguard in the study of dramatic art or dialogue is to note whether the process in the taking of a character is by assimilation or by imitation. This is very important, because it is only in low farce where imitation predominates; and if the imitative process is adopted, the highest tragedy is turned into farce, as is often the case with amateur performers.

Noble dramatic expression results from assimilation. It is only by imaginative insight and dramatic sympathy, causing the identification of ourselves with others, with conception of points of view and character, that dramatic instinct really has any play or expression.

MEMORABILIA.

AH, did you once see Shelley plain, and did he stop and speak to you,
And did you speak to him again ?   How strange it seems, and new !
But you were living before that, and also you are living after ;
And the memory I started at —   My starting moves your laughter !
I crossed a moor, with a name of its own and a certain use in the world, no
			doubt,
Yet a hand's-breath of it shines alone 'mid the blank miles round about :
For there I picked up on the heather and there I put inside my breast
A moulted feather, an eagle-feather ! well I forget the rest.

Browning.

FERDINAND AND MIRANDA.

> *Ferdinand.*   I do beseech you, —
> Chiefly that I might set it in my prayers, —
> What is your name ?
>   *Miranda.*   Miranda. — O my father !
> I have broke your hest to say so.
> *Fer.*					Admired Miranda !
> Indeed, the top of admiration ; worth
> What's dearest to the world ! Full many a lady
> I have eyed with best regard ; and many a time

The harmony of their tongues hath into bondage
Brought my too diligent ear : for several virtues
Have I liked several women ; never any
With so full soul, but some defect in her
Did quarrel with the noblest grace she owed,
And put it to the foil : but you, O you !
So perfect, and so peerless, are created
Of every creature's best.

 Mira.   I do not know
'One of my sex ; no woman's face remember,
Save, from my glass, my own ; nor have I seen
More that I may call men, than you, good friend,
And my dear father : how features are abroad
I am skill-less of ; but, by my modesty
(The jewel in my dower), I would not wish
Any companion in the world but you ;
Nor can imagination form a shape,
Besides yourself, to like of. But I prattle
Something too wildly, and my father's precepts
I therein do forget.

 Fer.   I am, in my condition,
A prince, Miranda ; I do think, a king
(I would, not so !) ; and would no more endure
This wooden slavery, than to suffer
The flesh-fly blow my mouth. — Hear my soul speak : —
The very instant that I saw you, did
My heart fly to your service ; there resides,
To make me slave to it ; and for your sake,
Am I this patient log-man.

 Mira.   Do you love me ?

 Fer. O heaven ! O earth ! bear witness to this sound,
And crown what I profess with kind event,
If I speak true : if hollowly, invert
What best is boded me to mischief ! I,
Beyond all limit of what else i' the world,
Do love, prize, honour you.

 Mira.   I am a fool
To weep at what I am glad of.

 Prospero. [*Aside.*]   Fair encounter
Of two most rare affections ! Heaven rain grace
On that which breeds between them !

 Fer.   Wherefore weep you ?

 Mira. At mine unworthiness, that dare not offer
What I desire to give ; and much less take

What I shall die to want.   But this is trifling ;
And all the more it seeks to hide itself,
The bigger bulk it shows.   Hence, bashful cunning !
And prompt me, plain and holy innocence !
I am your wife, if you will marry me ;
If not, I 'll die your maid : to be your fellow
You may deny me ; but I 'll be your servant,
Whether you will or no.

    Fer.   My mistress, dearest,
And I thus humble ever.

    Mira.   My husband, then ?

    Fer.   Ay, with a heart as willing
As bondage e'er of freedom : here 's my hand.

    Mira.   And mine, with my heart in 't : and now farewell,
Till half an hour hence.

    Fer.   A thousand thousand !

Tempest.   ——————   *Shakespeare.*

THE CAPTAIN AND THE TREASURER.

Kempthorn.   A dull life this, — a dull life, anyway !
Ready for sea ; the cargo all aboard,
Cleared for Barbadoes, and a fair wind blowing
From nor'-nor'-west ; and I, an idle lubber,
Laid neck and heels by that confounded bond !
I said to Ralph, says I, " What 's to be done ? "
Says he : " Just slip your hawser in the night ;
Sheer off, and pay it with the topsail, Simon."
But that won't do, because, you see, the owners
Somehow or other are mixed up with it.

              [*Enter* EDWARD BUTTER *with an ear-trumpet.*

    Butter.   Good-morning, Captain Kempthorn.

    Kemp.   Sir, to you.
You 've the advantage of me.   I don't know you.
What may I call your name ?

    Butter.   That 's not your name ?

    Kemp.   Yes, that 's my name.   What 's yours ?

    Butter.   My name is Butter.
I am the treasurer of the Commonwealth.

    Kemp.   Will you be seated ?

    Butter.   What say ?   Who 's conceited ?

    Kemp.   Will you sit down ?

    Butter.   O, thank you.

    Kemp.   Spread yourself
Upon this chair, sweet Butter.

Butter. [*Sitting down.*]   A fine morning.

Kemp.   Nothing 's the matter with it that I know of.
I have seen better, and I have seen worse.
The wind 's nor'-west.   That 's fair for them that sail.

Butter.   You need not speak so loud ; I understand you.
You sail to-day.

Kemp.   No, I don't sail to-day.
So, be it fair or foul, it matters not.
Say, will you smoke ?   There 's choice tobacco here.

Butter.   No, thank you.   It 's against the law to smoke.

Kemp.   Well, almost everything 's against the law
In this good town.   Give a wide berth to one thing,
You 're sure to fetch up soon on something else.

Butter.   And so you sail to-day for dear Old England ?
I am not one of those who think a sup
Of this New England air is better worth
Than a whole draught of our Old England's ale.

Kemp.   Nor I.   Give me the ale and keep the air.
But, as I said, I do not sail to-day.

Butter.   Ah, yes ; you sail to-day.

Kemp.   I 'm under bonds
To take some Quakers back to the Barbadoes ;
And one of them is banished, and another
Is sentenced to be hanged.

Butter.   No, all are pardoned,
All are set free by order of the Court ;
But some of them would fain return to England.
You must not take them.   Upon that condition
Your bond is cancelled.

Kemp.   Ah, the wind has shifted !
I pray you, do you speak officially ?

Butter.   I always speak officially.   To prove it,
Here is the bond.   [*Rising and giving a paper.*]

Kemp.   And here 's my hand upon it.
And, look you, when I say I 'll do a thing
The thing is done.   Am I now free to go ?

Butter.   What say ?

Kemp.   I say, confound the tedious man,
With his strange speaking-trumpet !   Can I go ?

Butter.   You 're free to go, by order of the Court.
Your servant, sir.   [*Exit.*

Kemp. [*Shouting from the window.*]   Swallow, ahoy !   Hallo !
If ever a man was happy to leave Boston,
That man is Simon Kempthorn of the Swallow !   [*Re-enter* BUTTER.

Butter.   Pray, did you call ?
Kemp.   Call ?   Yes, I hailed the Swallow.
Butter.   That's not my name.   My name is Edward Butter.
You need not speak so loud.
Kemp.   [*Shaking hands*].   Good-bye !   Good-bye !
Butter.   Your servant, sir.
Kemp.   And yours, a thousand times.   [*Exeunt.*
                                                 Longfellow.

XLVI. SPEAKING AND ACTING.

SPEAKING and acting are often considered antagonistic to each
other.   The actor has been advised never to speak upon the plat-
form, and the speaker warned against practising dialogues.   Mr.
Joseph Jefferson, in a lecture given at our two foremost univer-
sities, has said, "Actors fail as orators and orators as actors.   The
two arts go hand in hand so far as magnetism and intelligence are
concerned, but there comes a point where they diverge widely.
The actor is, or should be, impressionable and sensitive ; the orator
must have the power of impressing."   Accordingly, the true actor
is known by his capacity for listening rather than by his speaking,
while the speaker does not listen, but directly addresses, and seeks
to impress or dominate the attention and feeling of the audience.
The secret of acting consists mainly in the power to give attention to the ideas uttered by the interlocutor, and his "action"
is the response of imagination, feeling, and body to these ideas.

But while this is true, the actor must also speak as well as
listen ; he must have the power to change from the attitude of
hearer and to become a speaker ; and while the orator is always a
speaker, still, the secret of true oratoric delivery is his power to
receive spontaneous impressions from his own successive ideas.
He is the best speaker who is best able to give subjective attention to his own thought.   Each successive picture, each stage in
the processes of his thought, must cause a sensitive response.
The true speaker rarely dominates the attention of his audience
by mere force of will ; he wins attention by showing intense interest himself in the successive ideas which come to him.   In fact,
the secret of both oratory and action is attention.   The actor listens

objectively, the orator more subjectively. With an imaginative conception of the point of view and nature of some character, the actor gives his attention to his interlocutor, or to what his interlocutor is saying, showing by his action the effect of what he sees and hears. The orator, on the other hand, shows the effect of the discovery of successive ideas in his own mind. He displays a sensitive response to vivid conceptions which hold and direct the attention of his auditor also. The speaker wins sympathetic attention, and awakens the faculties of other minds by making them feel the action of the same faculties in himself.

One very common fault of speakers is a strenuous earnestness, or an earnestness that is volitional or physical rather than intellectual or emotional. True earnestness requires a mental balance, a co-ordinate response, from all the faculties. This can only be gained by yielding the whole nature to each successive idea or situation.

Dramatic instinct must be considered as something broader than acting. It must even be separated from stage representation. If dramatic instinct consist in the elements which have here been shown, — the power to see things from another's point of view; to feel the motives of men; to enter into an imaginative situation, and to feel the processes of thought and experience which would be the natural result upon a human being in such surroundings; to get out of the narrow circle of the individual and become a part of the race, — if it be all these, then it belongs to the orator fully as much as to the actor. In fact, it belongs to every human being, and is an element in human nature which is essential to all success, and needs development and normal direction.

Not only so, but if the orator speaks merely, he is apt to lose the fundamental elements of dramatic instinct, and the same is true of the actor. While speaking and acting are different, yet the student should practise both for assistance in the development of his dramatic instinct, and the better grasp of his chosen art.

The principle here involved is found in the relation of the imaginative arts to each other. The greatest artists occasionally practise a different art from their own for the sake of changing their point of view and finding out a new side to nature. They awaken thus their artistic powers, and discover any tendencies towards mannerisms or superficial conceptions of their work.

HENRY V. TO HIS TROOPS.

ONCE more unto the breach, dear friends, once more ;
Or close the wall up with our English dead !
In peace, there 's nothing so becomes a man,
As modest stillness and humility :
But when the blast of war blows in our ears,
Then imitate the action of the tiger ;
Stiffen the sinews, summon up the blood,
Disguise fair nature with hard favor'd rage,
Then lend the eye a terrible aspect ;
Let it pry through the portage of the head,
Like the brass cannon ; let the brow o'erwhelm it,
As fearfully as doth a galled rock
O'erhang and jutty his confounded base
Swill'd with the wild and wasteful ocean.
Now set the teeth, and stretch the nostril wide ;
Hold hard the breath, and bend up every spirit
To his full height. — On, on, you noblest English,
Whose blood is fet from fathers of war-proof,
Fathers, that, like so many Alexanders,
Have, in these parts, from morn till even fought,
And sheathed their swords for lack of argument.
Dishonor not your mothers : now attest,
That those, whom you called fathers, did beget you :
Be copy now to men of grosser blood,
And teach them how to war ! — and you, good yeomen,
Whose limbs were made in England, show us here
The mettle of your pasture ; let us swear
That you are worth your breeding, which I doubt not ;
For there is none of you so mean and base,
That hath not noble lustre in your eyes.
I see you stand like greyhounds in the slips,
Straining upon the start. The game 's afoot ;
Follow your spirit : and, upon this charge,
Cry — God for Harry ! England ! and Saint George !

Shakespeare

Webster called up an imaginary scene consistent with the facts in his speech on the murder of Mr. White, and allowed his mind and heart to be impressed by each successive conception. What actor ever received greater impressions from his interlocutor than Webster did from the scenes depicted by his imagination?

AN aged man, without an enemy in the world, in his own house, and in his own bed, is made the victim of a butcherly murder, for mere pay. Deep sleep had fallen on the destined victim, and on all beneath his roof. A healthful old man, to whom sleep was sweet — the first sound slumbers of the night hold him in their soft but strong embrace. The assassin enters through the window, already prepared, into an unoccupied apartment; with noiseless foot, he paces the lonely hall, half-lighted by the moon ; he winds up the ascent of the stairs, and reaches the door of the chamber. Of this he moves the lock, by soft and continued pressure, till it turns on its hinges; and he enters, and beholds his victim before him. The room was uncommonly light. The face of the innocent sleeper was turned from the murderer ; and the beams of the moon, resting on the gray locks of his aged temple, showed him where to strike. The fatal blow is given, and the victim passes, without a struggle or a motion, from the repose of sleep to the repose of death !

It is the assassin's purpose to make sure work ; and he yet plies the dagger, though it was obvious that life had been destroyed by the blow of the bludgeon. He even raises the aged arm, that he may not fail in his aim at the heart, and replaces it again over the wounds of the poniard ! To finish the picture, he explores the wrist for the pulse ! He feels it, and ascertains that it beats no longer! It is accomplished ! The deed is done ! He retreats, — retraces his steps to the window, passes through as he came in, and escapes. He has done the murder; no eye has seen him, no ear has heard him. The secret is his own, and he is safe! Ah, gentlemen, that was a dreadful mistake. Such a secret can be safe nowhere. The whole creation of God has neither nook nor corner where the guilty can bestow it, and say it is safe. . . . The guilty soul cannot keep its own secret. It is false to itself, — or, rather, it feels an irresistible impulse of conscience to be true to itself; it labors under its guilty possession, and knows not what to do with it. The human heart was not made for the residence of such an inhabitant; it finds itself preyed on by a torment which it dares not acknowledge to God or man. A vulture is devouring it, and it asks no sympathy or assistance either from heaven or earth. The secret which the murderer carries soon comes to possess him. . . . He feels it beating at his heart, rising to his throat, and demanding disclosure. He thinks the whole world sees it in his face, reads it in his eyes, and almost hears its workings in the very silence of his thoughts. It has become his master; it betrays his discretion; it breaks down his courage; it conquers his prudence. When suspicions from without begin to embarrass him, and the net of circumstances to entangle him, the fatal secret struggles with still greater violence to burst forth. It must be confessed; it will be confessed. There is no refuge from confession but in suicide, and suicide is confession.

Daniel Webster.

XLVII. MODES OF HISTRIONIC EXPRESSION.

ACTING and speaking are not the only modes of vocal delivery. Between these two extremes there have been many forms in nearly every age. Among the earliest of all public entertainments was the recitation of the epic, the lyric, and other poems at the Ionic feasts; and even the recitation from his histories by Herodotus, as some think, at the Olympian games, at any rate in Athens.

During the present century, there has been a great revival of public reading as a means of entertainment. It has gradually assumed many forms as practised by different artists. Charlotte Cushman, for example, whose readings can never be forgotten by those who heard them, especially her farewell course in the Boston Music Hall, which followed her farewell to the stage, nearly always read from a book, seated at a little table. Occasionally, she gave recitations or impersonation from Macbeth or her favorite plays; but these were rare. Her intensity, her great versatility and suggestiveness, the mobility of her face and flexibility of her voice, enabled her to suggest the deepest subtleties of the highest literature with perfect ease and repose. Many have followed in her steps. Professor Robert R. Raymond was one of the most illustrious readers of Shakespeare. Though reading from his book as closely as Charlotte Cushman, he stood, and rendered his characters with the whole body,—in many cases with the extreme pantomimic representation of acting. His greatest success was in the humorous parts of Shakespeare, which have possibly never received better interpretation.

One of the oldest forms of vocal rendering is recitation from memory. The reciter takes the attitude of the speaker, and everything is, in fact, given from the point of view of the orator.

This form has been practised in all the schools and colleges, and has been called declamation. It is chiefly a recitation from the orators,—a custom which we know came down to us from the Greeks, and with us has been gradually extended to include, as it did with the Greeks, the recitation of every form of poetry, and also of general literature.

Recently, there has grown up also another form of vocal rendering which is called impersonation. The impersonator either sits or stands, or does both; he uses his chair, his hat, coat, gloves, desk, or table occasionally as properties, acting each character with the fidelity of the stage. Frequently there is an exaggeration beyond what would appear on the stage of certain pantomimic bearings or vocal modulations, for the purpose of accentuating the opposition of characters to each other, which, of course, can only be done at moments, not by continuity, as in stage representation.

The monologue differs from impersonation in that the reader takes but one character, the story being constructed so as to suggest other characters indirectly by the speech of one. This has not been often practised except in France, where the leading actors with few exceptions have studied monologues and rendered them. Ten or twelve volumes in one series of monologues have been published during the past fifteen years. The two Coquelins are the chief representatives of this form of histrionic expression.

Each of these forms has had its advocates. Some have gone so far as to think that impersonations and monologues, or even recitations, are inartistic; that only public reading is true art. Others, however, advocate recitations, some, impersonations; but it must be borne in mind that all forms have their place. Each is adapted to certain occasions and to certain forms and grades of literary art. Any one of them may be lifted to an artistic plane, and most of them may be degraded to the lowest plane of farce. The principle is not the mode of the art, but the art principles that are embodied; everything must be consistent and harmonious. Even stage accentuations and exaggerations may be allowed for the purpose of a fuller interpretation; but such exaggerations must be simple and in harmony with the literary spirit of the selections rendered.

A reader like Charlotte Cushman must be more suggestive; and hence when there is the power of suggestion, as was the case with her, the greatest tragical works in the highest literature can be presented, which the impersonator hesitates to undertake. If, however, he understood the broader principles of art, and the highest possible control of voice and body, and was willing to be delicate and suggestive, the very noblest poetry could be rendered even as an impersonation, and especially as a monologue. The ordinary reader never renders such poems as Browning's " Saul," because neither his imagination nor feeling are sufficiently cultivated to appreciate them, nor his voice and vocal expression sufficiently trained to render them. At present, impersonation usually is confined to the plane of comedy, on account of its extreme representative character, and the taste of audiences. It lends itself very easily to the more popular forms of humorous representations.

XLVIII. ASSIMILATION AND HUMOR.

THERE are many discussions of the ludicrous, but none are adequate. The sense of the ridiculous is a kind of instinct, — an " example of unconscious reasoning." Some have taken great pains to explain that even judgment is the fundamental requisite of wit and humor; but the act of humorous perception is more or less a spontaneous, even an unconscious, process; it is, at any rate, immediate. The rendering of humor is important for the development of vocal expression. It secures free play in the action of the mind; it shows us the necessity of abandon, and of trusting in instinct.

The rendering of humor requires instinct, naturalness and simplicity, flexibility and elasticity of the voice, and that mercurial temperament which is the fundamental cause of flexibility and versatility in expression. True humor, especially, requires assimilation. It is always associated with the power to see things from various points of view, and with that joyous element in our nature which brings ease and freedom of action in the use of the voice, stimulates the circulation, quickens the breathing, opens the throat, and establishes right conditions of tone. It gives us also breadth of sympathy and keenness of sensibility. A sense of the incongruous prevents us from making blunders, and indirectly develops a sense of harmony and taste.

The rendering of noble humor also develops the power to read pathos. It is only a step from the sublime to the ridiculous, and one who has no sense of the ridiculous is pretty sure to take the step. The study of humor makes us conscious of the step, and so prevents us from taking it, and removes the fear of being ridiculous, which is one of the common causes of lack of power to express deep feeling.

There are special cases for which the study of humor is very necessary, as in the case of clergymen, or of any one who by his profession is tempted towards a special line of emotion. A clergyman is apt to take life so seriously, that his voice and vocal expression assume a cadence which becomes a mannerism. To prevent this, he needs to practise a great variety of emotions, so as to develop the gamut of vocal modulations and a vocabulary of his natural languages.

In the next place, the study of humor develops sympathy, or, at least, this is true of the higher kinds. There are, of course, kinds of wit which are cynical and sarcastic and to be avoided. The noblest humor is associated with the highest literature, and the *reductio ad absurdum* is one of the most effective means of progress in every age.

THE ORIGIN OF ROAST PIG.

MANKIND, says a Chinese manuscript, for the first seventy thousand ages ate their meal raw. This period is not obscurely hinted at by their great Confucius in the second chapter of his Mundane Mutations, where he designates a kind of golden age by the term Cho-fang, literally the Cooks' Holiday. The manuscript goes on to say, that the art of roasting, or rather boiling (which I take to be the elder brother) was accidentally discovered in the manner following. The swineherd Ho-ti, having gone out into the woods one morning, as his manner was, to collect mast for his hogs, left his cottage in the care of his eldest son, Bo-bo, a great lubberly boy, who being fond of playing with fire, as younkers of his age commonly are, let some sparks escape into a bundle of straw, which, kindling quickly, spread the conflagration over every part of their poor mansion, till it was reduced to ashes. What was of much more importance, a fine litter of new-farrowed pigs, no less than nine in number, perished. China pigs have been esteemed a luxury all over the East, from the remotest periods that we read of. Bo-bo was in the utmost consternation, as you may think, — not so much for the sake of the tenement, which his father and he could easily build up again with a few dry branches, and the labour of an hour or two, at any time, as for the loss of the pigs. While he was thinking what he should say to his father, and wringing his hands over the smoking remnants of one of those untimely sufferers, an odour assailed his nostrils, unlike any scent which he had before experienced. What could it proceed from ?— not from the burnt cottage —he had smelt that smell before; indeed, this was by no means the first accident of the kind which had occurred through the negligence of this unlucky young fire-brand. Much less did it resemble that of any known herb, weed, or flower. A premonitory moistening at the same time overflowed his nether lip. He knew not what to think. He next stooped down to feel the pig, if there were any signs of life in it. He burnt his fingers, and to cool them he applied them in his booby fashion to his mouth. Some of the crumbs of the scorched skin had come away with his fingers, and for the first time in his life (in the world's life, indeed, for before him no man had known it) he tasted — *crackling !* Again he felt and fumbled at the pig. It did not burn him so much now ; still he licked his fingers from a sort of habit. The truth at length broke into his slow understanding that it was the pig that smelt so, and the pig that tasted so delicious ; and surrendering himself up to the new-born pleasure, he fell to tearing up whole handfuls of the scorched skin with the flesh next it, and was cramming it down his throat in his beastly fashion, when his sire entered amid the smoking rafters, armed with retributory cudgel, and finding how affairs stood, began to rain blows upon the young rogue's shoulders, as thick as hail-stones, which Bo-bo heeded not any more than if they had been flies. The tickling pleasure, which he experienced in his lower regions, had rendered him quite callous to any inconveniences he might feel to those remote quarters.

"You graceless whelp, what have you got there devouring? Is it not enough that you have burnt me down three houses with your dog's tricks, but you must be eating fire, and I know not what! What have you got there, I say ?"

"O father, the pig, the pig! do come and taste how nice the burnt pig eats."

The ears of Ho-ti tingled with horror. He cursed his son, and he cursed himself that ever he should beget a son that should eat burnt pig.

Bo-bo, whose scent was wonderfully sharpened since morning, soon raked out another pig, and fairly rending it asunder, thrust the lesser half by main force into the fists of Ho-ti, still shouting out, " Eat, eat, eat the burnt pig, father, only taste — O Lord ! " — with such-like barbarous ejaculations, cramming all the while as if he would choke.

Ho-ti trembled in every joint while he grasped the abominable thing, wavering whether he should not put his son to death for an unnatural young monster, when the crackling scorching his fingers, as it had done his son's, and applying the same remedy to them, he in his turn tasted some of its flavour, which, make what sour mouths he would for pretence, proved not altogether displeasing to him. In conclusion, both father and son fairly sat down to the mess, and never left off till they had despatched all that remained of the litter.

Bo-bo was strictly enjoined not to let the secret escape, for the neighbours would certainly have stoned them for a couple of abominable wretches, who could think of improving upon the good meat which God had sent them. Nevertheless, strange stories got about. It was observed that Ho-ti's cottage was burnt down now more frequently than ever. Nothing but fires from this time forward. Some would break out in broad day, others in the night-time. As often as the sow farrowed, so sure was the house of Ho-ti to be in a blaze; and Ho-ti himself, which was the more remarkable, instead of chastising his son, seemed to grow more indulgent to him than ever. At length they were watched, the terrible mystery discovered, and father and son summoned to take their trial at Pekin, then an inconsiderable assize town. Evidence was given, the obnoxious food itself produced in court, and verdict about to be pronounced, when the foreman of the jury begged that some of the burnt pig, of which the culprits stood accused, might be handed into the box. He handled it, and they all handled it ; and burning their fingers, as Bo-bo and his father had done before them, and Nature prompting to each of them the same remedy, against the face of all the facts, and the clearest charge which judge had ever given, — to the surprise of the whole court, townsfolk, strangers, reporters, and all present, — without leaving the box, or any manner of consultation whatever, they brought in a verdict of Not Guilty.

The judge, who was a shrewd fellow, winked at the manifest iniquity of the decision; and when the court was dismissed, went privily, and bought up all the pigs that could be had for love or money. In a few days his Lordship's town house was observed to be on fire. The thing took wing, and now there was nothing to be seen but fire in every direction. Fuel and pigs grew enormously dear all over the district.

The insurance offices one and all shut up shop. People built slighter and slighter every day, until it was feared that the very science of architecture would in no long time be lost to the world. Thus this custom of firing houses continued, till, in process of time, a sage arose, like our Locke, who made a discovery, that the flesh of swine, or indeed of any other animal, might be cooked without the necessity of consuming a whole house to dress it. Then first began the rude form of a grid-iron. Roasting by the string or spit came in a century or two later, I forget in whose dynasty. By such slow degrees, do the most useful and seemingly the most obvious arts, make their way among mankind.

GEMINI AND VIRGO.

Some vast amount of years ago, ere all my youth had vanish'd from me,
A boy it was my lot to know, whom his familiar friends called Tommy.
I love to gaze upon a child ; a young bud bursting into blossom ;
Artless as Eve, yet unbeguiled, and agile as a young opossum ;
And such was he. A calm brow'd lad, yet mad, at moments, as a hatter ;
Why hatters as a race are mad I never knew, nor does it matter.
He was what nurses call a "limb ;" one of those small misguided creatures,
Who, tho' their intellects are dim, are one too many for their teachers ;
And, if you asked of him to say what twice ten was, or three times seven,
He'd glance (in quite a placid way) from heaven to earth, from earth to heaven ;
And smile, and look politely round, to catch a casual suggestion ;
But make no effort to propound any solution of the question.
And so not much esteemed was he of the authorities ; and therefore
He fraternized by chance with me, needing a somebody to care for.
And three fair summers did we twain live (as they say) and love together ;
And bore by turns the wholesome cane till our young skins became as leather ;
And carved our names on every desk, and tore our clothes, and inked our collars ;
And looked unique and picturesque, but not, it may be, model scholars.
We did much as we chose to do ; we'd never heard of Mrs. Grundy ;
All the theology we knew was that we might n't play on Sunday ;
And all the general truths, that cakes were to be bought at four a penny,
And that excruciating aches resulted if we ate too many ;
And seeing ignorance is bliss, and wisdom consequently folly,
The obvious result is this — that our two lives were very jolly.
At last the separation came. Real love at that time was the fashion ;
And by a horrid chance, the same young thing was, to us both, a passion.
Old Poser snorted like a horse ; his feet were large, his hands were pimply,
His manner, when excited, coarse : — but Miss P. was an angel simply.
She was a blushing, gushing thing ; all — more than all — my fancy painted ;
Once, when she helped me to a wing of goose, I thought I should have fainted.
The people said that she was blue ; but I was green, and loved her dearly.
She was approaching thirty-two ; and I was then eleven, nearly.

I did not love as others do (none ever did that I 've heard tell of);
My passion was a byword through the town she was, of course, the belle of;
Oh sweet — as to the toil-worn man the far-off sound of rippling river;
As to cadets in Hindostan the fleeting remnant of their liver —
To me was Anna; dear as gold that fills the miser's sunless coffers
As to the spinster, growing old, the thought, the dream, that she had offers.
I 'd sent her little gifts of fruit ; I 'd written lines to her as Venus ;
I 'd sworn unflinchingly to shoot the man who dared to come between us;
And it was you, my Thomas, you, the friend in whom my soul confided,
Who dared to gaze on her — to do, I may say, much the same as I did.
One night I *saw* him squeeze her hand ; there was no doubt about the matter ;
I said he must resign, or stand my vengeance — and he chose the latter.
We met, we "planted" blows on blows; we fought as long as we were able ;
My rival had a bottle-nose, and both my speaking eyes were sable.
When the school-bell cut short our strife Miss P. gave both of us a plaster ;
And in a week became the wife of Horace Nibbs, the writing-master. . . .
I loved her then — I 'd love her still, only one must not love Another's ;
But thou and I, my Tommy, will, when we again meet, meet as brothers.
It may be that in age one seeks peace only ; that the blood is brisker
In boys' veins than in theirs whose cheeks are partially obscured by whisker ;
Or that the growing ages steal the memories of past wrongs from us.
But this is certain — that I feel most friendly unto thee, O Thomas !
And wheresoe'er we meet again, on this or that side the equator,
If I 've not turned teetotaller then, and have wherewith to pay the waiter,
To thee I 'll drain the modest cup, ignite with thee the mild Havannah ;
And we will waft, while liquoring up, forgiveness to the heartless Anna.

C. S. Calverley.

XLIX. ASSIMILATION AND LANGUAGES.

THERE are three stages in the mastery of a foreign language: we
may be able to read it; when more familiar we may be able by
conscious translation to speak it; but we have truly mastered a
language only when we are able to think in its forms.

The great advantage in studying a language not our own, according to John Stuart Mill, is that " it prevents us from mistaking
words for things." Plato and Aristotle, he said, made this mistake
in their philosophy,—an error due to the fact that they had
mastered no language aside from their own.

There is an important principle here that applies not only to the
study of language, but to that of art. The painter who merely
paints is apt to cease to be an artist. He fails to realize the

importance of feeling; his art becomes a mere reproduction of natural objects. The musician who merely plays never rises higher than a mechanical performer in an orchestra. A man becomes an artist only by being able to express himself in more than one way.

The principle, however, applies with great force to the relation of thought to words. Very frequently, however, languages are so mechanically and artificially studied that the benefit spoken of by Mill is not realized. Students often develop a mere verbal memory. They merely study the language by grammatical rules. They aim only to understand the meaning embodied, and fail to enter into its spirit. Repeated attempts have been made to reform such mechanical methods in the study of languages, and to find a way to induce students to think in another tongue.

One of the most important aids to this end is the reciting of the best passages in the literature of the language we are studying. Vocal expression or recitation compels the student really to think in the language he speaks. He cannot stop with a mere understanding of the words. With any true conception of expression, he meditates over the passage which he is to recite, and endeavors to create imaginatively its successive conceptions and situations, and to assimilate its spirit. At any rate, he is compelled to master more completely the words, and is brought into a more immediate relationship to the processes of thought beneath them. He is compelled to use them as agents in the expression of thought and feeling. Every language has a melody of its own, and vocal expression will be of great advantage in conquering the difficulty of "accent." The student will find that this accent does not consist in the pronunciation of individual sounds or words; but that it is the manifestation of peculiar processes of thought and point of view, the genius which lies behind the words.

It has been well said that all great poetry implies utterance. It is the lack of true vocal expression, without doubt, that causes the roughness of modern poetry, and makes the difference between modern and ancient verse. The great poets have always bewailed the separation. Most of the great poets have hummed over and recited their own poetry. Tennyson's recitation of his own poems is no doubt one of the chief causes of the smoothness of his verse. The greatest lovers of Browning wish at times that he had hummed over his lines. They would certainly have been smoother.

If this be true of the poetry of our own language, it is also true of the poetry of a foreign tongue. We can hardly feel quantity and rhythmic movement without vocal expression. The pronunciation of a foreign language is one of the highest attainments. Practice in the recitation of the masterpieces of other languages will bring us more immediately into contact with the true spirit of poetry and the true genius of the language.

Besides, this "melody," as Beethoven said to Bettina, "gives *sensuous existence to poetry;* for does not the meaning of a poem become embodied in melody?" George Henry Lewes in his "Life of Goethe" has some valuable suggestions upon the inadequacy of all translations of poetry. "Words in poetry," he says, "are not, as words in prose, simple representatives of objects and ideas: they are part of an organic whole; they are tones in the harmony. Substitute other parts and the result is a monstrosity, as if an arm were substituted for a wing; substitute other tones, and you produce a discord. . . . Words are not only symbols of objects, but centres of associations; and their suggestiveness depends partly on their sound." If all this be true, vocal expression is necessary to the adequate comprehension or feeling of any poem, and especially when that poem is in a foreign language.

This method of studying other languages is also a great help to vocal expression. It develops the altruistic instinct; it exercises the mind in mastering another point of view, and so develops assimilation and dramatic instinct. It exercises a greater number of faculties and with greater intensity of action than the recitation of our own language. It makes the reader more careful, more self-possessed. It not only exercises the organs of articulation and thus improves the utterance, but it gives breadth of culture. It quickens the imagination and sympathy.

Not only should a student study and recite a poem in its native language with the true spirit of that language; it is also very important for him to make translations, and to recite these also. This will give him a subtle discrimination of words. It will enable him also to bring the results of the work he has done in another language into his own mother-tongue. The hard work of translation will furnish a deep realization of the nature of poetic expression. While it may not be possible to translate a poem adequately, reciting it in its native language will give the translator a better feeling of its metre and rhythm. Vocal expression will also assist criticism to find the weakness of any translation.

<table>
<tr><td>

LA VIE.

La vie est vaine ;
Un peu l'amour,
  Un peu de haine —
Et puis — bonjour !

La vie est brève ;
  Un peu d'espoir,
Un peu de rêve —
  Et puis — bonsoir !

Léon Montenacken.

</td><td>

LIFE.

Vain, vain is life ;
Some love and play,
  Some hate and strife
And then — good-day !

Short, short life seems ;
  Some hope and light,
A few bright dreams —
  And then — good-night !

</td></tr>
</table>

A little work, a little play
To keep us going — and so, good-day !

A little warmth, a little light
Of love's bestowing — and so, good-night !

A little fun to match the sorrow
Of each day's growing — and so, good morrow !

A little trust that when we die
We reap our sowing ! — And so, good-by !

Du Maurier.

ERLKÖNIG.

WER reitet so spät durch Nacht und Wind ?
Es ist der Vater mit seinem Kind' ;
Er hat den Knaben wohl in dem Arm ;
Er fasst ihn sicher, er hält ihn warm.

"Mein Sohn, was birgst du so bang dein Gesicht ?"
"Sieh'st, Vater, du den Erlkönig nicht ?
Den Erlenkönig mit Kron' und Schweif ?"
"Mein Sohn, es ist ein Nebelstreif."

"Du liebes Kind, komm, geh' mit mir !
Gar schöne Spiele spiel' ich mit dir :
Manch' bunte Blumen sind an dem Strand ;
Meine Mutter hat manch gülden Gewand."

"Mein Vater, mein Vater, und hörest du nicht,
Was Erlenkönig mir leise verspricht ?"
"Sei ruhig, bleibe ruhig, mein Kind !
In dürren Blättern säuselt der Wind."

" Willst, feiner Knabe, du mit mir geh'n ?
Meine Töchter sollen dich warten schön ;
Meine Töchter führen den nächtlichen Reih'n,
Und wiegen und tanzen und singen dich ein."

" Mein Vater, mein Vater, und siehst du nicht dort
Erlkönig's Töchter am düstern Ort ?"
" Mein Sohn, mein Sohn, ich seh' es genau ;
Es scheinen die alten Weiden so grau."

" Ich liebe dich, mich reizt deine schöne Gestalt ;
Und bist du nicht willig, so brauch' ich Gewalt."
" Mein Vater, mein Vater, jetzt fasst er mich an ;
Erlkönig hat mir ein Leid 's gethan."

Dem Vater grauset 's, er reitet geschwind ;
Er hält in den Armen das ächzende Kind ;
Erreicht den Hof mit Müh' und Noth ;
In seinen Armen das Kind war todt.

Goethe.

THE ERL-KING.

WHO rides so late through a night so wild ?
It is a father holding his child ;
He tenderly clasps him with his arm,
To hold him safe and to keep him warm.

" My boy, why thus dost thou hide thine eye ? "
" See'st thou not, father, the Erl-King nigh,
The Erl-King with his crown and his train ! "
" My son, it is only the mist from the rain."

" Come, lovely boy, come, go with me,
Such beautiful plays I will play with thee.
The flowers are bright with colors untold,
And my mother has for thee robes of gold."

" My father, my father, and do you not hear
What Erl-King promises low in my ear ? "
" Be still, draw closer, my child, my own ;
Among the dead leaves the wind makes moan."

" O lovely boy, wilt thou come and go ?
My daughters are waiting their sports to show.
They nightly lead their bands in glee ;
They will play and dance and sing with thee."

> "My father, my father, and see you not there
> His daughters glide through the misty air?"
> "My child, my child, I see it all plain;
> The willows wave and gleam through the rain."
>
> "I love thee; thy form has charmed me so,
> That, be you not willing, I force you to go."
> "O father, my father, so fast he lays hold;
> Erl-King has seized me with grasp so cold."
>
> The father groans, like the wind he rides wild,
> And clasps still closer the suffering child.
> He reaches home in doubt and dread:
> Clasped close in his arms the child was dead.

> EIN Fichtenbaum steht einsam im Norden auf kahler Höh'.
> Ihn schläfert; mit weisser Decke umhüllen ihn Eis und Schnee.
> Er träumt von einer Palme, die fern im Morgenland
> Einsam und schweigend trauert auf brennender Felsenwand.
>
> *Heine.*

THE TOMB AND THE ROSE.

> LA tombe dit à la rose:
> — Des pleurs dont l'aube t'arrose
> Que fais-tu, fleur des amours?
> La rose dit à la tombe:
> — Que fais-tu de ce qui tombe
> Dans ton gouffre ouvert toujours?
>
> La rose dit: Tombeau sombre,
> De ces pleurs je fais dans l'ombre
> Un parfum d'ambre et de miel.
> La tombe dit: Fleur plaintive,
> De chaque âme qui m'arrive
> Je fais un ange du ciel.
>
> *Victor Hugo.*

> "FAIR rose," the dark tomb said,
> "Dawn's tears above thee shed —
> What dost thou with them all?"
> The rose said to the tomb:
> "And thou, O gulf of gloom,
> With all that in thee fall?"
>
> The rose replied: "Dark tomb
> Those tears to sweet perfume
> I change while hid they lie."
> The tomb replied: "I take
> Each soul that comes and make
> An angel of the sky."

WANDERER'S NIGHT SONG.

> UEBER allen Gipfeln
> Ist Ruh,
> In allen Wipfeln
> Spürest du
> Kaum einen Hauch;
> Die Vögelein schweigen im Walde:
> Warte nur, balde
> Ruhest du auch.
>
> *Goethe.*

> O'ER all the hill-tops
> Is quiet now,
> In all the tree-tops
> Hearest thou
> Hardly a breath;
> The birds are asleep in the trees:
> Wait; soon like these
> Thou, too, shalt rest.
>
> *Longfellow.*

As illustrations for this exercise, "Erlkönig," by Goethe, is given in the original and in a translation. It is most dramatic, and well suited for recitation on account of the transitions, variety of emotions, subjective and objective elements, and intensity of feeling. It is simple in thought and diction, and hence very difficult to translate. A little poem in French is given, with a literal translation, side by side, and an adaptation of it by Du Maurier; also a short poem by Victor Hugo, with a translation.

L. FAULTS AND DANGERS IN DRAMATIC EXPRESSION.

On account of the universal misconception of the nature of dramatic instinct, there are many dangers into which a student is apt to fall, and many faults which he is liable to contract.

In the first place, many students have no appreciation whatever of the function of imagination in their work; sometimes they have contempt for the sublimest poetry, and refuse to do anything but rehearse plays or read pieces, usually of a low type.

Imagination is the first step toward assimilation. It is a spontaneous faculty; it creates, it realizes for each individual in its own way. It does not, like memory, merely receive impressions and mechanically reproduce them; it is the union of thought and passion; it is the mind of the heart; it is full of life, and is hence the essential element in dramatic instinct. There is little assimilation in memory, but there can be no imagination without assimilation. Imagination manifests as well as represents. It never imitates, — it identifies; it rouses passion and life.

Again, in the development of dramatic instinct, there is apt to be too much objective attention to mere differences in expression. There is frequently too great a desire for variety. The differences must be differences of situation, differences of thought, differences of feeling. Variety for the sake of variety is chaos. The only genuine variety is that which is expressive of unity; true variety is the result of unity, and of unity only. There must be direct opposition and harmonious relationship between each successive situation. It is unity in the midst of variety that is the secret of all beauty and the governing principle of all art; but it is especially the principle of dramatic art.

The student is liable to seek merely for skill, not for assimila tion. He is apt to study objective differences and to imitate these. Thus imitation is substituted for assimilation; desiring representa‑ tive contrasts and transitions, he seeks for them mechanically.

Again, students desire to rehearse dialogues merely. They learn every part mechanically, with little study or conception of character, little or no assimilation of the artistic spirit of the play, or the motives of the character they are to impersonate. They rehearse together, and trust for suggestion from stage managers or from the action of other characters. There is little characteriza‑ tion or dramatic instinct at present upon the stage. Rarely do we find such genuine assimilation as in Joseph Jefferson's Rip Van Winkle," Booth's "Hamlet," or the elder Salvini's "Othello." All dramatic expression is the manifestation of thought and passion. The processes of the mind must be revealed.

Another danger is the failure to distinguish between expression and exhibition. Dramatic art is considered as physical action simply. There is thus a failure to distinguish between show or theatrical display, and true expression. Dramatic art is directly antagonistic to show; it is not exhibition, but is a revelation of the mind, of spiritual force and life and movement.

Again, students often think that everything dramatic belongs to action, and hence endeavor to give exaggerated movements which are antagonistic to nature. They fail to realize that dramatic action is mental action; that action is dramatic only when it reveals the man; that dramatic action is not a superficial thing.

In giving such transitions, for example, as these, there is no time allowed for the mind to act between the phrases, and hence the changes, if any are made, are mechanical, sudden, and unnatural.

> HARK ! how 'mid their revelry
> They raise the battle‑cry ! — The clang of arms,
> And war, and victory for me ! Away
> With idle dreams ! Why, what to me are women ?
> Yet she — ah ! she is not like those at home,
> Loaded with clumsy ornaments, happy in bondage,
> With base caresses humbly seeking favor
> Of their base lords.

Again, there is a failure to recognize the fact that all dramatic expression is instinctive. We speak of dramatic instinct, and not of dramatic reasoning. There is an unconscious element in all dramatic expression. It is not even wholly voluntary; there are involuntary elements. Dramatic action is the result of assimilation, of sympathetic identification of ourselves with some idea, situation, or character. It depends upon imaginative insight and instinct.

Students often think that dramatic action consists in scenery, stage business, and odd make-ups; but that only is dramatic which is intense and true.

All true dramatic transitions are simple. Those writers, those speakers, who have been the most dramatic have been the simplest; declamatory speakers and stilted writers are never dramatic. Homeric simplicity, Shakespearian directness, and not oratorical display or declamation cause dramatic expression. Note, for example, Scott's "Maisie" (p. 349). How delicate, simple, and suggestive; — these elements make it truly dramatic.

The chief requisites, then, of dramatic vocal expression are simplicity, genuineness, a vivid imaginative realization of the spirit of the thought. The whole nature must be fully responsive to every idea, thought, situation, and character.

There is a universal misunderstanding as to what is dramatic. When a man reads the Scriptures, for example, with very sudden transitions and exaggerated representation or personation of each character, he is called too dramatic. The fact is, he is not dramatic at all, but theatric. He employs imitation, not assimilation.

One important danger in dramatic work is the substitution of the lower power of representation for the higher one of manifestation; the elimination of the imaginative, of the sympathetic elements, and the introduction of the merely imitative.

Again, there is danger in certain emotions. Many have a misconception of the nature of assuming another character. Hence their emotions are not genuine. They think that to be dramatic is to be somebody else and not themselves; they entirely overlook the fact that the very first requisite to being truly dramatic is to be able to be one's self, and that no one can really and truly assimilate another character until he has a certain conscious realization of his own. The higher the form of dramatic art the more this is true. The reader or the speaker must often be himself, and express himself as the chief character. He must be a sympathetic spectator of every event, and reveal his own point of view in contrast to that of others.

One of the great mistakes of public readers is that they eliminate all normal characters and accentuate the abnormal. This produces one-sidedness. The reader or impersonator in the arrangement of his program, or his abridgment of a play, must bear in mind that the abnormal has no place except in opposition to the normal, that the abnormal will itself fail to interest an audience deeply, if not directly contrasted with the normal. The high dramatic deals with the normal as well as with the abnormal. That is farce which deals with the abnormal alone.

Render the following grotesque poem, giving the dialect and other peculiarities of the characters, but making the deep feeling and dramatic situation predominate over all objective elements.

<h3 style="text-align:center">DANNY DEEVER.</h3>

"WHAT are the bugles blowin' for?" said Files-on-Parade.
"To turn you out, to turn you out," the Color-Sergeant said.
"What makes you look so white, so white?" said Files-on-Parade
"I'm dreadin' what I've got to watch," the Color-Sergeant said.
    For they're hangin' Danny Deever, you can hear the Dead March play,
    The regiment's in 'ollow square — they're hangin' him to-day ;
    They've taken of his buttons off an' cut his stripes away,
    An' they're hangin' Danny Deever in the mornin'.

"What makes the rear-rank breathe so 'ard?" said Files-on-Parade.
"It's bitter cold, it's bitter cold," the Color-Sergeant said.
"What makes that front rank man fall down?" says Files-on-Parade.
"A touch o' sun, a touch o' sun," the Color-Sergeant said.
    They are hangin' Danny Deever, they are marchin' of 'im round,
    They 'ave 'alted Danny Deever by 'is coffin on the ground ;
    An' 'e'll swing in 'arf a minute for a sneakin' shootin' hound —
    O they're hangin' Danny Deever in the mornin' !

"'Is cot was right-'and cot to mine," said Files-on-Parade.
"'E's sleepin' out an' far to-night," the Color-Sergeant said.
"I've drunk 'is beer a score o' times," said Files-on-Parade.
"'E's drinkin' bitter beer alone," the Color-Sergeant said.

They are hangin' Danny Deever, you must mark 'im to 'is place,
For 'e shot a comrade sleepin' — you must look 'im in the face ;
Nine 'undred of 'is county an' the regiment's disgrace,
While they 're hangin' Danny Deever in the mornin'.

" What 's that so black agin the sun ? " said Files-on-Parade.
" It 's Danny fightin' 'ard for life," the Color-Sergeant said.
" What 's that that whimpers over'ead ? " said Files-on-Parade.
" It 's Danny's soul that 's passin' now," the Color-Sergeant said.
For they 're done with Danny Deever, you can 'ear the quickstep play,
The regiment 's in column, an' they 're marchin' us away ;
Ho ! the young recruits are shakin', an' they 'll want their beer to-day,
After hangin' Danny Deever in the mornin'.

Rudyard Kipling.

LI. EMOTIONAL TRUTHFULNESS.

It is easier to explain the nature of thought than of emotion. To find an adequate method of developing noble feeling is one of the most difficult problems of education. The same difficulty meets us in the vocal expression of emotion.

Definiteness in emotional expression is not considered necessary by many. Those who are most punctilious in regard to pronunciation or the use of words, or who would condemn themselves very severely if they did not make an adequate definition of any thought, often fail to recognize the fact that they rarely, if ever, express a feeling with any truthfulness. Many educated men will read a psalm which is inherently joyous in a mournful tone, without any situation, and without any response to a true emotional point of view.

Among speakers the command of emotion is very inadequate. Many of them have practically no feeling, but give everything from a neutral or negative point of view. Some have one emotion which colors every thought they express; some have two, which alternate in a crude and meaningless fashion. Many sway from one emotional condition into another, independent of thought.

One method of developing the power to express emotion definitely and truthfully is to secure genuineness and simplicity in transitions. There must be no pretence of feeling. Each thought, each successive conception of the mind, must be felt simply and directly, and given with the most truthful actions of the voice.

The reader or speaker should especially avoid drifting. When once emotion has arisen, it is supremo for the time, and only by securing definite thought and imaginative action can the current of feeling be controlled and directed into new channels. Emotion acts naturally and re-acts rhythmically; hence the true imaginative or conceptive action of the mind causes variations in a current of emotion.

Every emotion has one subtle characteristic. There must be such an imaginative conception of a situation as will awaken feeling, and such genuine artistic insight as will enable the reader or speaker or actor to express definitely this one characteristic. This can be obtained only by careful, earnest, and long-continued practice. The expression of emotion must not be mechanical; it must be a free, natural, and spontaneous outflow.

The combat deepens. On, ye Brave who rush to glory, or the grave !
Wave, Munich, all thy banners wave, and charge with all thy chivalry !
Few, few shall part, where many meet ! The snow shall be their winding-sheet,
And every turf beneath their feet shall be a soldier's sepulchre.
 Hohenlinden.   *Campbell.*

There is a tendency in the transition of emotion to make changes which are not true; for example, in the preceding lines, there is no change of place; it is the same battle; only in the first lines, we are placed before the battle, and in the last two, after the battle. In the first two we sympathize with the heroic struggle, with the enthusiastic exhortation, we rejoice to see the march forward, we share the spirit of endeavor; but in the second, we gaze pathetically upon the fallen.

Now, in reading these lines there will be a tendency to make the first scene large and the last small, to make the first declamatory and impersonal, the second limited and personal. The right rendering of both keeps the scene as large in one case as in the other. The picture does not change in size, — it only changes in character, causing thus a definite change in feeling. The imagination is called upon to sustain certain elements and to change others. The tendency of an inartistic reader will be to change everything, and to give up the control of his power. This leads to chaotic and untruthful feeling and expression.

In every change of passion, there are certain continuous elements. A transition is like the wave of the sea: it is the same wave that rises and falls: there can be no true normal transition without sustaining certain conditions. Good art accents one specific change or action, which in this stanza is from sympathy with the struggle of the battle to sympathy for the dying; but the battle-field is the same, the number of men the same, while the heroic and intense control increases rather than diminishes.

It is the manifestation of only one change, as in this illustration, which gives power to expression. If we give up the heroic element of the first, and give mere sadness in the second, the true character of the piece is spoiled.

There is some such danger in all transitions, but especially in changing to sorrow. Sorrow tends to depression, and lack of control; hence there must be a special care to sustain the breadth and the nobility of the situation, and to preserve the intensity. Sadness is the passive characteristic of one who gives up to moods or feelings, but sorrow implies heroic struggle to carry a heavy burden. The first belongs to a weak character only, the second to a noble one. Everywhere we can find two things which are nearly alike, but which on closer examination are found to be wide apart. Only an expert can tell the difference between melted lead and melted silver; brass may be so polished as to look for a moment like gold. The same is true with many emotions. The unthinking, unimaginative speaker or reader substitutes antagonism for earnestness, extravagance for spontaneity, pity for sympathy. Indignation is noble, anger ignoble. Love is the most exalted emotion of a human being, sentimentality one of the lowest.

It is very important in the development of dramatic expression or truthfulness of feeling to practise the noblest emotions in contrast with those which are apparently akin to them, but are really widely apart. It is easy enough to come down a mountain; the difficulty is in climbing to the top. It is the expression of the normal and the noble that calls for the struggle; the abnormal is easy. To bring the abnormal into direct opposition to the noblest experience is the work of an artist.

Cultivated taste or artistic appreciation carefully distinguishes
emotions in tragedy from melodrama, comedy from farce or
burlesque. Truthful expression of emotion demands a recognition
of such distinctions on the part of the reader.

What is the predominant emotion in the following Ballad of the
Fleet? Is it heroism, melodramatic extravagance, or farcical
caricature? Would a public reader be justified in using tones
or movements which belong only to low characters and farcical
situations?

THE REVENGE.

AT Flores in the Azores Sir Richard Grenville lay,
And a pinnace, like a flutter'd bird, came flying from far away :
" Spanish ships of war at sea ! we have sighted fifty-three !"
Then sware Lord Thomas Howard : " 'Fore God I am no coward ;
But I cannot meet them here, for my ships are out of gear,
And the half my men are sick. I must fly, but follow quick.
We are six ships of the line ; can we fight with fifty-three ?"

Then spake Sir Richard Grenville : " I know you are no coward ;
You fly them for a moment to fight with them again.
But I 've ninety men and more that are lying sick ashore.
I should count myself the coward if I left them, my Lord Howard,
To these inquisition dogs and the devildoms of Spain."

So Lord Howard pass'd away with five ships of war that day,
Till he melted like a cloud in the silent summer heaven ;
But Sir Richard bore in hand all his sick men from the land
Very carefully and slow,
Men of Bideford in Devon,
And we laid them on the ballast down below ;
For we brought them all aboard,
And they blest him in their pain, that they were not left to Spain,
To the thumbscrew and the stake, for the glory of the Lord.

He had only a hundred seamen to work the ship and to fight,
And he sailed away from Flores till the Spaniard came in sight,
With his huge sea-castles heaving upon the weather bow.
" Shall we fight or shall we fly ?
Good Sir Richard, tell us now,
For to fight is but to die !
There 'll be little of us left by the time this sun be set."
And Sir Richard said again : " We be all good English men.
Let us bang these dogs of Seville, the children of the devil,
For I never turn'd my back upon Don or devil yet."

Sir Richard spoke and he laugh'd, and we roar'd a hurrah, and so
The little Revenge ran on sheer into the heart of the foe,
With her hundred fighters on deck, and her ninety sick below ;
For half of her fleet to the right and half to the left were seen,
And the little Revenge ran on thro' the long sea-lane between.

Thousands of their soldiers look'd down from their decks and laugh'd,
Thousands of their seamen made mock at the mad little craft
Running on and on, till delay'd
By their mountain-like San Philip that, of fifteen hundred tons,
And up-shadowing high above us with her yawning tiers of guns,
Took the breath from our sails, and we stay'd.

And while now the great San Philip hung above us like a cloud
Whence the thunderbolt will fall
Long and loud,
Four galleons drew away
From the Spanish fleet that day,
And two upon the larboard and two upon the starboard lay,
And the battle-thunder broke from them all.

But anon the great San Philip, she bethought herself and went
Having that within her womb that had left her ill content ;
And the rest they came aboard us, and they fought us hand to hand,
For a dozen times they came with their pikes and musqueteers,
And a dozen times we shook 'em off as a dog that shakes his ears
When he leaps from the water to the land.

And the sun went down, and the stars came out far over the summer sea,
But never a moment ceas'd the fight of the one and the fifty-three.
Ship after ship, the whole night long, their high-built galleons came,
Ship after ship, the whole night long, with her battle-thunder and flame ;
Ship after ship, the whole night long, drew back with her dead and her shame.
For some were sunk and many were shatter'd, and so could fight us no more —
God of battles, was ever a battle like this in the world before ?

For he said " Fight on ! fight on !"
Tho' his vessel was all but a wreck ;
And it chanced that, when half of the short summer night was gone,
With a grisly wound to be drest he had left the deck,
But a bullet struck him that was dressing it suddenly dead,
And himself he was wounded again in the side and the head,
And he said " Fight on ! fight on !"

And the night went down, and the sun smiled out far over the summer sea,
And the Spanish fleet with broken sides lay round us all in a ring ;
But they dared not touch us again, for they fear'd that we still could sting,
So they watch'd what the end would be.

And we had not fought them in vain,
But in perilous plight were we,
Seeing forty of our poor hundred were slain,
And half of the rest of us maim'd for life
In the crash of the cannonades and the desperate strife ;
And the sick men down in the hold were most of them stark and cold,
And the pikes were all broken or bent, and the powder was all of it spent;
And the masts and the rigging were lying over the side ;
But Sir Richard cried in his English pride,
" We have fought such a fight for a day and a night
As may never be fought again !
We have won great glory, my men !
And a day less or more
At sea or ashore
We die — does it matter when ?
Sink me the ship, Master Gunner — sink her, split her in twain !
Fall into the hands of God, not into the hands of Spain !"

And the gunner said, " Ay, ay," but the seamen made reply :
" We have children, we have wives,
And the Lord hath spared our lives.
We will make the Spaniard promise, if we yield, to let us go ;
We shall live to fight again, and to strike another blow."
And the lion lay there dying, and they yielded to the foe.

And the stately Spanish men to their flagship bore him then,
Where they laid him by the mast, old Sir Richard caught at last,
And they praised him to his face with their courtly foreign grace ;
But he rose upon their decks, and he cried :
" I have fought for Queen and Faith like a valiant man and true ;
I have only done my duty as a man is bound to do :
With a joyful spirit I Sir Richard Grenville die !"
And he fell upon their decks, and he died.

And they stared at the dead that had been so valiant and true,
And had holden the power and glory of Spain so cheap
That he dared her with one little ship and his English few ;
Was he devil or man ?   He was devil for aught they knew,
But they sank his body with honour down into the deep,
And they mann'd the Revenge with a swarthier alien crew,
And away she sail'd with her loss and long'd for her own ;
When a wind from the lands they had ruin'd awoke from sleep,
And the water began to heave and the weather to moan,
And or ever that evening ended a great gale blew,
And a wave like the wave that is raised by an earthquake grew,

Till it smote on their hulls and their sails and their masts and their flags,
And the whole sea plunged and fell on the shot-shatter'd navy of Spain,
And the little Revenge herself went down by the island crags
To be lost evermore in the main.

Tennyson.

The earnest student will struggle to define carefully in his vocal expression differences between the low and the high in emotion. Vocal expression is the direct language of emotion; and one reason why feeling is so little understood, so much despised in expression, is because its natural and direct expression is either so little or so carelessly studied.

THE PRIDE OF YOUTH.[1]

Proud Maisie is in the wood, walking so early;
Sweet Robin sits on the bush singing so rarely,
"Tell me, thou bonny bird, when shall I marry me?"
"When six braw gentlemen kirkward shall carry ye."
"Who makes the bridal bed, birdie, say truly?"
— "The gray-headed sexton that delves the grave duly.
The glowworm o'er grave and stone shall light thee steady ;
The owl from the steeple sing welcome, proud lady."

Sir W. Scott.

The refinement and differentiation of the feelings is one of the highest characteristics of taste and culture in an individual, of advance in the civilization of a nation or a race; hence, it is the most marked indication of noble expression in the speaker, reader, or actor.

The practice of emotion must always be connected with imaginative action. In expression, it is the imagination which chiefly acts as a stimulus to emotion. It is the power of the imagination

---

[1] Scott has given us nothing more complete and lovely than this little song, which unites simplicity and dramatic power to a wild-wood music of the rarest quality. No moral is drawn, far less any conscious analysis of feeling attempted: — the pathetic meaning is left to be suggested by the mere presentiment of the situation. A narrow criticism has often named this, which may be called the Homeric manner, superficial, from its apparent simple facility; but first rate excellence in it is in truth one of the least common triumphs of Poetry. — This style should be compared with what is not less perfect in its way, the searching out of inner feeling, the expression of hidden meanings, the revelation of the heart of Nature and of the Soul within the Soul, — the analytical method, in short, — most completely represented by Wordsworth and by Shelley.

Palgrave.

which elevates and ennobles the feeling. One hindrance to truth-ful feeling is vague, abstract, or unimaginative thinking. Truth-fulness of feeling depends upon simplicity and repose; emotion cannot be forced, nor can its expression be labored.

There must be no exaggeration or effort. The attention and interest to successive ideas must be genuine, so that every transi-tion will be truthful.

The various steps which have been laid down for the develop-ment of the imagination and of assimilation have aimed at secur-ing definiteness and truthfulness of feeling. If the steps are care-fully practised, little need be added regarding truthfulness of emotion.

LII. ORIGINALITY.

ALL the arts are one. They are but human endeavors to repre-sent or interpret nature; hence the fundamental principles govern-ing them are the same. It is not so correct to speak of several arts, as of several forms of art. This identity of " life and law " in art enables the specific artistic value of any one art product to be tested.

Vocal expression is an artistic act in the broad sense of the word. It calls into activity the whole man and requires especially imagi-nation and feeling. It is a human action which must be founded upon nature, but must be as ideal and noble as possible. It depends upon doing, and not merely upon knowing. For these reasons it belongs to the realm of artistic endeavor, and so its correctness and effectiveness must be judged by artistic laws.

In fact, the laws of art apply with more force to vocal expression than to other arts because these laws are derived from the direct study of the universal qualities of nature, and vocal expression is more intimately connected with nature than other arts. Some forms of art have more mechanical means or are more limited by materials, and hence show less direct application of the laws of nature.

Among the principles of art one has been named originality or spontaneity; but by this is not meant oddity, either in action, structure, or form. It means that the process is from within outward; that all the external accidents are the result of internal impulses, so that every expression has a character of its own. "The construction," says Professor Hudson, of literary structure, "must proceed from the heart outward, not the other way, and proceed in virtue of the inward life, not by any surface aggregation of parts, or by any outward principle or rule. In organic nature, every plant, every animal, however vast is the number of its species, is so kept from novelty and singularity, has an individual life of its own, which life is and must be original. It is the development from the germ, and the process of development is vital and works by selection and assimilation of matter in accordance with its inward nature. And so in art. The work to be original must grow from what the workman has inside of him and what he sees in Nature and natural facts around him, and not by imitation of what others have done for him. So growing, the work will, to be sure, take specific form and character. Nevertheless, it will have the elements of originality, too, in the right sense of the term, because it will have originated from the author's mind, just as the offspring originates from the parent; and the result will be not apparent superficial virtue, which is indeed a vice, but a solid, genuine, substantial virtue. That is, the thing will be just what it means, and will mean just what it says. Moreover, the greatness of the work, if it have any, will be more or less hidden in the order and temperance and harmony of the parts; so that the work will keep growing larger and richer to you, as you become familiar with it, whereas in the case of the thing made in an unoriginal way at a distance it will seem larger than it is, and will keep shrinking and warping as you draw nearer to it, and perhaps when you get fairly into it, will prove to be no substance at all, but only a mass of shrinking vapor, and if you undertake to grasp it, your hands will go through it as through a shadow."

Whatever words may be used to name this quality of art, it must be universally recognized as one of the first elements. Coleridge, in speaking of the form of Shakespeare's dramas and of the mistakes of the superficial critics of the past who objected to the form of Shakespeare's drama, has said: "The form is mechanic, when on any given material we impress a predetermined form, not necessarily arising out of the properties of the material; as when to a mass of wet clay we give whatever shape we wish it to retain when hardened. The organic form, on the other hand, is innate; it shapes as it develops itself from within, and the fulness of its development is one and the same with the perfection of its outward form. Nature, the prime genial artist, inexhaustible in diverse powers, is equally inexhaustible in forms: each exterior is the physiognomy of the being within, — its true nature reflected and thrown out from the concave mirror."

Schlegel has also said in reference to the same subject: "Form is mechanical when it is impressed upon any piece of matter by an outward operation, as an accidental addition without regard to the nature of the thing; as, for example, when we give any form at pleasure to a soft mass, to be retained after induration. Organic form, on the contrary, is innate; it unfolds itself from within, and attains its determinate character along with the full development of the germ. Such forms are found in nature universally, wherever living powers are in action. And in Art, — as well as in Nature, the supreme artist, — all genuine forms are organic, that is, are determined by the quality of the work. In short, the form is no other than a significant exterior, the physiognomy of a thing, — when not defaced by disturbing accidents, the speaking physiognomy, — which bears true witness of its hidden essence."

In every form of art there must be a suggestion of inward life. In nature all genuine forces are organic; that is, determined by an inner process. The external is not determined by the mechanical shaping or elimination, but seems to be an outgrowth. This is true of the expression of life and force in the universe. No two objects in nature are entirely alike, — no two leaves, no two flowers. Everything that grows has peculiar characteristics of its own.

There is no form of art or expression where this principle is in more need of application than in vocal expression. Imitation, as has been shown, is here most tempting, but most out of place. Delivery in vocal expression in its very nature is a direct revelation of the process and life of the personality of each individual man.

The style of men in writing may differ, but their style in delivery differs much more. Great artists paint differently, but no two people speak alike in conversation. It is that form of art where the mechanical is least applicable, and where the natural and spontaneous, the original and free, are the most important; but unfortunately where mechanical uniformity is often sought for and all originality eliminated.

Delivery is in its nature personal and free; and wherever there is a similarity between two persons in delivery, imitation or a mechanical method is to be suspected, and at any rate weakness is always the result.

It can be seen at once, therefore, that this principle of art is the most adequate means of testing assimilation. Whenever there is a mere representation of words, or a mere presentation of elements which have been aggregated in some way, monotony is the result. But the very moment there is direct assimilation of the truth, whenever the thought is really in the possession of the mind, the process by which the mind produces and feels it, has its immediate effect upon delivery.

Assimilation is thus the most direct road to genuineness, truthfulness, and naturalness. It must be the first and the last endeavor of the student.

LIII. UNITY.

In Nature all force and all life are related to a centre; and as art is founded upon the processes of Nature, organic unity must be its predominant law. Every good work of art must centre in itself, and must not appear to be a fragment or part of something else; it must have the appearance of a living organism. It is only by the sympathetic relationship of parts, that art or expression of any form is possible. Each detail must not only have a force and meaning of its own, it must also contribute to the meaning of the whole. All parts must unite to produce one impression. If some part of a building seems to have no organic connection with the whole, if the removal of this part would seem to improve the effect, then the building is inartistic. Details which are unnecessary to the general impression are elements of weakness.

Every part of a true work of art seems to be incapable of change.
Every word in a beautiful poem seems to be the inevitable result
of a hidden impulse of life.   Any part of a picture that gives the
impression of a spot is bad.   Even something which, in itself, is
beautiful, when it calls too much attention to itself, aside from the
real centre of the whole, violates the fundamental law of artistic
expression.

THE SONNET.

> Scorn not the Sonnet ; Critic, you have frowned,
> Mindless of its just honours ; with this key
> Shakespeare unlocked his heart ; the melody
> Of this small lute gave ease to Petrarch's wound ;
> A thousand times this pipe did Tasso sound ;
> With it Camoëns soothed an exile's grief ;
> The Sonnet glittered a gay myrtle leaf
> Amid the cypress with which Dante crowned
> His visionary brow : a glow-worm lamp,
> It cheered mild Spenser, called from Faeryland
> To struggle through dark ways ; and, when a damp
> Fell round the path of Milton, in his hand
> The Thing became a trumpet ; whence he blew
> Soul-animating strains — alas, too few !
>
> *Wordsworth.*

" Here," says Prof. Henry N. Hudson, of this sonnet, " we
have a place for everything and everything in its place.   There is
nothing involved, nothing ajar.   The parts are not only each true
and good and beautiful in themselves, but each is helpful to the
others, and all to the author's purpose.   Every allusion, every
image, every word, tells of the furtherance of his aim.   There need
nothing be added : there must nothing be taken away.   The argument at every step is clear and strong.   The poem begins, proceeds,
and ends just as it ought.   The understanding, the imagination,
the ear, are satisfied with the result."

This principle or law of unity applies with special force to
all forms of vocal expression.   It contains the greatest variety
of actions, mental, emotional, and physical; and the mind may
pass from extreme explosion to prostration, yet all must be expressed, and expressed in unity.   Delivery is the union of three
diverse languages, — words, tones, and actions.   Each of these is

also complex, and produced by a great variety of agents and modulations. The pantomimic element, for example, uses the eye, the feet, the hand, and the face, the torso and the head, the whole body, in short. If any one of these many agents is inconsistent in its action with the others, the whole expression is destroyed. Expression is possible only by their harmonious co-operation; whatever is unessential is not only unnecessary but positively injurious. Again, in vocal expression, inflection, the texture and color of the voice, the changes of pitch, and the degrees of loudness and rhythmic movement must all be brought into unity, or one modulation witnesses against the truthfulness of the others. So potent are the natural languages of tone and action that they may wholly belie the statement of the words, and in every such case, the instincts of men take the testimony of the natural languages in preference to that of words.

Again, unity depends not only upon the right relation of all parts, but upon a correspondence in the *degree* of activity. The degree of expression in the eye, for example, must justify the animation of the hand and the movement of the whole body upon the feet, the degree of change of pitch must justify the extent of the pause; the abruptness of the inflection must be consistent with the color of the tone.

Expression is not only complex in its simultaneous actions,— it is an art in time, that is, the elements do not change together; they have unity of movement. In fact, unity is chiefly gained by a right sequence of ideas and situations, and succession of actions or modulations.

To measure all these elements and to bring them by mechanical rule into organic unity is beyond the possibility of any human being. However plausible such a method may be, the experience of the race has shown it to be artificial and in violation of the principles of true vocal art. If vocal expression were a mechanical art, such a method might have place; but since it reveals the highest flights of imagination, the subtlest and noblest feeling, it must of all arts be the most spontaneous.

The only true method of securing unity and harmony in vocal expression is by genuine dramatic and imaginative assimilation.

The agents are too numerous, their actions too complex, the muscles to be controlled too varied, and often too unconscious and even involuntary, to be regulated and controlled in the same way that a piano player performs upon the keys. Dramatic action is always associated with dramatic instinct, and is a natural and not an artificial modulation of the agents of expression. The human body is a natural organism, united to which the soul comes into the world, and to the use of which it is impelled spontaneously. It is not a mechanism constructed by the art of man, which the performer must learn to play upon by laborious and conscious steps. The method of nature is direct; the central life must predominate over all, or there can be no unity. The imaginative and dramatic assimilation by which the thought and experience of the race are made a part of the living force of one human being, and every faculty and power of the speaker quickened into life, and every part of the body and every modulation of the voice trained to respond to the thinking and feeling soul, is the only method by which unity of expression can be obtained.

Unity has its beginning in the human soul. There are three elemental acts of man's being, — thinking, feeling, and choosing. The perfect man, according to Hegel, is the one in whom " thought and emotion are balanced by will." Unity and balance of these three elemental principles of a human being lie at the foundation of unity in expression.

These are often called " the three natures of man." This is a mistake. They are not isolated, but united. " The mind thinking is intellect; the mind feeling is sensibility; and the mind choosing is will." Still, perverted expression essentially disconnects them. Where there is a lack of any imaginative realization or assimilation, there is always one-sided expression of some form. Thought and emotion are not balanced. The will is isolated, and the man is mechanical; or thinking, and he is didactic and cold; or emotion, and he drifts, whines, or rants. In perfect expression the three are always in equipoise. The true speaker has the power to make any one of them predominate at any moment, but at the same time to keep the other two present in subordinate relations.

The various modulations of the body and of the voice have direct correspondence with these three elemental powers of being, — for example, inflection is more immediately the servant of man's rational nature; it reveals the process of thought. Rhythmic pulsation or touch manifests more the vital nature of man, while tone-color expresses more immediately the higher spiritual nature. These and other elements of vocal expression must be brought into harmonious co-operation. In noble expression, they all unite to cause one impression.

The highest unity can result only after the development or differentiation of all forms of expression. No element of the natural language can discharge the function of another; each has a function of its own, and must be trained to discharge this effectually. Then all can be harmoniously united. Unity implies diversity; only opposites can be united. The two hands are most unlike as well as most like, and hence are capable of unity. At every point they are in direct opposition to each other.

There are two great hindrances to unity, — variety for the sake of variety, and sameness. There is no unity where there is mere oneness or homogeneity. Unity is opposed both to sameness and to mere variety, to uniformity as well as to chaos.

To secure unity as the climax of assimilation requires thorough study and meditation over a poem, a story, a play, until the one situation, motive, or spirit shall fully dominate the reader.

The illustrations of unity are innumerable, and the same is true of exercises for its development. One important practice is for students to study some long poem, story, or play, and make an abridgment which shall embody its spirit, and render this abridgment with a unity of its own, but in harmony with the spirit of the whole work.

Transitions and variations must be studied as necessary steps to unity. Mechanical or mere volitional changes, however, are antagonistic to unity.

In a dramatic story or scene, unity of impression is often secured by the opposition of the first to the last. In the first part of such a scene, an emotion must often be accentuated for the sake of opposition and unity, or in order to give force to the effect of certain revelations. For example, Hamlet is very familiar with Rosencranz and Guildenstern when he first receives them. This emphasizes the reserve toward them when his suspicion is aroused. So in the scene of the play, he seems gay and careless at first, to accent the great passion at the disclosure of the king's guilt. Again, in the "Lady of Lyons," when Pauline enters the cottage, she must be full of the greatest joy; her love and her happiness must all be centred in Claude. Otherwise, the effect of the revelation cannot be shown. The rise of a wave of passion must be in proportion to its fall. There is danger of anticipating what is coming. Unity in dramatic movement can only be secured by vivid accentuation of each situation in opposition. Each specific event must be realized with its own spirit to bring it into unity with other events. All feeling is dependent upon imaginative contemplation. This must form a part of the preparation for all vocal rendering of noble literature. Such a feeling of the "spirit of the piece" should be awakened as to envelop all in one atmosphere, as well as to cause each idea to be definitely varied in relation to one dominant principle. The significance of the death of Lincoln, the feeling that awakes in the nation, must all be realized before any one can appreciate or conceive the poetic vision, or express the feeling in this intense outburst of passion.

O CAPTAIN, MY CAPTAIN!

O CAPTAIN, my Captain! our fearful trip is done;
The ship has weathered every rack, the prize we sought is won;
The port is near, the bells I hear, the people all exulting,
While follow eyes the steady keel, the vessel grim and daring;
But, O heart, heart, heart! O the bleeding drops of red,
Where on the deck my Captain lies, fallen cold and dead.

O Captain, my Captain! rise up and hear the bells;
Rise up — for you the flag is flung — for you the bugle trills,
For you bouquets and ribbon'd wreaths — for you the shores a-crowding;
For you they call, the swaying mass, their eager faces turning;
Here, Captain, dear father! this arm beneath your head!
It is some dream that on the deck, you 've fallen cold and dead.

My Captain does not answer, his lips are pale and still;
My Captain does not feel my arm, he has no pulse nor will;

The ship is anchor'd safe and sound, its voyage is closed and done;
From fearful trip the victor ship comes in with object won;
Exult, O shores, and ring, O bells! but I with mournful tread
Walk the deck my Captain lies, fallen cold and dead.

" On Lincoln."   *Walt Whitman.*

How each of the farewells of the two greatest English poets of
the century are permeated with one poetic situation, feeling, and
principle in harmony with the poet's life and work!

EPILOGUE TO ASOLANDO.

AT the midnight, in the silence of the sleep-time,
　　When you set your faucies free,
Will they pass to where — by death, fools think, imprisoned —
Low he lies who once so loved you, whom you loved so,
　　　　Pity me?

Oh to love so, be so loved, yet so mistaken!
　　What had I on earth to do
With the slothful, with the mawkish, the unmanly?
Like the aimless, helpless, hopeless, did I drivel,
　　　　Being who?

One who never turned his back, but marched breast forward,
　　Never doubted clouds would break,
Never dreamed, though right were worsted, wrong would triumph,
Held we fall to rise, are baffled to fight better,
　　　　Sleep to wake.

No, at noonday, in the battle of man's work-time,
　　Greet the unseen with a cheer!
Bid him forward, breast and back as either should be,
" Strive and thrive!" cry, " Speed, — fight on, fare ever
　　　　There as here!"

                                                    Browning.

CROSSING THE BAR.

SUNSET and evening star, and one clear call for me!
And may there be no moaning of the bar when I pnt out to sea,
But such a tide as moving seems asleep, too full for sound and foam,
When that which drew from out the boundless deep turns again home.

Twilight and evening bell, and after that the dark!
And may there be no sadness of farewell, when I embark;
For tho' from out our bourne of time and place the flood may bear me far,
I hope to see my Pilot face to face when I have crost the bar.

                                                    Tennyson.

This may be carried too far, as, even in these short poems, each idea changes the feeling. Reading all in one spirit does not mean a monotonous drift. Speakers often fail to make a point impressive from a misconception of unity. All is colored with one emotion; the great central emotion is anticipated, and there is no variation or movement of passion. The highest unity can be obtained only by sequence and opposition. Each idea must have its own character, and then it can be brought into true unity with others.

Unity is not only the highest quality of art and the climax of artistic endeavor, it is also a test of right methods of procedure in art work, especially in vocal expression. Where the method aims to regulate the modulations of the voice by rules, then inconsistencies and lack of organic coherence begin to take the place of that sense of life which lies at the heart of every true product of art. But where vocal expression is studied as a manifestation of the processes of thinking; where the teacher is able to see and to show a student, not only the chief fault in the action of the body and the voice, but its ultimate cause in the action of the mind; and where he is able to awaken genuine thinking and assimilation, to inspire imaginative action and dramatic instinct, — then one of the first results to follow is the truer energy of the student's faculties and powers, and the higher and more natural unity of the complex elements of his expression.

Words, as a form of expression, are symbolic or conventional representatives of ideas; but while speaking words, the voice is modulated, consciously or unconsciously, and reveals that which words cannot express. The changes of pitch, inflections, and textures manifest the process of thinking, the speaker's aims, feelings, convictions, and degree of interest, and his many attitudes towards ideas or his hearers. To reveal these elliptic and emotional relations is the function of vocal expression. Thus it is subjective, complex, and spontaneous, and hence less subject to rule and conscious regulation than any other artistic action of the human being. It reveals the deepest processes of thinking, the degrees and modes of assimilating and realizing truth, and hence more definitely than any other art, it shows the sincerity and genuineness of the man, his real character, his real interest, when rightly used; but when it is taught in an objective way, as an art, in obedience to rules, when it is taught as Grammar is taught, and an endeavor made to acquire modulations of the voice as words are acquired, and to make all modulations conform to rules, then vocal expression may, in a sense, become a foreign language, and its use a means of developing unnaturalness and affectation.

As vocal expression is the nearest to Nature of any artistic act, those qualities which are universally present in all Nature's processes, such as simplicity, ease, freedom, directness, repose, power, animation, and unity, are always found predominant. These qualities are the revelation of life, and must be developed by stimulating the life of the man, by awakening his powers to natural and intense activity, and by securing a sense of the passing of their activity into form or relation with other minds. If the thinking is genuine, if the assimilation is real, if the successive ideas and the feeling dominate the man at the instant he speaks, then expression is not a mere reproduction of memorized signs, a fossilized relic of what has been in the past, but the spontaneous life of the man bringing all the most delicate elements of expression into harmonious relationship to each other, to the speaker and to other minds. Voice and body are brought into unity, and even the elemental powers of being, — thinking, feeling, and choosing; then vocal modulations become living and true, and expression a revelation of the thought and experience of the man.

www.ingramcontent.com/pod-product-compliance
Lightning Source LLC
Chambersburg PA
CBHW021720110726
47902CB00005B/1273